THE CLOUDBUILDERS

And Other Marvels

The **DANCING TUATARA PRESS**
Books from **RAMBLE HOUSE**

CLASSICS OF HORROR

1 **Beast or Man!** — Sean M'Guire
2 **The Whistling Ancestors** — Richard E. Goddard
3 **The Shadow on the House** — Mark Hansom
4 **Sorcerer's Chessmen** — Mark Hansom
5 **The Wizard of Berner's Abbey** — Mark Hansom
6 **The Border Line** — Walter S. Masterman
7 **The Trail of the Cloven Hoof** — Arlton Eadie
8 **The Curse of Cantire** — Mark Hansom
9 **Reunion in Hell and Other Stories** — The Selected Stories of John H. Knox Vol. I
10 **The Ghost of Gaston Revere** — Mark Hansom
11 **The Tongueless Horror And Other Stories** — The Selected Weird Tales of Wyatt Blassingame Vol. I
12 **Master of Souls** — Mark Hansom
13 **Man Out of Hell and Other Stories** — The Selected Stories of John H. Knox Vol. II
14 **Lady of the Yellow Death and Other Stories** — Selected Weird Tales of Wyatt Blassingame Vol. II
15 **Satan's Sin House and Other Stories** — The Weird Tales of Wayne Rogers Vol. I
16 **Hostesses in Hell and Other Stories** — The Weird Tales of Russell Gray Vol. I
17 **Hands Out of Hell and Other Stories** — The Selected Stories of John H. Knox Vol. III
18 **Summer Camp for Corpses and Other Stories** — Weird Tales of Arthur L. Zagat Vol. I
19 **One Dreadful Night** — by Ronald S.L. Harding
20 **The Library of Death** — by Ronald S.L. Harding
21 **The Beautiful Dead and Other Stories** — The Weird Tales of Donald Dale
22 **Death Rocks the Cradle and Other Stories** — Weird Tales of Wayne Rogers Vol. II
23 **The Devil's Night Club and Other Stories** — Nat Schachner
24 **Mark of the Laughing Death and Other Stories** — Francis James
25 **The Strange Thirteen and Other Stories** — Richard B. Gamon
26 **The Unholy Goddess and Other Stories** — The Selected Weird Tales of Wyatt Blassingame Vol. III
27 **House of the Restless Dead and Other Stories** — Hugh B. Cave
28 **Tales of Terror & Torment Vol. 1** — Edited by John Pelan
29 **The Corpse Factory and Other Stories** — Arthur Leo Zagat
30 **The Great Orme Terror and Other Stories** — Garnett Radcliffe
31 **Freak Museum** — R. R. Ryan
32 **The Subjugated Beast** — R. R. Ryan
33 **Towers & Tortures** — Dexter Dayle
34 **The Antlered Man** — Edwy Searles Brooks
35 **When the Batman Thirsts** — Frederick C. Davis
36 **The Sorcery Club** — Elliot O'Donnell
37 **Tales of Terror and Torment Vol. 2** — Edited by John Pelan
38 **Mistress of Terror and Other Stories** — The Selected Weird Tales of Wyatt Blassingame Vol. IV
39 **The Place of Hairy Death and Other Stories** — An Anthony Rud Reader
40 **My Touch Brings Death** — The Weird Tales of Russell Gray Vol. II

CLASSICS OF SCIENCE FICTION AND FANTASY

1 **Chariots of San Fernando and Other Stories** — Malcolm Jameson
2 **The Story Writer and Other Stories** — Richard Wilson
3 **The House That Time Forgot and Other Stories** — Robert F. Young
4 **A Niche in Time and Other Stories** — William F. Temple
5 **Two Suns of Morcali and Other Stories** — Evelyn E. Smith
6 **Old Faithful and Other Stories** — Raymond Z. Gallun
7 **The Alien Envoy and Other Stories** — Malcolm Jameson
8 **The Man without a Planet and Other Stories** — Richard Wilson
9 **The Man Who was Secrett and Other Stories** — John Brunner
10 **The Cloudbuilders** — Colin Kapp

DAY KEENE IN THE DETECTIVE PULPS

1 **League of the Grateful Dead and Other Stories** — Day Keene in the Detective Pulps Vol. I
2 **We Are the Dead and Other Stories** — Day Keene in the Detective Pulps Vol. II
3 **Death March of the Dancing Dolls and Other Stories** — Day Keene in the Detective Pulps Vol. III
4 **The Case of the Bearded Bride and Other Stories** — Day Keene in the Detective Pulps Vol. IV
5 **A Corpse Walks in Brooklyn and Other Stories** — Day Keene in the Detective Pulps Vol. V

THE CLOUDBUILDERS

And Other Marvels

The Best of Colin Kapp

Volume #1

Colin Kapp

Edited and Introduced by

John Pelan

RAMBLE HOUSE

The Cloudbuilders, *New Writings in SF* #12, 1968
Ambassador to Verdammt, *Analog,* April 1968
The Railways on Cannis, *New Worlds,* 87 1959
The Subways of Tazoo, *New Writings in SF* #3 1964
The Pen and the Dark, *New Writings in SF* #8 1966
Getaway from Getawehi, *New Writings in SF* #16 1969
The Black Hole of Negrav, *New Writings in SF* #25 1975
Something in the City, *Analog,* November, 1984

ISBN 13: 978-1-60543-697-5

ISBN 10:1-60543-697-6

Cover Art: Gavin L. O'Keefe
Preparation: Kathy Pelan and Fender Tucker

Dancing Tuatara Press
John Pelan Presents:
Classics of Science Fiction & Fantasy Volume #10

THE CLOUDBUILDERS

And Other Marvels

TABLE OF CONTENTS

COLIN KAPP – ONE MAN NEW WAVE

Welcome to the expanded edition of *The Unorthodox Engineers!* As this is the product of print on demand publishing, this means that you've gone to some trouble to seek out this book. Perhaps you're one of the many readers who have been loyally following the series: "John Pelan Presents: Classics of SF & Fantasy" (in which case, allow me to express my thanks for your part in making this series a tremendous success!), or perhaps you were doing an internet search for "Colin Kapp", just in case there had been some new developments . . .

The latter scenario is a very viable possibility, as Colin Kapp's work is the sort that once encountered is likely to stick with the reader to the point that occasional internet searches for news of re-releases of his books or stories may well become part of one's routine. In my case, I've been awaiting the advent of this particular book for over thirty years! Having encountered Kapp's stories of Fritz van Noon and his team when they were first published, and like many, having missed out on the Dobson collection in 1979, this expanded edition has been the very top of my wish-list for books that don't exist (right up there with a collection of John Brunner's "Mr. Secrett" stories, the fourth Anthony Villiers novel from Alexei Panshin, and other books that but for vagaries in the publishing industry could be sitting on your shelf right now!)

When we think of British science fiction in the 1960s and 1970s we almost invariably think of the New Wave and names such as Aldiss, Ballard, Brunner, and Moorcock and *New Worlds* magazine which morphed from one of the best traditional science fiction magazines in the 1950s to an interesting sort of pop-culture *smorgasbord* in the 1960s that managed to showcase the best and worst attributes of the New Wave all at the same time. With all the fanfare and controversy surrounding *New Worlds* many readers (particularly those in the States) overlooked John Carnell's magazine series in book form (book-a-zine?), *New Writings in SF,* which is a real shame, for by definition it was more experimental in nature in that it had all the *feel* of being a magazine and in terms of quality it was consistently better than either *New Worlds* or *Science Fantasy.* What's more, some authors had the bulk of their best short fiction published there and nowhere else . . .

One such author was Colin Kapp . . . Oh, certainly U.S. readers got to see all of his novels, beginning with *The Dark Mind* in 1964. And later in his career much of his short fiction was published in both the US and UK, and by the late 1970s, if not exactly a household name, Colin Kapp had at least achieved the status of "featured author" in that he was always mentioned on a magazine's cover whenever he had a new story appearing.

Then in the 1980s the Colin Kapp was hired to author the *Cageworld* novels, a series set in the grand tradition of exploring humanity's future in epic fashion. A tradition that dates back to Olaf Stapledon's *Last and First Men* and is echoed in the current (and brilliant) saga of "the Great Ship" by Robert Reed. The sort of work that rekindles the sense of wonder in even the most jaded reader. Had Colin Kapp written nothing else besides *Cageworld,* he'd have earned a place in science fiction's collective memory on the strength of those books alone. However, there was a good deal more and we fans in the States got the short end of the stick as a great deal of Kapp's best work saw print only in the UK and only in John Carnell's *New Writings in SF.*

I'm usually pretty good about recalling who does me the good turn of introducing me to an author's work that I enjoy, but in the case of Colin Kapp, I can't be 100% sure of whom to thank . . . I'm pretty sure that it was a bookseller in the UK, most likely Andy Richards, though it just as easily could have been Simon Gosden or George Locke . . . In any event, I had read and thoroughly enjoyed *The Patterns of Chaos* and must have raved about it in a letter, asking if there were any other titles by this author that I should look for . . . My correspondent surprised me with the news that much of the author's best short fiction concerned a group of engineers using fantastic, but very logical methods to solve sfnal problems. Now under normal circumstances telling me that a series of stories are "written by a real scientist and concern the solution to engineering problems" is a good way to send me running in the other direction. Nowadays, when two of the best *writers* in the genre (Greg Egan and Alistair Reynolds) are scientists this may sound like an odd statement, but publishing was a different world back then and often as not a magazine editor would be so impressed with an individual's academic credentials or degree that they would overlook the fact that said individual wasn't really much of a writer. This was particularly true of the type of story that hinged on the resolution of a scientific puzzle for its plot (exactly the sort of tale that Kapp excelled at) . . .

However, I *had* already read *The Patterns of Chaos* and *The Wizard of Anharitte* as well as two of the three bonus stories included in this collection ("The Cloud Builders" and "Ambassador to Verdammt"), so I knew that Colin Kapp could write and *write well*, and furthermore, I trusted this bookseller, so in relatively short order a box containing a number of issues of *New Worlds* and a near-complete run of *New Writings in SF* showed up on the doorstep and I was now in possession of the first four episodes in the exploits of the "Unorthodox Engineers" (as well as a lot of other excellent material)!

Rarely has a story or stories so wildly *exceeded* my expectations . . . After all, I'd been briefed as to what the general idea was, and I knew Colin Kapp to be an author of no small skill and that he was literally in his sandbox when it came to working out the premises for these tales, so they *ought* to be good! But no, they were so much better than merely "good", that despite their UK-centric publishing history, I am still surprised that none of the tales made the final Nebula or Hugo ballots. Hyperbole? Not at all . . . With these (and several other pieces), Colin Kapp pulled off what only a very few authors seem capable of . . . He wrote what to my mind are the perfect *hard* science fiction stories. The definition I'm using is that these are all puzzle or gimmick stories, and were it not for the scientific background extrapolated, the problem would not exist and there would be no story.

That in itself is an impressive feat, but more importantly, these are all great *character driven* stories . . . Not only is the puzzle captivating, but you also care about what becomes of the characters. Ask any writer, developing a character that the reader cares about is the most difficult aspect of a short story. In a novel, you can literally follow a character from cradle to grave and come to either like or loathe as the author intends, in short story you have very little room to convey enough information about your protagonist for the reader to have a sense of who the character is and what makes them tick.

Doing the former is easy, however doing it well is rare . . . There are libraries full of unreadable "gimmick" stories wherein the solution to the puzzle is the entirety of the story. Doing the latter is also uncommon, though there are any number of very fine writers who set strong character-driven tales in an sfnal setting and achieve great results, certainly Harlan Ellison, Theodore Sturgeon, and Richard Wilson made careers at this, but the *science* in their stories was (to be kind) pretty thin. What Colin Kapp does as well as anyone ever has, is to combine strong characterization with scientific puzzles that will hold up to scrutiny by a panel of his peers in the engineering disciplines.

So how did this phenomenon come about? In an event that parallels the beginning of another of my favorite authors' career (Bob Leman), Kapp reveals in an interview conducted by Chris Morgan that one day upon returning home with the latest sf magazine, he expressed disgust with the contents and proclaimed that he could do better himself. Apparently, we have Betty Kapp to thank for sensibly making the suggestion that if he felt that way, perhaps he *should* give it a try. . .

The result was "Life Plan", which John Carnell accepted for *New Worlds*, with the request "please write some more." This was in 1958 and John Carnell remained a loyal customer throughout Kapp's career purchasing several more tales during his tenure as editor at *New Worlds* and picking up another dozen stories for his *New Writings in SF* series, which had the prestige of being issued in hardcover as well as paperback.

Successful in his profession as an electronics engineer, Kapp mentions being very seriously tempted to try writing full time, he also mentions that market forces at the time argued pretty strongly against doing so and when one looks back at the period, it's pretty clear that he made the right decision. The 1970s-1980s may seem to be a boom period for science fiction in terms of the number of titles released, but the sad reality is that with more books published, each individual book has a shorter window of opportunity to find its audience. For an author without an extensive and perpetually in-print back-list of twenty or so titles, these conditions almost ensure no individual book does more than (maybe) earning out its advance.

For any but the most prolific, these are not conditions conducive to supporting a family.

Taken as I was with the Unorthodox Engineers stories, I foolishly ignored the Dobson edition when it was released. The reason for this was that I simply couldn't imagine a US publisher not reissuing the book and doing a much better job of it than Dobson . . . (For some strange reason, from the 1960s-1980s most UK publishers seemed dedicated to producing their hardcovers with the cheapest, nastiest materials available. On the other hand, the paperbacks of the time with the various formats are generally sturdy and attractive volumes, printed on quality paper that will stand the test of time. Why this disparity? I can't begin to guess . . .)

Sadly, a US edition of *The Unorthodox Engineers* never appeared and US publishers started to subtly shift towards equating bulk with value and books started to become larger and larger as a matter of course, with the slender volumes of 50,000 to 60,000 words (once a standard), now a rarity. This perception still exists in the marketplace today to the point that my only concern when it came to producing this new edition of *The Unorthodox Engineers* was that it might be perceived as "too small" by our customers. I had the same concern with John Brunner's "Mr. Secrett" stories. In both cases, the solution was the same, I added two extra stories to each book that if not part of the series were at least thematically related to the point that they seem to belong there. In the case of this volume, it was a very easy selection as the two stories of the three bonus stories I've included were instrumental in my becoming a devotee of Colin Kapp's work, some forty years ago.

Our titular tale, "The Cloudbuilders" is one that may well be familiar to US readers, as it was included in the Wollheim/Carr *World's Best SF* for 1969, where Kapp appears alongside such familiar names as Vonnegut, Delaney, Aldiss, Carr, Silverberg, and Leiber. In 1969 the New Wave was at its very height in the US and the story that received the most attention was Delaney's "Time Considered as A Helix of Semi-Precious Stones". "The Cloudbuilders" is pure, classic Kapp, with a very believable society functioning under some interesting technological restraints and how its very growth and survival is carefully shepherded by the controlled release of technology known only to a select few. In other words, a very traditional science fiction story . . . I leave it to the reader to decide which story has better stood the test of time.

From "The Cloudbuilders" we go straight to the main portion of the collection, the four novelettes and one short story that comprised the original collection, *The Unorthodox Engineers.* The first story, "The Railways up on Cannis" (*New Worlds* UK 1959, *New Worlds* US 1960) does a splendid job of setting the stage for the series and introducing the brilliant and irrepressible Lieutenant Fritz van Noon. Despite being available to US readers, *New Worlds* (in paperback format) never really caught on. Readers weren't sure what to make of it, (was it a book, or was it a magazine? If the latter, then what was the schedule?) Unfortunately, these questions weren't addressed by the publisher, which pretty much assured that the US version of *New Worlds* would be doomed to failure. The end result was that a great opportunity to build an international fanbase fell by the wayside.

The next (and longer) installment didn't appear until four years later . . . By this time John Carnall had launched *New Writings in SF* and taken many of his regular contributors to *New Worlds* with him. Colin Kapp was on board with "The Night Flame" in the second issue, returning in the third with "The Subways of Tazoo". A longer and more ambitious piece, "Subways" also successfully portrays the remnants of a truly *alien* civilization adding the wrinkle of having to understand a completely non-human frame of reference as well as the remaining pieces of alien technology.

From this point on, the UE stories appeared sporadically in *New Writings in SF*, interspersed with other fine stories such as "Hunger Over Sweet Waters" and "The Imagination Trap". By the time that "The Black Hole of Negrav" (the fifth installment) appeared in the twenty-fifth volume of *New Writings in SF,* Kapp's career as a novelist was well-established and his short fiction familiar to readers on both sides of the Atlantic.

The Unorthodox Engineers as a series seems to have been a victim of bad timing and under-exposure. This bad luck seems to extend to the fictional characters as well . . . After pulling off four successful feats of unorthodox engineering, and saving his government untold billions of dollars, poor van Noon is still only a Lieutenant as "The Black Hole of Negrav" opens . . . One would think that after sixteen years a promotion of at least one rank might've been in order . . .

Despite my comments on the state of the marketplace in the late 1970s and early 1980s, there's certainly no reason to think that a US edition of *The Unorthodox Engineers* following the UK wouldn't have been successful and DAW would have seemed a likely outlet due to DAW being the publishers of *Cageworld.* Further, the top man at DAW, Donald

A.Wollheim had been instrumental in promoting Kapp to US readers by virtue of selecting both "The Verdammt Ambassador" and "The Cloudbuilders" for inclusion in his *World's Best Science Fiction* series during his tenure as the editor of Ace Books' science fiction line. Also, *Cageworld* was an *event*, on both sides of the pond . . . It isn't often that this sort of collaborative process is used to create a single book, let alone a series of four novels and anything released in 1982-1985 with the banner "By the author of Cageworld" would likely have done well.

For whatever reason, the opportunity to capitalize on *Cageworld* and build a larger audience for Colin Kapp's work came and went. While there were no additional "UE" stories, two very fine pieces "Something in the City" and "An Alternative to Salt" saw print in *Analog* in the mid-1980s. In any event, after a period of over thirty years, these excellent stories are available in both permanent hardcover format as well as attractive and inexpensive trade paperback. With a UK publisher preparing to issue e-books of several novels, it seems that Colin Kapp's work will be readily available to a new generation of readers.

On a less-happy note I have to report that the long-rumored-to-exist *sixth* Unorthodox Engineers story doesn't . . . (exist, that is), at least not in a usable form . . . I've been advised that the story *does* exist, but only in rough draft form and with notes of concern in the margins that the science postulated might not be workable and needs to be re-thought . . .

In stories where scientific accuracy plays such a key role, a weakness such as this could be fatal. That the author was concerned to the point that he felt that the whole premise might have to be re-worked makes the likelihood of a post-humous collaboration pretty unlikely. In my professional career I've been called on a time or two to polish up or finish work by an author who has passed on, but I'd be well and truly out of my depths in any project that involved the hard sciences. I'm afraid that we'll probably just have to concede that there are and always will be only five Unorthodox Engineers tales and leave it at that.

On a much brighter note, I can disclose that the UKs major publisher of SF, the venerable Victor Gollancz is embarking on an ambitious program of e-books, which will include a good deal of Kapp's work and further, that the contract for this collection also stipulated a *second volume of tales*, (which will likely see print in late-2013) and as I look over Mr. Kapp's bibliography, I see that there are certainly enough quality stories to make up a *third* volume of stories and I can't think of any reason why these collections shouldn't also come to pass. Then of course, there's also the "lost" novel *The Timewinders*. We know that it was purchased by Dobson and never released. It's now on my personal bucket list of books that I shall somehow cause to be published . . . As to how and when, at this point your guess is every bit as good as mine, but trust that I shall be working on it . . . Until then, I hope you enjoy these stories and the other Colin Kapp collection (coming next year) as much as I did when I first read them many years ago!

John Pelan
Somewhere Near Area 51
New Mexico, 2012

THE CLOUDBUILDERS

I.

Closer to the ground now, the field sounds and the forest sounds came up to him with the incredible clarity which never ceased to amaze even though he was no stranger to the air. With only the lightest of breezes, nothing disturbed the fidelity of birdsong and animal cry which reached up as he drifted overhead.

The area was not rich, but he judged it well-provisioned, and that in itself was fortune in these times. Having crossed the sparse lands of the north, and the slag-pits and black fissures which divided the plains, he could appreciate the green fertility and the sense of life abundant and thriving on the ground beneath him. And on the far horizon the great jagged teeth of mountains, falling to the sea, explained why Timor the Cloudbuilder had found it expedient to set his shipyards in this remote corner of the world. Apart from Timor's cloudships, there was no way in or out of this land. No way at all, unless one was brave enough or sufficiently foolish to risk the hazards of the sea.

Jacobi found the prospect rather pleasant. The sun was set high, yet not too hot for the meagre awning of the decking. The air was crisp and fresh, with a heady, crystal clarity which was balm to eyes and lungs alike. Beyond his reasonable expectation, the slight breezes drifted him as surely towards his destination as if he had set their course himself. This was a day for birds and gods and those who rode the ships the Cloudbuilders made.

There was bread and salt meat in his bag. In the sack was wine, sweet from last year's harvest and tangy with the living fruit. He prepared himself a meal. Above him, the single burner scarcely purred, its blue uniformity of flame no longer visible in the strong sunlight. On the treetops below, the shadow of the great air balloon flitted like Aphrodite's fingertip, lovingly, with an intangible caress. Jacobi had the feeling that he was going to like Catenor.

Although his height was falling slowly, he made no attempt to adjust the burner. For one thing there was little enough gas in the spheres after the last, long leg of his journey and he had a Cloudsman's natural sense of conservation. Secondly, the increasing incidence of farmland over forest suggested he was nearing his destination. By his reckoning, his present course should take him near enough to the shipyards to be seen by the lookout. He searched the scene carefully for the signal smoke which would indicate he had been sighted and give him guidance as to the most opportune time to land. But the fair winds which had carried him from Annonay had placed him near his destination days before he could have been reasonably expected and no lookout would be posted yet unless there were local ships due to return.

It was thus that he saw the clustered town of Catenor two miles to his right, and had already extinguished his burner, before the smoke columns rose to greet him. Choosing a likely field well clear of trees, Jacobi began to manipulate his descent. Gently he grasped the ropes that controlled the great leathern valves at the top of the balloon, venting some of the heated air which carried him, yet carefully retaining sufficient buoyancy to lighten the impact of landing.

With near-perfect conditions and the favour of the gods, his touchdown was light as a butterfly. As the ground took the weight of the decking, and the rigging began to slacken, he opened the valves to their fullest extent. The breeze carried the deflating balloon lazily sideways clear of the deck as it collapsed and emptied. The fabric was neatly folded and stowed by the time the carts came out to fetch him.

"Welcome to Catenor!" The yardsman from the leading cart held out a work-gnarled hand. "We didn't expect you quite so soon."

"The gods were kind," said Jacobi. "I'd allowed myself

three more days at least from Annonay."

The second cart drew up and the work of loading the balloon fabric, decking and ancillary equipment onto the flat drays was begun.

"And how is Lyons these days?" asked the yardsman.

"Prosperous but turbulent. But then, it always was. Do you know Lyons, then?"

"I was apprenticed there before I came to Catenor."

"Ah! That explains why your crew manhandle a ship Guild-fashion. Don't you miss being there?"

"No." The yardsman ran his fingers through the short stubble of his hair. "Lyons was not bad, but it doesn't have the promise of Catenor. The only sore in our sides here is the raiding."

"Raiding?"

"Cloud-pirates from beyond the mountains somewhere. They attack the villages once or twice a year, after beasts or grain or anything else they fancy. The last several times they've even come into Catenor and the yards. We've our own militia now, but they can't be everywhere at once. By the time we get a resistance force to the scene of an attack the chances are the raiders have taken what they wanted and gone back to the clouds again."

"Bad," said Jacobi. "What sort of ships are they using?"

"A mixed collection. Craft they've captured from all over Europe. Some good, some bad, but there's a rumour they've now got some with engines."

"Engines?" Jacobi was interested. "I've heard of them. There's a Cloudmaster in the Urals who fits engines in his craft. But their great weight destroys most of the advantages."

By this time the loading was complete. Jacobi swung onto the first cart as the patient dray-horses were urged back into life. His eyes alighted on several broad smoke columns rising from the fields about Catenor. He looked at his companion questioningly.

The yardsman was amused. "Oh, that? They're lighting the fires to roast oxen for the feast. Tonight you'll be the guest of honour in the town. It should be a feast worth remembering."

"I'm flattered," said Jacobi. "Do you always greet Journeymen like this?"

His companion laughed. "Not often. But first I have to deliver you to Timor. If you want a tip, don't bow down to him. He respects men who know their own minds and their own worth. He has neither time nor pity for fools. He's a hard man, but you'll find him the best Cloudmaster bar none."

"So I've heard."

"And with your help we'll one day build finer cloudships in Catenor than anything that Annonay can offer."

Timor's face was made of leather, which crinkled to expose a will of iron beneath. He took Jacobi's papers and inspected the seals closely before adding his own. The deeds accepted, Jacobi offered his dagger, as Guild-rule demanded. Timor's weatherbeaten face was crossed suddenly with disbelief. He reached for the instrument, then shook his head.

"Keep it on you, Journeyman. When the raiders come again you may have need of it."

"Cloudmaster, you know I can't do that." Jacobi was firm.

"Guild-rule requires I surrender my weapons to you. In law I am your servant and you my protector until my bond here is served. That is our contract and both you and the Guild have sealed it."

"Very well," Timor's eyes narrowed. "But not all laws made in Annonay will work in Catenor. If the raiders come and I thrust a weapon in your hands I expect you to use it. Either you accept that now or you'd best take your precious contract back to the Guild."

"Perhaps you should have hired a mercenary and not a journeyman?"

"Zeus!" Timor's face clouded with anger. "You call yourself a Cloudsman and you won't take arms even to protect yourself? What kind of cowards are they breeding in Annonay these days? There's no place for unarmed whelps and mewlings in my yards."

"Then your quarrel is with the Guild elders, not with me," said Jacobi quietly. "And if the raiders come, which is the harder thing to do—face them with drawn arms or with folded arms?"

"But where's the sense of it?"

"A Journeyman's duty is only to his calling. Any man may hire him who can pay the Guild the price. He dare not become partisan. His next bond may be with your enemy."

"Even with a cloud-pirate?"

"With any man who has the price. Guild-rule makes no distinctions between men."

The interlude had taken place within the portal of Timor's residence and therefore free from previous interruption. Its privacy was, however, terminated by a clamour from outside as the welcoming procession reached the door. Jacobi looked Timor straight in the eyes.

"Well, Cloudmaster, do you accept the contract, or do I return to Annonay?"

Outside, someone was calling Jacobi's name. A group of girls in the foreground were making giggled dares between themselves and looking into the doorway. The scene was all set for explosive carnival.

Timor pursed his leathern lips. "You stay, of course. If I let you go back to Annonay I doubt if the Guild will send me another. Nemesis take them! Still, the fault is mine. I insisted on a Journeyman of strong mind and strong arm. Now I find I can't stomach the one and can't use the other." The tanned texture of his face broke into a begrudged smile. "Welcome to Catenor, Jacobi. If you hold as firm to the rest of your contract as you have to this, I think I shall be well pleased."

All Catenor, it seemed, was going to the feast. And from the surrounding areas, wherever the word had spread, the country-dwellers came, by farm-cart, ox-cart, horseback and on foot, eager to join the revels.

It was an ideal night. Clear skies and a balmy warmth set a relaxing mood and the slight winds carried exciting hints of roast ox and wood-smoke into the town. Hanging lamps adorned the porches of the houses, and flaring torches, carried in procession or spread among the throng, lit the streets as bright as day. Wearing their brightest dresses, the girls stood out like radiant peacocks in the weaving light; and over all, Dionysus looked down from the clouds and rubbed his hands and smiled and nodded his approval.

Bred in more sophisticated climes, Jacobi was taken aback by the pagan enthusiasm of the gathering. There was a sense of shared relief from fears and deprivations of the past and this Jacobi found difficult to understand. Then suddenly the tide of emotions blossomed forth in a spontaneous flood of greeting and hilarious celebration which was way and above anything the situation seemed to warrant.

He was carried shoulder-high throughout the town and then out to the fields, where the ox-fires cast the cherry glow which made men resemble gods, and women, nymphs. Ale and wine flowed plentifully and the feast was a hilarious, barbaric, greedy parody of a meal. Afterwards, back to the ale wagons and wine casks and from thence again into the dancing town where everyone knew his name and treated him as a friend.

Although his impressions of the evening were of a continuing whirl of places, scenes and countless people, Jacobi gradually began to discern some faces which he saw more regularly than others. One of these belonged to a remarkably attractive dark-haired girl whose unrestrained vivacity had enlivened the feasting in the field. He remembered drinking wine with her later and a further meeting apparently by chance as he had re-entered the town.

Now she stood close to him, almost inviting his attention.

Jacobi did not believe in chance, nor in wasted opportunity. Taking advantage of the congenial melee in the street he moved to her, and drawing her into a corner, he kissed her. The responses of the girl were as anticipated, but the reaction of the local revellers was one of surprise and near embarrassment. They made him feel as if he had unknowingly performed some act of bravado reckless beyond anticipation even on such a night as this. Since he had been tasting unreluctant lips all evening, he found this disconcerting and inexplicable.

Then somebody cheered and the cheer spread. In a wave of laughter both he and the girl were raised shoulder high and carried triumphantly off through the crowds. Unfortunately the paths of their respective parties diverged and she was gradually lost to his sight. By the time he managed to escape again she was nowhere to be seen.

He did not bother to search too long. In the morning there would be time enough to make inquiries, but this was the time for enjoyment. He found another festive group and joined them gleefully, soon losing himself in the wine and the laughter and the sportive company. Finally he trekked with them back to the fields for further meat and song before settling near the warmth of one of the great fires, weary and immeasurably content. It had indeed been a feast worth remembering.

He had scarcely made himself comfortable and was sleepily pondering the crowded events of the day, when somebody splashed wine on his head. Irately he turned, to see the darkhaired girl darting away into the entwined shadows of the couples grouped around the dimming fire. He was now in no mood for a chase, and having found him he felt certain she would return. He lay back, but waited like a cat with muscles poised to spring. Another splash of wine and he whirled round with the speed of a tiger and caught at her wrist and held her. Laughingly she dropped the wine-cup and tried to tear herself away, then acquiesced.

"Tell me," Jacobi said, "do you always treat Journeymen this way in Catenor?"

"Not very often." Her eyes, reflecting firelight, were brimfull of impudence and mischief. "But then this is rather a special day.

"What makes this day so different from the others?"

"Your coming," she said simply. Something in her manner made him feel that this was no mere coquettish compliment. He pulled her down, then rolled over to the side.

"What's your name?"

"Melanie." She nestled up against him.

"Very well, Melanie. Now tell me why my coming makes this such a special day."

"Why?" She sat up, puzzled. "Because we've waited for you such a long time, that's why. For years Timor's wanted a Guild Journeyman to teach him how to build the new ships. The Guild offered him a hundred, but he preferred to wait for only Jacobi."

"He'd heard of me before?"

"Heard of you? Jacobi, what are you saying? Three years he's waited to buy your bond for the shipyards. In those three years the raiders have come here seven times. Thirty men are dead in the fighting and more women than I dare to count have been carried to their ships. That's the price we paid for waiting for Jacobi."

"I see." Jacobi did not see at all, but his experience led him to caution. When raiders attacked an otherwise static and feudal society, not all the men died at the raiders' hands and not all the women were carried unwillingly to the marauding cloudships. But his reputation in Catenor seemed unjustified. Other Journeymen had become legends by virtue of their knowledge or their skill or partisan approach. But his own dedication was to science. No one had a right to set him up as a demi-god.

"And you think that my coming here is going to change all that?" he asked at last.

She laughed. "Jacobi!"

"Yes?"

"You disappoint me. Are you going to talk all night?"

He pulled her closer. "Sorry! I've much to think about." He turned his mind to more certain aspects of his reputation. And by the morning she was far from disappointed.

II

Catenor was a clean and pleasant town, like most shipyard towns where methane gas was used to fuel the cloud craft. This was largely because the system of gas production placed a premium on decomposable organic waste.

The shipyards were a mile from the town and the road between the town and the yards held plentiful evidence of the enormous underground chambers into which was run the dross and all the field and farmyard waste and the spoilt ends of the harvest. From these chambers Timor extracted his gas for use or sale, and, in return for services received, he distributed the rich manures which kept the soil fertile for so many miles around.

Near the shipyards a small but rapid river turned the water-screws which powered Timor's reeking line-pumps. In the engine-shed proper the rattle and wheeze of the machinery treating and compressing the gas spoke of large and powerful atmospheric engines, but these were not visible from the road. The treated gas was forced into the strong but light-weight spheres which powered the burners of the cloudcraft. In recent pirate attacks the stock of spheres had been a prime target for the raiders, who both coveted the rich gas and were loath to leave behind undamaged any that they could not take. For this reason Timor kept his stocks of processed gas as low as practical and well protected behind a heavy stockade.

All of these things Jacobi noted as he walked that first morning from the town to the shipyards. With a knowledgeable eye he analysed each stage of Timor's establishment as he came upon it. Timor the Cloudmaster was one of the old tradition of Cloudsmen. With an approach almost wholly empirical he nevertheless constructed in his yards cloudcraft whose durability and range was the envy of many who were better technically endowed. Only the strong influence of the Guild had succeeded in producing craft superior to Timor's and now Timor was trying to even the balance by importing Guild knowledge and science to back his own skill and expertise. But it was an importation which promised to be more fruitful than ever Timor hoped.

Jacobi knew that by the end of his bond in Catenor the wheeze of the atmospheric engines would be replaced by the sharper hiss and rattle of high pressure steam reciprocating engines, and the steam-turbine would not be far away from discovery. At a guess, the waterscrews would also disappear, as new efficiencies in the gas compressors outstripped the capacity of the old line pumps to move sufficient gas from the tanks. Perhaps, with the shaft-power and the techniques and ideas he would leave behind him, some in Catenor would even begin to experiment with the unfamiliar concepts of a strange force called electricity. And these things would be incidental to his contribution to the methods of building cloudcraft.

It was less than an hour after dawn and a crisp chill still inhabited the air, but the yards were already alive with activity. Axemen were shaping spars and deck timbers with the sharp snick of steel on firm wood. Blacksmiths' forges glowed with the regular pulse of the bellows, and hammer and anvil chimed a chorus which had everything but melody. In the spinning shed the song of women denoted the satisfactory progress of making ropes and rigging. Only the fabric shed held its accustomed silence as sharp-eyed seamstresses sewed the myriad tiny stitches to form the seams in the fabric panels from which the great balloons were made.

Timor was in his office. Jacobi knocked and entered, a trifle hesitant after his first encounter with the Cloudmaster. True to his reputation, Timor wasted no time in coming to the point.

"Is it true, Jacobi, that in Annonay the Guild yards are building cloudships which have no need for burners?"

Jacobi nodded. "True enough. They are filled with a gas called hydrogen, which is lighter than the air itself. They have no need for heat."

"Lighter than air?" Timor seemed about to dispute the statement. Then he stopped and spread his hands. "If you say it, then it must be so. Tell me, do these ships stay buoyant permanently without the need for fuel?"

"They lose a little gas, which has to be replaced. But substantially it's so."

"I see!" Timor considered for a moment. "Then a ship that needs no fuel for buoyancy has an almost unlimited range, and the cost of flight is low?"

"Yes."

"But if they have all these advantages, why do we not see more of them?"

"One day we shall, when we know better how to build and handle them. At the moment they're dangerous and tiresome craft to fly. Because of their inbuilt buoyancy there is no easy control of ascent and descent as on a normal cloudcraft. They are not easily landed to wait for wind-change and they are more happily moored to towers than brought to the ground.

"Strange craft," said Timor thoughtfully. "Could we build one here in Catenor?"

"If you have coal, furnace builders and boilermakers, yes. You have already everything else that is needed."

"And you will show us how?"

"My knowledge is yours, Timor. But don't underestimate either the difficulties or the dangers of the venture."

"Difficulties and dangers are part of the stock in trade of a Cloudsman," said Timor. "But I"ll bear it in mind. Build me a hydrogen ship such as they build in Annonay. When it comes to flying it, I have some of the finest Cloudsmen alive. With their skill and your knowledge, we'll learn to tame it. If such ships can do what you describe, then craft from Catenor will one day circle the world."

Jacobi smiled slightly. "A noble ambition, Cloudmaster."

"Aye! But not an impossible one. By all accounts the ancients used to do it."

"So the legends have it."

"Legends?" Timor's eyes were direct and challenging. "I had heard that in Annonay the achievements of the ancients were more than legend."

Jacobi shrugged. "Of gods and ancients there are always many tales. For myself, I find it better use of time to study the craft of cloudships."

"Indeed?" Timor was critical. "Your reputation says otherwise. They credit you with much knowledge of the ancients' science. I suggest that cloudships are merely an exercise in application."

Jacobi faced Timor squarely. "An intriguing speculation, Cloudmaster."

"But a true one, eh? No, don't worry. All that passes within these walls is between us two alone. But if we're to work together it's better that we understand each other fully."

"I think we already understand each other, Cloudmaster. But I'd be interested to know what gave you the notion."

"Deduction. Journeymen from the Guild come always to teach—never to learn. So who teaches the Guild? Where does all the knowledge come from?"

"That you must ask the Guild elders."

"I already have, but they were even more devious than you. Nemesis take them! So I draw my own conclusions. I suspect they have some oracle, some means of access to the knowledge of the ancients."

"Even if it were true," said Jacobi, "what difference would it make?"

Timor spread his hands expressively. "Knowledge is power, Jacobi. And with that sort of knowledge available to them, the Guild ought to be the most powerful force in the world."

"But it isn't," said Jacobi mildly.

"It doesn't appear to be. And there's the mystery of it. The Guild is influential, yes, but they seem to do no more than instruct in the building of cloudcraft."

"Doesn't that rather tend to disprove your theory, then?"

"No." The Cloudmaster's shrewd eyes searched Jacobi's face carefully. "No, it rather tells me they have some very good reason for acting as they do. I should dearly love to know what the reason is. In fact, I intend to find out somehow. So let me warn you: Jacobi, if you want to keep your secret, maintain your guard carefully. Because there's more than I hold to this theory and some who would go to even greater lengths than I to find the answer."

The big trunk which was the centrepiece of his possessions had a covering of tough, tanned hide, deep-shone from years of burnishing and wax, patterned with brass studs and fitted with a massive hinge. The lock, a rare example of the artistry and skill of some craftsman worker in brass, was disfigured only where a thief had once used a crowbar in an abortive attempt to force it open. But Jacobi was unworried by the threat of attempted theft. Under the hide and the brass and the hints of underlying oak which showed at scuffed corners was a casket of forged vanadium steel and the wards and tumblers which guarded the lock were products of another age and not likely to yield to any tools or crafts available in Catenor.

He had deliberately sought lodgings in the town, away from the shipyards and from the living quarters usually provided. The gods had favoured his search and he had secured a high attic room, comfortably furnished, covering the entire area of the house. The several dormer windows admitted ample light by day and provided good views over the surrounding country. Now, under the rough-hewn beams of the low and sloping ceiling, he had a chance to be alone and unobserved. Jacobi checked the door, then opened the trunk and took out a device which he laid upon the table. He thumbed it into activity and waited impatiently for the go-ahead tell-tale to show.

"Jacobi calling Annonay ControI."

There was a moment"s hesitation before the device answered.

"Annonay Control answering." The voice was accompanied by a rushing background like the sound of waves on a seashore. "Come in, Jacobi. How's progress?

"Good," said Jacobi. "As we suspected, Timor has his suspicions about what the Guild is doing, but he's no idea how or why it's being done. Fortunately his curiosity is going to make him very receptive to new ideas. I suggest we push up the pace in Catenor just as fast as they can absorb it.

"Agreed," said the voice of Annonay Control. "Progress has been far too slow in Catenor and the west and too fast in Annonay. The discrepancy's beginning to show. There's even talk of moving the Guild yards out of Annonay to slow things down a bit."

"I guessed it might come to that," Jacobi said. "No matter how well you keep a secret, something always leaks. Catenor would be a good place for a new Guild yard if I can cut down the raiding."

"Is it that serious?"

"Not so far, but it threatens to become so. Apparently the raiders have got some craft with engines now and if they follow the advantage along the usual lines they could stifle Catenor before I can really get it started."

"I'II look into it. I doubt if the elders will sanction direct action against the raiders, but they'll probably give you discretionary powers to play the situation to the best advantage for Catenor."

"Discretionary powers would be all I'd need," said Jacobi. "I'll be in touch later."

"Right! I'll put this to the elders and see if I can get you a quick decision. And, Jacobi . . ."

"Yes?"

"Promise me something. You've a tough job ahead and we can't afford complications. Leave the women alone."

"Nemesis forbid that I touch one!" said Jacobi.

"That's no damned answer and you know it. I tell you, Jacobi, one day you're going to put a woman before Guild principles. And on that day you're going to make a mistake. But with the type of merchandise we're handling, we just daren't make mistakes. People have set the world on fire for much, much less."

Jacobi turned off the device, but looked at it thoughtfully for a long while before putting it away. Its compact heaviness stemmed largely from the crystal and ceramic blocks within: solid-state fully-integrated monolithic circuits and the imperishable Seebeck-effect fissile semiconductor generator techniques from the age of miracles. Yet to him the device was neither an anachronism nor was it futuristic. It was simply one of those accepted portions of life which, except in Guild circles, must forever remain in the shadows. And Jacobi was aware that the shadows folded more closely round him every day.

Finally he closed the trunk and locked it and lit the dim oil lamp, for the night was closing in. Somebody had left him roses in a vase on the table, and the scent, unnoticed until this moment, made him think of lips and wine and a girl called Melanie . . . Melanie with the night-dark hair and a way of making love which was scorching like the sun. Slowly the shadows grew in the dormer alcoves and extended from the huge, untidy beams until the symbolism of the room became an exacting analogue of his life and his projected future. And at that point Jacobi reacted to his unreasoning compulsion—and left the room in search of life and light.

There was a tavern off the main street where the sounds of cheerful expression exceeded the capacity of the brew house to keep it confined. The light and the laughter and the music spilled from the doors and windows in a friendly tide which spread across the gutter and irresistibly attracted his feet. Entering, he chanced upon the yardsman who had met him on his arrival in Catenor. The fellow greeted him heartily, ordered ale, then drew Jacobi aside conspiratorially.

"You're a rare lad, Jacobi. You know, you'd quite a reputation even before you arrived. But you've a better'n now or worse'n, depending on how you look at it." He nudged Jacobi in the ribs with his elbow.

"You're way ahead of me," said Jacobi guardedly. "I'd been drinking much. What did I do?"

"Do?" The yardsman nudged him again. "There's not many men in Catenor who'd dare lay Timor's daughter—even if she'd give them the chance, which she wouldn't."

"Timor's daughter? You mean the girl Melanie is Timor's daughter?"

"Zeus! Do you mean you didn't know it? I'll wager Timor's not been able to find you today, else you'd not be left in doubt."

"I spent most of the day with him," said Jacobi. "But he never said a word of it. Perhaps he doesn't know."

The yardsman's brow clouded. "Nothing happens in Catenor that Timor doesn't know. Take a tip from me, lad. Tread very warily. Timor and his daughter were both stamped from the same clay. They neither of them give anything except that they expect back a great deal more for it. Just ask yourself, Jacobi, what is it they're expecting to get from you." The yardsman turned back to his friends. "Here, lads, what do you make of this . . ."

Jacobi joined them in the drinking and the friendly badinage, while some more serious part of his mind attempted to analyse the situation. He ignored his previous feelings of pride because he realized now that the conquest had been too easy. Last night she had been the hunter and he the hunted - and Timor had held his peace about it. Or had he? Jacobi held the memory of the shrewd eyes on his face and the voice which said: ". . . and some who would go to even greater lengths than I to find the answer."

But just how much did Timor expect to get in return for his daughter?

III

Timor fetched a master black-iron boilermaker from his workplace near the forests. The furnace makers came a hundred miles by cloudcraft on the first good winds, listened to Jacobi's proposal, and shook their heads. Then they decided to stay. Jacobi, fighting the lack of established technology which a Guild yard would have given him, was patient. He modified and simplified his designs to suit the tools and skills available, hoping that he could achieve his aim without sacrificing safety. He alone was conscious of the more subtle aspects of the exercise. Given the need for a product and the certainty that it could be made, the techniques for its production would grow like seeds in men's minds. If he could manage to build one plant for producing hydrogen in Catenor, then others would far more easily be able to build similar plants in the future.

For the quantity and purity of the hydrogen he needed, he decided to build two complementary plants: an ironsteam retort for producing the hydrogen itself, and a water-gas generator to regenerate the sponge-iron bed in the retort. An alternative scheme to produce hydrogen also directly from water-gas he dismissed because of the practical difficulties of building scrubbers to remove the unwanted carbon di- and monoxides.

A small coke-making plant was also necessary and he planned to contain some of the coal-gas by-product both to assist in heating his retorts and also to introduce the inhabitants of Catenor to its uses. Thus an offshoot of his work would be the founding of at least one new basic industry in Catenor which would grow in time without his further intervention.

Absorbed in the problems of planning such an ambitious venture and one which involved him as designer, inventor, overseer and the source of almost all the knowledge it required, Jacobi almost daily worked himself to a standstill. He frequently slept on the site amid the tools and drawings, being too tired even to journey to his room in Catenor. Under these conditions he almost forgot the dark-haired Melanie, having neither the time nor the energy for pursuit or conquest. After many days of such activity, Timor, fearing for Jacobi's health, ordered him to rest. Jacobi went to his room at midday and slept the twenty-four hours round.

He awoke to the scent of roses from the fresh blooms on the table and leaped rapidly out of bed, realizing that someone had visited him while he slept. He found no sign of the intruder, however, except that yesterday's dead rose petals had been swept into the basket. Checking the door, he turned to the trunk and set the communication device on the table. As he pressed the switch the print-out slot at the bottom began to issue a white card. He picked it up and read its legend.

—ANNONAY CONTROL TO JACOBI—URGENT—GUILD APPROVES YOU FULL DISCRETIONARY POWERS AGAINST RAIDERS—IMPERATIVE UPGRADING OF CATENOR PROCEEDS AS PLANNED—ANNONAY SITUATION IMBALANCE

BECOMING CRITICAL—END—

Jacobi was about to make verbal contact with Annonay, then thought better of it. Even in the daylight, another wrap of shadows seemed to close around his shoulders and he was suddenly depressed at the sheer weight of the obligations which were pressing on his head. Some beast inside him clawed out to establish a personal freedom which he knew he might never attain. Guild merchandise was indeed a dangerous and heavy weight to carry.

A footstep on the stair leading to his attic broke his reverie. He locked the device securely in the trunk before he dared open the door. It was Melanie, with kisses, fresh pies, bread and wine. Jacobi, having just awakened from sleep, had not realized how great was his appetite. And later, as the setting sun red-bloomed the ceiling with its light, they both sat down to eat.

It was only afterwards, when Melanie had gone, that Jacobi looked for the white card bearing the message from Annonay—and found that it was missing. In this he sensed he had already made a mistake of the kind about which Annonay had warned. But even so, he reckoned that he had gained the best of the bargain from the unintended contract. He knew now that Timor's curiosity must be as insatiable as was his daughter's passion for love. And these were both factors he could use to the Guild's or his own advantage.

Having ensured that the construction of the hydrogen plant was well started, Jacobi turned his attention to the making of the hydrogen ship itself. This was not so difficult, since most of the techniques were common with those Timor already used. But the work involved a lot of calculations which were foreign to Timor's empirical approach. In design detail, too, there were alterations to be made. Jacobi insisted that the iron links and bolt eyes normally employed round the deck-yoke be replaced by fixtures of wrought brass, to eliminate the possible danger from sparks. He wanted a mooring tower, too, but he originally dismissed the idea because, without engines available, he knew that once the craft had left the tower no wind, however favourable, could ever drift it back to that precise point for mooring. But Timor over-ruled the objection, and ordered the tallest firs to be cut from the forest and trimmed and erected to make a scaffold of sufficient height to launch the ship.

The coke-making plant was the first thing in operation. Timor was more interested in the tar than in the coal-gas itself, but Jacobi made lime-light burners which were far brighter than the torches used round the yards, and the yardsmen were quick to adopt them. Meanwhile his stocks of coke grew to a useful volume.

It was during this period that the raiders made their next appearance. Jacobi was in the yards with Timor, explaining details of how hydrogen could be safely conveyed from the retort to the ship. Above them a dark and sultry sky showed the imminence of rain. The yards were already apprehensive. This was the raiding season and a low cloud-belt with suitable winds formed the most advantageous conditions and cover for the cloud raiders. Lookouts had already been posted on the towers and no one was surprised to hear the horns and the cries of: "Raiders ho!"

Typical of their pattern of attack, the raiders had travelled far and were now returning on home winds. Thus they could descend at will, secure their prize, and escape to the clouds again safe in the knowledge that any who dared to follow must drift into the dangerous mountain region which was raider's territory. Had they attempted a raid while borne on outward winds, Timor's crews would have taken to the air and followed them into some final battle precipitated by the lesser range of the marauding cloudcraft. But no craft from Timor's yards had ever returned once having entered the mountains.

The lookouts were eagle-sharp in their perception and both Timor and Jacobi had to scan the sky to locate the points already identified as raiding craft. Timor saw them first and uttered an oath of annoyance.

"The carrion!" he said. "Only three, but this time they've

got engines. Where's our defence against that?"

The question was rhetorical and Jacobi made no answer. His searching eyes found the objects and even at that range he could see that Timor was right. At the rear of each deck squatted a black bulk of mechanism with a shaft trailing crude wings which flailed huge circles in the air. The effect of the wings was slight, but for combat the ability to move even slightly faster than the wind, or to resist it, gave its possessor a crucial advantage. Timor's craft, like all normal cloudships, had control of ascent and descent, but for speed and direction they were utterly dependent on the winds.

The raiders, however, had a further advantage. Besides conferring a degree of control over the speed, the engines also gave a limited manoeuvrability. This was being demonstrated now. Their ships were not following the wind but moving cross-wind at a slow angle so as to bring their course more nearly over the shipyards. To achieve this they were using canvas keels on a framework set aslant under the decking, which, combined with the thrust from the rotating wings, angled their ships untidily crabwise but gave them some choice of direction.

Jacobi could sense Timor's mixed anger and interest as the unorthodox craft drifted nearer to his yards. This was certainly not a raiding party. With only three ships, each carrying but a handful of men, they would have fared badly had they attempted to land. More probably it was a scouting expedition assessing the potentialities of the harvest in preparation for a future raid. Given fair winds they would come again one day soon with a hundred ships or more, armed and able to take whatever they needed or fancied.

"Jacobi." The Cloudmaster had moved to his side, still gazing at the ships in the sky. "If I could get one of those engines, could you make it work for me?"

"Yes. Or copy it and build more. But they're too heavy for your kind of voyaging. You need too much gas for the burners in order to maintain buoyancy. That limits your range."

"But your hydrogen ship could carry one without limiting its range."

"True!"

"Good!" Timor had come to a sudden decision. He dashed across the yards yelling orders to his crews. At first Jacobi failed to understand his intention, but suddenly the import of the conversation struck home to him.

At four points in the yards tethered craft, with balloons filled and ground-based auxiliary burners idling, had been prepared for flight and were waiting for a wind-change that would drift them southeast with cargoes of pigs for sale. The squeal of swine being hastily released into the yards and the running flurry of men told of a rapidly conceived change of purpose. Shipborne burners flared high and luminous as scratch crews hastened to prepare the ships for flight. As the craft were readied Timor bade them stay as he watched the speed and direction of the raiders' ships above, anxious not to rise too soon and be carried by the wind helplessly out of the field of battle.

Jacobi moved too, as soon as he realized what Timor meant to do. The dark cloud-cover and the impending rain gave him a sudden inspiration. He ran to the workshop wherein he kept his tools and personal belongings. In his satchel was a waterproof pouch, tight-folded and bound to form a seal. He hooked the pouch to his belt and took out also a short rodlike weapon with a grip to fit his hand. Then he ran back to where Timor's cloudcraft still strained at their moorings. Noting the position of the raiders, he chose the ship he judged most likely to make a near interception and climbed aboard, swinging up the rigging like a monkey.

Timor was on the decking and saw him pass. He raised a quizzical eyebrow and seemed to shout something, but no words came to Jacobi's ears. Jacobi reached the fabric of the balloon and continued on up the rigging net outside the huge envelope, his toes digging into the soft fabric belly. Then, at Timor's signal, the mooring ropes were axed, and the four cloudships rose from the yards in slow unison in an attempt to intercept and come to grips with the raiders.

It was a good attempt, but one doomed to failure from the start. The air in Timor's balloons had grown over-hot in the period of waiting and the craft rose at a faster than usual rate. Though the burners were quickly doused, Timor's ships achieved the altitude of the raiders too soon, and continued rising. Some of Timor's men had crossbows, but the punctures made by steel shafts in the fabric of the raiders' balloons were too small to do material damage. Likewise they were too high and too distant to accurately find targets on the raiders' decks. Their only chance was to try and close the separation to a point where they could ensnare the raiders' rigging with barbed grapples and haul the vessels together.

Frantically Timor's ships vented air in an attempt to fall closer to the raiders' level. But the process was slow and the enemy craft had abruptly changed course. Since he could control only the height and not the position of his craft, the situation was out of Timor's hands. The raiders' new direction was calculated to take them out of grapple and bowshot range in the shortest possible time, and, incidentally, proved the superiority of engines in combat or defence.

Almost atop the balloon now, with his feet wedged securely between the fabric and the rigging, Jacobi waited, watching the raiders' ships behind and below wheel to the new course which Timor would be unable to follow. Then his heart leaped as he saw the implications of the move. Given luck, the right-hand ship of the three, moving slowly sideways and at a speed slightly greater than that of the wind, would soon pass reasonably close below the craft on which he sat. He opened his waterproof pouch with particular care, then took up the weapon with the hand-grip and bent it savagely.

The mechanism clicked satisfactorily and he straightened it and opened the breech. In the pouch were darts with long, thin, metal splines and a curious head. He fitted one into the weapon and sighted it on the raiders' balloon, waiting his opportunity. A few rainspots thudding on the fabric around him reminded him to close the pouch securely. For some minutes it seemed as if his plan might come to nothing. The target craft on which his attention was centred was drawing rapidly off of their course and the venting of the balloon on which he rode was reducing the height difference without bringing them closer together.

He finally judged the approach of the two ships to be about the nearest that they would achieve, though the range was still too far for certainty. Raising his weapon he took careful aim at the target balloon. The weapon responded with the *phut* of released air, but there was no way of knowing if his dart had found a target or fallen into empty air. Swiftly he reloaded and re-primed his weapon and sent his darts winging one by one. Above them the rainclouds hovered dark and the forests below were still and saddened by shades of black. Now only time would tell if his missiles had found their intended place of lodging.

He became aware slowly that he was not alone. Timor had climbed the rigging on the other side and had been watching his activities with interest. He moved round and took Jacobi's weapon and examined it curiously.

"If crossbows can't get me an engine, what chance d'you think you have with this? Or was it crows you were after?" The last sentence was less of a question than a probe for further information.

Jacobi maintained a bland face. "Gaining an engine is your affair, Timor. Never let it be said that a Cloudmaster looks for help of a whelp or mewling. And even the crows were cleverer than I."

Timor scanned him narrowly. Although they were by this time at roughly the same level as the raiders' balloons, the divergent paths of the two forces had placed their distance apart too far now even for bowshot. But Jacobi continued to follow the progress of his quarry closely.

"You're up to some mischief," said Timor. "Else you'd not have come."

"I?" Innocently.

"Yes, Jacobi. There's far more to your scheming than the building of cloudcraft."

"Do you have any complaints about the way I serve my bond?"

"Quite the contrary. You've achieved more progress in a

few weeks than most men accomplish in a lifetime. That's what makes me suspicious. It doesn't escape me that everything you do has at least two purposes."

"Nemesis take the thought! How badly do you want that engine?"

"If I cannot match the raiders in the sky then I had better stop shipbuilding in Catenor."

"That's what I thought," said Jacobi. "When the raiders are far enough crosswind they'll stop using their engines—they take too much fuel to use for other than short manoeuvres. After that they'll drift with the winds and rely on us not following them into the mountains. Maintain your height and stay with them. It could just be that one of them won't get that far."

"I see!" Timor's eyes were like bright steel coins in wrinkled pigskin purses. "They didn't tell me that prognostication was also one of your talents."

"I'm no adept. I could do with a little assistance."

"In what way?"

"Pray for rain," said Jacobi.

IV

As Jacobi had predicted, the raiding ships, having drawn far enough crosswind to be free from molestation, stopped their engines and drifted with the same winds that carried Timor's ships. Thus there was a period of enforced stalemate during which the pirate ships strove to gain height, and Timor's ships to follow them.

Jacobi maintained his station atop the balloon, watching the growing rainclouds and the darkening ridges of the mountains towards which they were being carried. Under the mountains the broad estuary of the river showed like a band of steel dividing the fertile lands from the grey rock slopes.

Time was becoming important. If the rain came before the drifting forces reached the river, they would most probably gain their prize. But if it held off for longer, then the raiders would drift home to the sanctuary of the mountains and

Timor would not dare to follow them across the water. If Timor's ships crossed to the mountains they would isolate themselves from help or return on the ground and would have to set-down in the mountain reaches to await a wind-change. This might well involve a long encampment, and, due to the haste of their departure, the party had come recklessly unprovisioned. Further, falling into raiders' territory they could expect no help or mercy from pirates anxious to add new cloudcraft to their stolen fleet.

But a closer misfortune was at hand for Timor's ship. In the yards the cloudcraft had been readied, waiting for wind-change using ground-based auxiliary burners to conserve the gas charge in the flight spheres. The latter had been standing near the craft and had been hastily coupled when the emergency ascent began. Unfortunately something had been overlooked. The sphere of gas powering the burner on which their buoyancy depended broke suddenly from its straps and plummeted downward. The loss of its weight shot the ship rapidly skyward before it began its slow, inevitable fall as the air in the balloon grew cooler.

Jacobi felt the ship lift as the sphere fell away and the cries of dismay from below explained the nature of the mishap. He could have wept with frustration, for the growing patter of raindrops indicated that, the gods willing, a few minutes longer might have placed the raiders' ship and its engine at their mercy. Nor was he deceived as to the seriousness of the situation facing Timor's vessel.

He felt the rigging under him slacken and his weight begin to sink into the fabric as the warm air inside the balloon grew less supporting. The men from the deck below were climbing now to join him, the safest place aboard a crashing cloudship being above the fabric, with something beneath to cushion the impact of landing and less chance of being smothered by the collapsing envelope. But at this height their chance of survival was less than even and fear inhabited their eyes.

Their companion ships, seeing their plight; began to fall also—initially faster since they could afford to vent hot air, while Timor could not. Timor's concern was to retain every vestige of buoyancy which the cooling air in the balloon could give them, but they were still dangerously high and he had no real hope of succeeding. Jacobi stayed aloft a moment longer, watching the craft in which he was sure his darts were buried and praying for effect from the now freely falling rain.

The gods were suddenly pleased. From the balloon and rigging of the raiders' ship patches of fire sprang up, clearly visible even from the growing distance. The fires were quickly extinguished, but were sufficiently damaging to make holes in the fabric through which a man might have put his head. Then the crippled raider too began to fall.

The plight of Timor's craft was now perilous indeed. The angle of their descent threatened to drift them across the water to strike the mountain's foot with killing force and Timor dared not sharpen the angle by venting air, since this could only have increased their speed of impact. Summing up the situation rapidly, Jacobi clambered untidily down the slackening rigging and found Timor alone on the decking.

Timor forced a wry smile at his appearance. "What now, Journeyman? Does the Guild have answers for this situation too?"

"Yes," said Jacobi. "Get those men down and do as I do. It's our only chance."

Climbing back up the rigging to the point where the ropes just cleared the bottom of the envelope, he reached through the lines with a blade and slashed at the fabric. Timor watched him for one second before divining his purpose, then moved like a fury, cursing and slashing with his knife, and calling to the rest of the crew to do likewise. As the great circle was cut from the bottom of the balloon, the burner and its harness fell away. Shorn of this weight and open to the air, the half-balloon flowered outward like a giant mushroom within the confines of the rigging, its speed of descent checking perceptibly.

Then Jacobi directed their attention downwards and they cut the main ropes holding them at the lowest possible points. The decking fell dramatically away, leaving the men suspended in the rigging with the giant fabric mushroom now wildly unstable and threatening to spill air and collapse. But with the help of the gods and under the lashing of Timor's blasphemous tongue they managed to re-locate their weight and maintain the stability of their precious canopy. Again their speed was checked, but even then several of them would have come to harm had they not fallen into the waters of the estuary.

As his head broke the surface of the water, Jacobi struggled and freed himself from the ropes and rigging and struck out for the nearest land. He was a poor swimmer and he seriously doubted his ability to swim the distance. Certainly he had no capacity to go back and ensure that the others were free and able to escape. He swam doggedly towards a clump of trees which was all he could see of the shore, hoping that the cramp which so frequently terminated his swimming would not strike before he could reach safety.

For a long while his efforts seemed unable to decrease his distance from the trees and he began to lose hope. He was tiring rapidly with the unaccustomed exercise and his swimming had become a mode of spasmodic snatches at the water, wasteful of energy and unhelpful towards progress. Then cramp knotted the muscles in his right leg and in a momentary panic he twisted and sank untidily and painfully in the water.

He came up gasping for breath and spitting water and perilously near to drowning. But strong hands seized his shoulders and he allowed himself to float and be drawn by the arm towards the shore. Then he was commanded to put down his feet and he found himself standing with the water waist high on the soft sands. His rescuer supported him on his arm until Jacobi had managed to overcome the cramp in his legs sufficiently to limp his way to dry land.

Exhausted, Jacobi sank onto the bank for a while, then looked about. As far as he could gather, all the members of the ship's crew were now safely ashore. He noticed Timor farther along the bank, face down on his arms and covered in mud from the low basin through which he had crawled from the water. Even from a distance he could see Timor's shoulders moving convulsively, and, fearing that the Cloudmaster was ill, Jacobi ran to him and turned him over. But it was laughter that racked Timor's frame. Seeing Jacobi, he stopped and sat up and clapped a huge and muddy arm around the Journeyman's shoulder.

"By the gods, Jacobi, for a non-combatant you do a remarkable line in warfare and survival!"

Jacobi sat down beside him. "Did you think then that all that came from Annonay was academic?"

"No. I expected common sense as well. But not miracles. What did you do to the raiders' ship?"

"I shot darts at them tipped with a metal called sodium. The sodium was coated to protect it in my pouch, but when exposed to moisture the coat dissolved and the metal caught fire."

"Metal caught fire?" Timor looked at him quickly, then shrugged. "Strange tools for a Guild Journeyman, to be sure. Do they have a peaceful use as well?"

"No."

"I thought not," said Timor. "I always knew there was more to the Guild than sweetness and light. What now of your claim to be non-partisan?"

"I fired those darts in the Guild's interests, not in yours."

"I see! And how do you in Catenor determine what is in the interests of the Guild?"

"You already know that, Timor—or if you don't, ask Melanie."

"Zeus!" said Timor ruefully. "I should have known better than to bandy words with you." He searched in his soaking clothes for a pocket and from this he produced the wet and crumpled remains of what once had been Jacobi's message card from Annonay. "Nemesis take all double-devious journeymen! I've wronged you, Jacobi lad, and I freely admit it. I was suspicious of you and your overt cleverness. I still am, but I know now it's working in my favour. You build me a new ship, destroy my enemy and save my life. For that I repay you by doubting your motives and stealing your messages."

"And lending me your daughter," said Jacobi mischievously.

Timor's smile broke through again. "You won't be drawn, will you, Jacobi. I respect you for that, though I'm damned if I'll let the matter rest."

Soon they heard the horns through the thicknesses of the forest and answered with loud cries, having no horns of their own with which to answer. Fortunately they were heard and soon located by the crews of Timor's other ships which had made safe landing. A camp had been established and a brushwood fire had been started, the wet wood being kindled with methane from a flight sphere.

The remains of the damaged raiders' ship were found caught in the trees about two miles away. The crew were dead and the deck was torn and splintered, but the precious engine was almost intact and easily recoverable. Timor himself directed its lowering to the ground, with patient care. For him this was the start of a new era in Catenor and he would permit no risk which might endanger his prize. Finally the job was done and the engine, still on torn fragments of decking, was gently laid on the forest loam to await the drays from Catenor to carry it back to the yards.

When Jacobi examined the mechanism he found, not the crude gas engine he had expected, but a fairly advanced diesel, and he then knew for a certainty just how serious the situation in Annonay had become.

With Timor now even more solidly behind him, Jacobi now found himself in almost complete control of the Catenor yards and work on the hydrogen ship project moved ahead at a furious pace. The hydrogen plant was completed and ready for testing long before the ship itself had been constructed. Jacobi's daily round was long, arduous and exacting, but he found time to go to Catenor each evening to relax and see Melanie. After three weeks, and with her father's blessing, she chose to become his mistress and moved in with him in the high attic room. Thus stabilized, Jacobi put his mind and hands solidly to work.

The stormclouds of trouble brewing over Annonay left him largely untouched. Guild merchandise was explosive media and needed to be handled with caution even by those bred in its service. An uncontrolled leak of advance technology from Annonay into a world not yet prepared to receive it had given great advantages to an unscrupulous few and public opinion had swung sharply against the Guild. This was a breach of confidence which only time itself could heal. In the meantime the Guild had no option but to reduce the scope of its operations in Annonay to that of building established forms of cloud craft.

Six weeks later Jacobi's project was complete. The hydrogen plant was fully operational and a competent crew had been instructed in its use. The ship itself, now containing on its deck the diesel engine and a fair reserve of fuel, lay at the foot of the mooring scaffold waiting for the charge of gas which would make it buoyant without burners. The wings which the raiders had used on the engine had gone and in their place a wooden propeller occupied the shaft, while a system of rudders had been provided for direction. Tomorrow was to be the day of the first light. Jacobi's last checks gave him confidence that the venture would be a success. He returned to Melanie full of confidence.

Against Guild-rule, he had no longer made a secret of his communication device since Melanie had moved in. Now it stood permanently on a small table ready for his nightly contact with Annonay. Melanie left the instrument severely alone, realizing, by some instinct, that it was part of another age and had powers and contents whose secrets she would never comprehend. This factor, more than anything, brought home to Jacobi the separation which would always be between them and wrapped the insufferable shades of isolation more firmly round his shoulders.

This day when he arrived home she complained that the instrument had been clicking to itself as if trying to attract attention. Jacobi inspected the message store. The tell-tale indicated that something was contained therein, so he activated the print-out. He was both prepared and yet unprepared for the message he received.

—TECHNICAL INFORMATION RETRIEVAL CENTER NEW YORK—VIA SATELLITE LINK AND LA GAUDE SUB-CENTRE— TO JACOBI IN CATENOR—MESSAGE BEGINS QUOTE CRISIS SITUATION—RIOTING IN ANNONAY—GUILD YARDS ABANDONED—EUROPEAN OPERATIONS ENDANGERED—IMPERATIVE YOU SECURE CATENOR FOR NEW GUILD YARD—NEGOTIATE TIMOR ANY BASIS UNQUOTE—END MESSAGE—

—YORKTOWN CONTROL—

Jacobi caught the card in his hand and, after scanning it briefly, he slipped it into his pocket without a word to Melanie. Later he tried to raise Annonay Control on verbal contact, but received nothing but static from a distant storm. As the message had implied, the Annonay installation was finished. Whether later historians would see this as the end of an era which failed, or merely as a temporary setback to one of the braver ventures of mankind, was now largely in his own hands. But his hands were already tired from continuous overwork and the brain which guided them was likewise tired of too much knowing, too much thinking, too many obligations and a brand of loneliness which held him apart from Melanie even in the throes of love.

He found suddenly that he needed time to think, to question seriously, perhaps for the first time in his life, whether the purpose for which the Guild existed was an ideal worth what it demanded of him. It would be too easy to slip into the pattern of life at Catenor, to marry Melanie, to raise children, to build cloudcraft in Timor's yards and to forget the Guild and its intrigues and obligations and its dedication to an abstraction called posterity. He remembered acutely the whip of his own anger against those who had inexplicably weakened and deserted. Only now could he see how immature it was to judge until one had oneself been tested and how little you could predict of your own reactions under the duress of emotion and overwork.

Melanie must have intuitively sensed the conflict within him and how crucially she was involved, for she drew him to her and soothed him and when they fell to making love it was tenderly and with a great consideration utterly unlike the passionate consummations of the past. Jacobi drifted into sleep still in her arms, but restlessly, his dreams confused with vaulted banks of microfilm and microfiche and ranks of reading-screens, video playback monitors and electron flying-spot decoders. Again the voice of his mentor led him through the complex concepts of computerized normal text awareness and reconstructed in painstaking detail the elements of computer programming for data retrieval. When he awoke, over-hot and unrested, to the sound of horns and cries of: "Raiders ho!" he had some difficulty in determining reality from dreaming.

His confusion was enhanced by the fact that he knew that a pirate raid at such a time was a near impossibility. Firstly, the raiders never came in darkness and secondly the winds had set to outwind as far as the raiders were concerned. It would have taken a very confident raider—or a very mad one—to land in Catenor under such conditions. Or a very powerful group of raiders!

The last thought crystallized as a shattering possibility. Knowing that Timor had both a Journeyman and an engine, the raiders could have realized that opposition from Timor's sector was destined to become increasingly stiffer; ending as such developments must, in the final destruction of random raiding forces. The logical counter-move in such circumstances was a massed strike with all available manpower to stifle the potential opposition while it was still in embryo. That meant the yards would be the focal point of the attack, and destruction, not plunder, would be the object of the exercise.

Then Jacobi knew that his previous conflict had been resolved. He could see now that the opposite to the Guild's principle was a sort of painful barbarian anarchy—a hangover of the last dark age out of which they were still trying to claw their way. He dressed hastily, and Melanie, waking after him, sat up in a spasm of panic and clutched at his wrist.

"Jacobi, don't leave me!"

He drew his arm away carefully. "I have to get to the yards, Melanie. You know that."

"Yes."

She knew that he had to go but hoped that something in his makeup and his feeling for her would cause him to stay. As he reached the door he turned and the tears in her eyes accused him of betrayal. He had to close the door resolutely behind him to shut out her sobs as she collapsed back on the pillow. Had he listened further he too was sure he might have stayed.

The streets were full of running men, townsmen and yardsmen and the Catenor militia gathering together, and over all the sounds of horns calling from somewhere out in the night. Jacobi, having declined to adopt a partisan approach, had no set point of rendezvous and for this he was suddenly glad. He took the quietest alleys leading out of town, then along the road to the yards, setting up a good jog-trot the whole distance. Behind him he could hear carts setting out from Catenor, while, in front, watch-fires were being lighted around the yard perimeters by the yardsmen on duty. At this point he saw no sign of the raiders and had only the horns' evidence that they indeed had come.

At the yard gates he was stopped by a yardsman with a pike and forced back into a circle of firelight for recognition. His vitriolic condemnation of the delay was a performance worthy of Timor himself and a gate was immediately drawn open for him to enter. Inside the yards he had the place to himself and this suited his purpose well. He was halfway through to his destination when heavy fighting broke out near the gas stockade and a burst of flame pointed the pattern of the raiders' approach to the menace of the Catenor yards.

At the foot of the scaffold lay the components of his precious hydrogen ship. Tomorrow it should have proudly risen to shape and then taken flight for all in Catenor to see the progress in shipbuilding. Tonight it was a neat-stacked fold of fabric, rope and canvas above the deck which housed the engine. He knew precisely what he had to do. He pulled the drain plug from the fuel tank and allowed the crude oils to flow out onto the decking. When he was reasonably sure the deck and ropes were saturated he took a burner igniter and some chaff and encouraged a small fire which he threw bodily onto the oil-soaked decking. The resultant flare, which encompassed deck, fabric, rigging and scaffold, gave pause to raider and defender alike. But the hydrogen ship stood no chance of becoming a raiders' prize.

V

Catenor underestimated the raiders badly. Apparently in temporary collusion with several other pirate parties, over a hundred and fifty ships had landed in the vicinity and it was a toughened, ruthless army which hit Catenor and the yards that night. By morning the fight was nearly over. Using a feint attack on the yards as a diversion, the main spearhead of the raiders' forces had gone straight into Catenor with one specific purpose—hostages. The women and children had been herded like cattle out into the fields and any who opposed had been slain without mercy. Pockets of resistance in the town had been burned down or smoked out and nearly a quarter of Catenor was smoking ruins at the coming of the dawn.

Deceived by this pattern of tactics and embittered by the savagery of the attack, Timor, who held the yards intact save for the gas stockade, refused to surrender his installation. The raiders sent him the limbless torso of a young girl and promised him another every hour until he gave in. Soon ragged white flags flew upon the lookout towers and the raiders had their way. Jacobi stood with arms folded and watched, knowing that he alone would have to win the battle that the rest of Catenor had lost. The message of the mutilated child's body was not lost on him. Guild-rule or no Guild-rule, a Journeyman made partisan by witness to such an atrocity was no mean enemy.

Jacobi foresaw the coming developments even if Timor did not. The Cloudmaster, his face full-thunder, went out to meet the raiding chief and his aides. They knocked him down in the dust and kicked him and passed on into the yards dragging a captive behind them. The captive was Melanie, hands bound and scolding like a fury. They made a rope halter and tethered her to a post like any common beast.

"Where's the Journeyman?"

"Here." Jacobi came forward, arms folded.

"Ah!" The raiders' leader, a bearded giant called Dacon, signalled swift acknowledgment. "You would be Jacobi. We've heard of you." He nodded in the direction of Melanie, straining at her bonds. "In fact we know a great deal about what motivates Catenor. The woman is primary hostage to ensure your cooperation."

"The Guild is not amenable to blackmail," said Jacobi. "Neither does it operate under duress. As a Cloudsman, if you have a reasonable claim to Guild service, you shall receive it. Otherwise you may rot."

"Service? You damned whelp!" Dacon blazed with anger. "It's not service we want from you—it's hydrogen."

"Hydrogen? In those sacks?" Jacobi looked across the fields to where the raiding cloud craft were scattered across the fields.

"Yes, in those, Journeyman."

"No," said Jacobi flatly. "If you want hydrogen you'd best buy a Journeyman-at-bond from the Guild. There's more to hydrogen flight than filling cloudships."

"Zeus! I could afford three hundred men for the price of one Guild bond. But why should I bother when you will provide it free of charge?"

"The Guild does nothing free of charge. If you want hydrogen you'll pay Guild price."

Jacobi turned and walked deliberately away towards Timor's office. After a dozen paces he was caught and swung roughly round again to face the raiding chief.

"You mistake your position here, Journeyman. Are we to

treat you with presents as we did with Timor?"

"No," said Jacobi, "it is you who mistake your position.

You can't kill everyone in Catenor, because you're outnumbered by several to one. Only your hostages protect you. But if you continue your atrocities on the hostages they won't constitute protection any more. When that point comes the population will tear you apart with their bare hands if necessary."

Dacon was amused. "It was scarcely our intention to settle here."

"You've some small craft out there," said Jacobi, nodding to the field, "and you've already come a fair way. Don't tell me you've fuel enough for your burners to carry the whole of you right across the plains."

"No," said Dacon, discomfited by the accuracy of Jacobi's summary. "Hence our interest in hydrogen. With it we can dispense with using fuel."

"And save at Guild price you'll get no hydrogen from me."

"I think we shall," Dacon looked towards Melanie. "Yon's a pretty girl and ripe too. I'd imagine you'd hear her screaming a long ways from here if we put our minds to it."

Jacobi faced him squarely. "Try it. See how many women you have to torture or how many children you need to mutilate before you precipitate the bloodbath you cannot possibly hope to win." He spat contemptuously on the cloud-pirate's ankles, then turned his back and walked away, praying the shadows of Guild responsibility would clog his ears with clay and poke the eyes out of his imagination. Every step he took was a determined effort and every muscle movement demanded voluntary control as if, in the interim, he'd forgotten how to walk. He reached the stairs leading to Timor's office and had ascended the first three steps before he dared to turn. Behind him there had been no sound at all.

Dacon had followed and was ten paces off, standing now looking up at Jacobi.

"Very well, Journeyman! What is the Guild price for hydrogen?"

"Simply that, when you have it, you leave Catenor immediately. No more killing, no rape, no hostages and no women to be taken."

"Only that?" Dacon's face registered his disbelief. "I don't follow your reasoning, Journeyman. Where's the Guild gain in that?"

"That's the Guild affair. Do you want to pay more?"

"No. I accept the price. In return for my ships filled with hydrogen I will see it goes as you ask. But we came here for a reason—and that was to destroy Timor's yards. You say nothing of that in your bargain."

Jacobi shrugged. "Leave the hydrogen plant undamaged, but with the rest you may do as you will. It's no concern of mine."

Timor had come back into the yards, his mouth bloody and shorn of the aura of control and authority he normally carried about him, he seemed to have aged incredibly. Now he was but an old and beaten man, ignored by the raiders and unable to surmount the circumstances which had befallen him. He found his daughter tethered to a post and tried to interfere, but the pirates merely threatened the girl with a knife and he moved on helplessly. Then he saw Jacobi and Dacon and came hesitantly across the yards to know what they were saying.

He could not have caught the words but must have guessed the gist of the conversation, for suddenly he roared with anger and drew himself back to something of his old stature.

"Jacobi, by the gods, I'll make no bargains with murderers!"

"The bargain is already struck in the Guild's name," said Jacobi.

"Then the Guild will have to fulfil it. You'll get no aid from Catenor."

"I need the crew to make hydrogen."

"Any man of mine who helps you will have a sorry time living in these parts hereafter. And you'll likely find it healthier yourself to leave if you assist this hell-spawn."

"Then get back with the women and children," said Jacobi, "because you've entered your second childhood all too sudden." He turned to Dacon. "Find me men and I'll instruct them what to do. Start bringing your craft here to the yards and have plenty of tethers prepared."

"They'll get no hydrogen here." Timor pushed his way past the pirate and started up the steps towards Jacobi and there was murder in his eyes.

This time it was Jacobi who knocked Timor into the dust.

The word spread fast and support for Timor was unanimous among the men of Catenor. No yardsman would cooperate with the raiders, even under the threat of death, and the raiders finally cleared them from the yards. In the town feeling against Jacobi ran high for his quisling activities, though he had no opportunity to explain the bargain he had struck, nor did he attempt to do so. Melanie was one of the last of Timor's people to leave the yards. They took her, unbound now and silent, back to the rest of the women. Her only action as she passed through the gate was to spit in Jacobi's face and look at him, not in anger, as might have been expected, but with disgust and repugnance, such as one reserves for something unspeakably obscene.

The reasoning behind Jacobi's unpopularity was obvious.

Having already some craft with engines, the raiders had a great superiority in flight. With hydrogen also, they would be untouchable. Not only Catenor but the entire province would be permanently wide-open to plunder and rape and no man might raise his hand against the raiders for fear of massive retribution. This, coupled with the loss of Timor's yards, would settle the area back into the fringes of the dark ages of lawless poverty and fear from which it had so painfully striven to emerge.

Despite their loose and lawless association, the raiders were remarkably efficient when there was work to be done. All were expert Cloudsmen and many were ex-yardsmen dispossessed of their jobs by attitude or circumstance. Contrary to his expectation, Jacobi found no difficulty in instructing a raiding crew to work the hydrogen plant and well-organized dray-crews soon had the first ships in position ready for filling. As the first ships received their charge they were weighted with sand and hauled clear of the workings to allow new craft to be brought in.

With some one hundred and fifty balloons to fill, progress was slow and Jacobi initially doubted if the coal stocks would be sufficient. But by continuous operation of the cokemaking plant to ensure the most efficient yield, plus the stock of coke he had already accumulated, he managed to find the majority of the gas he needed. Several of the raiders' smaller craft he rejected as unsuitable for filling and these the raiders burned rather than leave them in Catenor.

The whole operation took three days. In that time the hostages had been permitted to slowly filter back into the town without further molestation. The raiders' pickets in the town had been withdrawn in stages and the pirate manpower was now almost entirely concentrated in the yards. The yards themselves were being systematically destroyed: the forges smashed, the fabric and rigging sheds burned, the methane chambers holed and the pumps and pipework bent and broken. Through the devastation Timor wandered daily without hindrance, watching his lifetime's work being reduced to rubble. Occasionally he came near to Jacobi and stood in silent witness, his face completely without expression.

All was complete by late afternoon on the third day. Since control of altitude in the gas-filled cloudships could not easily be attained without loss of hydrogen, Jacobi had suggested that the assorted ships could be kept more closely together by loosely roping the craft in groups, The idea of a cloudcity of associated craft appealed to the raiders and thus it was mainly in three groups of linked ships that the raiders departed on a slow wind. Dacon's and a few of the larger ships were unroped and these remained as a rear-guard until the main force was well aloft.

Timor's people and the citizens of Catenor kept well away during the hours of departure, presumably not wishing to incite an incident unnecessarily. But they were black on the fields between Catenor and the yards, watching and waiting. Dacon observed the slowly advancing horde with some amusement. When the raiders went, Jacobi would be left the sole occupant of the remains of what had once been the shipyards of Catenor—and Jacobi was not very popular.

As a final gesture the pirate called Jacobi to his side and nodded to the taut, human tide crossing the fields. "How about it, Journeyman? Do you fancy becoming a cloudpirate? We could make use of your talents and you've a hard welcome coming to you when your friends arrive. We've not left them enough solid wood to make a gallows, but doubtless they'll be satisfied with stoning."

"Thanks," said Jacobi, "but I'll take my chances here. I'll wager I'll live long enough to serve out my bond."

Dacon raised an inquiring eyebrow. "Then you've more faith in human nature than I. Farewell, Journeyman, and take care of that hydrogen plant. One day we may have need of more, and then we'll be back."

"I'll ask Timor to be sure to keep it hot for you," said Jacobi. "There's little enough else left for him to do."

With the raiders gone, Jacobi sat on a pile of rubble and watched the departing ships rise to become mere shadows in the clouds, then fade to nothing. Their disappearance was so absolute that they might well never have existed. But the solid witness of their recent tenure was unmistakable. The once proud shipyards of Catenor were now rubble and ash heaps and desolation. Somewhere to the fore was a small grave where the remains of a murdered child had been roughly buried in a shroud, the ends of which still showed above the ground. Around Catenor there would be more graves still. If Jacobi had ever again needed a reminder that the Guild ideal was the only way, then the stark picture about him would long serve to trigger his reactions.

He was aware from the almost silent sounds of entry that the townsfolk and yardsmen had reached the yards and he sensed rather than saw that Timor was at their head. He did not bother to turn and face them because any attempt at explanation from him would have been wasted words. Whatever they intended to do to him they would do regardless. So he sat and listened to their curiously wakelike approach and so was completely unprepared for the hand which fell suddenly on his shoulder.

"Peace, Jacobi!" It was Timor, his eyes on the clouds where the raiders had last been seen. "I think I know what you've done." He sat on the rubble beside the Journeyman. "Promise me not many of them will be alive by morning."

Jacobi turned to look into Timor's old, steel eyes. "Not more than about three dozen, I expect."

"Aye! And how many of them were here?"

"Nearly six hundred."

"Aye!" said Timor again, considering the enormity of the coming event. "For a non-combatant, Jacobi, you make a terrible enemy. How will they go?"

"After sundown, when the atmosphere cools, they'll lose height," said Jacobi. "Because I forgot to instruct them better, some of them will attempt to light their burners. Those ships will either catch fire or explode. Those roped together with them will likely go also."

"And if they should forbear to light their burners?"

"Then every ship has somewhere in its rigging one of my sodium darts. Perhaps tomorrow or the day beyond they'll find rain or cloud moisture sufficient for the purpose. If six of those six hundred are alive later than three days from now it'll be only because the gods have blessed them. Is that revenge enough for you, Cloudmaster?"

"Revenge, aye!" The Cloudmaster looked moodily about the ruined yards. "But not compensation. There'll be hard times in Catenor before we make cloudships here again."

As he spoke there was the sound of muffled thunder from above. Glancing upwards they saw a cloud light up, rose-tinted from within, followed by more thunder. Then away across the fields things fell burning from the sky through the cloud cover. Then whole ships came falling, wreathed in flame, and the black dots of men precipitated into death. There was no telling how many, but for fifteen incredible minutes the display continued and the fields were bright with fires against the growing dusk. Perhaps a third of the raiding armada fell in that time and those which escaped carried the sodium seed of their own death unknowingly somewhere in the rigging. Guild-rule or no Guild-rule, a Journeyman made partisan by witness to atrocity was no mean enemy.

Despite their grief and their losses, the citizens of Catenor celebrated Jacobi's victory that night. For the first time in memory the threat of raiders had been removed completely from the town. The loss of the yards and the death of some of their kinfolk saddened the occasion but did not quiet its expression. But this time Jacobi was restrained and unable to lose himself in the revels. The weight of Guild obligation now firmly entrapped his shoulders and its veil of shadows was suffocating about his face. As with Timor, the recent events had aged him greatly, and he was beginning to discern what loads the Guild elders habitually took upon themselves.

He took himself early from the celebrations and sought Timor at his house. The Cloudmaster was resting. His face, under the light from the dim oil lamp, was more lined and more aged than Jacobi ever remembered seeing it before. His old, shrewd eyes, however, had lost none of their steely comprehension.

"It's not a social call that brings you here at this hour, Jacobi."

"No. I want to buy your shipyards for the Guild."

Timor shrugged. "I have no shipyards. Only heaps of rubble."

"All the better. It will save us the work of demolition. The ships we want to build here will have no use for fabric and rigging."

"You speak in riddles," said Timor tiredly. "There are no such ships as those. But anyway, state your terms."

"The Guild will pay fair price for your yards as they stood before the raiders came. A Guild cell will be established here and you will become a Guild elder. All your former staff here will be guaranteed employment and many more besides. Also the Guild will set up schools, libraries, hospitals, factories, and whatever Catenor requires to develop as the industrial and commercial capital of Europe."

Timor considered this in silence for a long time, then:

"You bargain in the same way you fight, Jacobi—without compromise."

"Then it's a bargain?"

"It's a bargain. I'd be a fool to refuse. But in point you buy nothing from me but the knowledge and hand-skills of a few hundred craftsmen."

"That's all I need," said Jacobi. "From that all the rest will follow."

"And if I'm to become an elder of the Guild does that mean I also learn from whence the Guild gets it knowledge?"

"Its administration will be part of your responsibility," said Jacobi. "The ancients had machines they called computers which could read and be aware of what they read. They crystallized vast libraries down to strips of film and reels of tape and gave the computers access to these stores of information. A man could ask for all that was ever known of a subject and the machines would give it to him. Then, when the last dark age began, the ancients sealed down their equipments and left them for us."

"So this is the oracle from which the Guild gets its knowledge?"

"Something more tangible than an oracle, but it works as well. Journeymen are educated from birth in Guild schools where the level of knowledge taught from computer information is roughly two centuries ahead of the times in which we live."

"Then the purpose of the Guild is not to advance the art of building cloudcraft, but simply to spread this knowledge?"

"Just that," said Jacobi. "But to spread it in such a way that its introduction doesn't cause more misery than it relieves. Knowledge is power and we have no wish to create powerful tyrants through our own efforts."

"But why pretend to concentrate on cloudcraft?"

"It's a good cover and it presents an advancing technology that automatically scatters about it a lot of other skills and trades. In this way the Guild can re-fashion whole communities without anyone even suspecting the cause of the transformation."

"I suspected," said Timor quietly. "That's why Catenor waited three whole years for Jacobi. You see, I insisted on having nothing but the best."

Leaving Timor's house, Jacobi turned by a long route across the fields around the town, half fearing to put into action the next move because of the years of involvement which it would bring upon him. Along the dark ways, with only occasional moonlight to guide him, he chanced upon courting couples neglecting the rejoicing in the town for more deep and personal approaches. Momentarily he wished that Melanie was by his side, but he stamped the regret angrily from his mind, knowing that dreams separated by two centuries of technical education can never quite be reconciled.

Looking outward, he began to make his plans. The old shipyards, together with the farm adjoining, would make a landing strip—grass at first, and start with biplanes. Later—much later—concrete runways for the jets. Thus would a new breed of cloud craft rise out of Catenor. And one day, perhaps, even spacecraft. . . .

His steps took him back to the attic. It seemed now as empty and impersonal as his life. Melanie had no use for either since the night the raiders came. The message store of his communicator issued a single interrogatory symbol, indicating that the device had been contacted in his absence and a reply was awaited. Jacobi thought for a moment, then opened the keyboard in the top and typed his message slowly, noticing his hands were shaking.

JACOBI—CATENOR—TO TIRC YORKTOWN NEW YORK VIA LA GAUDE AND SATELLITE LINK—MESSAGE BEGINS QUOTE CATENOR YARDS DESTROYED BY RAIDERS—TOWN AND POPULATION SUBSTANTIALLY INTACT—RAIDERS DESTROYED—INSIST IMMEDIATE UPGRADING CATENOR TO PHASER FIVE LEVEL IMPERATIVE ELSE YOU LOSE EUROPE UNQUOTE—

JACOBI—CATENOR

The reaction was immediate. Before he could take his fingers from the keyboard the print-out began to spill words as if in a frenzy.

TIRC NEW YORK TO JACOBI URGENT—GOOD DECISION IF YOU CAN HANDLE IT—GUILD ALREADY APPROVED PHASE FIVE IN CATENOR—MASSIVE AID WILL BE ROUTED TO YOU VIA HELIUM DIRIGIBLES—ALL EUROPEAN OPERATIONS NOW CENTERED ON CATENOR UNDER CONTROL—GOOD LUCK—HOW DOES IT FEEL TO BE RUNNING YOUR OWN CIVILIZATION QUERY—

Jacobi's fingers returned to the keyboard, and after establishing contact codes he typed one further word in answer:

—HELL—

AMBASSADOR TO VERDAMNT

"Welcome to Verdammt, Lieutenant." Captain Administrator Lionel Prellen extended a hand to the new arrival.

Space Technician Lieutenant Sinclair ignored the hand and saluted gravely. "I understand that the Space Territories Administration on Verdammt has requested Naval assistance in providing a landing grid and subspace beacon to permit an F.T.L. liner to make touchdown."

"That's correct," said Prellen.

"We wish to land a V.I.P. at present on the F.T.L. liner. You appear to possess the only grid capable of being assembled here in time to arrest that liner and bring her down safely."

The lieutenant eyed him speculatively for a moment. "In consequence of this request, Admiral Melk has detailed the *S.N.V. Gemini* to stay in immediate orbit around Verdammt and ferry down a pre-structured grid, generators, and beacon equipment for ground assembly. The arrangement is that you are to provide facilities and labor, while I am detailed to supervise the assembly and give technical assistance."

"Excellent!" said Prellen. "We couldn't have asked for a better arrangement. But you don't look too happy about it, Lieutenant."

"Since you ask, Captain, I'm not. The Navy has a great deal in hand these days, and tying-up the *Gemini* for twenty days while your grid is assembled is not my idea of maximum utilization of resources."

Prellen shrugged. "Then the Navy had only to refuse. It was, after all, only an interservice request for assistance."

"The admiral felt it was a legitimate request only if the importance of the operation justified the cost and wastage. He was not then in a position to judge the merits of the case. I'd like to ask you, Captain, is it justified?"

"I think so," said Prellen, evenly.

"And fortunately, I don't have to answer that sort of question either for you or for Admiral Melk. My responsibility is to the Space Territories Administration on Terra. But since you've raised the question, the V.I.P. we're interested in landing here is the first Terran Ambassador to Verdammt."

"Ambassador?" Sinclair struggled with his disbelief. "Correct me if I'm wrong, Captain, but the Space Manual lists Verdammt as having no indigenous life form of sufficient intelligence to facilitate or comprehend any form of sociological contact."

"And both you and the Space Manual are wrong," said Prellen. He returned to his desk and sat behind it wearily. "You're both dead wrong. Verdammt has a highly intelligent life form—just how intelligent we don't yet know, but it may well be vastly superior to ourselves. The trouble is that the initial ratings were carried out using the Manneschen scale, which is based on Terran-oriented concepts of intelligence. The life form here is anything but Terran-oriented. In fact, in Terran terms, it is completely unintelligible."

"Yet you consider it intelligent?"

"I do, considering intelligence on the broader definition of ability to consciously manipulate environment, the Unbekannt are at least equal to ourselves. How, or why, they manipulate their environment is as yet beyond us, but the fact that they can, and do, is something we cannot deny. That's why Verdammt rates an Ambassador, and it's he and his staff we wish to land from the F.T.L. So now I want a clear decision from you, Lieutenant: do I get my landing grid and beacon?"

"You'll get them," Sinclair said tersely. "That had already been decided. But with a proviso. The request was to be investigated from every angle, and if found not to be completely justified, the admiral is prepared to refer the whole case back to Terra."

"You mean it's a good platform for playing interservice

politics to Admiral Melk's advantage," Prellen said shrewdly.

Sinclair stiffened. "The first ferry will be landing in the morning with a foundation material, and the work can start immediately. This afternoon I'd like to do a site survey."

"I'll put you in touch with my engineering officer," Prellen said. "He'll give you all the help you need. But what about you? Are you quartering on the *Gemini*?"

"Unfortunately, no. I'm resident here until the assignment is complete."

"Then I'll offer you a cabin aboard our humble base ship *S.V. Maxwell*. It won't be up to Naval standards, but it's more convenient than a prefabricated shack."

"In the Navy . . ." began Sinclair, then changed his mind.

"I know what they do in the Navy," said Prellen, "but I put it to you that on Verdammt you'll be glad to have the hull of a spaceship between you and the outside during the long and noisy nights."

"I'll be pleased to accept your hospitality," said the lieutenant without enthusiasm. "I've no doubt there's a lot more to Verdammt than is recorded in the Space Manual."

"You could say that twenty-three times over," Prellen said, "and you'd still be only hovering on the edge of the truth."

If Sinclair had had any reservations about quartering in the *Maxwell* he lost them at ten minutes past ten, Verdammt standard time, that evening. Scorning the officer's mess, he sought out the radio room and spent the evening carefully drafting and encoding his report to Admiral Melk and his schedule of operations to the *S.N.V. Gemini*. This done, he had returned to his cabin and prepared for sleep.

His preparations were disturbed by the sudden screech of something sliding down the outside of the hull, and then the solid *clomp-clomp* of whatever it was apparently ascending the hull again with leaden feet. After some thought he dismissed the incident with a shrug and was almost in his bunk when the noises returned. This time the *clomp-clomp* went down and the screeching up. This was followed by other sounds completely beyond definition; the sensation of gentle rocking as though the ship was being raised and lowered slightly in its shock-absorbing mounts.

Although the phenomena had all the makings of a first-class disaster he was unable to detect any signs of panic or emergency action from the rest of the ship so he decided to investigate. Throwing open the door he bumped straight into Anton Wald, the S.T.A. psychologist to whom he had been introduced at dinner.

"Ah!" said Wald. "I was just coming to tell you not to worry."

"What's happening out there?"

"It's only the Unbekannt," said Wald mildly.

"What are they doing—attacking?"

"I don't think so. I honestly don't know what they're doing. It's just something they do now and then for their usual unfathomable reasons. I suppose it pleases them, and it doesn't do us harm, so we let them get on with it."

Sinclair was baffled. "You mean you don't post guards to keep them away?"

"We don't want to keep them away. We're here to study them."

"But they're tearing the ship apart!"

"No," said Wald. "You'll find this peculiar, but they do no damage and they don't even leave a trace of their activities. You won't find as much as a footprint out there in the morning."

"But the noise!"

"So?" Wald shrugged. "What would you have us do? Go out and shoot a dozen? Certainly they're alien, but with that level of intelligence, any attack by us on such a pretext would be morally indefensible. Anyway, I have a sneaking idea that, if they wished to attack us, they could do it in ways against which we'd have no conceivable defense. I don't think I'd care to start a shooting match with the Unbekannt."

"I see," said Sinclair, in a voice which betrayed that he didn't see at all. He turned back into his cabin, closing the door, and resigned himself to a sleepless night. Whatever mysterious rite the Unbekannt were performing on the hull it certainly had sound as an integral part. And Unbekannt sounds were like nothing ever heard before.

Sinclair's first action of the morning was to make an inspection of the outside of the ship. He was reasonably certain that the noises of the previous night could not possibly have been performed without considerable damage to the hull. To his amazement, there was no sign even of scratches on the surface oxide of the outer skin, nor were there any footprints, or signs of disturbance, in the sand.

In spite of his incredulity, or perhaps because of it, Sinclair became intrigued by the problem, remembering the rocking motion which had been imparted to the ship, and remembering that the vessel itself probably weighed better than a hundred thousand Terran tons. It was difficult to imagine how such forces could have been applied to the ship without leaving any trace, and even more difficult to imagine what was the significance of its accomplishment.

The base ship and its three supply auxiliaries stood in a clearing perhaps four square kilometers in area, beyond which the native Verdammt brushland began its unvarying pattern on all sides. The clearing was artificial and included an area of prefabricated hutments and the site where it was proposed to erect the landing grid. From an engineer's point of view this was an excellent arrangement, with all the available supplies and resources concentrated at a point close to the grid site.

The first ferry arrived strictly on schedule, and Sinclair was quickly occupied attending to unloading details and in liaison with the commanders of the working squads. But from time to time he raised his head and looked deeply into the tantalizing fringes of surrounding brush, wondering if the Unbekannt were out there watching the new activity and what, if anything, they were understanding of it.

Occasionally something flickered against the brushland background, but always too quickly, or too inconveniently, to be seen except out of the corners of his eyes. Gradually, however, he became convinced of the Unbekannt watching from the edges of the brush and making occasional forays a few meters into the clearing, presumably to gain a better view.

It was nearing the close of the work period before he managed to get away to find Wald. The latter was in his office in a prefabricated shack, looking morosely at a curiously wrought crystalline tablet which appeared to flicker and restructure itself even as he turned it in his hands. As Sinclair entered, Wald passed the object carefully to him for examination.

"What is it?" Sinclair asked at last.

"Damned if I know," said Wald. "It's something the Unbekannt left here, but whether to eat it, watch it, sit on it, listen to it, or whatever, we don't know. I sometimes wonder if we ever shall. It could be anything from a crystalline computer to a piece of abstract art . . . or something so far beyond our comprehension that the human race may never understand or need one."

"About the Unbekannt," said Sinclair. "Are they hostile in any way?"

"Physically, no. I think they're as anxious as we are to establish communication. But it's in that very fact their danger lies."

"I don't understand," said Sinclair.

"No, I didn't think you would. Think for a moment about the concept *alien.* The Unbekannt are so alien that almost nothing about them approaches anything that we are able to comprehend. They are so far removed from our concepts of a life form as to not only be unintelligible but also completely unimaginable. So, how do you begin to comprehend something beyond the realms of your own imagination? The answer is simple: you can't."

"But surely that depends solely upon the scope of the individual mind."

"Not really. Human experience itself limits the individual imagination to a reference frame outside of which it is difficult to handle concepts, because there are no analogies and no coordinates you can use to formulate, or retain, the idea.

A concept outside the reference frame doesn't mean anything."

"I still don't see the danger," Sinclair said.

The psychologist looked up sagely. "To accept the Unbekannt as reality you have to deny all your own education and experience. They don't mean a thing in our terms, so you have to try to adopt theirs. Stress and disorientation will result. The human brain doesn't react very kindly to that form of pressure. The mildest result is confusion, the direst is complete withdrawal from the conflict—cataleptic shock. That's why I suggest you check with me before you attempt any personal contacts with the Unbekannt. We can't afford to lose you. Not until we've got our grid."

"That's just the point," said Sinclair. "In view of all this I can see no conceivable reason to have an Ambassador on Verdammt until after you've managed to reach some comprehension of the Unbekannt."

"And you resent it, don't you?"

"What do you think!" Sinclair spun swiftly on his heel. "You're damn right I resent it! I resent being sent to this God-forsaken place to install a landing grid and a beacon for a bureaucratic wangle. A wangle that has misled the S.T.A. into believing that this planet requires an ambassador to deal with a life form with which he will never be able to communicate."

"Have you finished, Mr. Sinclair?" Prellen's voice came coldly.

Sinclair, who had not noticed his entrance, swung back wildly.

"No, I haven't finished! If you want my opinion . . ."

"I don't want your opinion," said Prellen flatly. "I don't want anything from you other than an operative landing grid and an accurately aligned subspace beacon. It may interest you to know, that it was Dr. Wald's own work on Unbekannt psychology, which decided the Space Territories Administration to send an Ambassador to Verdammt, and the timing of the operation and the method of delivering the appointee, were decided by myself."

"You?"

"Yes. Sorry to disappoint you, Sinclair, but we captain administrators do administrate sometimes. So you see, no graft in high places, no bureaucratic wangling, no sinecures. Simply a technical report, an agreement, and a schedule of operation."

Sinclair's face was frank with disbelief.

"I don't believe you, and I don't think Admiral Melk will either.

"Candidly, I'm going to end my report to him with the recommendation that this whole affair be investigated."

"I find it difficult," Prellen said carefully, "to believe that, in view of what you tell me about the pressure of work, the admiral still has nothing better to do than play politics."

"Prellen, I don't have to take that sort of remark from you!"

"And I don't have to take this sort of insolence from you," said Prellen dangerously. "I'd like to remind you that, until the ambassador takes over, the conduct of Terran affairs on this planet is entirely my responsibility. Temporarily, I represent the legally constituted authority. Do you know what that means on an unfederated Rim world?"

"I'll tell him," said Wald with malicious pleasure, "since there's a great deal of his education they omitted at the Space Academy—such as manners and the gentle art of knowing when to stop. In Terran affairs the captain's power is absolute. And that includes the power of life and death. So, if you'd take a suggestion from me, I'd recommend you to close your mouth before something gets into it—such as my boot."

"You shouldn't have said that, Anton," said Prellen when Sinclair had gone. "Melk's got enough on us already without threats of physical violence to his staff."

Wald grinned affably. "You'd have said it yourself if you hadn't been bound by what passes for protocol."

"Of all the rotten luck, this is the worst," said Prellen. "Out of the entire strength of the Navy they had to send us one of Admiral Melk's satellite pets. There's going to be hell to pay for this anyway, without Melk causing a stir, but I'd hoped to make it a *fait accompli* before the storm broke. If we can only hold things down that long, we may well get away with it; but if Sinclair raises too much trouble now, the whole affair is liable to blow up in our faces."

Slowly the grid took shape. The pre-structured sections which were brought by ferry were being assembled high and easily. Then the generators arrived, and their squat and heavy forms were compacted into the base of the structure, there to connect with the conductor chains which confined the grid-flux within the web of intricate spars. The immense bright needle of the subspace beacon arrived as a single unit and was set up alongside the grid. A prefabricated shack had been placed nearby, and it was here that Sinclair was installing the transmitter that, operating through the beacon needle, would call the F.T.L. liner out of subspace and guide it down on the featherbed flux field of the grid.

Prellen daily checked the progress of the construction and carefully compared the estimated time of completion with the computer predictions of the position of the liner moving at faster than light speeds across the universe towards them. He was acutely conscious of the relatively narrow time margins with which they had to contend, and he was greatly relieved to find that Sinclair's antagonism towards the aims of the project in no way impaired his ability to control the rapid construction of the grid.

In no small way Prellen was impressed by the immaculate efficiency of the Naval ferry team who delivered exactly the right component to the right position at the precise time it was required, and Sinclair's efficiency was no less in his organization of the placing and assembly. Sinclair's secondary operation of sending detailed reports in code to Admiral Melk on the aims and operation of the S.T.A. establishment was more disturbing. The situation on Verdammt was sufficiently unique to demand quite a radical approach to the problem of establishing communication with its inhabitants, and Prellen was uncomfortably aware that political pressures on Terra could well be shaped to destroy the delicate balance of the extra-sociological experiment he had planned.

He was discussing this very point with Wald one evening when Sinclair came in. His face was alive with jubilation and his hand clutched the transfax print which was the obvious source of his mood. As he caught sight of Wald he nodded with satisfaction.

"I'm glad I've caught the two of you together, because I want to continue a previous conversation. Subject: the Ambassador."

"Go on!" said Prellen, with a glance at Wald. "I take it that you have some further information, no doubt from Admiral Melk."

"I have indeed, Captain Prellen. The admiral is having this whole affair investigated, but as a preview, he's sent me the names of the Ambassador and his party aboard the F.T.L."

"He needn't have bothered," said Prellen tiredly. "I could have given you the same information, if you'd been civil enough to ask."

"Even the name of the Ambassador—you do know the name, don't you?"

"Yes," said Prellen slowly. "It's Prellen. He happens to be my son."

"So you admit it!"

"I make it a policy never to deny those of my children born in wedlock."

Sinclair was incensed by his lack of concern.

"You know what I mean! Do you wish me to enlarge on this expose of string pulling?"

Prellen shot Wald a quick look. "We're naturally interested in the extent of your information," he said guardedly.

"I rather thought you would be. Shall I go into some further details, such as the fact that the embassy staff consists of five women and no men. An interesting piece of personnel selection, that. Need I continue?"

Prellen held up his hand. "No, that will do for now. I don't know how Admiral Melk came by the information, but it's accurate as far as it goes. But tell me, Sinclair, exactly what do you personally hope to gain out of this extracurricular exercise?"

"Are you thinking of buying me off?"

"I wasn't making any offers, but I'm sure you do have a price."

"What makes you so certain, Captain?"

"It's self-evident," said Prellen. "It must be money or promotion, because you've certainly never heard of a thing called principles."

"You dare speak to *me* of principles?"

"Yes," said Prellen, "and one day you'll understand just what my principles are. Until then I can only hope that you do a better job at engineering than you do at mudslinging, because if you don't, that F.T.L. liner is going to make a hell of a mess when it makes planetfall."

Something dark and shapeless landed with a thud on the translucent dome of the beacon shack, scrabbled furiously down the curving slope with the screech of something imaginable as sliding claws, and leaped from the bottom of the canopy into the sheltering brush. The noise of its passage set Sinclair's teeth on edge. He looked up savagely as the episode was repeated by a second and then a third body. The fourth provided a variation; hitting the canopy low, it achieved the patently impossible by sliding up the dome and disappearing from his ken as it reached the apex.

Sinclair was halfway to the door when he remembered Wald's injunction, and turned to the communicator instead.

"Dr. Wald, there's something playing on the roof of the beacon shack here. I think it must be the Unbekannt."

"Very likely," said Wald. "It's about time they started putting you through the maze."

"Maze?"

"Rat-maze—primary reaction test for experimental animals. Basic stimulus and response stuff. They've assessed most of us here in the past and got tired of it. As a technician, you're different, and I suspect they're now trying to get the measure of you."

"By playing silly-devils on the roof?" Sinclair was incredulous. "What can they hope to learn by that?"

"I've no idea," said Wald. "I warned you that they were beyond comprehension. It's fairly clear, however, that they have no more chance of understanding us than we have of understanding them. Each is trying to assess the other by their own standards, and I doubt if our reactions to them make any more sense than theirs to us. It's a classical nonlogical situation with no answers."

"If I can get my hands on one, I'll soon give you a few answers," said Sinclair.

"It would be interesting to see if that's true," said Wald. "But I don't advise you to try it. How do you know, Sinclair, that one of them out there has not just had a similar thought about you?"

"A damn monkey?"

"Ah! So you've already fallen into the trap!" said Waldo "Because you've never been able to see one clearly you've assumed for yourself they're like monkeys—a limited Terran concept. Factually, they have vastly less in common with monkeys than we do. So your worst danger is in your own false preconceptions."

Even over the communicator Wald heard the fifth Unbekannt start its variant alien dance across the plastic roof, and Sinclair's conversation terminated in a shout of wrath before the connection was broken. Wald held the silent handset speculatively for a moment or two, then nodded at some inner musing.

"By the great paunch of Admiral Melk," he said irreverently to nobody in particular, "some people never take no for an answer."

Opening the door of the beacon shack, Sinclair looked outside. The shack was near the edge of the clearing, and only a broad path separated it from the nearest fringes of waving brush. A screech across the roof warned him of the passage of another Unbekannt, and enabled him to judge the direction of its motion with sufficient precision at least to be able to see the blur which descended and skittered away to the cover of the foliage. He gained no impression of height or form, but judged its mass to be encouragingly less than his own, although its speed and agility were phenomenal.

He turned back inside the door, and his fingers closed on a meter length of titanium stock from which he had cut the commutator segments of the beacon. He balanced it thoughtfully for a moment in his fingers, not knowing what sort of force could be applied to the Unbekannt without becoming lethal. Then he took the rod in his hand and went outside to wait.

For a long time nothing happened. The quivering, twilling sounds of the smaller brush-land life came to him with startling clarity, and the chill, moist breath of the vegetation closed around his neck like the wrap of a filmy scarf. Finally he heard a screeching across the roof, and, mentally calculating the time and position of descent, he moved back to the wall and waited with rod poised. Precisely where anticipated, the blur dropped like a stone from the roof—and Sinclair struck.

He was never afterwards able to decipher, or describe, what happened next. The impression was not that of hitting a soft, moving body, but of unexpectedly striking a block of stone. The shock transmitted to his fingers by the bar numbed them with pain, and he dropped the metal in anguish. Something spat at him, or shone at him, or did something alien and incomprehensible and a wave of nausea and disorientation spun his body with almost physical force.

Then the Unbekannt stopped in front of him. Sinclair fought his way out of his confusion and immediately returned to it as his mind strove to reconcile what he saw with what he considered remotely possible. The shattering absurdity of what his eyes perceived tallied in no way with any of the very wide range of things he was prepared to see. And by the time he had climbed back out of the mental abyss of the impossible, his alien antagonist had disappeared.

He stood for a few moments collecting his wits, then looked about. No Unbekannt was visible, but an unformed flickering deeper in the brush suggested that they had not gone far away. Then he heard again the familiar screech and turned to look for his rod.

It was only then, in an agony of shock, that he realized just how far out of his depth he was. For the length of titanium had become rolled and wrought into some marvellously alien and intricate design. His hands were shaking as he picked it up and noted the complexity of closed loops, the immaculate formation of which would have involved a Terran craftsman in many hours of patient labour and the use of an electron-beam welder. But this marvel had been produced in the split-second between the moment the metal had left his fingers and the time it had reached the ground. And it was perfectly cold to the touch.

The phenomenon made no sort of engineering sense at all. It was both impossible and factual simultaneously. And it was this, more than anything else he had encountered on Verdammt that made him sweat and wonder and suddenly to feel afraid. Taking hold of the remainder of the rod, he turned and deliberately followed the Unbekannt out into the brush.

"Sinclair's gone." Wald found Prellen in the chartroom of the Maxwell.

"Gone where?" Prellen was immediately alert.

"I don't know. Out into the brush, I think."

"Damn!" said Prellen. "That means he's probably gone to see for himself what the Unbekannt are like. As much as I dislike the Navy, I don't think it's good politics to return their technicians in a state of shock—and that's the certain result of such a contact on his somewhat rigid mentality. Anyway, the F.T.L. is only sixteen light-hours out. We've got to get that idiot back, Anton, before he damages himself."

"No," said Wald solidly. "I've got to get that idiot back, I know. But, if he's been gone as long as I think he has, he'll be in it pretty deep by now. Too deep even for you. I'll take a couple of the psych team and a triple dose of mescalin. If we don't come back, *don't* come out and try to find us."

"Is it really that bad in the deep areas?"

"It's worse," said Waldo "You've got the statistics on nervous breakdowns for the exploratory teams. Try working that out as a percentage of total personnel turnover."

Prellen smiled wryly. "I already have," he said. "Very well, you're the doctor. Anything you need in the way of support?"

"Only a few prayers and a hell of an imagination," said Wald dryly. "They're the only factors which seem to count out there."

"Then I wish you luck," said Prellen. "Oh, and Anton . . .!"

"Yes?"

"I don't know what encouraged Sinclair to go out there alone, but if he comes to any harm as the result of one of your exercises in psychology, you know the way I'll have to play it."

"I'd not expect it otherwise," said Waldo "But, Captain, you'd have an awful job assembling the proof!"

The brushland bore no discernible paths, but the springiness of the palmate stems enabled him to pass in any direction with the minimum of diversions. Sinclair mentally noted the position of the sun as he started to walk, choosing to follow an area of visual unquiet which hung low in the distant foliage. This patch of indefinable flux in the brush apparently sensed his coming and moved ahead of him, sometimes with a surprising burst of speed, yet never moving so far away that it was out of his sight.

Whether it was an individual Unbekannt, or a group of them, he had no means of knowing, and why the aliens registered only as a flicker was a factor which even his training in physics did nothing to explain.

The only familiar aspect of the situation was the suggestion of a lure, or an invitation, to follow. Since Wald had refuted the suggestion that the Unbekannt were physically dangerous, Sinclair felt no great trepidation about following the aliens to whatever destination they were mindful to take him.

Psychologically, however, he now was not so certain of his

ground. His brief encounter with the Unbekannt had severely shaken his confidence in the span of his own imagination, and had pointed up Wald's lecture on the more insidious dangers of alien contact. But the possibility of gleaning at least a hint of the technology by which the titanium bar had been cold-formed in milliseconds into its present intricacy of design was something irresistibly attractive to him.

After an hour of such journeyings, he stopped, suddenly worried by a stroke of illusion. He received the curious sensation that momentarily great towers had existed in front of and about him—towers which had risen and vanished with such rapidity that the impression was little more than subliminal. Yet such was the quality of the phenomenon that it was stamped with an unmistakable aura of reality. Stock still now, he surveyed the area of brush hoping to find something which could have triggered the fantasy. The brushland remained the same, quietly moving yet unchanged.

Then hell engulfed him. Suddenly he was plunged into the centre of some dark, grinding enormity which might have been the intestines of an engine from the weapon shops of the damned. Or it might have been to Cro-Magnon or Neanderthal man as one of his own cities would have been. His mind shrieked at the unendurable savagery of the impressions which reeked of noise and dirt and turbulence and intolerable power.

Then the scene was gone as raping hyper-metropolis as far beyond his comprehension and endurance part of some clattering, overwhelmingly as it had arisen. The only turbulence remaining was that in his startled brain, and the only noise that of his ringing ears still reacting to the shock. And with a mounting terror in his heart, he waited with a transfixed fascination for what he feared was yet to come.

With uncomprehending eyes Sinclair attempted to follow the series of montages and mirages of scenes and symbols which flowed around and over him. Having no means of telling imagery from physical fact he had to force his mind not to attempt to comprehend or interpret, only to record. But even so, some psychosomatic reflex gripped at his stomach, and numbed his head with dizziness. Bewilderingly his surroundings achieved apparently impossible transpositions from the gloomy shadows of some huge Satanic complex to the white-hot negativeness of an isolated point of desert, then to an icy darkness punctuated by random coloured shards so unimaginably out of perspective that he had to close his eyes in order to suffer them. And again the images blended and blurred and reformed, gaining substance and alien, incomprehensible meaning by keying some nonhuman semantic trigger which racked him with emotions which his body was not constructed to experience.

His first shocked impression had been that of movement, of being thrown in some inertialess way into a series of different, imbecilic, quasi-environments. Later, some more rational portion of his mind re-appraised the sensations and thrust upon him the half-formed concept that he was factually motionless and that these fantastic quasi-environments were actually being created and dissolved around him.

He remembered that Prellen had defined intelligence with reference to the Unbekannt as the conscious ability to manipulate environment.

Dimly, he began to perceive the truism that, given time, all environments, whether by manipulation or natural causes, must change; and that the unimaginable flux and transformation around him was different mainly in pace from any human situation.

For a frantic moment he felt a single point of understanding with the Unbekannt, but in experimentally allowing his mind license to follow it, he lost the concept and found himself in a wilderness of unchartable madness.

His senses were screaming from the overload of unpredictable sensations, which gave rise to great fatigue and a sense of imminent collapse. His feet were restrained by a nightmare leadenness, and the whole structure of concept and analogy, which he had built for himself as a protective rationalization, was beginning to split open about his head. He knew that, if he cracked now and allowed the mad disorder to flow into his mind unfiltered, he would lose touch with reality and be forced to retreat down paths from which there might be no returning.

He did not see Wald and the two psych men as they closed in, moving like men underwater across the shifting nightmare wastes. Only when they touched him did he withdraw his transfixed consciousness from the imbecile panorama and attempt to re-establish contact. He could not make the breakthrough, but he stood submissively while they used a hypodermic gun on his arm. After a short while the Unbekannt became more real to him and less overwhelming; the quasi-environments grew more understandable and more pregnant with their incredible truths—which somehow he was never quite able to capture and retain.

And they led him away out of the insane realms into the slowly quieter brushland which had itself become seeded with patterns and contrasts of shade and colour which hinted of, but never quite revealed, entrances to the vaster region of consciousness and the creatures which dwelt beyond.

It was touchdown time minus two hours when they finally brought Sinclair out of sedation and led him, still trembling with reaction, to make the final adjustments to the apparatus and to activate the grid. Wald stayed with him, assisting in the simpler operations, and watching him constantly with a kind of pained sympathy. Finally Sinclair indicated that the task was finished, and turned to the doctor with a wan smile.

"I have to thank you for getting me out of there. I can't say you didn't warn me."

Wald dismissed the incident with a shrug. "How do you feel now?"

"Jumbled and . . . confused. Somehow, I don't think I'll ever be the same again after that."

Wald nodded. "Hell, isn't it, having a headful of concepts and no way to communicate them? You went in too deep and without preparation. Normally we use drugs which leave you reasonably objective while minimizing the strain on the imagination. It's the only way to survive out there."

"But how can anything so utterly impossible have existence?"

"I've no doubt," said Wald, "they're asking the same sort of question about us, and with about as much hope of finding an answer. The truth is that neither of us are impossibilities; we merely exceed the limitations in the minds of the others. One or both of us, as a species, has got to find a way of making a readjustment if we're ever to achieve any sort of understanding."

The two were now standing outside the beacon shack watching the grid which was deceptively tranquil in spite of the force of the focused flux field which spiralled from it up into the exosphere. At tropospheric levels the unusual Verdammt clouds had congregated in response to the bright puncture which the concentrated force field had stabbed through the ionized zones of the upper atmosphere, and an unknown thunder throbbed at high altitudes. But, at ground level, the atmosphere remained serene and even the blue corona discharge from the needle of the beacon seemed muted and subdued.

"I think you can appreciate now," said Wald, "how trapped we are in the web of the things we know. We limit our imagination by hedging our reference frame with a pattern of probabilities and possibilities. We can't comprehend or communicate with the Unbekannt because they run contrary to the whole structure of our assimilated logic. The only conceivable bridge between the two cultures would be to take a human mind, which hasn't been forced too rigidly into the mould of our own logical concepts, and expose it simultaneously to both cultures in the hope that it can learn to accept, if not reconcile, the two mutually contradictory sets of values."

"If there was an individual with such a mind . . ."

"I think there is," said Waldo. "Just one such is our ambassador."

Somewhere a bell began to spell out a set of regular, isolated pulses. Sinclair looked at his chronometer.

"Twenty seconds to contact," he said.

All attention was now focused on the high beam of power which projected from the grid into the sky. No matter how familiar one was with the process, it was a sight which never lost its fascination. At one instant the immense F.T.L. liner was carving its way through subspace at a near-infinite velocity; the next it would emerge into normal spacetime and be strung, poised and at rest, on the gridbeam like a compass needle on a pin. It was a miracle to which no one ever became reconciled.

Sinclair said "Now!" and the bell broke into an uninterrupted clatter. Simultaneously the ship appeared, far lower than had been anticipated, but still within safety margins. The super-sonic shock of its arrival smacked at the ground with the force of a blow, and a brief thunderstorm crackled and flared in its wake, accompanied by the inevitable dense precipitation which the onlookers accepted stoically as part of the arrival ceremony.

Slowly, as though on an invisible thread, the ship descended obediently to a featherbed touchdown atop the cradle of the grid. After a period of apparent inactivity, the bottom hatches opened and a winched cage was run up to facilitate off-loading. As the cage reached the ground there was a general movement in its direction from the waiting assembly.

Wald looked at Sinclair. "Finished here? I'll take you down and introduce you to the ambassador."

Sinclair looked at the coverall he was wearing. "I'm scarcely dressed."

"No matter. We're not sticklers for formality in the S.T.A."

They walked down to where the knot of people at the foot of the grid was beginning to break up as the ambassador's party moved on.

As the range closed Sinclair stopped as though puzzled, then picked up the pace again and clutched at the doctor's arm.

"Are you serious about this?"

"About what?" Wald's expression was all innocence.

"About the ambassador. . . Tell me it's some sort of joke."

"If you think it's a joke, you have a weird sense of humour."

"But a baby—No wonder you needed the grid for a soft touchdown."

"William Arthur Prellen," said Wald, "Ambassador Designate to the Space Territory of Verdammt. Age . . . twenty-seven days, or thereabouts. He's getting a bit old for the job, but he's the best chance we have of establishing contact with the Unbekannt. We intend to bring him into contact with them with sufficient frequency and for sufficient lengths of time that his formative mind grows to accept them equally with ourselves. What's the matter? You're looking a bit grim. Don't tell me you've just realized the S.T.A. isn't as soft a service as it appears?"

Remembering his own experiences in contact with the Unbekannt, Sinclair was feeling rather sick. "And you really think you have a chance of doing it this way?"

"Just a chance," said Wald, "and it's a dangerous one at that. Dangerous to young Prellen and to those who put him there. This could well be Admiral Melk's greatest victory."

"He'll never know," said Sinclair. "Not from me, anyway. I never dreamed you'd risk so much!"

"And the Unbekannt," said Waldo "That crystal in my office . . . did I mention that it grows a little every day? I suspect it's an embryo Unbekannt. Their ambassador to us, so to speak. It would seem we've already achieved that first point of understanding."

THE RAILWAYS ON CANNIS

"Colonel Ivan Nash to see you, Sir."

Colonel Belling frowned. "Ivan Nash? I thought he was on Cannis with the occupation force. Anyway, show him in."

"Too late!" said Nash from the doorway. "I'm already in. Can't wait on ceremony, you know. I've got a peace to run."

"Good to see you, Ivan! What brings you to Terra?"

"Briefly," said Nash, "it's the railways up on Cannis."

Belling waved his visitor into a chair and issued him a drink.

"I fear I'm a little out of touch," he said. "I didn't think railways were quite in your line."

"No?" Nash filled his pipe carefully. "How much do you know about Cannis anyway?"

"Not much. Gravity, atmosphere and climate roughly earth-normal. Population rated human equivalent on the Manneschen scale. Oh yes, and volcanoes!"

"Precisely," said Nash drily. "Let us not forget the volcanoes. Cannis-four is a young world with a very thin crust. Volcanic activity is widespread and generally severe. Fire-blowholes about a dozen metres in diameter can force up anywhere at any time. They raise sharp-edged slag cases from ten to a hundred metres in height. That's why there are no roads on Cannis."

"Quite a place," commented Belling, refilling the glasses.

"Quite a place and quite a people." Nash studied the ceiling reflectively. "Tough as nails and as perverse and changeable as the hell-hole that spawned them. Considering there's not a two-hundred metre diameter of flat space anywhere on the whole damned planet it's highly remarkable that any form of civilisation ever managed to evolve, let alone one that managed to kick itself into space."

"I had wondered about that."

"Well you might. The Canians are an extremely clever race. They're craftsmen, hobbyists and gadgeteers of the highest calibre. They built up a highly effective mechanical culture by trial and error and empirical method. But they have no true science as such."

"So?"

Ivan Nash paused. "So we blasted the hell out of Cannis during the war and now they don't have sufficient continuity or technology to get back on their own feet. If you knock a cockeyed culture like that to pieces how, in the name of Thunder, do you get it together again?"

"I don't know," said Belling, quite honestly.

"And neither do I. They're a heck of a nice people when you get to know them. The fact that they picked on Sirates to colonize when we were already there was just bad luck. That's why our presence on Cannis is more of a rehabilitation job than an occupation proper. If we let them down we throw them back a thousand years."

Belling whistled. "As bad as that, eh?"

"Worse. With their present production and distributing capacity they'd have difficulty in maintaining more than twenty per cent of their population at a minimum survival level without our help. And help all the way from Terra is a mighty expensive item. We have to stand them on their own feet fast."

"So you want reconstruction engineers?" asked Belling.

"No, I already have engineers. Unfortunately it doesn't work. Advanced technology is not very suited to patching up a string and hairpin culture. The gulf between our technology and their technique is too great. What I need are specialists with a peculiar kind of skill. That's why I came to you."

"The entire engineering reserve is at your disposal," said Billing. "You name 'em; I've got 'em. What do you want?"

"My main concern is with the railways. With no roads or airstrips, the railways alone give cohesion and life to their scattered society. Without it they cannot survive."

"So you want railway engineers?"

"No," said Nash sadly, "they wouldn't be a molecule of use."

"How come?"

"Man!" said Nash in a voice of awe and wonder. "Did you ever see the railways up on Cannis? It's a shunter's nightmare, a plate-layer's conception of hell. From an engineer's point of view it's a complete and utter impossibility."

"Somebody must have constructed it originally."

"Yes, a myriad crazy, bug-brained innovators, each working on a separate part to an entirely different specification and for conflicting reasons. It's a completely lunatic system which breaks every known law of elementary railway technique."

"Then," said Belling wearily, "if you don't want engineers what do you want?"

"I want to borrow the U.E. squad," said Nash steadily.

Belling winced. "Are you serious?"

"Deadly."

"You realize what the U.E. squad could do to a situation like this?"

"I realize it's a dangerous thing to try, but desperate ills need desperate remedies. It's the last chance we have to save Cannis."

"If I were you," said Belling sadly, "I'd resign."

Lieutenant Fritz Van Noon of the U.E. squad faced his superior warily.

"I've got news for you," said Colonel Belling. "As you know I was against the formation of the U.E. squad right from the start. I may be wrong but I don't recant. The whole subject of Unorthodox Engineering has never sat very easily on my conscience. However, I think you've won your point."

"You mean that Operation Hyperon is going through?"

"Just that, but there is a proviso. You have to keep the squad in operational trim until Hyperon is ready by accepting assignments outside this reserve. Colonel Nash has already made a specific request for your services."

"I'm grateful," said Fritz warily, "but there's a distinct odour of an ulterior motive here somewhere."

Belling smiled wolfishly. "There is indeed. Tell me, Fritz, do you know anything about railways?"

"No, sir, not a blessed thing."

"Then you'd better get yourself a book or something. You've just been appointed controller of public railways on Cannis-four. U.E. goes with you."

"Cannis-four? Where in Jupiter is that?"

"It's the only habitable planet in the Cannis sector. It's the closest approximation to hell I've been able to locate."

"I thank you for the sentiment, sir."

"And I appreciate your tact, Fritz. You know, it's no easy task running a specialist engineering reserve. Always you get the one engineer in a thousand who should never have got out of kindergarten, let alone graduated. With a reserve strength like ours it's inevitable that we should have collected more than our fair quota of screwballs. The problem has always been to place them in positions where they aren't actively dangerous. Now I don't have to worry. Anybody who engages U.E. does so at their own risk."

"Which statement reveals a deplorable lack of insight," said Fritz Van Noon. "I devised U.E. to provide an outlet for those engineers whose imagination carried them beyond the ordinary."

"I know," said Belling drily. "I've seen some of your extraordinary engineering. I can only assume that taking you to Cannis to rehabilitate what was recently enemy territory is some ingenious form of war reparation. And Fritz—"

"Sir?"

"Take it easy on Ivan Nash. He's a friend of mine, and he doesn't suffer fools gladly. Try pulling some of those stunts you've pulled on me and you'll probably spend the rest of your career in a Canian jail—in irons."

"You can trust me, sir. After all, U.E. has a reputation to maintain."

"That's precisely what I was afraid of. Now get the hell out of here, I'm going to have a ball!"

The landing at Hellsport Base did nothing to endear Fritz to the planet. The transfer ferry entered the guiding radio cage at a tangent, failed to equalize, and bucked and ricochetted from beam to beam until the crew abandoned the automatics and dropped her to the ground under manual control. The ferry touched down with the motors out of synchronisation, spun crazily, and overheated the landing pit before it finally swayed to rest. That meant two hours of waiting whilst the water jets strove to cool the hull and bedrock of the base.

Jacko Hine, his second in command, met him at the spaceport bar.

Jacko and a small contingent of U.E. had been sent ahead to make a preliminary survey of the position. The summary of the reconnaissance was proclaimed by Jacko's crestfallen attitude and by the way his hair began to grey.

"How does it look?" asked Fritz.

Jacko looked at him seriously for a second or two. "Grim," he said. "If I'd tried to figure out an assignment which would prove U.E. to be a bunch of useless, incompetent layouts I couldn't have made a better choice."

"I thought that was it!" said Fritz. "Friend Belling was too sugarsweet on handing out this offering. Anyway this gives us a chance to prove him wrong once and for all."

"Does it? Open your pretty shell-like ear and I'll pour in a few home truths about Cannis railways. Item: no part of the system has been in operation for at least five years. Those parts of the installation which survived the terran 'verter bombs during the war have either fallen down of their own accord or else suffered from volcanoes."

Fritz choked on his drink and had to be patted on the back. "Volcanoes?" he queried finally.

"Sure. Small ones. They keep on coming all the time. Even at the heyday of the Cannis railway approximately one fifth of the total rail length was always out of commission due to volcanic activity. After five years without maintenance or repair the damage and confusion is simply catastrophic.

Nash's engineers rebuilt five kilometres of new track and suspension last year and two volcanoes ruined it within a week."

"Go on," said Fritz grimly.

"Item," said Jacko. "All the new steel has to come from Terra. Delivery delay is a little under two years and a ship can't deliver more than a hundred tons at a time. The Canians have a good malleable iron but it won't harden. It's all right for rails and short supports but the tensile strength is too low to allow its use for major engineering projects."

"Enough!" said Fritz. "The rest of the misery I will discover for myself. All this weeping is playing havoc with the flavour of the beer. I'm seeing Colonel Nash this afternoon, and after that I want to set some railway."

"In that case," said Jacko, "you'll need another drink."

Colonel Nash was waiting for him at Cannis H.Q. There was a certain air of reserve between the two officers which Fritz found vaguely familiar.

"I take it you've read the dossier on Cannis," said Nash. "How does it strike you as a job?"

Fritz shrugged. "That depends on the type of co-operation we get."

"You get whatever you want. This is a last-ditch stand. The rehabilitation is costing us infinitely more than did the war. We can't afford to play conquering heroes."

"What I want," said Fritz, "is simple. I just want that we should be left alone—very much alone."

"How do you mean? Discipline, administration, or what?"

"Everything. Just set us down at a rail point about a hundred kilometres out and then forget us."

"This is damned irregular," said Nash. "After all, you are an army unit. What about supplies, for instance?"

"We'll find our own."

"And steel—you can't build a railway without steel."

"Lack of essentials never yet troubled an unorthodox engineer."

"But this is ridiculous!" said Nash. "I didn't fetch you out from Terra just so you could go play cards in the wilderness."

"Look," said Fritz quietly, "you want a railway. You've proven that orthodox methods can't provide it. Now do I get a crack at it the unorthodox way or do you return to Terra and admit the job has you beaten?"

"Get out!" said Nash angrily. "Get out of my sight as quickly as possible. I'll leave you alone, but I promise you one thing . . . the next time you enter Hellsport it had better be on a train, else I'll nail you for insubordination and bust you so low you'll have to say 'sir' to a private."

"Thank you!" said Fritz Van Noon. "That's all I wanted to know."

They came across the structure silhouetted against the orange-yellow sky. It reminded Fritz of nothing so much as a rotting seaside pier propped awkwardly on random legs clear of the broken terrain below. Jacko had a rope ladder tied to the structure, since the original sling and hoist access had rotted beyond repair. The two climbed gingerly to the platform overhead, brushing the rusting piles and girders, and being showered with dirt from the gaps in the dark decking.

Above the decks the desolation grew. It was a crumbling, grotesque parody of a structure whose impotence in style and form was rendered more alien and yet artistic by the vagaries of slow corrosion. It was like a surrealistic film-set for a comedy of horrors which nobody dared to make. And on the far side, characteristically askew, was a sign board in Canian characters, and after, scrawled in chalk in terran hand, the legend: "Hellsport Terminus. The end of the line."

"It reminds me," said Jacko, "of a card house set on a sea of rusty spaghetti."

Fritz frowned and mooched dismally through the festoons of rusty iron and threadbare cable. "What hit it?" he asked at last.

"Nothing." Jacko guided him away from a bed-plate which had rusted to an extent where an uncautious foot might easily penetrate into the depths below. He pointed to a slag cone, now cold, which had burst through the tracks at mid-point across the terminus, ruining two tracks completely and half filling the remainder of the terminus with light volcanic ash. "Apart from the inquisitive volcano everything is just as it was when the last trains went north in the war. Believe me, they'd be using this installation now—only the trains never came back."

"Can't say I blame the trains," said Fritz moodily. "You mean to tell me this rotting junk heap is still in functional order?"

"By Canian standards, yes."

"Tell me," said Fritz testily, "did they have remarkably small trains or is this multiple-rail stuff some sort of gimmick?"

"I asked about that. Seems that each branch line had its own gauge and some had several according to who built them. At a terminus like this you have to accommodate anything which comes, so you run one track inside another nice and tidily. One snag through—you should see what it does to the points."

Fritz shuddered visibly despite the warm afternoon air. "I'd better see the worst, I suppose."

They walked out from the terminus to the huge switching grid which served to integrate the various branch lines entering the terminus. There was nearly a kilometre of patch-work mechanical desolation, overhued with rust and complex beyond belief. Gantries and galleries were solid with cranks and levers, bars and linkages, rods, and handwound helical springs. Cloth covered cables and solenoids had dropped their sickly bitumen under the coercion of many summer's suns, and now lay bleached white and ugly across the rotting spans like the bones of some alien skeleton.

Fritz viewed the scene with increasing dismay. Jacko leaned heavily on a stanchion and eyed his discomfort with a perverse humour.

"We're doing fine," said Fritz. "We've got ourselves a station complete with a volcano, a marshalling yard which shouldn't exist outside of a bad dream, six branch lines which don't go anywhere, and no trains to try out anyway. Add the fact that we can't get any steel and the probability that anything we do build will be ruined by more volcanoes within six months, and I surmise we are well and truly up a gum tree. You don't know whether to blow the whole lot up and start again or to leave it as an object lesson on how not to build a railway."

"Now who's being conventional?" chided Jacko. "I should have thought that this morass of mechanical ingenuity would have gladdened your heart no end."

"No," said Fritz, "and I'll tell you why. You see, its builders paid no attention to basics. There is a certain idiot futility about building something destined for sure destruction. Even a bodger must work to the principle of the greatest return for the very minimum of effort. That is why the Cannis railway is not only unsound but also needlessly complicated.

"Take this switching grid, for instance. It's not only vulnerable but it's largely unnecessary. It's designed to be completely automatic, self-routing, self-isolating, self-signalling and probably foolproof. Even Terran cyber-controlled railways have nothing to match this except in theory. But the faults result from limited vision. We could have done the whole thing with about a tenth of the parts and twice the reliability."

"We may have to," said Jacko. He pointed outwards across the tracks to where thick motes of dust and cinder were dancing in the sun. "Unless I miss my guess there's another volcano coming through down there."

"I want," said Fritz Van Noon, "to start about a hundred kilometres out on something nice and simple. We should have both engines and the necessary technique by the time we get back to Hellsport. What type of engines did they use, anyway?"

Jacko drew a deep breath. "You're not going to believe this," he said warily, "but the engines were even stranger than the tracks: The Juara engine was a steamer run on dried resins. Two locomotives from Manin were sort of battery-electric jobs. One from Nath came home on some kind of super gyroscope, and the Callin locomotive was an I.C. engine run on alcohol made by fermenting bean husks. Apart from that the rest were pretty unconventional."

"You don't say!" said Fritz drily. "The Canians seem to have set out to beat us at our own game. Talk about unorthodox engineering! We're a set of ruddy amateurs compared to them."

"I doubt it," said Jacko. "In my youth I thought I was the world's worst crackpot screwball. Then I met up with you and found that, in comparison, I was merely a sane, sensible, hardworking engineer. I never got over the disappointment of that hour of realization. I have a feeling the Canians will find themselves in a similar predicament. Under the heavy hand of Fritz Van Noon the Cannis railway will never be the same again."

"Thank you for that sly vote of confidence," said Fritz. "Now this is what I propose to do. I want you to take a 'copter to the Callin area, find the locomotive and bring it back to there—" He stabbed his finger on the map. "There's a two kilometre break in the track there where a 'verter bomb caught up with it. I'm taking the rest of U.E. to that point to try and repair the break. If we can, it will give us a workable area down as far as Juara. I want to complete that run before the Callin hean harvest is ripe. That gives us about two months."

"Two kilometres of new track in two months? You're off your rocker!"

"Naturally," said Fritz. "Else I wouldn't be running U.E."

The township of Juara lay on a crest of sullen rock. The shelf of granite had reduced the volcanic activity of the region to a tolerable level, and made habitation possible at the expense of the fertility of the soil. The railhead was untouched, but as the line swung again northwest and then north of the plateau it entered a low basin where the slag-cases, dunned with vegetation, stood up thick and tall like armless trees in some fantastic petrified forest.

This was a bad point for the rail. From the air it was obvious by the tortuous twisting of the route that the line had been diverted from disaster and rebuilt at least a dozen times. Occasional sections were completely isolated from the remains of the existing track and lay as forlorn crescents of rotting railway awaiting trains that could never come.

Six kilometres out from Juara was the break. A 'verter bomb dropped casually in the vicinity by a terran stratocraft had left its usual trademark. The railway had literally been shaken to pieces. For nearly two kilometres the remnants of twisted girderwork and trestles sprawled on the broken ground, tied together with the soft iron of the rails. North again by over forty kilometres lay Callin and the fertile mountains of Cansoon.

In the centre of the break Fritz ordered down the 'coptors, and the aero-sleds rendezvoused to drop the heavier equipment. The fragile, alloy Knudsen huts were hastily assembled and staggered, two by two, between the tall volcano spires. Prefabricated workshops were completed in record time as soon as the dino-dozer had cleared a sufficient site. The packaged forge and the rolling mill were rolled on air cushions to key points on the site.

Working feverishly and without obvious direction, the engineers of U.E. carved themselves a base on the alien territory and settled themselves in. By nightfall a new functional township had arisen beneath the dark towers of Cannis.

Fritz was well pleased with the achievement. Its success was marked by a subtlety which would have passed all but the keenest of observers. For U.E. was not a team as such; it was a collection of individuals. Nobody planned or directed, except in the very broadest way, but each engineer was trained to analyse the salient points of an operation and to guide his own activities to achieve the maximum effect. It was the myth of anarchy on a practical, productive scale—and it worked! The patient genius of Fritz Van Noon had wrought a philosophic miracle.

It was on the first day that Malu arrived. He strolled into the base at the crack of dawn, a thin brown Canian with the dark liquid eyes and the quick, birdlike movements that characterised his race. All Canians are inquisitive to a fault, and a casual inspection of any work in progress is part of the scheme of things. After poking and probing into every conceivable crevice he went from hut to hut harrying the occupants with atrocious pidgin Galactea. He found nobody who could understand him until he came across Harris, who not only spoke Galactea but also fluent Canian. Harris realised the worth of the contact and hurried him off to meet Fritz.

"This is Malu," said Harris. "He's a local engineer. He wants to know what he can do to help with the railways."

Fritz smiled acknowledgement. "Can he find me any local labour?" Harris translated, and a heated discussion followed. Finally he turned back to Fritz. "He says that he can get plenty of labour but that the Canians won't work in gangs under direction. They're strictly free-lance or they don't work at all."

"I thought this would happen," said Fritz. "Point out that it's their harvest we're trying to get to Juara. It's no skin off our nose if it doesn't go through. Also they obviously don't have the skill or the ability to do the job themselves else they'd have done it already."

"I already said that, but it's no dice. They're an independent lot of cusses. They'd sooner starve than suffer direction."

"Come to think of it," said Fritz, "come to think of it; so would we. Hell, I'll take a chance! Let them all come. It may never look like a railway but I guarantee it'll be a lot of fun trying."

By this time Malu had wandered off to examine some new aspect of the Knudsen huts. He was obviously worried by the alloy hulks, and came back for a long and excited argument with Harris.

"He's worried about the Knudsens," said Harris. "Says we mustn't build directly on the ground."

"Why ever not? There's no flooding hereabouts and the site is reasonably level."

"That's not the point. Malu says the lichen is temperature sensitive. It turns brown where a hot spot is developing. It gives you about a ten hour indication of when to move house. If you build on the ground you can't see the lichen underneath."

Fritz relaxed. "I've already thought of that. Between each pair of huts we have a thermo-couple buried. The alarms are automatic and don't need watching. Besides which, they're not affected by the sun and rain as is the lichen. Anyway you can't put a Knudsen hut on stilts—it'd fall to bits."

Harris translated to Malu, who shrugged resignedly and walked away wagging his head from side to side.

"He says it won't work," said Harris. "He coined a phrase: "people who live in magnesium huts shouldn't dare volcanoes!"

"Jupiter! That was all I needed!" said Fritz Van Noon.

Curiously enough the combination of Canian and U.E. personnel worked rather well. The natives knew their own limitations and did not attempt an operation or to handle an unfamiliar tool until they were sure of their competence. The U.E. squad became the lead team, breaking new ground, and the Canians seconded in careful emulation of their instructors.

By the end of the second day a huge stretch of track had been cleared, the rails returned to the rolling mill, and trestles and undamaged span girders stacked ready for reassembly. Ingots of malleable iron were manhandled down the line from Juara, and the forge and rolling mill worked continuous shifts to shape the soft metal which had to serve instead of steel.

The U.E. metallurgist was going quietly crazy trying to figure out why the Canian iron refused to harden. He finally decided it was due to the perverse allotropic form of the native carbon, and broke down an electrolytic refining cell of terran origin to gain a less temperamental sample of the element. Two pounds of this steel prepared in the laboratory exhibited a cold-short brittleness of such degree that it was rendered into iron filings by a few taps of a hammer. Increasing the silicon content and using Canian carbon he obtained a steel of the same tensile strength as lead. At this point he broke down and wept bitterly, then went out and joined in the construction work.

On the fourth night Fritz was awakened by the babble of voices outside his door. He dragged himself from his bunk, opened the door and stepped out. He immediately fell over Jacko who was prostrate on his stomach in front of the threshold probing the ground with the aid of a spot lamp. Malu and two fellow Canians were watching the proceedings from a discrete distance.

"Hell!" said Fritz. "Is this your idea of a joke?"

Jacko rubbed his posterior with an aggrieved air. "Hell," he said, "is an apt description of our destination if we don't leave this spot pronto. Your hut is nicely located on a hot-spot."

"What?" Fritz felt a sudden tremor of the ground beneath his feet and caught a wisp of the sulphurous fumes issuing from widening fissures in the ground. They had scarcely covered twenty metres before the hut exploded in a riot of brilliant fire. At a safe distance they turned and watched the point where a new volcano burned live at the very spot where Fritz had been sleeping not four minutes earlier.

"One up to Cannis!" said Fritz grimly. "It's getting to be a personal fight with no holds barred. Well, if that's the way Cannis wants it then I can fight dirty too."

Jacko surveyed the furious gout of fire before him. "I thought you were fixing a thermocouple alarm?"

"We did," said Fritz. "Platinum, platinum-rhodium couples at three metres depth. That must be where we fell down. Hot sulphur and silicates are poison to a platinum-alloy thermocouple. It must have gone open-circuit before it could operate the alarm. It was a mischance in a million but one we can't afford to risk again. The rest of the Knudsens will have to be jacked up somehow."

"Can we afford the time?" asked Jacko. "We have to get the harvest through to Juara. Can't we simply use another type of thermocouple?"

"No, we tried that. The soil is too corrosive, and a shielded couple isn't sufficiently sensitive. Either we raise the huts or we risk frying in our beds. I don't fancy waking in the morning and finding myself done brown on both sides. And I'm still going through to Juara on time even if it's over your dead body."

"I was afraid of that. By the way, I brought you back an engine. As a prime-mover it would make a very good potting-shed, but the fuel is simply superb."

Much of the track itself was recoverable since the low speeds and traffic density of the line would make no great demands on the quality of the rail. A great deal of the girderwork from the spans was likewise capable of reclamation. Only the trestles had suffered badly. Four out of five were a total write-off and, due to the great allowances needed by reason of the poor quality of the metal, rebuilding ate deeply into the available stocks of iron. As the work progressed it became painfully obvious that no more than half of the break could be completed because of the lack of trestles.

Fritz refused to be disheartened, and laid his advance plans with a quiet precision and a secrecy which involved the confidence only of Harris and Malu, who were given special missions to perform. Everyone else grew despondent, and even Jacko's customary pessimism seemed justified when the hot-spot appeared.

"Where is it?" asked Fritz.

"Right," said Jacko, "where it will do the most damage. Under our new track and right in the centre of a span. Three days and the whole lot will be down again. How the heck can you build a railway under these terms?"

"You can't," said Fritz. "That's why we're going to alter the terms. Take my advice, Jacko, never try to buck the system. If it's big enough to break you, try helping it on its way."

"Sophistry," said Jacko. "You can't stop a volcano."

"Can't I? Cannis and I have a lot in common. We both think the same way—mean and underhand. It's a policy of kicking the enemy while he's down. That way you get the greatest results for the least effort. This is a personal fight and no she-dog of a planet is going to put one over on Fritz

Van Noon."

Jacko shook his head sadly. "Let's face it, Fritz. We're licked. We can't go any further without terran steel and we can't hold on to what we have done. There's no disgrace in folding up before a physical impossibility."

"I've told you before," said Fritz sternly, "there's no such thing as a physical impossibility. A limitation is a state of mind not a question of fact. An aeroplane was a physical impossibility until men's minds learned how to tame the concept."

"Is lack of steel and a surplus of volcanoes also a state of mind?"

"Certainly—if you regard them as limitations."

"Very well," said Jacko, "come and prove your point."

By the time they arrived at the span the hot-spot was beginning to break. Even as they watched, the ground belched and broke as the angry pressures blew the topsoil apart. Then came a heavier explosion, the ground flew back and a column of fire spurted irregularly through a spray of liquid, incandescent magma, which congealed around the blowhole to form the foundations of the cone. Not fifteen metres above, the span appeared to dance in the stream of heated gasses, and was blackened and scorched by the leaping blasts.

Ensign Harris came over at a run, clasping a mortar projector to his chest, and was followed by Malu and two engineers carrying a rack of mortar bombs. They set up the projector at a reasonable distance and proceeded to prime the bombs.

"Are you crazy?" asked Jacko.

"Yes," said Fritz. "That's my forte. I want to see what happens if we put a mortar bomb smack inside that crater. You're the weapons expert. Can you do that without damage to the trestles?"

Jacko estimated the position silently. "The bomb I can manage, but the trestles will be in the care of their own peculiar deities."

The result was even more spectacular than anticipated. The bomb rose in a brief arc and fell with careful precision into the mouth of the flaming cone. A split instant of hesitation and then hell itself was unleashed. The pyramid of toffee magma split wide with a murderous roar; gouts of flame and incandescent lava boiled and foamed high into the air and collapsed into a storm of white-hot cinders and writhing jets of burning gas. At the base, where the cone had stood, the blowhole angrily vomited a widening pool of boiling lava like some grotesque festering sore.

"Another?" asked Jacko.

Fritz nodded. "We might as well be fried sheep as roast lambs."

The second bomb, too, was carefully placed. This time the lava rose like a living wall and plunged outward, splashing and streaming its magnificent debris up to thirty metres from the seething well. A sheet of roaring flame rose up with frenzied fingers and enveloped the protesting members of the rail-span overhead.

The blast of heat and awesome fury sent the watchers scurrying for shelter, with Harris fearing for the safety of his remaining bombs. Only Fritz stayed put, his clothes smouldering, shielding his eyes with his hands and overcome with the enormity of the havoc he had wrought. Then the flaming torches died and the white-hot spume grew less. The lava pool became a darkening puddle of red toffee, shot with occasional bursts of recalescent heat and overhung with the will-o-the wisp of burning sulphur.

"One up to me," said Fritz Van Noon.

By morning the remains of the volcano held no visible sign of life.

The lava had spread into a vast rippled puddle of rock, still hot but solid enough to hear a man's weight. Already the lichen was beginning its assault on the cooler regions, eager to begin the symbiosis with the grass to follow.

Jacko had the calculations finished by the time that Fritz was ready to inspect.

"Fritz, you're a ruddy genius! There's enough material in this puddle to make two average-size volcanoes in this district. That mean's we've cleared it out completely. With a hit of luck they won't have another volcano here for the next sixty years. Unless a volcano happens right under a trestle leg we can treat it the same as this one. That simplifies life no end."

"Precisely," said Fritz. "But it's the trestle legs I'm worried about. Pile-driving those base supports makes the trestles rather vulnerable. What happens to your railway if your trestles suffer a high mortality rate?"

"I think we quit," said Jacko candidly.

"Not on your life," said Fritz. "We've got enemies. If U.E. goes home in defeat they'll try and break us for sure. Between us we run the largest collection of screwballs and technical malcontents in the whole terran service. Not one of them would be happy about returning to honest engineering while they can stay with us and play forsaken children's games under the minimum of effectual supervision. We just can't let them down. Besides which, there's more than the Cannis railway at stake!"

"I guess you're right," said Jacko. "But look at the problem. We can't put a straight track run on the ground because of the cones in the way. Even if we could it would take years to level up the site. Therefore we build on trestles and spans over the rocks and smaller cones. That makes sense even if it looks grotesque. But you can't stop a volcano which comes up under a trestle. Even the Canians never found a way round that."

"I can," said Fritz slowly. "But it's a dangerous thing to try. You see, there is one place on Cannis where a volcano never rises."

"I doubt it."

"But it's perfectly true. A weathered volcano may break and fall, but a new volcano never rises where an old one still stands. Pressure difference, I suppose."

He broke off suddenly with a puzzled frown.

"I thought I heard a 'coptor. Were we expecting any visitors?"

Jacko found a pair of field glasses and studied the 'coptor

now visible on the horizon.

"Trouble!" he said. "Looks like the administration has found out where we are. That's a deputation from Hellsport unless I'm very much mistaken."

"Heck!" said Fritz. "Can't you head them off? I've got work to do. I bet it's that lousy planning group come to foul things up."

There were two terran civilians in the 'coptor. The taller of the two was obviously the spokesman, whilst his companion appeared to be some kind of technical consultant. On the way down from the landing raft they made a rather pointed inspection of the piles of girder and angle which littered the camp, and the short man took it upon himself to explain to his companion certain niceties of railway construction which Fritz appeared to have overlooked. By the time they reached the office they were clearly in the mood for business.

"I'm Eldrick, Planning and Coordination," said the tall civilian. "I think you would be Mr. Noon."

"Lieutenant Van Noon," corrected Fritz wearily. "I told you over the radio-phone not to waste your time on a trip out here."

Eldrick smiled tolerantly. "I think you misunderstood our purpose. We are the group which co-ordinates the efforts of all units on Cannis to ensure that the maximum effort is concentrated in the right direction. We are here to help you."

"When U.E. needs help," said Fritz, "it helps itself. That's the prime function of U.E. We're independent, unco-ordinated, unorthodox, and generally fireproof—and what's more I have a certificate to prove it."

Eldrick was unmoved. "I still think you're making a mistake."

Fritz threw up his hands in a passable imitation of a man going berserk.

"The whole Cannis episode is a mistake. Even this misbegotten planet is some blatant cosmological error. If you think you can create order out of chaos with a slip-stick and a schedule of spare parts then you have no idea of the complexities involved."

"Have you?" asked Eldrick pointedly. "What about steel! You can't build a railway without steel. There are priorities to be arranged, specifications to be agreed, orders to be placed on Terra. Organization is essential to the well-being of any major endeavour."

"Organization," said Fritz, "is the last refuge of a tired mind. It's a bumbling, mechanical substitute for initiative. I can't wait twenty months for terran steel even if it is cut to size and neatly drilled to specification. If I haven't got steel then I'll use something else, never ask me what."

"I regard that as a very foolish and unnecessary attitude."

"That foolish attitude of creation out of necessity," said Fritz heatedly, "is the power and the reason that placed Mankind above the animals. Without it we'd still be scratching fleas off each other's backs. Now I must trouble you to leave."

"Very well," said Eldrick, "but if necessity is the mother of invention then you are in for a highly creative time. I've had a look at your constructions here, and if you think you can get a line through to Hellsport inside ten years you're either a genius or a fool."

"Was that wise," asked Jacko, watching the 'coptor lift-off for Hellsport. "I mean, throwing him out like that."

"No," said Fritz. "But, by Heaven, it felt good! These planners make my blood boil. Civilization runs at a quarter pace because of the blind dictum that everything must be organized according to the book."

"I suppose it has its virtues, though." Jacko was thoughtful. "After all, look at the Canians. They can't muster a sufficiently collective effort to repair their own railways."

"And for why? Because they're running on the wrong philosophy. They can't do it because they're trying to reinstate the railways as they used to be. That's not the right attitude. There is no logic which says a problem has to be solved in the same way as it was done previously. The Cannis railway was a product of its own time—and times change. If you haven't the means to do what the other fellow did, then forget it and try something else."

"That's what I like about you," said Jacko. "You consistently move in the opposite direction to everyone else. I seem to remember you were about to show us how to build a volcano-proof trestle without actually using any steel."

Fritz smiled mischievously. "Suppose we forget about trestles. Can you salvage enough scrap to manage the spans and the rails?"

"Sure. That I can find, but if it's not a rude question how do you figure to hold them up? Will power?"

"No, volcanoes, dead ones. Lop off the tops and what have you got? Natural pillars of rock which will last a lifetime. Strap on a yoke, sling the spans between them and you have your railway."

"Crazy like a fox!" said Jacko. "It would work, of course—over a very short section, but I suppose that tired little brain of yours didn't also figure out how to manoeuvre a string of volcanoes into a straight line roughly approximating the way we want to go? Or do we build a crazy zig-zag track and use triangular trains?"

"No," said Fritz, "although the idea did occur to me. Also a proverb about Mohammed and the mountain."

"Now I know you're nuts," said Jacko. "If you haven't got volcanoes then you haven't got any, and there's nothing you can do about it."

"Is that so? Then I think you have something yet to learn. This may not be one of the most brilliant moments of my career but it may well prove to be the most spectacular."

At the end of the line, where the next trestle ought to have been, Harrison, and Fanning, the U.E. geologist, had the mobile drilling rig assembled. Fanning was taking core samples from the drill and shaking his head sadly.

"I don't like this, Fritz. We've penetrated to forty metres and the stuff is coming up hotter than hell. I should hate the drill to break into a high pressure region."

"How near are we to a molten layer?"

"Can't tell exactly, but the sonic depth-probe puts it at about seventy metres, plus or minus ten."

"Near enough," said Fritz. "If the stuff the drill is picking up is fusible I think we can stop right here."

Fanning mopped his brow and began to withdraw the drill. When it was out they collapsed the drilling rig, and the dino-dozer hauled it from the site.

Then Harris returned dragging several metal cylinders with obvious caution. Fritz waved everyone away from the drilling, adjusted something on one of the cylinders and heaved it end first down the well. Nothing happened except that after about a minute thick yellow smoke began to issue from the hole. Fritz cursed and, approaching warily, dropped another cylinder after the first.

He scarcely got away in time. There was a crack like the voice of thunder, and a ball of violent, sparking incandescence screamed into the sky. Then flames jetted up, a scorching burst of fire leaping from the soil like some fantastic blow-torch. Molten magma, entrained in the superheated gasses, was hurled high in the air and descended as a scatter of singeing hail driven on the light cross-winds.

The onlookers fled in confusion far from the terrible well. By the time that Fritz reached shelter his uniform was smouldering in a dozen places and his face and hands were red from exposure to the heat and covered with superficial burns from the searing fall-out. Jacko had fared little better, having waited to make sure that Fritz was able to escape. They sat down on a broken slag-case, dabbing balm from a first-aid pack on their burns and watching the hectic blast as it roared with unimagined ferocity.

Slowly the cone began to form as lava congealed around the flaming throat, and the fiery torch rode up with slow magnificence as the cone became a candle and then a tower with a bright and angry beacon at the top.

"Voila!" said Fritz. "I give you a volcano."

"Hell. I'll give you volcanoes!" said Jacko, dabbing at his burns.

"Next time you try this Guy Fawkes stunt you're strictly on your own. What the heck did you drop down that hole?"

Fritz smiled. "A Kellung super-thermite bomb—and a cylinder of oxygen for luck. The intense heat generated by the bomb just above a bed of active igneous magma was more than sufficient to release the volcano. This time the process was channelled by the bore-hole, so we got a cone instead of a puddle."

"Per ardua ad asbestos!" said Jocko ruefully. "Are you seriously suggesting we do this all the way to Hellsport?"

"Only where we have to," said Fritz. "And even that will take more Kellung bombs than we can come-by honestly. Fortunately there's a way round that. Up on the Juara shelf is the Command weapon stores. They've more Kellung bombs there than we're ever likely to need."

"But will they let us have them?"

"No," said Fritz, "but that's never stopped Harris before."

Three days later the new volcano was extinct. A crazy scaffold was set up round the cone and the top neatly truncated with power chisels and pneumatic drills. As a structure it stood supremely suited for its job. This siliceous rock had set like concrete, and had it been cast deliberately by hand it could not have stood more straight or firm. The yoke was placed around the cone top and secured by hooks into the narrow crater. Prefabricated spans were trimmed to length and joined up to the existing structure. The result was the finest trestle that Cannis had ever possessed.

For U.E. it was an hour of jubilation. The forgotten gimmicks and the half-formed innovations suddenly leaped to new promise now it was certain the line was going through. At the end of a three week burst of energy the last rail of Juara was bolted into place. The locomotive returned to Callin with improvised rolling-stock and two days later chugged triumphantly through to Juara with the first load of the finest bean harvest for years.

Then it blew itself to bits.

"And something else," said Jacko. "They've just arrested

Harris at the Command weapons store. So we won't be using Kellungs any more."

It was summer in Hellsport. Flies and dust thickened the air, whilst the humid heat was relentless and intolerable. Even in the air-conditioned sanctuary of the Command H.Q. the dust crept through the filters and the humidity defied the monitors to hold the moisture content and the pressure down.

When the shouting began Colonel Ivan Nash grew irate with this newest source of irritation. He called a native courier to find the meaning of the outrage.

"They say, *Lazib*," said the native, with sly humour, "that a train comes in from Juara bearing the greatest man on Cannis."

"Nonsense!" said Nash irritably. "There are no trains left on the Juara-Callin line."

"That may be true, *Lazib*," said the Canian, with his tongue in his cheek, "but something is coming down the line. Look, you can see it for yourself."

Nash released the clamps and flung open the window, wincing at the blast of dust and heat which invaded the room. He found his field glasses and scanned the railway, which seemed to be dancing in the slow heat-haze. Something was coming down the Juara line, but the distance and. the dust conspired to make identification impossible. Only when it grew nearer were the details of the vehicle displayed.

Nash choked and closed the window with a clang. The "train" bore a curious resemblance to a service trooping-helicopter, minus rotors, and slung on a low truck, the wheels of which were broad grooved rollers. Various items of machinery were slung about the outside of the strange assembly, and in front walked a Canian with quick, birdlike movements, hopping from sleeper to sleeper and carrying a big red flag.

The train entered the terminus, reversed to another rail, then shuttled back and forwards just to show the proficiency of its roller wheels in manoeuvring on any gauge of line. The Canians went wild with enthusiasm, and shouted and cheered until Nash thought his head was going to split. He was still starring from the window when Fritz Van Noon came into the room.

Colonel Nash considered him silently. “All right, Fritz, you win—so far. I never thought you’d make it. Too bad you had to step out of line to do it.”

“You didn’t exactly help,” said Fritz. “I thought we were finished when you had Ensign Harris arrested for stealing Kellung bombs. Fortunately Malu, our tame Canian genius, cooked us up a substitute using Canian rocket fuel.”

“I know,” said Nash. “I had my spies up there. A very worthy effort. Too bad I have to throw the book at you. Unorthodox engineering I could learn to stand, but brigandry is a very different matter.”

“Is it?” asked Fritz. “I have a warrant here authorising the release of Ensign Harris. It’s neatly signed, sealed and counter signed by Terran GenCom.”

“No dice!” said Nash. “I mean to court-martial Harris good and proper. Even GenCom can’t dictate to me on the internal administration of my own sector. With any luck Harris will still be in jail when the sun goes cold. And as soon as I can get evidence of complicity you’ll go up beside him. Weapon stealing is a capital offence. Besides which—” he said accusingly, “—you haven’t had time to get GenCom confirmation on a release warrant.”

“No need,” said Fritz complacently. “Release warrants for Ensign Harris are part of our standard equipment. We always stock up before starting on a mission.”

Nash was shocked. “You mean to say that this man’s conduct is officially condoned?”

“Condoned?” Fritz chuckled. “As far as I am aware the only crime Harris committed was to get caught. For that I will personally reprimand him.”

“But this is preposterous!” said Nash. “The man’s a criminal thief.”

“Precisely. That’s his speciality. It took us a long time to find a crook of his calibre. He’s the man who broke the First National Bullion Bank and got away with a quarter of a million pounds."

"This gets worse and worse," said Nash, his voice rising with disbelief. "Do you mean to say you employ a known criminal because of his prowess at breaking and entering? What sort of trade classification do you call that?"

"Quartermaster," said Fritz, with obvious enjoyment. "We want equipment and supplies, he has to beg, borrow or steal to provide them. It's a point of honour that he never comes by anything through the proper channels."

"But in the name of Mercy, why?" Nash sensed he was losing ground.

"It's part of the fundamental philosophy behind U.E."

Nash chewed his moustache nervously. "I've been warned about getting into an argument with you."

He returned to the desk and poured himself a drink. On second thoughts he offered it to Fritz and poured himself another.

"I don't doubt you can explain," he said heavily. "I don't doubt your ability to talk your way out of anything. I'm just warning you it'd better be good. If I'm not convinced I'll have every man-jack of yours in irons before the morning,"

"I think not," said Fritz. "I'm afraid you've been the victim of a slight deception. That crazy gang of bodgers of mine is not quite what it seems. This may be unethical, but if you attempted to take any action against us you'd be out of the army so fast you wouldn't have time to change your hat."

"I warn you . . ." said Nash grimly.

"Hear me out first," said Fritz. "Have you heard of Operation Hyperon."

Nash nodded. "The deep-space penetration project. Two million light years and no possibility of return."

"Precisely. Well, U.E. is the lead team that's going."

"I don't think I understand. Is this some sort of joke?"

"No, sir, very far from it. You see, in a deep-space probe you can't afford to carry anything but men and the very minimum of equipment which will ensure survival. There are no supply ships, no machine shops, and no reference libraries at two million light years from Terra.

"So what type of men do you send? Physicists who are lost without a laboratory? Engineers who can't obtain any steel? No, you send the men who can make a plough out of a tree-trunk, a stone and a length of creeper. You send the men who have made a lifetime's habit of turning anything they could lay their hands on to their own peculiar advantage."

"And that's the philosophical concept behind U.E.?"

"Just that," said Fritz. "Ours is an age of highly complex technology. Specialization and standardization are the key-words of our civilization. But as the starships spread us further across the galaxies the strings which tie us to the centres of order and knowledge tend to become a bit tenuous. You can't take your technology with you. Things come unknit."

"A masterpiece of understatement," said Nash. "Even on Cannis we created a technological monster. We tried to apply terran know-how without having the facilities to back us. It didn't work."

"Just so," said Fritz, "hence U.E. This is an experimental team chosen to a pattern decided after years of psycho-research. It's a completely flexible approach with no precepts sacred except that the end justifies the means. We have built a team which can construct the nucleus of a functional civilisation out of bits of string and matchsticks if necessary. Our coming to Cannis was simply an exercise."

Nash picked up the phone and dialled a number.

"Bring Ensign Harris to my office immediately—and forget the guards, I'm ordering his immediate release. That's right, you idiot, I said 'release'! Oh yes, and bring up another bottle of Scotch—no, make it a crate. We're going to have a party."

"Thank you," said Fritz Van Noon, bodger extraordinary.

THE SUBWAYS OF TAZOO

"Lieutenant Van Noon, report to Colonel Belling's office."

"Damn!" Fritz Van Noon glared at the loudspeaker. "Sounds as though Belling's back and on the warpath again."

"Can you wonder?" Jacko Hine helped him out from under the miscellanea of half-assembled pieces. "Let's face it, Fritz, some of our recent projects have come unstuck in a rather spectacular manner."

"True," said Fritz, "but never let it be said that the Unorthodox Engineers have produced a damp squib. Always our results have exceeded our wildest expectations."

"Or Belling's wildest fears," said Jacko morosely.

As Fritz entered the office Colonel Belling half raised himself from his chair in greeting. "Ah, Van Noon! Just the fellow I wanted to see."

"Sir?" asked Fritz suspiciously. Colonel Belling was not a man given to cordiality towards his subordinates.

Belling smiled wolfishly. "I've just returned from the General Staff conference. Since you reinstated the railways up on Cannis even the Old Man has been forced to admit that there may be occasions when unorthodox engineering has its virtues. For my part I felt impelled to point out that I'm trying to run a specialist engineering reserve, and that carrying the can for a complete squad of engineering illegitimates was not strictly within my terms of reference. As I explained, always I get stuck with the one engineer in a thousand who should never have left kindergarten, let alone graduated. The only repository I have for these mechanical misfits is the U.E. squad, where the damage they can do, if not exactly nullified, is at least anticipated."

"Isn't that a little unfair, sir? I mean . . ."

"I know just what you mean, Fritz, and I don't accept it. Engineering is a discipline, but the brand you apply is strictly delinquent. The outcome of the conference was that Colonel Nash, whom I'm beginning to suspect has masochistic tendencies, has volunteered to take the U.E. squad on the Tazoon enterprise."

Fritz considered this for a moment. "Exactly what are they doing on Tazoo, sir?"

"Supporting an archaeological team. Life on Tazoo is now extinct, but evidence tends to show that it once held a civilization as highly developed or more so than our own. In terms of knowledge to be gained it is probably the greatest find that space has ever given to us. It is doubtful if the Tazoons were human or even humanoid, and they became extinct at least two million years ago. Our problem is to pick up the remains of a complex mechanical culture as alien and as old as that and attempt to understand it for what it was."

"I shouldn't have thought that was too difficult, sir."

"No, Fritz, I never supposed you would. That's partly the reason you're going. Your inverted-sideways approach is the nearest thing to an alien technology that we've got. That makes you a specialist."

"Thank you, sir," said Fritz warily. "And the other part of the reason we're going?"

"The climatic conditions on Tazoo are such hell that the average rugged ground-cat has a useful working life of about two weeks. That means the archaeologists can't explore enough from base to get at the really big finds they are certain exist. Fritz, I want you to provide them with transport to where they'll be most use—and if you don't, you'd better find another engineering reserve to come back to, because if you come back here . . ."

"I know," said Fritz unhappily, "you'll make me wish I'd opted to transfer my retirement pay to Tazoo."

"You know, Fritz," said Colonel Belling, "for a moment we reached a point of real understanding there. I think I'm going to rather enjoy the thoughts of you and the U.E. squad sweating it out in a hell-spot like Tazoo."

Touchdown on Tazoo. The transfer ferry had no viewports and afforded no opportunity for its passengers to receive a preview of their destination. Even the ground-cat which rendezvoused at the landing site close-coupled its hatches with the ferry's air lock before the transfer of passengers and goods began. In the cabin of the ground-cat, shutters likewise obscured the view and cheated Fritz of his moment of revelation.

"Allow me to introduce myself," said the cabin's occupant. "The name is Philip Nevill, Archaeologist in Charge."

"Van Noon," said Fritz. "Engineer extraordinary—and this is Jacko Hine, one of my staff."

Nevill grinned affably. "Your reputation preceded you, my boy. Frankly, when I heard of you I persuaded Colonel Nash to get you here at any cost. There are things on Tazoo it'll take a very liberal mind indeed to understand."

The ground-cat struggled away from the ferry, its engine coughing in asthmatic complaint.

"So I've heard," said Fritz. "Look, do you mind if I open the shutter for a second? I'd like to know the worst right from the start."

"Help yourself," said Nevill, "but I promise you it's a passion you'll soon lose."

Fritz fought the shutter from the window and peered out for his first glimpse of Tazoo. Heavy cloudbanks filtered the furious sunlight to a brilliant monochromatic red which hurt his eyes and rendered all colours as shades of red or the darkest, sooty black. The terrain itself was nothing but a lumpy, featureless waste as far as the eye could see.

"Satisfied?" asked Nevill.

Fritz dropped the shutter back with a clang and closed his eyes.

"Painful, isn't it?" asked Nevill. "Normal endurance is about forty minutes before red-blindness sets in. Very bad for the eyes, to say nothing of the psychological effects. Incidentally, the ultraviolet radiation for two hours after dawn and two hours before sunset is strong enough to take the skin off you in about three minutes flat."

"Charming!" said Fritz. "And what's it like at midday?"

Nevill raised his eyes to the ceiling. "Ruddy awful!" he said.

At the blare of the ground-cat's horn Nevill opened the shutter again. "There's the base—way over yonder."

Fritz scowled at the blood-red panorama. Perhaps half a kilometre away was the base, like a cluster of cherries half-submerged in a waste of pink icing.

"Underground, eh? A very sensible precaution."

"It isn't underground," said Nevill in a slightly aggrieved tone. "It's a surface installation."

"But I don't see anything but some almighty balls of mud."

"They're standard Knudsen huts with a protective skin on. There's a sandstorm that whips up every night which would sandblast an unprotected Knudsen to a skeleton before dawn. We spray each hut weekly with a highly plasticized poly-polymer which is reasonably abrasive resistant. The plastic traps some of the sand and this materially increases its resistance, but builds up and completely ruins the shape."

Abruptly the engine of the ground-cat coughed and died. Nevill held a rapid exchange over the intercom with the driver.

"Engine's gone," he said finally. "Either the carburettor's etched away or the damn sand has got into the cylinders—or both. Anyway, the cat is a write-off for all practical purposes, so there's nothing for it but to walk—and it's too near evening for that to be funny."

They descended from the cabin, Fritz and Jacko choking quietly in the acrid air which caught at their noses and made their lungs feel raw. Nevill, acclimatized, was surveying the sky anxiously. Above them the swirling cloudbanks, blood-red trailing into purple and black, plunged across the darkening sky so low that Fritz had an almost compulsive desire to put up his hands to see if he could touch them. There must have been a high wind above, for the cloudrace was certainly moving at better than a hundred kilometres an hour, yet on the ground the warm humidity was deathly still, as though a sheet of glass insulated them from the driving turbulence.

Nevill was worried. "Looks like a storm," he said.

"Is that bad?" asked Fritz.

"Only if you're unlucky enough to be out in it. Let's hope it's a wet storm. They're decidedly uncomfortable, but not usually fatal if you can get to shelter quickly enough."

"Why, what happens?"

"Nothing spectacular if you can find shelter from a hundred kilometre per hour damp sandstorm and if you happen to have sufficient alkali available to neutralize the rain on your skin."

"Neutralize the rain?" said Fritz, his voice rising. "What the blazes is in it?"

"Oh, about five per cent sulphuric acid plus a trace of hydrogen chloride with a little free ionized chlorine. Stings like hell, but it's better than a dry storm."

"I'll buy it," Fritz said helplessly. "If a wet sandstorm is equal to an accelerated metal descaling process, what's a dry storm equal to?"

By now Nevill was deeply concerned, scanning the furious cloudrace with worried and experienced eyes. They were still three hundred metres from the nearest part of the base, with Jacko and the driver close behind.

"I think you're going to have a practical demonstration of a dry storm, Fritz. If the smell of ozone becomes intolerable or if you hear anything like a bee buzzing don't hesitate—just drop to the ground as fast as you are able. If you can find a hollow then roll into it, otherwise don't bother—but whatever you do, be quick."

"A bee buzzing?"

"Air ionization path, the prelude to a lightning bolt. There's a few mega-megavolt not many metres up in the cloudrace, and it packs a current that can not only char a man but also fuse him very neatly into the sand. The carbon from the body reduces a great many metal oxides in the ground so that the resultant slag forms a remarkable range of glasses."

"Forget the chemistry," said Fritz hastily. "I never could see myself making a very convincing paperweight."

"Then drop!" said Nevill, suiting action to the words.

They all dropped to the ground. Fritz's nose didn't have time to detect the ozone, virtually paralysed as it was by the existing acridity, but his ears did register the sudden buzz which Nevill had anticipated by a half second. Then the lightning bolt, a blaze of vivid energy a mere thirty metres distant, spat like a column of angry fire rising to the heavens. The noise and the shock-wave of its passing stunned them momentarily. By the time they had collected their wits only a generous patch of fused sand and a choking concentration of ozone marked the spot where the bolt had struck.

"Bad!" said Nevill. "Worst I've seen. It's striking low ground, which means we have no possible cover out here. Best throw away any metal you may have on you and try to crawl back nearer to the cat—but for Pete's sake keep your heads low."

Another bolt of lightning, bigger and nearer than the first, stabbed into the sand behind them like the bursting of a shell, followed by three almost simultaneously in the near vicinity.

Desperately slowly the party crawled back towards the cat, which stood as the pitifully-low high-spot of this particular area of terrain. On all sides of them now the jagged lightning cut into the ground with burning shafts of vicious energy, like the arrows of retribution fired by some crazed electric god. Then a shaft burned down on the cat itself. The fantastic current fused the metal into a white-hot bauble which was ripped open by the expanding air within. Before their horrified eyes the cat sank like a lead toy thrown on to glowing embers, and became a dirty, slag-shot puddle of mixed metal and silicates alloying with the red sand of Tazoo.

Then mercifully it began to rain. Nevill turned his face to the stinging, acrid precipitation and let out a howl of pure relief. A few seconds later they were running like half-blinded madmen through the corrosive waters in the direction of the base camp, heedless now of the cracking lightning which had withdrawn to the edge of the rain belt. They were fortunately within a few steps of the base when the wall of sharp, abrasive sand, whipped to fury by a fantastic driving wind, bore down upon them out of the deep purples of the approaching night.

TWO

"Welcome to Tazoo, Lieutenant!" Colonel Nash beckoned him into the office.

Fritz explored the still-smarting skin on his face and hands, and was still painfully aware of the puffiness around his eyes. "Thank you, Colonel. That was quite an initiation ceremony out there!"

Colonel Nash smiled fleetingly. "Unpremeditated, I assure you, but the weather is part of the reason you're here. A ground-cat is the toughest machine available, but as you saw for yourself it is totally incapable of standing up to the environment. The low pH of the celestial waters conspires with the sand to etch and tear the guts out of any transportation contrivance we've yet imported to Tazoo. When you consider atmospheric chlorine, hydrogen chloride, free sulphuric acid and ozone, plus high humidity and extreme ultraviolet radiation together with an additional nightly sandblast, you can guess that corrosion prevention is not the least of our troubles."

Fritz shuddered involuntarily.

"I must admit," said Nash, "that I haven't always seen eye to eye with you before on the subject of unorthodox engineering, but if you can solve our transport problem I shall at least be open to persuasion. Certainly no orthodox engineers can give us transport on Tazoo at a cost less than the total budget for the entire enterprise."

"What facilities have we?" asked Fritz.

"On Tazoo—anything you can find. If you need anything shipped out from Terra you'll need a damn good case to get it because of shipping costs. Certainly we can't afford to bring any more vehicles out here. Now it's up to you to delve into your unorthodoxy and come up with something practical."

"How is the Tazoon enterprise going?" asked Fritz.

"Slowly," said Nash, "largely because of the aforementioned transport limitations. Nevill's team have uncovered a lot of architectural monstrosities, but the real prize will come if they can find some of the Tazoon mechanical artifacts. If they do, and if they are one half as weird as the rest of the finds so far, it will require all of your peculiar genius to identify and interpret them. We're expecting to find some very unorthodox engineering from a culture which died before the end of the Pliocene period on Terra."

"What signs are there to indicate that they had a highly scientific culture?" asked Fritz. "Surely the finds so far don't indicate very much."

"The preliminary survey party found signs that the Tazoons had reached both of the Tazoon satellites, and we're reasonably certain that they also reached the next planet sunward in this system and actually established a base there."

"All this sounds highly promising," said Fritz. "But two million years is a long time. Would there be anything left of machines and mechanisms after such a period?"

"Nevill theorizes that to develop a high-level functional civilization the Tazoons must have had some pretty good engineers who would have been making due allowance for the make-up of the Tazoon atmosphere. Furthermore, the moist conditions don't penetrate very far down into the sand, so that the deeper an artefact is buried the greater are its chances of almost infinite survival. Deep exploration at a really promising site should give us a slice of Tazoon civilization in a very reasonable state of preservation. We need only one good site to justify the whole Tazoon enterprise."

The next day Fritz found Philip Nevill in the Archaeological H.Q., apparently none the worse for his previous day's exposure.

"Hullo, Fritz, my boy! What can we do for you?"

"I hope you can answer a question. Do you know what happened to the Tazoons themselves—I mean, why did they become extinct so swiftly when they had achieved such an apparently high technological level?"

Nevill scowled. "You're equating technology with the ability to manipulate environment and thus ensure a higher survival potential. Well, I'm afraid I can't answer that. Indications are that they abandoned the populated areas enmasse and migrated towards the equatorial regions. From distribution figures it looks as though the entire population set out for the tropics and were decimated on the way. This suggests they were fleeing from something biologically intolerable which claimed a great number in flight."

"Drastic climatic change?" asked Fritz.

"Climatic, no—environmental, possibly. We looked for evidence of major climatic changes, but there's nothing significant that we can trace. The only thing that is recent, geologically speaking, is the sand."

"The sand?"

"Mm! Probably the result of some ecological imbalance. The major plains appear to have once included prolific forests such as are still to be found in places around the temperate belts. For some reason, drought or fire or blight perhaps, these forests died. The results were typically Terran in their pattern."

"Soil erosion?"

"Yes, and on a catastrophic scale. Once the sand got to work on the unprotected soil nothing thereafter got the chance to germinate. We're still picking up viable seeds from the deep diggings, but all the shallow seeds are either dead or had started growth and been uprooted."

"When did this happen—the erosion?"

"We can't tell with certainty, but it appears to slightly predate the extinction of the Tazoons themselves. Whether these two factors are related is something only further research can prove. Does that answer your question?"

"Yes, but only to pose another," said Fritz. "I don't understand how any culture technically able to explore the neighbouring satellites could have been wiped out by anything as foreseeable and reversible as soil erosion. And why migrate to the tropics when the soil fertility remained in the temperate belts?"

"I don't know," said Nevill. "It's a difficult problem. The Tazoons were not even humanoid, and the probability is that neither their physiology nor their logic had anything in common with our own. It could be misleading if we attempted to interpret their actions by simple extrapolation of what we might have done in similar circumstances."

"A good point," said Fritz. "I don't necessarily agree with it, but I'll bear it in mind. Thanks, Philip, you've given me something to think about."

Having established that the U.E. squad was reasonably well quartered, Fritz turned his attention to the transport problem. This brought him back to Jacko who had compiled a transport survey which he presented with as much enthusiasm as if it had been his own death warrant.

"We're in trouble, Fritz. Of the hundred ground-cats originally provided for the enterprise only twenty are still functioning. Two hundred hours operating life on Tazoo reduces a cat to a condition where you couldn't sell it for scrap value. By sorting bits and pieces we could probably reconstruct another five cats, but we can only reckon on a maximum of six thousand operating-cat-hours before we start walking."

Fritz stared disconsolately at a virgin notebook. "What about tractors and heavy equipment?"

"They're not too bad—but only by virtue of the fact that most of them are still in sealed crates. Once they're broken out there's no reason to suppose they'll last any longer than the cats do. This combination of corrosion and abrasion is something to which I'd not cheerfully expose a clockwork mouse."

"I take your point," said Fritz. "As I see the present requirements it doesn't give us much over a sixty-day transport potential. What protection can we give to the cats to extend their working life?"

"A lot of a vehicle we can plastic coat, as they do with the Knudsens. The engines are a more difficult problem. Some genius thought of providing them with standard aluminium-alloy turbine housings, and what the Tazoon atmosphere does to the alloy makes my flesh creep. Even the vitreous liners devitrify and release particles of silica into the bearings."

"Don't bother to describe," said Fritz, "what silica does to the bearings. I think we have to face the fact that while we might save most of the cats themselves we aren't going to be able to save many of the engines. We could devise a system of enclosing the engines in an inert atmosphere but I doubt if we have the facilities here to do a permanent job. We then also need a supply of controlled pH, moisture free oxygen for the air intake. I think we could produce that by electrolysis, but I doubt if we can handle it in sufficient quantities to be of much value."

"And so on *ad infinitum*," said Jacko ruefully.

Fritz nodded. "Let's try it anyway. I want two cats modified. Plastic spray them everywhere possible, and seal the engine compartment and fill it with a nitrogen and hydrogen mixture of non-ignitable composition. Get our micro-Linde column working for the nitrogen and make an electrolysis plant for the hydrogen. You'll need both the Linde and the electrolytic plant to get enough oxygen for the air-supply for the engine intakes, and you'd better dilute the oxygen with any nitrogen you can spare, then adjust the turbines to run on that."

"And what do I keep the oxygen in?" asked Jacko.

"They've a fair supply of the plastic poly-polymer they use for spraying the huts. It shouldn't be beyond our capacity to blow a gasbag from that."

"It all sounds feasible," said Jacko, "but I doubt the capacity of the micro-Linde to give us all the nitrogen we need."

"So do I," said Fritz, 'that's why I said to modify two cats only. There's plenty of other things to try, but this is the most obvious, and we've neither time nor the resources to start nitrogen fixation in a big way." He went to the window, opened the shutter and stared moodily out at the red and featureless wasteland.

"Sand," he said. "Nothing but sand, fine-grained, abrasive

and all-pervading. What we need, Jacko, is something completely new in the way of transport on Tazoo. I wonder what the Tazoons themselves employed."

Three days later and the modification of the cats was in full swing when the telephone rang.

"Van Noon speaking."

"Fritz, Nevill here. I've got some work for you."

"Bring it over," said Fritz. "A little more won't make much difference. "

"Right. Be with you in about ten minutes. It's one of these Tazoon mechanisms we've been looking for."

"Now you have me interested," said Fritz. "Exactly what is it?"

"That's what I want you to tell me."

Ten minutes later Nevill arrived and ceremonially knocked out his pipe on the threshold in deference to a large no-smoking notice over the jury-rigged electrolysis plant. Then he signalled to his assistants who dragged a large object into the hut and dropped it on the floor. Fritz looked at it dubiously.

"I think you've come to the wrong department. It looks like the great grandaddy of an alien chicken wishbone once belonging to some grandaddy alien chicken. Why not present it to the biology boys?"

"I did," said Nevill, "but they sent it right back with the message that you were responsible for investigating machinery."

"Machinery?" Fritz surveyed the acquisition moodily. "Have you tried it on the catering department? Perhaps they could turn it into some sort of broth."

"Machinery," said Nevill firmly. "And I'll tell you why. It isn't animal, it's vegetable—Tazoon ironwood to be precise. Also, it didn't grow that way. It was manufactured, or at least trimmed to shape, as witness the tooling marks. Furthermore, the Tazoons were plenty fond of them because the Southern plain out yonder has them at an estimated density of nearly half a million to the square kilometre."

Fritz choked for a full half minute. "Half a million?"

Nevill nodded. "And that plain is pretty big. If the sampling we have done is representative of the whole area there could be something like five thousand million of those on that one plain alone. I know the Tazoons were alien beyond our conception of the word, but I just can't see them producing that many just for the hell of it. That would be an exercise akin to paving the Sahara desert with pencil sharpeners. It's my belief that the wishbones are something functional. I want you to tell me what they were and what their function was."

Fritz nodded. "I'll let you have a preliminary report in a day or so, but if that's a machine I should hate to see their idea of a great big alien chicken wishbone."

After Nevill had left, Fritz spent a quiet hour examining the wishbone from all angles and going all over the surface of it with a magnifying glass looking for clues as to its function. Then Jacko had the wishbone hauled to the workshop for a more thorough examination. He reported back when the work was completed.

"I think we have something here, Fritz. You know those nodules on the inner surfaces, well, the fluoroscope shows a dark mass of some foreign material in each. If you're agreeable we're proposing to cut one out and see what it is."

"Start cutting," Fritz said, "because if this is a sample of Tazoon engineering then the sooner we start to come to grips with it the better."

Reluctantly the bandsaw cut into the ancient ironwood. Halfway through, the blade screeched complainingly on some hard inclusion. Then the nodule became detached, and from inside it Jacko shook a large, bright crystal on to the table.

"I thought as much," said Fritz. "There are metal fibres in the structure of the wishbone and metallized facets on the crystal. On this evidence I'd say this was some form of piezo-electric device. And see how the crystal is drilled—do you suppose there could have been strings across the wishbone?"

Jacko counted the nodules equal on both sides. "Lord, a harp!" he said in a voice heavy with incredulity.

"Or a sound-transducer," said Fritz. "There are common electrical paths through the ironwood, and connections to the crystals. If you applied an alternating current to those contacts, the crystals would excite the strings in sympathy according to the resonant frequency of the particular system. I wonder what on earth it would sound like? Jacko, start restringing what's left of this thing while I sort out a power amplifier and a few bits and pieces. Together we can make some be-eautiful music."

"Right," said Jacko, "but if your conception of music is anything like your engineering I'm going to take time out to make some earplugs too."

THREE

It took three hours to complete the assembly. Fritz disappeared to the communications hut and returned with an assortment of equipment which he appeared to assemble more by inspiration than by design. When everything was ready he switched on. The first results were shattering, and the electronics needed drastic revision before a reasonably tolerable result was obtained.

After some final adjustments Fritz pronounced himself satisfied with the results and dropped into a chair to listen attentively, his gaze wandering to the open shutter and the blood-red sunset trailing nakedly beyond.

"Listen to it, Jacko!" said Fritz happily. "Alien and beautiful beyond recall."

"I might just point out," said Jacko, "that if somebody attempted to re-string a two-million years old grand piano with stranded cable and without any idea of the scale and pitch involved, the results would sound equally alien."

"I'm in no mood to quibble with one who possesses such a tiny soul," said Fritz. "To me this is music such as the ancient Tazoons knew it as they walked hand in hand in the eyeless evenings of old Tazoo. Can't you imagine it, Jacko, this incredible music voiced by a million harps in the blood-red twilight of this alien land?"

"It makes my head ache," said Jacko. "What are you feeding into the blasted thing, anyway?"

Fritz coughed. "Actually it's the telemetry signals from the satellite monitoring the Tazoon ionosphere, but the harp contributes about five-hundred per cent distortion, so you never know it from music."

"I can't help feeling distinctly uneasy," said Jacko, "about the notion of anybody wanting half a million crazy self-playing harps to the square kilometre. No culture could be that fond of music and yet survive."

"They didn't survive. And we can't yet hope to understand so alien a culture. If you want a parallel, think of all the millions of personal transistor radios taken to the beaches on Terra on a public holiday. Think how much simpler life would be if they erected loudspeakers at four-foot intervals on all beaches and made full-time listening compulsory instead of merely unavoidable." Despite the warmth Jacko shuddered visibly and closed his eyes, while the complex tones of the harp sang strangely with unfathomable harmonies which did curious things to his stomach. "I'm beginning to get the idea," he said, "exactly why the Tazoons decided to migrate. Listening to this, I get precisely the same urge myself."

At that moment the door was flung open and Nevill, eyes aglow with jubilation, burst into the hut.

"Fritz, we've done it! A real find at last. To judge from the extent of our soundings we seem to have hit upon the location of a whole damn Tazoon city under the sand."

Fritz bounded up with enthusiasm. "Congratulations, Philip! This sounds like the breakthrough we've been waiting for. Exactly where is this site?"

"Under our very noses—about twenty kilometres east of here. I tell you, Fritz, my boy, there's a real metropolis down there."

He stopped, aware for the first time of the singing harp.

"What in the name of Thunder is that?"

"A genuine Tazoon harp in action," said Fritz modestly. "Don't you like it?"

"No," said Nevill, "because it isn't right. Nobody, however alien, would want more than one of anything that sounds like that. Besides"—he mopped the moisture which had risen on his brow—"the Tazoons had very small ear cavities. Their audible range was undoubtedly, in the medium ultrasonic. Frankly they could never have heard anything pitched as low as that. Sorry! Try and make it do something else like lighting fires or something."

And so saying, he was gone, leaving Fritz looking miserably at his equipment and trying to avoid Jacko's eyes.

"All right," said Fritz, "so even I can't always be right first time." He turned off the amplifier disconsolately. "I still think it was a good idea."

"That's the second of your good ideas that has run off the rails today," said Jacko, fingering his ears.

"Second?" Fritz looked mildly surprised.

"Yes, I forgot to tell you. Your idea for obtaining pure nitrogen for the cats by fractional distillation in the micro-Linde didn't solve the problem, it merely transferred it. The blasted Tazoon atmosphere's eaten the guts out of the Linde compressor."

"That was all I needed to make my day!" said Fritz. "You'd better get the boys together, Jacko. I want every repairable ground-cat and tractor prepared for operation, and as much heavy lifting and moving tackle as we can acquire."

"What are you planning, Fritz?"

"Let's face it, Jacko, we can't keep enough transport in service to do the daily forty-kilometre round-trips to the new site for very long. If that's a major site they've found there won't be much point in having a base camp this far distant. The logical thing to do is expend all our resources, moving the whole base to the new site."

"Are you crazy?" asked Jacko. "It'd take months to dismantle this lot and transport it that far."

"I said nothing about dismantling. A Knudsen hut is a unit structure. It is capable of being moved as a whole. Can you think of any reason why we shouldn't just attach a cat or tractor to each hut and haul it bodily over the sand to the new site?"

"Yes, Colonel Nash and the base psychiatrist, to name only two. A Knudsen could never stand a belting like that and finish in one piece."

"Ordinarily, no, but these have been covered with alternate layers of resin and sand to a thickness which has become ridiculous. Dammit, Jacko, you've got a metal and sand-filled resin laminate there which must have all of a hundred and fifty times the strength of the original hut."

"You're dead right, of course," said Jacko. "But I'm going to love thinking of you trying to explain it to Colonel Nash."

"All right," said Nash at last. "You can start moving the base just as soon as the necessary cables and services have been laid. I don't need to remind you that everything has to be fully secured by sundown. And I warn you that if anything goes wrong . . ."

He leaned back speculatively for a moment.

"You know, Fritz, I must confess I'm disappointed. I'd expected great things from unorthodoxy, but when it comes to the point you can't even promise to keep a decent transport system in operation."

"A snowflake," Fritz protested, "wouldn't stand much chance in Hell unless you had a ton of refrigeration equipment alongside. The fault is not being in Hell, but in being a snowflake. You've got a roughly similar position with your cats on Tazoo. A suitable cat could easily be designed for these conditions, but it would need Terran resources to build it and a long haul to bring it out here. The cost would be astronomical. The limitation is in associating transport with the idea of a ground-cat."

"I'm perfectly aware of that," said Nash. "In fact it's the reason I sent for you. You have the reputation for producing the impossible at very short notice. All right—I challenge you to produce."

"Miracles we perform immediately," said Fritz quietly. "The impossible takes a little longer. After all, we've only been here a week."

Nash watched him narrowly for a moment. "Fritz, frankly I don't believe anybody has the remotest chance of doing what I ask, but I'm calling your bluff. If you have any sort of transport running on Tazoo in three months' time I'll be glad to take back all the harsh things I've ever said about UE. If you don't I'll have to send you back to Terra. The Tazoon enterprise wasn't designed to carry any dead weight."

"It's a challenge I'll accept," said Fritz, "but don't expect to equate transportation with any vehicular form you're used to, because the chances are a million to one against it looking like anything you've ever seen before."

Jacko was waiting for him outside the office.

"Bad?" he asked.

"Not good," said Fritz. "We've got three months to crack the transport problem or get kicked out as a bunch of nogood layabouts. The honour—even the continuance of U.E.—is very much at stake. Somehow we've got to contrive some sort of vehicle, and this in the face of the fact that we have no source of constructional material capable of withstanding the Tazoon environment."

"So where do we go from here, Fritz?"

"Damned if I know. You go and check the arrangements for the big move. I'm going over to the site to see how friend Nevill is doing. He may have dug up a little inspiration out there—and Heaven knows I could use a little right now."

Nevill saw the cat drawing across the rouge desert, and came to the edge of the workings to await Fritz's arrival.

"How're things going, Philip?"

"Wonderful, my boy. We knew we had a major find, but this—this is paradise! We're going straight down on a major city by the look of it, and the stuff on the lower levels where the sand is dry is in a perfect state of preservation. Some of the three-storied buildings are so sound that we'll be able to use them for our own purposes. I tell you, Fritz, the Tazoon enterprise looks like paying off about two million per cent interest. The complete analysis of the stuff found here will occupy generations."

Fritz gazed down into the broad quarry which was the site of the workings. On every hand the feverish activity of the archaeological teams pointed a measure of the excitement and enthusiasm which infected everyone concerned. The shifts had been voluntarily lengthened, but even so, the end of the short period had to be declared a compulsory cessation of work lest those on the trail of such immeasurable archaeological delights should endanger their health by continuing until they dropped from exhaustion.

Here and there alien towers were already exposed above the sand, unimaginable obelisks of incomprehensible architecture, curiously distorted and decayed by time and the ravages of wind and sand. Some, the sand shored back to greater depths, were firmer on the lower levels, and the architecture was even more marvellously and more inconceivably wrought. Occasionally, vertical pits descended at points where logic had decreed there lay something more intriguing or exciting or yielding greater bounty for the effort it entailed.

Fritz was fascinated beyond measure. The clawing otherworldliness drew his imagination on with an inescapable lure. As an engineer he fought to tame the logic of the structures which were being uncovered before him, but something in his soul, poesy perhaps, denied him an identification of parts and trapped him in the wonder of the whole. He was the technologist who came for a dispassionate analysis and stayed to worship.

With great resolve he wrenched his mind from its journeyings and looked at Nevill appealingly. The latter patted him on the shoulder sympathetically. "I know, my boy," he said. "It takes us all like that. It's both wonderful and sad to be uncovering the remains of so great a culture; wonderful because the culture was so great, and sad because we find their city empty of the creatures who created it."

"Why the hell did they have to go?" asked Fritz. "After they'd got all this way? They had mastered their environment to a degree comparable to ourselves, then in the space of a few short centuries they faded and died away and the sand moved in and covered all their marvels. But for what reason did they go? It's something we must discover lest it also comes upon us."

FOUR

By sundown the last hut had been transferred to its new position near the workings. The day had been one of great activity intermixed with frustration. As Fritz had foreseen the huts had proved themselves capable of being moved bodily across the sand, but the condition of the cats and tractors was such that the path of the move was plainly marked with a trail of abandoned vehicles spread broadly across the sandy steppes. Indeed, by the end of the day only five cats remained in operation.

After organizing a team to recover any repairable cats, Jacko went to look for Fritz and found him in the workshop idly strumming the Tazoon harp with the air of a man evoking the muses as an aid to inspiration.

"You know, Jacko, I wish I could work out what happened to the Tazoons. I simply can't understand why such a highly advanced and organized culture should suddenly fall to pieces. There's no suggestion of a major war, and there's not sufficient radioactive material on the planet to make a nuclear holocaust a possibility. It's a highly disturbing thought that a catastrophe which could destroy a race with that level of technology could leave so little trace. It's as though they suddenly closed up their cities and walked out to die on a mass trek to the equator."

"What about famine?" asked Jacko.

"Possibly. That's virtually what Nevill suggested—widespread soil erosion. For some reason the major forests in this zone died suddenly. That rather suggests a prolonged drought—but you'd think a major technology fighting for survival could cope with even that. The sea is an atrocious mineral stew, but I'm willing to bet you could distil enough water to maintain a pretty fair agricultural belt if the need arose."

"But without nuclear energy where would you get that sort of power?" asked Jacko. "Distillation of sea-water on that scale would take a great deal of energy."

"Power!" Fritz sat up. "Now there's an idea! Come to think of it, where did they get their power from anyway? Let's put a few facts together. We know that at a certain stage in the history of Tazoo something happened—something which in the span of a couple of centuries destroyed the civilized inhabitants of the planet. Curiously, the wildlife forms survived for a considerable time afterwards, and some are still to be found in the forest belts. Now the basic difference between civilized and wild-life forms is that the former are power dependent animals while the latter are not. Jacko, my dear fellow, you may have hit upon something there."

"It's just a gift," said Jacko modestly.

"Then seeing it didn't cost you anything, see if you can stretch it a little further. Let's play for a moment with the assumption that the Tazoons had become power-dependent animals—as we have ourselves. What would their basic source of energy have been if it could have failed suddenly and disastrously?"

"Oil or natural gas, perhaps," said Jacko.

"Not very convincing. By all appearances the Tazoons were great power users. From what Nevill's uncovered recently I'd say the power consumption in this area alone must have been quite fantastic even by Terran standards. Now, you don't develop a heavy power-consuming technology unless you've a good idea that you have the resources to maintain it. To do otherwise would be technological suicide."

"That's assuming they thought about the problem in the same way that a human being would."

"I wouldn't know about human beings," said Fritz drily, "but engineers I do know about, and their thought processes must be essentially similar whether they have one head or six. There are an infinite number of ways of solving any engineering problem, but the simpler answers will always look familiar. It's just the nature of the beast. Give a ten-armed

Dingbat a head of steam and tell him to convert it into electrical energy. I don't care what the influence of his racial characteristics, training or personal geometry, somewhere, at some point, he's going to fall into a chain of logic familiar to engineers of similar calibre anywhere. Ergo, I don't think we can go far wrong if we tackle this problem from our own standpoint, and currently we are assuming they had a power supply which appeared infallible yet failed. Now we need to know what was the source of that energy. If we knew that maybe we could work out why it stopped."

The telephone rang and Fritz answered it. Nevill had been searching for him.

"Fritz, I'd like to see you first thing in the morning. There's something I want you to take a look at."

"Right! Something promising?"

"I imagine so. The team has just uncovered something which looks like the entrance to a mine of some sort. Perhaps you'd like to look it over."

"We'll be there first thing," said Fritz.

"What's up?" asked Jacko.

"Nevill's team have discovered what he thinks may be the entrance to a mine."

"In the centre of a city?"

"The same question occurred to me," said Fritz. "I don't think that a mine is particularly probable, though it might just be connected with our lost energy source—or he may have stumbled on something I've been looking for myself."

"What's that?"

"Jacko, in a city as large and as complex as this one appears to be, where's the logical place to put the bulk passenger transport system?"

"Underground," said Jacko, "same as always."

"Precisely, and that's what I'm hoping Nevill's hit upon."

"God!" said Jacko. "An alien subway scarcely bears thinking about."

Further in from the door they had to use flashlights. Here the sand had not penetrated so deeply, and by the time they had reached the head of the shaft only a brief dusting covered the floor.

The shaft was equipped with the normal Tazoon-type stairway—a central pole with round horizontal bars set in a helix, but on a broader pattern than they had encountered hitherto and with a deeper pitch. Such a stairway was not adapted to human physiology, but it was traversable—just—by those with climbing experience or suicidal tendencies. Jacko had neither.

"Down?" he enquired, his flashlight failing to probe the darkness of the alien depths.

"Down," said Fritz. "Where's your sense of adventure?"

"It remained firmly embedded in my childhood," said Jacko, "along with the sense necessary not to get into situations like this."

"Down!" said Fritz firmly, and suited actions to his words. Together they climbed down perhaps one hundred metres.

Since it was impossible both to climb and hold a flashlight, this was accomplished in total darkness, and the steady rhythm of the climb from bar to bar exercised its own almost hypnotic fascination. Both had to stand for many seconds at the bottom to re-orientate their senses.

The preservation of the passageways at that level was remarkable and probably complete, and the air was cooler and less aggressive than above. Remarkable also was the dryness of the connecting tunnels which had lain for so long at such a depth, indicating the complete lack of a water table above the level of the deep-welled seas of Tazoo. The walls here were of metal, curiously wrought in a manner which might have been functional or might have been symbolic; and the alien strangeness of a completely artificial Tazoon environment gripped at their hearts with a half fear which had nothing to do with self-preservation. For the first time they felt the full impact of standing in the presence of the logical but unimaginable achievements of a culture which had no common roots with their own. They could vaguely comprehend but never predict the unfolding of the unearthly technology which surrounded them.

Machines or effigies, they had no means of knowing which, stood like dark, mute sentries in the uncertain, shifting shadows of the flashlamp's beam; the tortuous walls and fluted ceilings were channelled and moulded with a thousand metal mouths connected to unguessable throats for unfathomable reasons—only the floor approximated its Terran counterpart, having a common engineering function of providing an unimpeded pedestrian passageway.

They turned another corner and stopped abruptly when the flashlamps' beams soared into empty darkness and encountered nothing. Their consternation was relieved by the realization that they were now looking along the length of a vastly greater tunnel than any they had so far traversed. Vaguely they could trace the complex vaulted roof rising to its apex in a series of panels shaped to some intriguing algebraic equation. At their feet the floor continued unchanged as far as the flash-beams could reveal, while to their right the level dropped abruptly perhaps two metres to form a channel of about seven metres width. Beyond the channel rose the walls again arching upwards.

"Are you thinking what I'm thinking?" asked Fritz.

"Uh!" said Jacko. "No matter how you build it, a subway station is a subway station is a subway station, and this is just one such."

"Good man," said Fritz. "I want to have a look at the rails."

Together they surveyed the channel, probing minutely with their flashlights.

"No lines," said Jacko at last, his voice tinged with disappointment. "It could be that we're wrong about this place. Perhaps a sewer . . ."

"I'm not wrong," said Fritz. "I'd know a subway when I found one even if I was deaf, blind and shut up in a box. It's part of the chemistry of whatever genes conspire to make an engineer. Here, help me down, I want to explore."

"Don't you think we'd better go back and get some reinforcements?" said Jacko. Fritz had started along the channel to where it entered a somewhat smaller tunnel undeniably reminiscent of a Terran subway. "For Heaven's sake, Fritz, you don't know what you might find in there!"

"What's eating you, Jacko? Not losing your nerve all of a sudden?"

"No, it's just that walking down a tunnel that might contain an emergent subway train goes against my finer sensibilities—even if it is two million years behind schedule."

Fritz took fifteen paces into the tunnel and let out a whoop which paralysed Jacko with fright.

"Jacko, get down here quick! I've found one."

"Found one what?" asked" Jacko when he had regained control of his vocal cords.

"A train, you idiot. I've found a blessed train! Fetch the other lamp."

Against his better judgment Jacko dropped into the channel and followed Fritz into the tunnel. Then with a churning stomach and racing brain he examined the artifact which barred their further entry.

"That," he asked finally, "is a train?"

"It can't be anything else," said Fritz, not very happily.

"It doesn't appear to be a signal box and there's not much point in having a wrought-iron summer house this far underground. It appears to be the right shape to fit the tunnel so it's probably either a highly ornate tunnelling machine or else it's a train."

"Alien!" said Jacko in awe. "The connotations of that word get lost by common usage. It doesn't begin to convey the mind-twisting sense that everything you know and believe has been scrunched up and re-sorted by a different kind of logic. These people had different values and different basics, and it makes the mind squirm even trying to re-adjust."

"They didn't have different basics," said Fritz, "they merely had a different emphasis on the relative values of the same old basics. We can't yet try to comprehend the culture, but when it comes to unravelling their engineering I think we shall find we have a great deal in common."

"Like an iron-lace potting-shed without wheels or tracks which we presume to be a train simply because it doesn't appear to be anything else?"

"Just so," said Fritz. "We have to separate the mechanics from the culture. As far as we've gone we've found very few Tazoon applications of principles of which we were completely ignorant. Of course, they were streets ahead of us in some fields and curiously lacking in others—they had no organic chemistry, for instance. But they don't appear to have dabbled in the occult, so if that's a train it's only a matter of time before we find out what made it go."

Cautiously they squeezed down between the curious vehicle and the tunnel wall, the better to examine the structure's complexity and strangeness.

"It's a crazy, twisted birdcage," said Jacko finally. "An appliance for containing crazy, twisted birds."

Fritz looked up from the complex of curiously wrought mechanisms. "We'd better get some more lights down here, and muster some of the squad. I want this insane dumpling-container taken to pieces and put together again when I've had a chance to examine the pieces."

"Cannibalization I can understand," said Jacko, "but why the resurrection?"

"Because," said Fritz Van Noon, "if it's the last thing I do I'm going to put the subways of Tazoo back in operation. We obviously can't build a transportation system on the surface, but here we have a ready-made nucleus which already goes halfway to meet the problem."

"I demand to be invalided out of the Service on the grounds of insanity," said Jacko, "your insanity. I thought we'd had enough of railways up on Cannis."

"That was different," said Fritz. "There we were merely up against physical obstacles such as errant volcanoes. This is specifically an exercise in matching technologies. All we have to do is to determine which part of the railway system moves and which part is intended to stay still. That shouldn't be too difficult, now should it?"

"Not when reduced to such basic terms," Jacko agreed dourly. "But I know you. You never realize when you're beaten."

"I've told you before," said Fritz sternly, 'there's no such thing as a physical impossibility. A limitation is a state of mind, not a question of fact. Here we are faced with the work of a completely alien race who nevertheless had a technological and scientific level roughly comparable to our own. Providing we hold that one fact paramount we ought to be able to unscramble any device this planet has to offer and make it function for our own service if we wish."

"Providing one thing holds good," said Jacko. "We have first to be able to recognize a thing for what it is. It's no good dismantling a Tazoon milk-strainer if we're under the impression that it ought to be a transistor superhet—or *vice-versa*, come to think of it."

FIVE

Fritz reported back to Philip Nevill. The latter listened to the details of the find with the air of suppressed jubilation which was rapidly becoming his permanent expression. Then he ran his fingers through his untidy hair and searched for his pipe with a distracted grin.

"Fritz, my boy, this is perfectly marvellous. What a day we've had! We've opened up so many promising new lines of research that the whole damned thing is getting out of hand. We could do with five hundred trained archaeologists to digest the meat in this lot, and even then we couldn't do more than scratch the surface. The impact of building techniques alone on Terra is going to be fantastic, and when the whole complex is assembled into Terran know-how its impact on the human race will be so great that our own culture will never be quite the same again.

"If you really want to make your mark on the enterprise, then take over this subway completely, because I shan't be able to get round to it for five years at least. Do a complete technical run-down on it, as detailed as you like. Do anything you like with it which won't impair its archaeological value. All I ask is a comprehensive progress report in time for each data shipment to Terra."

"Fair enough!" said Fritz. "I want to open up the buildings

directly above the station to look for ancillaries."

Nevill glanced at his sketch map and drew a line through two diagrammatical blocks. "It's all yours," he said, "but don't drive yourself daft trying to comprehend too much too fast. You'll find you have to absorb Tazoon environments rather than understand them. Sooner or later the pieces fit themselves into place. And Heaven knows there's enough pieces available for fitting—a jigsaw embracing the life and work of a complete culture."

"We've just got ourselves a subway," said Fritz, as he rejoined Jacko at the workings. "We're going to open up the building here and see what's inside."

"Who's we?" asked Jacko suspiciously.

"You," said Fritz. "I'm going below again to see if I can trace any control sequence running up from below. I want you to go in there and see if you can find anything similar running down. We'll meet at the end of the shift and compare notes. You know what to look for—cable groupings or anything which suggests that it might have a control or power function."

"You're really set on this, aren't you?" Jacko said. "About using it, I mean."

"Certainly," said Fritz. "Let's face it, if Fritz Van Noon can't restart an alien subway then who in the universe would you expect to be able to do it?"

"I was afraid you'd ask that," said Jacko.

An hour later they met again at the portals of the building.

"There's a sort of power and control complex which appears to come down somewhere near the further end here," said Fritz.

Jacko nodded. "I picked up the end of that," he said. "There's a channel running through the basement of the building, and the complex rises into that, and is then split into sections which are fed to the floors above."

"What's it like in there?" asked Fritz.

"Weird," said Jacko. "There's no other word to describe it. It's like the epitaph to an insane, overgrown spider with a compulsive spite against inverted single-head broaching presses."

"Thank you," said Fritz. "I can imagine it all too clearly."

Jacko's description of the basement of the building was, if anything, an understatement. The ground floor proved inconceivably worse, and the situation deteriorated rapidly as they ascended to the higher floors. The subway had possessed the crude simplicity of a functional unit, but the detail and complexity of the levels in the building above defied analysis or description. For a long time no object which they examined provided any sort of clue as to its function, and they traversed the cluttered levels with an increasing sense of dismay and frustration. As with most of the larger buildings only the top storeys had suffered any considerable decay, and the sand and damp had not penetrated into the interiors to any great extent, so that the state of preservation on the levels in which they were interested was excellent.

Fritz's spirits were nearing their lowest ebb as he battled with an ocean of incomprehensibilities, until he entered the final gallery. Here he stopped, groping for form in the alien pattern, then seized a glimpse of illuminated understanding and fanned it into a flame.

"Jacko! Do you know what this is? Don't you see—electrical control gear."

Jacko was unimpressed. "If this is their idea of electrical control gear I should hate to see their version of a collection of crazy, twisted maypoles."

"It doesn't matter," said Fritz. "The approach may be alien, but the underlying logic is inescapable. Unless I miss my guess this is an automatic switching system, and from its complexity I should think it's pretty comprehensive. It may even be the only switching system for the whole of the Tazoon subways. You realize what that means?"

"About fifteen years' circuit analysis," said Jacko morosely.

"No. Look at the condition of this stuff. The preservation is as good here as it is in the subway itself. The chances are it's still functional. We'd only have to re-connect the power to get the whole thing back into operation."

"Perish the thought!" said Jacko. "I may be a bit naive, but assuming—just for the sake of argument—that what we've found is a subway, where would you get the energy to power it? Subways need a lot of power, and if the Tazoons ran out of it how are you going to find it?"

"We'll worry about that later. It may not be easy, but I have one advantage the Tazoons didn't have—access to the complete technologies and resources of a scientific culture which was completely alien to the Tazoons. I don't doubt that Colonel Nash could be persuaded to bring an MHD oscillating-plasma generator out from Terra, but that's a last resort. As an unorthodox engineer I'd prefer to locate the original Tazoon power source and see if a completely fresh engineering approach could start it producing again."

"So what's the plan?" asked Jacko.

"Get Harris and a couple of the electrical boys to join me here to try and analyse the circuit logic. Meanwhile you take the rest of the squad below and start dismantling the train. Between us we should discover enough about the way the Tazoons handled electricity and mechanisms to have a fair idea of how to make these pieces work."

"You think so?" asked Jacko. "I still haven't forgotten what you did to that ruddy harp."

Fritz's team did indeed manage to establish a certain amount of circuit logic, and once a few principles were known the work progressed rapidly. They concentrated mainly on the huge switching columns, swiftly realizing that what at first sight could be mistaken for relative crudity was in fact an ingenious and sophisticated short-cut technique to solve a highly complex sequence-switching problem. Among other things they discovered that the assembly was probably built to handle alternating current with an efficiency peaking at about ten kilocycles a second, although such periodicity seemed unlikely in practice. The current handling capacity of the assembly was staggeringly high. Breakdown voltages too were high, but afforded no real clues as to the normal operating potentials. Safety precautions against unshielded conductors were non-existent, and they were forced to the conclusion that either the equipment was designed to operate unattended or else the physiology of the Tazoons had rendered them immune to electric shocks which would be lethal to their Terran counterparts. The apparatus which logically should have been metering equipment, however, made no sense at all.

Somebody was soon at work rigging up a communicator to connect the switching gallery with the subway below. When the line was functional Jacko was the first to make a call.

"Fritz, we've run into a snag on this train dismantling project. We can't get the blasted thing apart. Tell me I'm crazy if you like, but I'd swear the train was cast as a whole and not fabricated—moving parts included."

"Cast in a pattern of that complexity in steel?" asked Fritz incredulously.

"Not steel," said Jacko. "titanium, unless I judge my metals wrong."

"That only makes it worse," said Fritz. "Come to think of it, we were being a bit naive expecting a two-million-year extinct culture to leave something which could be dismantled with a hammer and a pair of Stillsons. Is there no hope at all?"

"We could take an atomic-hydrogen torch or a cutting laser and chop it into two-inch slices, but I doubt if Nevill would react favourably to the idea."

"Come to think of it," said Fritz, "neither would I. Better abandon the project, Jacko, and come back up here. I think I've got a better idea anyway."

"What are you planning now, Fritz?"

"I'm looking at it this way: there are two ways of making a piece of equipment yield the secret of its function—you can dismantle it and worry the principle out of its components, or you can simply set it operating."

"I hope I'm misunderstanding you," said Jacko. "For one ghastly moment I had the idea you were proposing to re-start the Tazoon subway without knowing how it worked."

"I was proposing just that. Can you think of a faster way of finding out how it works than by seeing it in action?"

"Is one allowed to resign from the project?" asked Jacko. "Or is suicide the only logical form of escape?"

"You can also be beaten to death by your superior officer, if you're really smitten with an escapist death-wish. We think we've unscrambled the power lines in the gallery here and we've made a guess at what should prove to be the main input lines."

"So?"

"So I want to trace them back to source. Then we can start investigating whether or not we can re-start the native power producing plant. I want every man I can get employed on tracing those lines, Jacko, and I want you to supervise personally. Remember, we have to get the whole thing operational inside three months if we're to beat Nash's deadline."

"I still think it's a waste of time," said Jacko. "If we're right that the Tazoon civilization collapsed because of lack of power, what chance have we of finding it some two million years later?"

"I suspect the answer is quantitative," said Fritz. "They were trying to run a civilization, we're trying only to run a subway. I'd estimate our requirements at perhaps one ten-millionth of theirs or less. Viewed in that light it doesn't seem too difficult a task, now does it?"

SIX

Nevill's team had concentrated on clearing only the tops of the taller buildings. Generally the sand penetration into the interiors was not total, and thus they had access to large modules of Tazoon architectural environment without having to wait for the total clearance which ultimately would follow as resources became available. Once gaining the interior of a building they were relatively free to explore the entire contents of the lower levels. Archaeologically the finds were so incredibly lush that complete classification and analysis would take many decades, and the method therefore used was to set up specialist study groups to make a complete analysis of certain typical areas as a guide to rapidly separating the unique from the mundane when new areas were opened up. Representative samples were carefully crated for transport to Terra, where a more exhaustive examination would be undertaken.

For the next two weeks Fritz himself was kept fully employed in his role as authority on alien science and technology, and the sheer mass of work confronting him could have kept him comfortably occupied for several lifetimes at least. It was now painfully obvious that the staff of the Tazoon enterprise could have been increased a hundredfold and still the finds would have been more numerous than the researchers. Fritz's own work in the field was hampered by the fact that he was working without assistance, the entire complement of the U.E. squad being devoted to locating the elusive power source from which the Tazoons had derived their supply.

On this latter point even Nevill had been unable to offer any help. Although detailed maps of the sectors of the buried city were beginning to be built up there was nothing in them which suggested any power generation or distribution facilities. This was not conclusive, because in very few areas had it yet been possible to excavate below the level of the basic terrain on which the city had been built, and what lay underneath was still a subject for conjecture, but the pattern of conductors disappearing into the depths was sufficient to convince Fritz that whatever the source it was probably not located within the city confines. Jacko's report did not appear to illuminate the situation.

"I tell you, Fritz, that main power input cable you gave us was nothing of the sort. For fifteen blasted days we've traced that thing. A cable it may be, but it's a distribution circuit if it's anything at all."

Fritz scowled. "Are you sure you didn't lose it and pick up another cable in error?"

"Do me a favour!" said Jacko. "We were feeding a signal into the thing at the switching house and picking it up all the way down the cable. I tell you that thing is a distribution complex originating, not terminating, at the subway building."

Fritz sat up sharply. "Distributing power where?"

"I hate to tell you this, but it covers a fair proportion of the Southern plain. The cable divides and sub-divides *ad infinitum* as far as we can tell. We counted divisions into roughly forty thousand pairs and that still left a fair majority—but we gave up when we found what was at the end of a dozen or so of the minor pairs. I'll give you three guesses . . ."

"Don't tell me," said Fritz. "I can imagine . . . ruddy great Tazoon harps."

"Harps, harps and nothing but harps, and never a string between them. Listening to music I could understand, but can you seriously maintain that they installed five thousand million loudspeakers across the plain just so that they could listen to the trains? Nobody could be *that* alien!"

Fritz thumped the table. "Jacko, you're a ruddy genius!"

"Am I?" Jacko blinked.

"Yes. You've given me the clue I needed. Get the squad together, Jacko, we're going to re-start the subways of Tazoo."

Ten weeks of the precious three months of Colonel Nash's ultimatum had elapsed before they were in a position to make the preliminary tests. The intervening period had been one of furious activity for the U.E. personnel, and one over which Fritz had draped a veil of secrecy such that nobody outside of his group had any idea of the direction of his slowly unfolding plans. But on the final evening everything was ready. Fresh cables of Terran newness threaded their way out of the subway entrance; and on the platform two dozen floodlights illuminated the mechanical achievements of a culture which had passed two million years before, and shone into the tunnel to light a vehicle which had stopped in that position at the same time that on Terra elephants were native to the Sussex Downs and the evolving ancestors of man had yet to distinguish themselves from their animal counterparts.

Shortly before sunset Fritz and his team assembled at the subway building. Already the calm stasis of the day was beginning to tremble with unease as the riding cloudrace overhead broke lower, heralding the nightly windy torment of the land. This was no lull before the storm but an increasing tension, a tight coil being further tightened to the inevitable breaking point which was the lash of the sand-filled gale. As the storm broke they hastened inside.

Fritz found himself more than slightly in awe of the thing he contemplated doing. Immaculate as was the preservation of these Tazoon artefacts he could not help remembering, as an engineer, the patterns of low temperature creep, the grain growth, the diffusion—all the degradation of properties which fabricated metals might be heir to after two million years of rest. Fortunately the Tazoons had understood their materials and their atmosphere well, and apparently had built to last, with a success which was phenomenal.

In any case, Fritz was now committed. Sentiment and curiosity apart, the very continuance of the U.E. depended on his ability to re-activate the subway. He could not draw back now even though the whole place threaten to crumble about his head in a welter of dust and thunder.

As was his custom when there were unavoidable risks to be taken, Fritz alone attended the array of instruments set up in the subway proper. Jacko was in the switching gallery on the other end of the communicator, in a hastily conceived control set-up which included the rest of the relevant monitoring instruments they had been able to piece together from the inadequate supplies brought to Tazoo. Jacko, uncomfortably aware of the danger of Fritz's position, had sought to dissuade his superior from being present for the actual test run, but Fritz, foreseeing the cataclysmic damage to the installation which might result from the experiment, had decided to be present to gain first-hand experience of the principles of operation which might by their own employment become hopelessly obscured.

Five minutes to zero hour, and Fritz took a last check on

his instruments. He had already signalled Jacko to begin preliminary switching when he heard footsteps and voices echoing in the corridors leading to the platform. He snatched up the communicator.

"Hold it, Jacko. I think I've got company. Do nothing until you hear from me."

"Right," said Jacko. "But it's none of our boys down there, I promise you."

"No," said Fritz, "but unless I mistake the gruff undertones it's Colonel Nash and his aides. I'll have to get rid of them, of course. We'd get ourselves a bad name if we knocked off all of the top brass in one go." He slammed down the handset and marched up the platform just as Nash and his retinue arrived.

"Lieutenant Van Noon," said Nash icily, "I have just been informed of your intention of trying to re-start the Tazoon subway this evening. As this is a project of the first magnitude I think I should have been more directly informed."

"You will be, sir, as soon as we have anything to report."

"I don't think you quite appreciate my point," said Nash. "If you succeed in this it will be the very first Tazoon mechanical artifact of any moment to have been re-started. As such it is a rather—er—historical occasion. Naturally I'd have liked to have been asked to be present."

"And I don't think you quite appreciate my point," said Fritz. "There comes a point in the progress of any project which is usually obscured by a notice reading: *Danger, Engineers Testing*. As far as we know the Tazoon subway is intact and perfectly preserved. Fom an engineering point of view there is no reason why we can't switch on the current and have it back in operation as it last was two million years ago."

"Well?" asked Nash ominously. "What's the problem then?"

"Just this," said Fritz. "How do we know that what was normal for the Tazoons is even remotely tolerable for us? The power input for this one sector of the line is quite fantastic by Terran standards. The Tazoons don't appear to have been fools about the efficiency of power conversion, so I can only conclude that Tazoon subway operation was a pretty hectic procedure. When they throw the master switch upstairs we shall have a sample of Tazoon mechanical environment in the raw. I don't want anybody down here at that moment who isn't absolutely essential to the success of the operation."

Colonel Nash snorted with irritation. "The best available information to date indicates that the Tazoons were small-boned, avian and somewhat fragile creatures. I am perfectly certain that officers of the Terran Exploratory task force are able to tolerate the conditions in a deserted subway every bit as well as its former occupants. But if you happen to be so unsure of your mechanical aptitude why don't you switch things on a piece at a time?"

"Because," said Fritz, "as far as we can tell the whole system is interlocked back to a master computing house of such complexity that it will take all of ten years to unravel the individual controls. For reasons best known to themselves the Tazoons did not appear to have been in favour of local circuit isolators, so we have to accept the whole or nothing at all. I'm making a formal request, sir, for you to leave. If you remain I can't be responsible for the consequences."

"Are you staying, Lieutenant?"

"Yes, sir."

"Then we stay too. I appreciate it's your show, but I think you're over-stressing the danger angle."

"Very well," said Fritz. "But remember it was your decision." He returned wearily to his communication point. "Jacko, prepare to switch on."

"Have they gone?"

"No, they insist on staying to see the fireworks."

"Ouch! I hope you know what you're doing."

"If I did," said Fritz, "the chances are that there's nothing on Tazoo which could persuade me to stay on this platform while you throw that switch. Bring the current up to a maximum over thirty seconds and hold it there for three minutes. If you can't contact me on the communicator immediately you've switched off again then get down here fast with all the emergency equipment you've got."

"Right," said Jacko. "And good luck! I'm giving you a count-down of ten . . ."

SEVEN

If Fritz Van Noon was prepared for the worst experience of his life he was still unprepared for the sheer intensity and quality of the impressions which assaulted him. The whole tunnel cavity lit up in a kaleidoscope of lights of unbelievable colour-range and brilliance. The air grew rapidly and uncomfortably hot and choking with acrid vapours which his lungs could not accept and which burned his skin like the breath of a playful blowlamp.

But it was the noise that dug furrows in his soul. A series of rising screams from a dozen mechanical throats passed up through the audible range and into the low ultrasonic, causing dust fires to break out at intervals along the platform. Devices hammered and clattered and chattered in a cacophony which clawed at his eardrums with red-hot needles. Literally every fragment of the installation vibrated or resonated or contributed in some way to the atmosphere of screaming, explosive thunder. Ominously, the train which Fritz had stationed himself to watch, held motionless for a full minute then discharged itself in a rumbling, grinding ricochet into the station and down the further tunnel, accompanied by a cataclysmic roar which contained all the acoustic qualities of a continuous collision with an unending series of cheap tin tea-trays.

Scarcely had the first train disappeared from view than another skeleton juggernaut hurled itself upon the station and drove a hectic and furious path straight down the line and was gone before his senses could properly interpret its arrival. Fritz cringed before the shock-wave of its passing and watched his precious monitoring instruments scatter in all directions. He ground his teeth in mental pain at the sound of the mechanical anguish of tortured metal biting into tortured metal. Sparks and white-hot fragments showered the platform and peppered his coverall with a pattern of small singed holes.

Colonel Nash and his entourage were now crouched against the wall further down the platform, white-faced and with their hands over their ears, while some noise-making instrument above aimed horrific noises at their heads. Under their feet the dust smouldered with a repulsive miasmatic odour, reminiscent of kakodyle and mercaptan, which had to be smelled to be believed.

Before Fritz had time to realize the smile that blossomed in his bosom yet another train entered the station, this one fighting to halt itself with a spine-chilling screech of unseen brakes which fought valiantly to kill the horrible momentum. Fritz gritted his teeth and watched its progress right to the last shuddering halt. With his monitoring equipment out of action he was forced to estimate the vehicle's speed mentally and make a rough guess at the forces which would act on the passengers of a vehicle involved in such a drastic reduction of speed. The answer told him more about the physiology of the Tazoons than Nevill had deduced in the previous twelve months.

Abruptly the power died and his eyes were forced to adapt to the relative dimness of the Terran floodlights. His ears still whistled and ached from their recent battering, and the intolerable heat and humidity made him feel like the occupant of some outlandish Turkish bath. Colonel Nash climbed unsteadily to his feet, a perfectly unreadable expression on his face, and picked his way carefully around the heaps of smouldering dust on the platform. His aides, lacking his aplomb, openly betrayed their relief at the end of the ordeal and hastened to the exit.

Nash made straight for Fritz.

"Van Noon."

"Sir?" Fritz saluted briefly while trying to balance a previous audio-frequency spectrum analyser which was in danger of falling off the platform into the channel.

"I owe you an apology," said Nash. "Lord, that was ruddy

awful! But you've given me grounds for thought. I'm not saying you didn't warn me—but where in hell did you get all that power?"

"I'll be reporting on that, sir, as soon as I've tidied a few details."

"Very well," said Nash. "There'll be a Staff conference at three o'clock tomorrow in my office. I'd appreciate your answer then."

He turned and strode off, while Fritz became aware of the communicator buzzing urgently.

"Fritz, are you all right?"

"Only just," said Fritz. "It was grim. Everything was at least five times as fast as its Terran counterpart and about twenty times as noisy, to say nothing of the heat. If that's a sample of a deserted Tazoon subway in operation I hope I never have to suffer one during the rush hour."

"I've got news for you," said Jacko. "We had switching trouble up here on the temporary lines we rigged. According to our calculations we were only able to supply forty-three per cent of the total estimated loading. If you'll hang on for a moment I'll give you a test run at a hundred per cent loading."

"Don't bother," said Fritz hastily. "For that I'd need some repeaters and telemetry equipment plus a few unattended TV cameras. I'm not staying here for a hundred per cent loading run."

"Did you discover anything?"

"Enough. Initially the potential weakness of this system will be confined mainly to its passengers. The Tazoons were apparently using an adaptation of an A.C. linear motor for traction, with the bottom of the channel as the reactive element. On the same principle they use A.C. magnetic flux repulsion to lift the train clear of the ground so that they're virtually hovering on a magnetic flux field. I suspect the same principle should be operating on each side to centre the train with respect to the tunnel walls, only we didn't have enough current to make it fully effective. Come to think of it, it's a damn clever idea, with the train held in a mechanically frictionless supporting field with only inertia, air-resistance and eddy-current losses to be overcome by the traction system. I can't yet see how the current pickup is arranged, but that's probably inductive too. Suffice it to say we can soon adapt it to our own purposes."

"Good," said Jacko, "only I can't see that by so doing we're going to produce what we set out to achieve. They asked for a transport system and we're offering a subway with all that connotes in the way of limited routes and limited points of access. How long do you think that is going to satisfy Nevill?"

"For at least a lifetime, I should think," said Fritz. "The building of a subway is a dramatic achievement in the history of any culture, requiring, as it does, the co-ordination of a considerable quantity of technological resources. Ergo, you only build subways to connect points which are sufficiently important to warrant such endeavour. Give Nevill a functional subway under this city and he will have immediate and convenient access to all those points of the city which the Tazoons themselves thought worth while making accessible. You not only have a transport system but a considerable pointer to the psychology and cultural habits of the Tazoons themselves."

When Fritz arrived at the Staff conference he had the feeling that the rest of the meeting must have been convened about an hour earlier, for the assembly was already engaged in earnest discussion at the time of his arrival. Nevill was leafing forlornly through a formidable pile of notes, reading abstracts, and Colonel Nash was in the chair.

"Ah, Lieutenant, take a seat. We hope you are going to tell us how you came by that impressive source of energy which enabled you to put on that display last evening in the subway."

"I can do more than that," said Fritz. "I think I can add considerably to our knowledge of the Tazoons themselves. But let us start with the harps—Tazoon harps. I suddenly realized what they were."

"And what was that?"

"MechanoeIectric energy converters—piezo-electric generators, if you like. The harps are merely assemblies of high-efficiency piezo-electric crystals operated by the vibrating strings of the harp. The strings are made to vibrate by the passage of the Tazoon night winds."

"I'm no scientist," said Nash, "but I would have thought that piezo-electric effects were scarcely of sufficient magnitude to be useful for energy conversion on that scale."

"A common misconception," said Fritz. "Even our relatively undeveloped Terran ferroelectric ceramics are capable of something better than a power generating density of sixteen watts per square centimetre, which has solar cells beaten hollow. The Tazoon crystals are capable of an output of eighty watts per square centimetre and a conversion efficiency of better than ninety-five per cent, an efficiency markedly better than even the most advanced Terran M.H.D. oscillating-plasma reactors. Mechanoelectric conversion has always been a highly promising line of development, but hampered by the fact that on Terra there was a scarcity of large-scale sources of mechanical energy of useful frequency. The Tazoons made ultra large scale use of medium-level energy by utilizing the winds to activate the harp strings. A Tazoon harp in a typical night wind is capable of an output approaching two kilowatt. This comes out to around a megawatt of power for each square kilometre of plain equipped with harps."

"Are you sure of this, Fritz?" asked Nevill.

"Perfectly sure. We powered the subway by re-stringing some of the harps out on the plains there."

"But doesn't the output vary with the force of the wind?"

"Yes, but with the harps ranged over a wide area the variations average out fairly well."

"But how did they obtain their power when there was no wind?"

"They didn't," said Fritz. "We've found nothing which would indicate any attempt to store the power nor any suggestion of an alternative supply. When the wind stopped, everything stopped. Thus by habit if not by nature the Tazoons were probably nocturnal."

"But this is ridiculous," said Nevill. "I still can't conceive that they would fill whole plains with electrical generating transducers."

"Why not? They had no particular use for the great outdoors. By and large their native environment was intolerable to them."

Nevill sat up sharply. "That's a highly speculative statement to make. How do you arrive at that conclusion?"

"Simple," said Fritz. "Firstly, they were nearly blind, hence the need for such inordinately intense lighting such as we found on the subway. If my calculation is correct even Tazoo at mid-day was a pretty dull affair to their eyes. Secondly, the temperature the subway reached was so far above ambient that it's a reasonable guess that they couldn't tolerate outside temperatures for very long. They had a very low body mass and presumably chilled rapidly."

"Incredible!" said Nevill. "I knew they were small-boned, but body mass . . ."

"If you'd seen the rates of acceleration and deceleration of a Tazoon subway train you'd soon see that only creatures of small body mass could survive it."

"All right," said Nash, "you seem to have all the answers. Perhaps you also know why the Tazoons became extinct?"

"I could make a good guess. Even more than ourselves the Tazoons were power dependent animals, for the aforementioned reasons. They had reached a point where they couldn't exist without power for light and heat, having presumably reached an evolutionary dead-end which had put them out of phase, so to speak, with their native environment. Now remember that they depended on power from the harps, not having any great resources of alternative fuels, either fossil or nuclear. Remember also that the harp frames were made of ironwood from the trees of the forests which used to adorn the plains. I suggest they increased their power generating areas at the expense of the trees until at some point they encountered soil erosion. Normally soil erosion is reversible if the right steps are taken to combat it, but . . ."

"Well?" said Nash.

"Soil erosion led to sand and the sand and wind conspired to form a sandblast which abraded and destroyed the strings of the harps. The failure of the harps meant loss of power—the very power essential to bring in the purified sea-water necessary to help combat the soil erosion. The process developed into a vicious circle—more sand, less harps; less harps, more sand, and so on *ad infinitum*, every day the situation worsening as the sand robbed them of the power they needed to combat its formation. When the sand grew deep enough it even prevented ironwood seeds from rooting, so the rest of the forests gradually died also. The Tazoons, faced with a gradual but unalterable loss of power, took the only course open to them—they tried to migrate to the tropical regions where the climate was life-supporting without the need for power. History seems to record that very few of them ever got there, which is not surprising when you consider that the night-wind was certainly capable of blowing a Tazoon clean into the air."

There was several moments' silence. "And the harps?" asked Nash. "That was their sole means of power generation?"

"We have found nothing which would indicate otherwise."

"What a pity! Philip Nevill had just succeeded in persuading me to lend support for a rather ambitious project. Consequent upon your demonstration of both power production and a potential source of transport, Philip was proposing to re-establish the Tazoon city, initially to cater for archaeologists interested in extra-terrestrial work, but later as a permanent colony and as a supply base for ships moving out to the Rim."

"You mean to re-populate the place—turn it back into a living city?"

"Given time, yes. If possible also irrigate the deserts and reclaim some of the wasteland. It's a great pity you have such admirable reasons why it can't be done."

"But it can be done," said Fritz. "Given time and sufficient labour to repair the harps there's enough energy out there to power the whole city and a dozen others."

"But I thought the sandblast . . ."

" . . . ruined the harp strings. Yes, it did . . . but that was before the advent of Fritz Van Noon. The Tazoons probably used a plain metal wire, possibly titanium, which was susceptible to abrasion. Remember they had no organic chemistry to speak off hence no plastics. We're using a high tensile and extremely tough steel wire and a polysilicone elastomer coating over it, which is a highly abrasion-resistant combination and should give many years' service without trouble. Unfortunately it damps the vibrations considerably—but then, we don't need the degree of either heat or light which the Tazoons found necessary."

"And you really believe the Tazoons became extinct because of the lack of a suitably coated wire?"

"Yes," said Fritz, "just that. And let it be a lesson to ourselves. We don't know what factors in our own technology may be lacking when it comes to meeting some new and unexpected crisis. Our development is probably as one-sided as the Tazoons, but in another direction. Therefore nothing but benefit can come from the complete assimilation of every phase of Tazoon science and technology into our own. If colonization can do that, then I'll see you have the power to colonize."

"For the want of a nail . . ." said Nevill speculatively.

"Fritz," said Nash. "I've been meaning to speak to you about the possibility of permanently establishing U.E. as a branch of the Terran Exploratory task force instead of merely a section of the Engineering Reserve. How would you react to that? Of course, it would mean promotion . . ."

"I should personally welcome the idea, sir," said Fritz, "but I fear I've already accepted another assignment on Tiberius Two. They're trying to establish a mono-rail system there."

"I see," said Nash. "And just what is there about a monorail system on Tiberius Two that requires your peculiar talents?"

Fritz coughed discreetly. "I understand it's something to do with their gravity. Apparently it changes direction by seventy degrees every Tuesday and Thursday morning," he said, reaching for his cap.

THE PEN AND THE DARK

The scudder slid through candy-floss clouds of cirrus and strato-cumulus so extremely Earthlike in formation that even the scudder's well-travelled occupants felt a twinge of nostalgia for home. Far below, the green and gilded fields proudly displayed the rich bust of the planet Ithica ripening in the rays of the G-type primary. The occasional sprawl of town or metropolis betrayed the Terran origin of Ithica's inhabitants and the results of their desire to recreate the image of a far-off homeworld. With a little imagination this could easily have been mistaken for one of the rarer spots on Earth.

But when the scudder cleared the haze of the cloud formation, the black and fearsome thing which reared above them was decidedly not of Earth.

Caught on a sudden and curious down-draught, the scudder dived steeply and then went into a mammoth power-climb that took it soaring into a wide and safe helical orbit around and finally above the hideous patch of darkness.

"So that's it!" said Lieutenant Fritz Van Noon.

Dr. Maxwell Courtney nodded. "That's it. That's what we call the Dark. What you see now is the mushroom dome. It's all of twenty-five kilometres across, and as near indestructible as anything we've ever encountered. We put a nuclear Hell-raiser down on to it and nothing happened at all."

Van Noon raised a swift eyebrow. "Nothing?"

"We know the device exploded, because we were able to detect the start of the priming flash. After that—nothing. The Dark absorbed every quantum of energy released. It swallowed the whole damn lot and never so much as flickered."

"And you say that aliens put it there?"

"So the records read. About two hundred terrayears ago—

long before we re-established contact with Ithica. It would seem some sort of alien vessel made a touchdown on the edge of the city, stayed a night, then vanished as abruptly as it had come. But in its place it left this pillar of darkness, and nobody has ever found out why they left it or what it's supposed to do. There's a great many theories about it, but none which completely explains the facts. Some think that it soaks up energy and transmits it elsewhere. Some think it's contra-terrene. It's even suggested that an alien colony lives inside it."

"And what's your own opinion?" asked Van Noon.

Courtney shrugged. "After three years of scientific examination I still don't know what to think. At some time or another I've held most of the current physical theories only to discard them for another."

"Is it uniform right the way down?"

"It's really shaped like a bolt," said Courtney. "The shaft proper is about seven kilometres in diameter and about thirty kilometres high. It is capped by the mushroom head here which extends out to about twenty-five kilometres in diameter and apparently defines the region of the Pen."

"The Pen?" Van Noon looked up from his notes. "What's that?"

Courtney smiled fleetingly. "Sorry! That's local terminology. I mean the apparent penumbral shadow of reduced effects which surrounds the pillar of Dark. It's a twilight region about nine kilometres average depth, the outer reaches of which are easily penetrable, and the inner regions connect with the Dark. It has an interesting subclimate too—but you'll see that for yourself later."

Van Noon scowled. "And you have no idea at all what the Dark is made of?"

Courtney spread his hands. "It's commonly assumed to be contra-terrene, as I said, but I don't think the hypothesis holds water in the face of all the evidence. But God-alone knows what it really is. Even the Pen raises some nice problems in physics which don't have answers in any of the textbooks we know."

"All right," said Van Noon. "I'd like to take a closer look at it first and come back to you when I've some idea of what questions to ask."

"I rather hoped you'd do it that way," Courtney said. "We've assembled such a mass of data on the Dark that we don't know if we've lost our way in our own erudition. That's why we asked for some of you Unorthodox Engineering chaps to come out to Ithica to supply a fresh approach. The answer may be so damned obvious that we can't see it for the weight of the maths intervening."

"And the primary object of the exercise is what?" Courtney glanced from the window at the monstrous column of darkness which reared its head high over the landscape. "I don't know. Study it, use it, get rid of it—it's an alien paradox, Fritz, and I don't think anyone with an ounce of science in his makeup can let it rest there doing nothing but soaking up the sun."

"What's the general topography of the Dark area, Jacko?"

Jacko Hine of the Unorthodox Engineers unrolled his sheaf of maps. "This is the position of the Dark, and the area I've coloured shows the extent of the Pen. As you can see, the whole is centred on the edge of what used to be the city of Bethlem."

"Is the city still there?"

"Its ruins are. The present city of New Bethlem has moved southwards, but in and around the Pen the remains of the old city still exist. Nobody lives there now. If you'd been into the Pen you'd understand why."

"You've been in, then? What's it like?"

"Weird," said Jacko. "It's cold and dull, but the sensations aren't the usual ones of coldness and dullness. This is a different feeling entirely. I can't quite explain it, but there's something wrong with the physics of the place."

"Then I think I'd better start there. Where's the rest of the U.E. squad?"

"Doing some preliminary fact-finding at the edge of the Pen. I suggest we can contact them as we go in, and see what they've found."

"No," said Van Noon. "I'd sooner contact them on the way out. I want my first impressions of the Pen to be a direct personal experience. I need to get the 'feel' of the thing—because I have a suspicion that this problem is going to be cracked by intuition rather than by observation. Maxwell Courtney's no fool, and he and his team have been gathering facts for three years now. There's no sense in repeating what they've already done, so I'm going to play it my way."

"I was rather afraid of that," said Jacko, following in his wake.

The edgeland was an area dominated by the ruins of the old city. The transport took them to the very perimeter of the Pen, and here they dismounted. Van Noon surveyed the phenomenon thoughtfully.

The termination of the Pen was sharp, precise, and unwavering. At one point the magnificent sunshine of Ithica baked the dust golden and ripened dark berries on the hanks of hackberry-like scrub. A centimetre away the summer changed abruptly to a dark winter, shadowed and uninviting, and such scrub as grew within its bounds was thin and gnarled and bore no fruit at all.

Above them the wall of shade rose vertically until it disappeared into the cloud-ring which clung stubbornly round the sombre column. Looking into the Pen, Van Noon gained the impression of gradually increasing coldness and bleakness and gloom until, in the centre, he could just detect the absolute blackness of the great pillar of the Dark. Cautiously he extended a hand into the boundary of the Pen and withdrew it, experiencing the strange chill on his skin.

"Very curious," he said. "What strikes you most about this, Jacko?"

"Lack of interaction between the warmth outside and the cold inside."

"Precisely. At a guess there's a temperature fall of fifteen degrees centigrade over a distance of one centimetre. Now there's plenty of heat capacity available out here, so why doesn't the warmth penetrate farther into the Pen?"

"There's only one answer. The heat is being removed."

"Yes, but I don't see how. Even if you postulate that in the centre of the Pen is an area of absolute zero temperature you would still expect to get a graduated temperature rise at the boundary and not a sharp transition such as you have here."

"So?" Jacko looked at him expectantly.

"So I can see how to achieve the inverse of this situation using, for instance, a collimated beam of infra-red heat. But a collimated shaft of coldness is something very new indeed. As you remarked, Jacko, there's something wrong with the physics of this place."

With swift resolution Van Noon stepped through the perimeter and into the Pen. Jacko pulled up his collar and followed him in. The contrast was staggering. Whereas a few seconds previously the Ithican warmth had been sufficient to bring them to a gentle sweat, they now stood shivering with the curious chill which inhabited the Pen. Van Noon was looking with amazement at the dreary landscape and subclimate of the Pen interior.

The bright Ithican sunlight did not penetrate. The internal winter continued sheer up to the outer wall, and such light as there was filtered downwards from a dirty, leaden cloudbase trapped within the Pen itself. Even looking sunward, no sign of the Ithican primary could be seen, though it should have been clearly visible, and its apparent loss was not explicable in terms of haze or diffraction.

The sun-toasted ruins which stood outside the Pen continued inside as a depressing waste of rotting bricks and slimed timbers, forming forgotten streets on which even the sparse and miserable vegetation had not much cared to grow. A few furred rodents scattered at their approach, with an attitude of resignation, as if self-preservation here was a matter about which one thought twice.

Van Noon was sampling his surroundings with the detachment of a scientist, yet using his own body in lieu of instrumentation. The process went on for several minutes before he came to a conclusion.

"What do you feel, Jacko?"

"Cold."

"Anything else?"

"Yes, dull. I don't know if it's physical or psychological, but every action seems to demand too much effort."

"You're right there," said Fritz. "I found the same thing myself and I don't think it's psychological. It's almost as if every form of energy here was negated or opposed."

He picked up a stone. "Watch! I want to throw it through the window in the old wall over there."

He threw the stone with practised ease, having judged its weight to a nicety. But the stone lost speed rapidly and fell in a limp trajectory to the muddied soil several metres short of its intended target.

"See what I mean?" said Van Noon. "That stone, accelerated to the velocity at which I released it, should at least have hit the wall. But it didn't. It acted as a lighter body might have done on travelling through these conditions—or as a body of its actual weight might have done had it somehow lost kinetic energy during flight. How do you lose kinetic energy from a body in flight, Jacko?"

"You can't *lose* it," said Jacko. "You can only react it against something—friction, air-resistance, and so on—in which case the energy leaves the system in some other form, usually heat. The energy itself is never lost, only converted."

"But here it wasn't,' said Van Noon. "I wasn't throwing against a headwind, and the air in here is no more dense than outside after allowing for temperature and humidity differences. So whatever stopped that stone wasn't a normal reaction to flight. And I can find no evidence of abnormal gravity or coriolis effects. That stone just progressively lost energy. Mass times velocity doesn't seem to equal momentum in the Pen—and that's a hell of a smack at the textbooks you and I were raised on."

"Working outside the textbooks never worried you before," said Jacko. "Let's get out of this place, Fritz. It's giving me the creeps."

"In a minute, Jacko. I'd like to explore a bit farther in first."

They walked together down the remains of a long-forgotten road, treading wearily on the slimed cobbles of the surface. The environment was desolate and forlorn, with an air of perpetual dampness and slow rot and reluctant fungus. As they penetrated to greater depths the gloom grew perceptibly greater, and the cold chill reached a degree where it would have been unwise to remain too long without the protection of additional clothing. Vegetable and animal life were here almost completely absent, and the slime and fungus showed plainly that even the lower life-forms were maintaining their hold only with the greatest difficulty. Even organic decay had not progressed far after two centuries of perpetual winter.

"What are we looking for, Fritz?"

"I don't know, Jacko. It's the feel of this cold that has me puzzled. I don't feel I'm cold just because the environment is cold. I feel I'm cold because my body is radiating more heat than it should at these temperatures. To judge from the feel of my skin it's about five degrees below freezing point here."

"Agreed," said Jacko. "Well below freezing, certainly."

"Then just an observation," said Van Noon. "Why aren't the puddles of water frozen? It's my guess that a thermometer wouldn't give much below ten centigrade. It's the same effect that we encountered at the perimeter of the Pen—radiant heat being opposed by something only explicable as radiant cold."

"I don't understand that, Fritz. After all, cold is only the absence of heat."

"I wonder," said Van Noon, "if that isn't a limitation to thinking which we've imposed upon ourselves. What happens if we postulate a phenomenon called contra-heat, which we treat as the conventional electromagnetic heat radiation but with the signs reversed?"

"There's no such animal," objected Jacko.

"No? Fetch some equipment in here and compare the radiant heat loss against temperature and I think you'll find there is. There has to be. There's nothing else you could set up in an equation which would go half way to meeting all the facts."

Something crackled and spat unexpectedly behind them with a sound like a multiple pistol shot. They whirled round and stopped in quick amazement. Between them and their path out of the Pen was quite the smallest and darkest and lowest thundercloud they had ever seen. The bottom of the cloud hung probably not more than thirty metres above the ground, and its inky-black consistency made them think of vapours other than those of the air, though this was probably a trick of light and circumstance.

But it was the lightning which gave them pause to think: vicious arcs between ground and cloud which started to stab with all the anticipated brilliance and fire but which were curiously extinguished by some constrictive phenomenon which pinched the plasma and quenched the arc. The result was a staccato "pop" instead of a thunderclap, and a rate of lightning repetition which occasionally generated a continuous tearing noise rather than the usual sounds of storm. But there was no doubting the destructive potential of the lightning bolts.

Moved by unfelt winds, the thundercloud was drawing rapidly nearer, and Van Noon was more than a little apprehensive.

"Better find some shelter, Jacko. This could be dangerous."

They looked about them. The ruins of a hovel, partly roofed with sloped and perilous slates, provided the nearest offer of sanctuary. This they accepted, and squatted within the miserable, damp, boxlike walls while the cloud moved overhead. Lightning stabbed at the path outside with a viciousness which seemed to contain some element of personal malice, but finally it passed. The cloud went spitting and snarl-ing on towards the pillar of the Dark, and Van Noon and Jacko emerged to watch its progress.

"I'll teach Maxwell Courtney to speak of 'interesting sub-climate'," said Van Noon ominously. "Let's get out of here, Jacko."

"You know, Fritz, I was just about to suggest the self-same thing myself."

"That was what they call a rogue storm," said Courtney. "In the Pen you meet them quite a lot. They seem to form and disperse almost spontaneously, but while they last they can be very dangerous. They always travel fast, and always in straight lines. If caught in the open we avoid them by simply running out of the way."

They were seated in Courtney's office in New Bethlem, and the broad windows of the room opened to a distant view of the Pen and its core of Dark. Courtney's desk faced the window as if to give him a constant reminder of the broad enigma to which his life was currently dedicated. The attitude of his visitors' chairs showed that they were no less aware of the dominating influence of the looming column of shades.

"Well," said Van Noon. "We've gathered a little data of our own on a preliminary survey, and I'm told you have acquired data by the ton. That puts you in a good position for answering questions, and me for asking them."

"Ask away," said Courtney. "I don't pretend to have all the answers, but I can do you a nice line in inexplicable facts."

"What can you tell me about anti-energy or contra-energy effects?"

Courtney whistled softly. "That's a piece of fast thinking, Fritz. It took us two years before we could bring ourselves to consider the hypothesis seriously. But I know what you're thinking. Most of the physical effects observed in the Pen can be satisfactorily explained only by thinking in terms of polar opposition—negation by precisely defined effects of exactly opposite character. The fact that these opposite effects are completely unknown to nature outside the Pen doesn't necessarily invalidate the case for their existence inside the Pen. The very nature of the Pen and the Dark is obviously extra-physical, or we'd not have a problem in the first place."

"Precisely!" said Van Noon. "But you do admit the possibility of contra-energy?"

Courtney spread his hands. "I admit it as a possibility. It's certainly a basic premise which fits all the observed facts in the Pen. But it's only one premise among many, and it doesn't have much to commend it when you consider it a little deeper."

"Go on," said Van Noon.

"Let's take an extreme case," said Courtney. "You can prove it for yourself, or take my word for it, that the difference between the Pen and the dark is purely one of degree. Whereas energy negation in the Pen is only partial, that of the Dark is absolute."

"I'll take your word for it. I'd guessed it anyway."

"Good. Now consider this: no matter what intensity, character, or type of energy we have applied to the Dark, we have had no discernible effect upon it, nor have we been able to pass any energy through even a thin sector of it. We have encountered absolute negation, Fritz, of any energy applied in any way. If you stick to your contra theory the implications are too complex to be true, and rather frightening."

"I think I understand you," said Van Noon, "but I'd rather hear it your way."

"I'll put it as simply as I can. If we fire a projectile at it, according to your theory that projectile needs to be met precisely at the perimeter of the Dark by what is effectively a counter projectile of identical mass travelling at an identical velocity to a precisely identical point. That makes too many coincidences for my orthodox-type stomach. And again, suppose we use X-ray bombardment or any other form of radiation. For precise negation this would need to be met at the identical point by contra radiation of the same intensity, wavelength, and phase as that which we apply. Either the Dark is an extremely broadband transmitter capable of producing any type of force, energy, intensity, and phase of radiation at any point on its perimeter at any instant Without prior notice—accurately and instantaneously—or else the Dark is full of little green men with an uncanny knack of anticipating our test programme and arranging their contra facilities to suit."

"I get the point," said Fritz. "How do you arrange to fire a projectile to meet an unexpected projectile head-on with precisely matched mass and velocity and to an impact position predetermined to an accuracy of plus or minus a few microns? It can't be done. You've shaken some of my confidence, but you still haven't encompassed the impossible."

"No? Then I'll do so right away. For your contra theory to be true, the Dark would need to be a dynamic entity. It must necessarily give out exactly as much energy as it receives, for the negation to be complete. It's been here for two hundred years, Fritz. Now calculate two hundred years of radiant energy from the Ithican sun alone and then add what we've flung at it in the last three years of experiment. You'll see that it would need the energy resources of a small star in order to have the reserves to meet any demand. We dropped a nuclear Hell-raiser on it, and a Hell-raiser is a planet-buster, remember. What sort of power supply could conceivably meet a demand like that instantaneously?"

"I don't know," said Van Noon, "but we can't yet claim to know the ultimate in power sources. But very soon I intend to find a way into the Dark, and then perhaps we'll find out."

"You can't do it, Fritz. There isn't a ghost of a chance of penetrating into the Dark."

"I think there is. And I think I know the very way in which it might be done."

"Whatever made you say that?" asked Jacko anxiously, as they left the room.

"It's a feeling I have," said Van Noon. "I said I was going to play this by intuition, and right now my intuition tells me that the Pen and the Dark are contra-energy effects."

"In spite of what Courtney said?"

"Certainly. I must admit he had a nice point about the projectile needing to be met effectively by a contra projectile if the contra-energy theory was to be maintained. It wouldn't actually need to be met by a contra projectile, but merely by an opposing force of the right sort applied in the right place at the right time. I don't doubt that Courtney's correct that such a negation is necessary to substantiate the contra theory.

But I do suspect that his data on absolute negation is not quite as complete as he imagines."

"In what way, Fritz?"

"Well, I can't conceive of a continuous pattern of negative energy which could deal with any sort of force or radiation applied at any point at any time. I can, however, conceive of a pattern of contra radiation or effect which is selectively produced in response to a particular stimulus at a particular point. But you see what this involves?"

"No," said Jacko.

"It involves detection, analysis, and synthesis of a contra effect. Three steps—which must necessitate some sort of time-lag. Courtney has established that any applied energy is negated—but I doubt if it can be negated instantaneously. The three steps may be completed in nano-seconds, but I'm quite sure that a time-lag must exist. Now I want to go into the Pen, right up to the Dark perimeter, and see if we can prove or disprove this."

"And if we prove it?"

"Then I think we'll have a way to drive a tunnel into the Dark and see what's inside."

Jacko lost his power of speech as his mind strove to contain the enormity of the project. Fritz shot him an amused glance, and continued.

"There's a particular reason I want to go in, Jacko. There's a second principle involved in this detection, analysis, contra-synthesis set-up which you might not have thought of. Something else is implied . . . and that something is some form of guiding intelligence."

They had chosen heavy caterpillar crawlers for their transport into the Pen. The choice was determined not only by the fact that a tracked vehicle was an advantage over the broken terrain but also for the reason that the vehicles possessed magnificently powerful engines and an ample reserve of power. Three crawlers were obtained for the expedition; one to run well ahead, one to act as reserve, and one to stay well in the rear with sufficient rescue equipment to recover either of the leading crawlers should the deeper Pen effects exceed the capacity of the engines to keep the vehicles in motion.

Clothing for the party had been chosen for a simple property—thermal insulation. Although the actual temperature of the deep Pen probably did not reach freezing point it was essential to insulate the radiant heat of a man's body against the contra-heat effect which would otherwise have striven to reduce the temperature of a man to the ambient point, with lethal effect. In this way the cold of the Pen differed from normal cold, and the expeditionary figures were clad as though for a journey to the arctic.

Once clear into the outer perimeter of the Pen and out of the strong Ithican sunshine, the expedition began to appreciate the clothing which up to that point had caused them a barely tolerable condition of overheating. Now, as the light faded and the chill of the perpetual winter closed around them, they grew more comfortable. But the underlying seriousness of the venture was pointed-up by a change in the engine note to a more laboured level as both the functioning of the engine and the momentum of the vehicle were affected by the contra elements of the Pen.

The leading crawler carried the bulk of the equipment, especially the precious lasers with which it was hoped to establish the existence of a time lag in the Dark phenomena. Van Noon was captaining the vehicle, Jacko was driving, and Pederson, an observer sent by Courtney, completed the party. Van Noon had intended their route to follow a road indicated on the old maps as running for nearly two kilometres straight in the direction of the axis of the Dark. The intention was abandoned quickly on finding that a building of considerable proportions had collapsed, turning part of the road into an unnavigable pile of masonry. The maps were forgotten and a new route was improvised as the situation demanded, having regard to the abilities of the crawler and taking advantage of the opportunities presented by the slow erosion of the Pen environment on the fabric of the old town.

The light from the trapped cloudbase became increasingly leaden and dull until, at about five kilometres in from the perimeter of the Pen, Jacko was forced to switch on the headlamps. Their effect was negligible. Such light as they produced was robbed by some contra effect in the Pen environment and did little to disperse the muddy gloom. Van Noon had anticipated this and had a searchlight mounted on the roof of the crawler. The intensity of light from this was sufficient to permit their passage through the damp, dilapidated, ghost-like streets of Bethlem to within two kilometres of the Dark itself. Then that illumination too became inadequate.

"Better get out, Jacko, and let's estimate the situation," said Van Noon.

They descended, conscious of the acute contra-heat coldness which searched at their shrouded faces and probed at their wrists and ankles. They were conscious too, now, of contra-momentum, which gave an entirely false impression of the density of the air, since the effect was remarkably like trying to move under water.

Pederson joined them, and they made a brief survey of the situation. Whereas from a greater distance the column of the Dark had been clearly visible, it was now merged into the claylike blankness of scene which made it scarcely distinguishable as a separate entity. Jacko tried the radio communicator, but the instrument was dead save for some rare static from a distant rogue storm. The magnetic compass also had become nonfunctional much earlier, and though the gyro compass still purred unhappily in its box its readings were questionable in view of the conditions under which it was operating.

The quality of light from the cloudbase was curious and unreal. Effectively the light from above should have given them far greater incident and reflected illumination than they actually experienced. This drastic attenuation of the light should have been explicable in terms of fog or haze, but nothing such existed, and their inexpressibly dreary state of near-night had no explanation save for that of an alien opposition to the fundamental laws of physics.

"What are we going to do, Fritz?" Jacko's own attempt to

resolve the situation had reached an impasse.

Van Noon looked back, hoping for an indication as to whether or not the second crawler had been able to follow their tortuous route to the spot. No evidence was forthcoming, so he shrugged his shoulders.

"You two can vote me down if you want to, but I propose that we choose the most likely direction for the Dark and just drive blind until we hit it or stop."

"I'm with you," said Jacko. "What about you, Pederson?"

"Count me in. I've no ambition to walk back on my own."

They re-entered the crawler. Having decided on the most probable direction of the Dark, Jacko orientated the vehicle, locked the tracks on synchronization, and proceeded to drive straight into the unknown.

The journey was a driver's conception of Hell, a nightmare route across unfamiliar territory, effectively blind, and with no warning of what obstacle might halt or jolt them. Added to this was the rising resistance to movement, both on the part of the vehicle and of its occupants. Inside the driving cab even the instrument lights had become impossible to see, and the penetrating coldness finalized the depression which was settling over the spearhead of the expedition. Once or twice Jacko questioned whether they ought to attempt to turn back. Van Noon chided him gently and looked only ahead to the point where the darkness ought to terminate in a meeting with the absolute of the Dark.

Constantly the vehicle rolled and bucked, and canted at dangerous angles as it encountered broken walls or piles of debris in its path. Sometimes it stopped with a bruising shock against some obstacle beyond its power to move. Jacko was skilful in such emergencies and withdrew the vehicle from each such predicament without stalling the engine, knowing that a stopped engine this far into the Pen would never be restarted. Bruised, and in constant danger from masonry from grazed walls crushing the cab, they endured the journey patiently; although with various deviations from the course which the presence of unsurmountable obstacles forced on Jacko, they had no certain idea if they were still headed towards the Dark at all.

Then came the moment they had been dreading. In pitch darkness now, the crawler came to a sudden halt against something immovable. The tracks churned the soft floor uselessly for a half second, and then the engine stalled before Jacko could throw the vehicle in reverse. He tried the ignition cycle in vain, but the contra effects were too powerful to permit the heavy engine to be restarted. The silence grew absolute save for the tick-tick of metal cooling rapidly and Fritz's voice cursing in a strangely muted way.

"End of the line," said Jacko finally.

Van Noon opened the door. "As we've managed to get here we may as well see where we are," he said.

They climbed out. Their powerful torches were about as useful as glow-worms, and permitted an examination of no object more distant than about a quarter of a metre. Beyond this was darkness in all directions except directly vertical, where a muddied stain across the sky mocked them with its inability to provide any useful illumination on the ground. Van Noon searched around him and picked up a short length of rotting timber with which he cast about in the darkness on all sides. Then he called urgently.

"Jacko, are you near the crawler?"

"I am," said Pederson. "Just by the cab door." He banged the metal, which returned a dull and unrewarding thud. Like their voices, the sound was strangely attenuated.

"Good! Now, Jacko, can you place yourself by sound in a line between our two voices?"

Jacko moved somewhere in the darkness. "I think I'm there."

"Right. Now we're three in a line, with Pederson on the right, you central, and myself on the left. As far as I can make out, about three paces ahead of us is the Dark. Find something to probe it with, and don't touch it even with your gloves. Maintain your orientation carefully so that you don't lose direction and walk into it. It could be very dangerous to touch."

They advanced slowly, Pederson tapping the side of the

crawler for identification, and Fritz and Jacko talking so that the sound of voices gave their relative positions. Even so, Jacko got there first. His probe was a shard of splintered ceramic with which he was striking before him as though at some anticipated enemy. Contra-momentum made this a difficult movement to achieve, and the darkness added to the soup-like resistance to movement, giving the whole situation a dream-like character without the visual qualities of the conventional nightmare.

Then Jacko hit the Dark. It was detectable by its complete negation of the force with which he struck it. And it returned no sound, and in this way was distinguishable from any ordinary obstacle struck with force.

"Got it," said Jacko. "But that knocking sound you hear is my knees. I admit I'm frightened of this thing, Fritz."

"I'm not exactly keen on it, either," said Van Noon. "But this is what we came to see. It's a pity we can't see it now we've got here. Have you any suggestions, Pederson?"

"I've just discovered the Dark is what we ran the crawler into. . . No wonder it didn't move."

An ominous and familiar staccato rattle made them turn.

A rogue storm, travelling towards them and parallel to the wall of the Dark, was making its passage known by its peculiarly pinched lightning. Because of attenuation, the lightning and thunder had been undetectable even from a short distance, and the storm was almost upon them before they were aware it existed. There was no time to seek shelter. They flung themselves down on the damp earth at the foot of the Dark and waited for it to pass. It sprayed the area with quenched fire as it went, doing no damage to them, but the intensity of the arcs was such that momentarily they had a clear picture of their situation.

The Dark was just in front of them, a sheer wall of unblemished black-velvet nothingness, impossibly perfect. The crawler had nosed head-on up to the black wall, and its tracks were pressed hard against the exterior. On all other sides of them lay the ghost-suburb of desolate ruins, the reflecting white teeth of broken masonry contrasting with the wet, black soilstones of the earth.

As soon as the worst of the storm was over they climbed back to their feet.

"What are you going to do, Fritz? Try the lasers?"

"I don't know." Fritz had moved back to the crawler and was examining the tracks in contact with the Dark by the spasmodic light of the rapidly waning storm. "I don't think we need to, Jacko. I think I've got my answer. You see, it did take time for the Dark to analyse and apply a counterforce to stop the crawler. But that fraction of a second was sufficient for something significant to happen. The crawler tracks have penetrated very slightly into the Dark."

It was impossible for the others to verify Van Noon's statement since the light from the storm had rapidly become eclipsed by the strength of the contra effects. The combined output of searchlight and torches failed to re-establish the point, and the lasers refused to function from the crawler's emergency power supply. But Van Noon was sufficiently convinced of what he had seen to regard the expedition as a success.

"All we have to do now is to get back to tell the tale," said Jacko, unhappily.

They started back by the only means available—they walked. For the first half kilometre they stumbled blindly through the darkness and the nightmare of contra-momentum. The coldness, too, was becoming serious now that they were exposed for a long period without the protection of the crawler cab. But gradually their eyes, accustomed to complete darkness, began to discern light like the first touch of dawn, and with the returning ability to see, they no longer blundered into blind paths in the ruins from which they had to retreat by sense of touch alone. And the contra-effects grew slightly less, so that their pace progressively improved as they made their way out of the deep Pen regions.

Two kilometres away from the Dark they came across the crushed path that their own crawler had made on its way in, and this they followed gratefully. Shortly they found the second crawler, abandoned, and with its engine stalled and cold. The third crawler was patrolling a broad front along a road about three kilometres radius from the Dark perimeter. They were hailed and taken aboard for the last part of the journey through the growing light and finally out into the unbearably bright gold sunset of an lthican evening.

Courtney was there to greet them. His team had spent the day re-running exploratory tests, but this time with particular reference to the onset-time of negation. His results amply confirmed Van Noon's experience. There was a time-lag on the introduction of any energy phenomenon to the Dark or the Pen before negation set in. The exact period of the lag varied with the type of phenomenon, but was greatest for applied physical force.

The Ithican government, sensing promise in the issue, had already granted almost unlimited facilities to aid any practical application of the idea. On Van Noon's behalf Courtney had accepted the challenge, and the party rode with buoyant spirits back to New Bethlem where work on the next phase of Fritz's plans against the Dark were just about to begin.

"A tunnel?" said Jacko.

"Strictly speaking," said Van Noon, "I had in mind something more in the nature of a horizontal well, but I think a tunnel is a fair description."

"And just how do you propose to sink a horizontal well into the Dark?"

"Frankly, I don't see much difficulty. We take an ordinary iron pipe of sufficient dimension to permit the passage of a man—and just knock it in."

"Crazy like a fox!" said Jacko. "We're talking about the Dark—the great energy negator. In the name of Moses, how do you just knock a pipe into that?"

"I thought I'd already demonstrated that," said Fritz. "There's a time-lag before the onset of negation. Apply a pile driver or something to your pipe and hit it once and it will penetrate the Dark; just a little before the detection, analysis, contra synthesis has a chance to stop it. Then the negation will be applied and stop the tube going in any farther, and the system will reach stasis. The contra-force obviously cannot continue to be applied after the original force has ceased to operate, so the force, contra-force balance will then relax."

"So?"

"So then you hit your pipe again and drive it in a little more. And so on. And providing you work on a completely random and non-predictable basis there's no chance of the contra-force being applied in anticipation. I suspect that only if we set up a standard repetition rate will we meet with complete and instantaneous negation of the force that we apply."

"So we knock in our tube. Then what?"

"It depends on what we find. The Dark may be a solid or it may be a thin-wall phenomenon. If it's a solid we shall not gain much except for a little knowledge. But if it's thin-wall, then we might have a chance to look inside."

"From which you're assuming that the Dark effect won't penetrate inside the pipe."

"I think it may to some extent, but take any physical phenomenon and place an inch of steel in front of it and you always get some modification or attenuation, if not a complete shutoff. I don't see that the situation should be materially different for contra-physical phenomena. With a bit of luck we should be able to get through."

"What do you think's inside there, Fritz?"

"As I see it, Jacko, some form of intelligence, but I wouldn't like to guess any closer than that. Whether the Dark is some cosmic amoeba or has inside it a complex of little green men is something I intend to find out. Are you with me?"

"I'm right behind you," said Jacko. "But don't ask me to be the first man through that ruddy pipe."

By the time that Courtney returned to the base camp a few days later Van Noon's plans were fairly well advanced. Fritz described the scheme briefly. Courtney was intrigued but doubtful.

"I don't see," he said, "how you're going to drive a pipe of that diameter into the Dark—remembering that the driving has to be done in the deep Pen area where the contra-momentum is killing. You'd never get a horizontal pile driver to work under those conditions."

"No. We've already taken care of that point by taking a new line entirely. We're going to fire it in."

"Fire it?"

"Yes. Attach the free end of the pipe to what is effectively a large-bore gun or reaction chamber with an open muzzle pointing away from the Dark. In the gun we fire a high-explosive charge and let the recoil of the apparatus drive the pipe against the Dark. According to my calculations, a series of explosive shocks should have the right sort of driving characteristics for the job. How does it sound as an idea?"

"It could work," admitted Courtney. "Unless we're up against something we don't know about yet. How far have you got with the project?"

"We've managed to get the lengths of pipe into the Dark area, and the gun chamber is there also. There's trouble keeping handling equipment working so far into the Pen, but we've managed somehow. We should be ready to start firing sometime tomorrow. Have you been able to get the extra stuff I asked for?"

"Most of it's outside on the carriers, and the generators will arrive in the morning. Here's the radiation monitor, trolley-mounted as specified. I only hope it fits into the pipe."

"I'll try it out," said Van Noon. "I can run it through our test length and if it doesn't fit we can modify it before it goes into the Pen."

He wheeled the small apparatus-laden trolley to the length of pipe that ran down the workshop where they had been fabricating the gun chamber. The trolley fitted easily into the interior of the pipe and, to give himself a little practice, he crawled in after it and pushed it before him. The iron confines of the pipe returned the roar of the small casters with a noise like a train speeding through a tunnel. When Van Noon reached the far end he found that Jacko had returned and was peering anxiously down the pipe.

"Why the sound effects, Fritz?"

"Eh? Oh, this? It's the radiation detector. It's obvious that even the iron of the pipe can't do more than attenuate some wavelengths of the electromagnetic spectrum—and the same presumably applies to the contra spectrum. So just to be on the safe side Courtney has knocked up a combined range monitor which should cover anything likely to be dangerous but not detectable by our own senses. I don't expect that we'll encounter any such radiation, but it's better to be safe than sterile."

"Agreed," said Jacko. "We're taking enough chances with the unknown already. I've just come back out of the Pen, and we're right on schedule. The first firing can take place at mid-day tomorrow."

"I'll be there," said Fritz. "I'm particularly interested in knowing what happens to the core which we leave in the pipe. If the Dark is true radiation-type phenomena, there won't be any core material. But if it's something else, we may have to think again."

The null-pressure suits obtained from Space Command were far more suitable for working under deep Pen conditions than the expeditionary clothing had been. Specifically designed for work on asteroids and similar bodies under a pressure dome but exposed to extremes of stellar heat and cold, the suits were the finest flexibilized radiation foils that had yet been devised. In the Pen, of course, no pressurized dome was needed, but the suits ensured that the searching fingers of contra-heat were no longer a danger or of major discomfort to the U.E. squad.

But the drag of the contra-momentum was not so easily avoided. Close to the wall of the Dark it exhibited an almost treacle-like resistance to movement which was common to both men and machines alike. The adaptations of technique needed for working in an environment possessing such a high quasi-viscosity were numerous, but the combined ingenuity of the Unorthodox Engineering squad was equal to the challenge. Somehow the impossible had been accomplished, and the structural components of Van Noon's tunnel had been patiently sworn into place ready for the projected penetration of the Dark.

"Ready to fire?"

Jacko nodded. "First shot in thirty seconds."

They were watching the scene by the light of two large, continuously operating lasers which Courtney had managed to obtain. These were directed on the point where the leading end of the pipe was pressed hard against the Dark perimeter. The illumination, spread slightly by deliberate diffusion with mesh screens, was adequate despite the contra-radiation loss. The backscatter illumination was also quite useful around the working area, but was attenuated sharply and unnaturally with distance. The power for the lasers had to be derived from outside the Pen via cable, and the contra-electrical loss was such that two large generators were needed to drive sufficient energy in to keep the lasers in operation.

The first shot was fired. The sound of the explosion was incredibly muted, and the tongue of flame from the reaction chamber was quickly quenched and drained. Van Noon examined the junction between the pipe and the Dark.

"I think it's working, Jacko. Only millimetres so far, but it's definitely going in. Keep firing rapidly but erratically. Let me know when you're in about a metre. Then I want to go down inside the pipe and see if any sort of core is left."

By reason of good organization on Jacko's part they had penetrated a metre by late afternoon. Then the gun chamber was removed to allow access to the free end of the pipe. Van Noon had a line measured to a pipe's length minus one metre, and one end he left clamped to the free end of the pipe while he took the rest of the line inside to give him an indication of his position. Ten minutes later he came out jubilant.

"No core material, Jacko. The pipe is clear to the very end, and then the Dark begins again. That means we've got a metre of clear tunnel already and no complications so far. Now I want firings to continue right round the clock, as close-spaced as possible without setting up a standard repetition rate. If you scatter the charges round the area a bit so that each has to be fetched from a slightly different distance, that should be sufficient. But I want the depth of penetration per shot carefully watched, and if it varies very much from the existing rate, cease firing and let me know."

It took forty hours to drive the first length of pipe into the Dark. By this time a second length had been added to the first and there were indications that the depth of penetration per shot was increasing. The second was driven home in twenty-five hours, partly due to the decreasing resistance it encountered, and partly due to the increasing proficiency of the shot-firers.

The third pipe was inserted in seventeen hours, and the fourth, in twelve. The time for subsequent pipes decreased in rough proportion. The tenth went half way, and then the indications were that no great resistance was being offered to it by the Dark since the assembly of pipes now moved forward the full theoretical distance per shot that they would have moved in the Pen itself. Jacko brought his charts to Van Noon.

"I think we're through, Fritz. These seem to show that the Dark is a relatively thin-wall phenomenon with its effects decreasing with depth of penetration and reaching virtually zero at about ninety-five metres. God alone knows what's at the other end."

"Take the gun chamber off, Jacko, but be careful in case something unexpected comes out of the pipe. If nothing happens in half an hour then I'm going through to have a look."

Nothing did happen. The end of the pipe protruding from the Dark remained empty, silent and cold; and there was no way of telling what lay at the far end. A laser directed down the pipe returned nothing but light-scatter from walls and motes of dust. The only factor of note was a strong current of air entering the pipe as though to equalize some unexplained deficiency in pressure.

Finally Van Noon hoisted the radiation trolley into the pipe and followed it in.

"I'm going down a bit, Jacko, for a preliminary survey.

Stand by with some weapons in case I come out fast with something after me."

"Nothing doing!" said Jacko. "If you're going down that pipe, then I'm coming too."

"That's what I hoped you'd say," said Fritz. "Let's get on with it. The situation won't improve itself by waiting."

He crawled into the pipe. With some misgivings, Jacko followed him in. Ahead of Fritz the radiation trolley clattered on the iron and raised a multitude of clamorous echoes which engulfed them in a tide of sound. Inside the pipe the contra-sound attenuation apparently did not operate to anything like the same degree as that encountered in the Pen. The radiation monitor gave no indication of any increase in rate above the slow background count, and they considered it safe to continue.

Occasionally Van Noon stopped and let the echoes die, but nothing else disturbed the silence except their own breathing and their own awkward movements in the confines of the pipe. Then after what seemed an eternity of crawling the clatter of the trolley ceased again and Van Noon stopped and half twisted himself to look back.

"Jacko," he said urgently, "think very carefully. Are you absolutely sure how many lengths of pipe we drove into the Dark?"

"A ruddy fine time to be concerned about the economics of the project."

"Hang the economics! Are you sure?"

"Certainly. Ten in all. Why?"

"I've been counting the joins. I'm now in the twelfth pipe, that's why."

"Don't make jokes like that, Fritz. You'll give me heart failure."

"I wasn't joking. The casters on the trolley drop into the flange gap at every join, and I have to ease them over. That's what made me start counting how many joins I'd passed."

"So you're now in the twelfth pipe out of the original ten," said Jacko, still not fully convinced. "That's quite a trick! How do you explain it, Fritz?"

"Contra-iron pipe," said Van Noon. "Lord! I thought it was a joke when Courtney suggested that they stopped a projectile with a contra projectile. But it appears it wasn't. They do just that. They tried to stop our pipe with a length of contra-iron pipe so precisely similar that I'd not have noticed the difference had I not been counting. What type of creatures could do that, Jacko—almost instantaneously?"

"I don't know," said Jacko. "But I'm afraid of them."

"You and me both. To work a trick like that must demand a technology centuries ahead of ours. But even so, I've a feeling we've got them worried."

"Why's that?"

"Because if they were still operating at full efficiency there's something we'd logically have met in this pipe before now—a contra-radiation monitoring trolley pushed by a contra Fritz Van Noon."

"We're way out of our depth, Fritz," said Jacko finally. Are you still going on?"

"If you're still following."

"I'm still behind you, but I'm darned if I know why. I've followed you into some crazy situations before, but this has the lot beaten."

They moved on, the roar of the trolley casters echoing and reverberating around them and occasionally stopping as Fritz eased the little wheels over a flange gap.

"Just entering pipe nineteen," said Van Noon finally. "If they provided as many as we did then there's only one to go."

"See anything yet?"

"Not an atom."

"I was just thinking, Fritz. It'd be a neat nick if they'd connected an infinity of pipes together. We could go on crawling through here till Judgment Day."

"Good point, Jacko. We'll reconsider the position when we get to the end of number twenty."

Again the trolley roared and stopped.

"Just entering pipe twenty," said Van Noon.

"Let's get it over with," said Jacko. "I feel like a godevil working overtime."

"Right. This is it!"

The trolley was moving slowly now, with Fritz concentrating on every centimetre of its progress, using the feel of the iron instead of eyes. There was no way to measure distance in the darkness. The only way was to crawl and to hope that one remembered the feeling of crawling a length of pipe. Then a sudden cessation of noise, with the echoes slowly sinking around them.

"End of pipe," said Van Noon. "But there's no resistance. The trolley is half way out of the end but I still can't see a thing. I'm going to let the trolley go and see what happens."

There was a brief scrape of metal on metal, and the thump of something on the pipe.

"It fell down," said Van Noon, "but not very far. I can still feel it with my hand. And something else. . . There's no contra-momentum out here. I can move quite freely. It isn't even very cold. It must mean we're well inside the wall of the Dark. I wonder if the torch will work."

The torch did work. In the darkness the light touched the interior of the pipe with an intensity that was momentarily dazzling. Projected outwards, the beam was clearly visible but it contacted nothing that reflected except the wet, brown stones of the earth, and the radiation trolley fallen on its side. Ostensibly they were looking into night, bare and empty, but Fritz was not convinced.

"This isn't darkness," said Van Noon. "It's more like veils of darkness. . . thin layers of contra-light. See how the torch beam falls off in discrete quanta. I'm going out there, Jacko, to see if I can make head or tail of this. You stay by the pipe with a torch ready to guide me back. I'd very much like to find out who or what it was that put ten pipes on the end of ours."

"And I'm going to wish you luck," Jacko said. "I'm not at all sure I want to know." Van Noon dropped to the ground. The soil underfoot was an obvious continuation of the old town terrain. His torch illuminated the stony earth for many metres in front of him, but it was useless when directed horizontally in any direction because of the apparent lack of anything to reflect the light.

But he was right in his observation that the intensity of the light was stepped-down by curtaining veils of something. As he approached a veil he could see a distinct drop in the brightness of the beam as it was intercepted by something dark and nebulous. He reached the veil and touched it, curiously. His fingers encountered nothing, and he walked through it without sensation. Looking back, he was glad still to be able to see the light from Jacko's torch, but he knew that if he passed through many veils even that would be lost to him.

But the situation changed without warning. The fifth veil was not insubstantial at all. It was a film of something like dark, thin-blown glass, and he shattered it with his torch because he had not known of its solidity. And as it shattered, light from beyond spilled out through the broken edges and he had the briefest glimpse of the scene of gold-hazed wonder. . . and then the air exploded in his face.

And even the explosion was unreal. The blast caught him not from in front but from behind and above, moving towards the explosion rather than from it. It tumbled him forward and pinned his body to the ground with a great pressure. Desperately he fought to raise his neck and shoulders for a further glimpse of the creatures who lived in their sanctuary deep inside the hollow Dark. He wanted a better look at the godlike machines they controlled, now rising high like gossamer and congregating in the golden light as they swept magnificently upwards almost faster than the eye could follow. But a sheet of flame crackled and tore across the vastness of the area and whipped high in an angry, explosive tide.

A shockfront of pressure tore him from the ground, then dropped him cruelly. Despite the hurt he fought to retain consciousness and turn and watch the exodus of the gods. But the forces acting on him were too great. Instead he was swamped by darkness.

His next impression was that of Courtney's face and the sense of lapsed hours. He felt bruised and shaken, but not seriously hurt. He was lying in the open, and the Ithican sky above was broadly trailed with the colours of the sunset.

Courtney came up and put a folded coat beneath his head and a blanket over his body.

"Take it easy, Fritz. There's a doctor on his way."

Van Noon smiled wanly. He tried to sit up, then thought better of it. "Is this where the Dark was, or did you get me out."

Courtney sat down beside him. "The Dark's gone, Fritz. I don't know what you did, but you certainly made a good job of it. The whole darn thing imploded. It was a fantastic sight. The Dark and the Pen drew up together, then spiralized like a whirlwind. There was a blast which broke every window in New Bethlehem . . . and then the whole complex just disappeared."

"I know what did it," said Van Noon. "Our atmosphere reacted with theirs with a sort of mutual destructiveness. It was the total reaction of mass with mass—complete consumption of both and no by-product. It was our tunnel let the air through, and I broke the last seal by accident. And once the reaction started, nothing could stop it."

"So it was contra-terrene!" said Courtney.

"Deep inside, yes. And I'd guess that the purpose of the Dark was to act as a form of barrier against the contra world outside—an insulator separating the opposed atomic conditions. They must have tried to maintain it against penetration by every trick they knew. But what damned them was a simple slip of logic. They stopped a hollow object with a hollow object. . . and forgot the hole inside. But even so, we were lucky to get through."

"Lucky?"

"Yes," said Fritz. "We were operating on the wrong principle. There was no detection, analysis, synthesis reaction involved. There didn't need to be, not the way they did it."

"I don't follow, Fritz."

"I missed the point myself at first, but there's only one logical answer to the detection and negation of any phenomena applied anywhere at any time . . . They did it with mirrors."

"Mirrors?"

"Yes. Not ordinary mirrors, of course, but using a reflecting principle capable of producing the exact and true physical inverse of whatever comes into its field—a mirror that works not only with light but over the entire region of physical and force phenomena, including matter itself."

"My God!" said Courtney. "It's a fascinating concept."

"I'd give anything to know the mechanics of it," said Van Noon. "The reflector wasn't a simple plane, it was a three-dimensional cavity about ninety metres deep between the inner and outer walls. And somehow in that space were reproduced contra-physical objects rather than mere images. And in our innocence we had the temerity to bore right through the 'glass' to the back."

"That's where you have me puzzled by this mirror hypothesis, Fritz. It doesn't seem to fit the facts. Your breakthrough was dependent on the assumed detection-analysis synthesis trinity, and it worked. But the theory assumed a delay time was inherent. But a mirror has no time-lag. Its returned image is instantaneous."

"That's not true," objected Van Noon. "The image returned by a mirror is never instantaneous. Light travels from the object to the glass at a finite velocity, and through the glass at a different but also finite velocity. So the image returned to the object is always delayed in time by just twice the time it takes light to reach the reflector. We were lucky in that in their contra mirror the effect was even more pronounced for the type of phenomenon in which we were interested."

Courtney absorbed this in silence for a moment or two. Then: "What put you on to the idea, Fritz?"

"Primarily your point about their power output having to match the total power input from all sources. It seemed improbable they would have chosen such a dynamic and wasteful method of maintaining a long-term defence. But a reflection principle has no such disadvantage. A mirror returns only when it receives. It needs no power to return the image. And when I got into the cavity and found nothing there but the image-iron pipes by which we'd just arrived, I knew that reflection was the only answer. But like a damn fool I went and blundered through the 'silvering' on the back of this mirror."

He leaned back momentarily and closed his eyes, trying to recapture an image in his own head. "What happened to them, Maxwell? Did they get away?"

Courtney turned his head to look at the sunset.

"No. They didn't make it, Fritz. They reached the stratosphere in those machines of theirs, but then they exploded. Thank God the power release was too high to do much damage!"

"It's a pity," said Fritz. "I'd sooner have got to know them than have destroyed them. We could have learnt an awful lot from people who could build mirrors like that."

"Had they been inclined to teach," said Courtney, "but in two hundred years they never attempted even to make a contact. I think that they were so far ahead of us that we were merely as ants to them."

Van Noon sat up painfully and looked around. "By the way, what happened to Jacko?"

"He's a little bruised and dazed, but nothing serious. Apparently the implosive blast shot him out of the pipe like a cork out of a bottle. He swears you did it on purpose."

"I saw them go," said Van Noon, "and they were like golden gods flying back to Olympus. I would never have done a thing like that on purpose. Do you suppose we'll ever know why they were here?"

"I doubt it," said Courtney. "And even if they'd tried to tell us, I doubt our capacity to have understood. Try explaining the uses and construction of a Dewar flask to an ant—and see who gets tired first."

GETAWAY FROM GETAWEHI

One

"Colonel Nash has just checked out of the spaceport, sir. Says he'll be with you in about half an hour. He's bringing a Commander Brumas with him."

"Coming to see me?" Colonel Belling cast a thoughtful glance at the wallclock. "He didn't happen to say what he wanted?"

"No, sir." The Port Liaison Officer was apologetic. "But he was in one hell of a hurry. The Navy virtually commandeered the field to give the ship priority clearance to land. They even used heat-shielded tenders to start offloading passengers before the pit was halfways cool. Looks like some sort of emergency. It's not often they risk landing a heavy cruiser at a metropolitan spaceport."

"A heavy cruiser?"

"Navy craft—one of the biggest. The Labship *Tycho Brahe*, no less."

"Was it in trouble?"

"Not apparently. But I think Colonel Nash was. When the Port Marshal went out to meet him off the tender the Colonel shouted 'Get away!' or something like that, and ran up the walkway like he was jet assisted."

"Thanks for calling." Belling cut the connection to the spaceport and turned back to the wallclock speculatively. Then he picked up the handset again.

"Duty room . . . Is Lieutenant Van Noon still in the depot?"

"Yes, sir. But he's due to check out in a few minutes on twenty-one days leave."

"Stop him. He's not to leave without my personal authority. Put him under arrest if necessary, but don't let him go."

"Understood, Colonel. What's the charge this time?"

"No charge. Just hold him until I send for him. I have a slight feeling that Colonel Nash isn't the only one who's going to be in trouble."

"Glad to see you, Ivan!" Belling held out his hand. "You know, I haven't seen you since you went to Tazoo."

"Tazoo?" Nash mopped his perspiring brow. "I wish to hell I was still on Tazoo."

"Oh? I gathered it was a bit of a hell-hole."

"The galaxy's worst—or so I thought. But that was before I came across Getawehi."

"Getawehi? What's wrong with Getawehi?"

"That's just the problem," said Nash, with a look of resignation. "I'm damned if I know what's wrong with Getawehi. I can't even talk about it without sounding irrational. That's why I asked Commander Brumas along. He's handling the Navy's side of the Getawehi project and a saner man you couldn't wish to meet. He doesn't find it easy to talk about Getawehi either. For that reason he's come armed with a taped record which shows some of his peculiar problems. I think he'd better state his case first."

"You have me intrigued," said Belling. "The entire resources of the General Engineering Reserve are at your service. If you can broadly define your problem, I'll call up one of our specialists who may be able to assist."

"Forget your specialists," said Nash heavily. "Get that nutter Van Noon up here. This is the type of outwards-facing-interior problem that only he knows how to handle."

"You know," said Belling, "I had the feeling this was going to be one of those days as soon as I heard you were coming." He reached for the handset again.

"Duty room . . . Is Van Noon available?"

"Yes, sir. Under close arrest. He had to be restrained from leaving. Do you wish to enter a charge sheet?"

"No. Just get him up here fast. And while you're at it, drop a noose over Sergeant Hine and the rest of the UE squad. I have a feeling we may be lucky enough to be rid of the whole damn lot by morning."

"You sent for me, sir?" Lieutenant Fritz Van Noon entered the office cautiously.

"Yes, Fritz." Colonel Belling motioned Van Noon towards a chair. "Sorry to have to cancel your leave, but something very important has come up. Colonel Nash you already know, but I want you to meet Commander Brumas, currently heading the Navy's Space-Engineering Research team. He has an emergency on his hands." He turned to his visitor. "Commander, this is Fritz Van Noon, who runs our Unorthodox Engineering group."

Despite his obvious agitation, the naval officer relaxed somewhat at Fritz's entry. He had evidently found Colonel Belling's approach to his problems no more comforting than those of his own Service authorities.

"What's on your mind, Commander?" asked Van Noon.

"Getawehi." Brumas said it with the air of a man who has repeated a story so many times that he is sure that by now the whole world must be familiar with its details.

"Getawehi? Sounds like an insect repellent."

"No such luck. It's a planet and one of the most Godlost territories in space. We've a twenty-man construction team trapped down there, and we can't lift them off."

"And you think the Engineering Reserve might be able to help you?" Van Noon shot a quick look at Colonel Belling—who was apparently finding some innocent amusement in the ceiling, to judge from the expression on his face and the elevation of his eyeballs.

"Not the Engineering Reserve," corrected Brumas sharply. "Specifically the Unorthodox Engineers. The other kind we already have, but after exposure to Getawehi problems they tend to go down with nervous breakdowns like they were infectious. No, this is a far-out situation, and it's going to take some intensely screwball ideas to solve it."

"Then you're on to the right person," said Belling maliciously.

“Exactly what’s so special about Getawehi?” asked Fritz.

Brumas mopped his brow. “Let me give you the background first. There’s a big joint-service science project called Ixion on at the moment. The Navy’s part was to land and assemble an equipment project on Getawehi. Superficially it seemed a simple job. It proved to be the biggest balls-up in Naval history. Not only have we been unable to complete the assignment, but we’ve also lost most of our equipment and left our construction team stranded on Getawehi. If we can do nothing else, we have at least to find a way to get the team off.”

“I don’t quite see what the UE group can do that Space Rescue can’t.”

“No—but then you haven’t been to Getawehi. The whole planet’s a rotten cosmological joke. Everything about Getawehi is sideways-up. From its orbital velocity and apparent mass it has no business even being in its present orbit around its primary, Geta. And not content with being a complete mathematical absurdity, its own rotation is subject to such peculiar perturbations and variations that its progress can only be described as lolloping. It doesn’t even have a stable period of rotation.”

“You must appreciate I’m supposed to be on leave,” said Van Noon warily.

Brumas was unswerving. “But it’s only when you take a closer look at Getawehi that the real peculiarities of the planet begin to emerge. Take, for instance, the dance of the drunken rocket.”

Van Noon looked appealingly towards Colonel Belling, but the latter avoided meeting his eyes and busied himself with loading the videotape projector.

The screen brightened to show a stereo close-up of the planet’s surface, a view obviously taken from a spacecraft in a precarious synchronous orbit. Under the cameras the terrain of Getawehi was nothing remarkable. On the screen an ashen-grey soil, spotted with wisps of heather, purple fern and palmaceous grasses, gave way reluctantly to the edge of a grey, rock-strewn steppe—a typical patch of ecological poverty in the cosmological scheme.

"This is the spot," said Brumas, "where the first team made touchdown. The prognosis was favourable. Getawehi had a breathable atmosphere at tolerable pressure, no predatory animals above the size of a mouse, and temperatures well within the range of working suits."

"I've still got twenty-one days due to me," said Van Noon plaintively.

Brumas ignored the interruption. "I'm replaying the recording at ten times its actual speed, so that the effect will appear exaggerated. What you will see is only one example of the kind of tricks that Getawehi has up its sleeve. In a few moments you will see the landing of the ferry rocket. At this playback speed the actual transit time will appear quite brief, but we are mainly interested in what happened after it landed."

The actual moment of touchdown was obscured by a swiftly-subsiding dustcloud, which cleared to show the rocket standing firmly on its landing legs but leaning at a decided angle from the vertical.

For the first time, Van Noon began to take an active interest.

"Odd!" he said.

"It gets more odd the farther it goes," Brumas assured him. "As a matter of interest, it's the only ship we've been able to put down without it toppling. Not that that did very much good."

From the vantage point of the camera almost vertically overhead in space, the legs of the rocket could be seen to be firm, but the angle at which the nose-cone faced the sky changed direction and deviated in angle in the most alarming way.

"At this point we assumed," said Brumas, "that what we were observing was the failure of one or more shock absorbers on the legs, and a hunting pneumatic servo trying to compensate. But it isn't true."

"No," said Van Noon. "I didn't think it would be."

"What makes you say that?"

"The rocket's centre of gravity. Even with a weighted base—which you haven't got on a ferry rocket—you couldn't lean it at that angle to the vertical without it falling over."

"Very good!" approved Brumas. "So what's your reaction to that little paradox?"

"I feel sick."

"I mean seriously . . .?"

"I was being serious. If the rocket hasn't toppled it can only be because its centre of gravity hasn't been greatly displaced by the angle at which it's leaning. There's only one set of conditions where that would be possible."

"Which is?"

"That the gravitational attraction of Getawehi is not perpendicular to the surface of the planet. On Getawehi, 'up' is not only angled from the geocentric vertical, but it's even subject to short-period changes of direction."

"This boy's brilliant!" said Brumas, glancing at Belling. "Now, Fritz, leaving aside the fact that gravity variations on that scale are a physical impossibility, let's see how you do on the next bit."

"You mean there's more?"

"I haven't started yet. This is only by way of introduction. You name the impossible, and Getawehi has it."

The nose-cone of the rocket swung to encompass three hundred degrees of arc in as many seconds, then the whole space vehicle gave a skip and a stagger, spun completely about on one landing leg, then re-established itself about a ship's diameter away from its original position.

"Ingenious!" said Fritz Van Noon.

"Isn't it? I thought you'd be intrigued. But the worst is yet to come."

Having found its legs, so to speak, the rocket adopted a fairly rapid series of gyratory steps while miraculously remaining approximately vertical. Its path was increasingly haloed by a ring of escaping crewmen, like frenzied ants encircling a honeypot. Each step the ship took was preceded by the curious hop-skip motion with which it had preluded its new mode of transport. Its continuing drunken dance through the fern banks soon carried it out on to the edge of the steppe. There it abruptly disappeared from view except for an unmoving brown stain.

Brumas swore and stopped the projector. “Sorry about that! I’ll give you that last sequence again at true speed.”

“It might help,” said Van Noon morosely. “An inebriated rocket I could learn to live with, but I know from bitter experience that the abrupt removal of half a billion credits of Government money invariably needs a good explanation.”

After a brief interval the rocket re-appeared, moving now at its actual speed and engaged in the last of its strides through the fern and out on to the plain. The extreme angle of its tilt was clearly visible, and its last swivel-round was remarkably controlled considering the vehicle’s thousand tonne Terran deadweight.

As the landing carriage touched the plain’s edge, one leg folded beneath its burden. The rocket tipped sideways and began to fall. But more than falling, the whole ship appeared to dissolve as it toppled, the debris melting like candlewax dropped on a hot stove. There was a brief flare, scarcely visible in Geta’s strong sunlight, then there was nothing left of the vessel save for a large area of brown metallic stain on the sand-ash and a few chunky ceramic tube components which survived the remarkable fate of the rest of the ship.

For a long time Van Noon was silent. Then finally he spoke. “That was quite some trick,” he said. “How’s it done?”

“I’ll go into that later,” said Brumas. “Right now the point at issue is that we’ve a job to do on Getawehi—a job we’ve started but can’t finish. We’ve three supply ships orbiting the planet which we daren’t instruct to make planetfall for obvious reasons. And we’ve a twenty-man construction team stranded on Getawehi which we can’t lift off. We’ve had a hundred per cent mortality rate on transfer ferries attempting touchdown, and we can’t even communicate with the ground force except by line-of-sight laser channel, due to radio interference.”

"All of which adds up to one heck of a problem," said Van Noon.

"Precisely!" Brumas and Colonel Nash exchanged glances. "But as I said, this is only the introduction. Colonel Nash is the one who has the real problems."

Two

The thunder died as the Labship *Tycho Brahe*, having cleared the necessary seventeen thousand astronomical units, transmuted easily into its hyperspace analogue and fled through the weird corridors of the dimensionless continua. Aboard, it was time for relaxation. Navigation towards Geta held few of the problems of astronavigation which would have complicated the reaching of a star within the confines of the Milky Way. Far out from the edge of the Galaxy, where the great tides of emptiness washed against the brave Rim stars, the farther galaxies hung like incredibly distant islands in an ocean of darkness. In the intervening void, a million light-years from anywhere, one solitary star formed an unmistakeable beacon in the emptiness of space. This was the primary Geta, a cosmological odd-man-out, jealously nursing its wilful satellite, the lone planet called Getawehi.

As the vibration of the planetary drive faded from the fabric of the ship, Van Noon forsook the computer and traced his second in command to the radio room.

"Colonel Nash wants to see us, Jacko. At last we're going to get a briefing on Project Ixion."

Jacko Hine was not impressed. "If it's all the same to you, Fritz, I'd rather get off here and start walking home. The more I learn about Getawehi the crazier it all becomes."

"Why? What's the matter now?"

"I've been checking the recordings to see why Brumas thought it necessary to use a laser channel to communicate with the ground force. I found the answer. In addition to an enormous magnetic field, Getawehi has an output of radio mush which exceeds that from Terra by about nineteen hundred to one."

Van Noon stopped abruptly. "Synchrotron emission or static?"

Jacko dropped the wire spools on the table. "Neither. Modulated carrier waves. There's no doubt of it. Long waves, short waves, v.h.f., u.h.f., and damn nigh into the X-ray band. You name it, and Getawehi has it. And some of those transmitters pack a punch which would make a Terran mega cast station look like a spark transmitter."

Van Noon began to look rather grey. "But there can't be any such transmitters on Getawehi. Hell, Jacko, it's uninhabited. There's no life form on Getawehi with an intelligence much above a jack-rabbit. So who's doing the broadcasting—ants?"

"I wouldn't know. But I can say that the radio output from the surface, mainly broadband carriers modulated by random noise, constitutes an almost perfect radio blanket."

"But it's damn ridiculous! Radio galaxies I have heard of, but what the heck am I supposed to make of a radio planet? It can't be a case of synchrotron emission, because you don't get that sort of electron energy on a habitable planet. Anyway, it wouldn't give you a modulated carrier. But what's left? Nothing much less than an array of conventional transmitting equipments—which is impossible—and even if it weren't, you'd still need power to get that sort of output. You can't get that by rubbing two pieces of lichen together."

Jacko smiled ruefully. "It makes a change to hear you condemn something as impossible. What's happened to the spirit of sweet unorthodoxy this morning?"

"It's gone a trifle sour on me. Hell, Jacko, Brumas has a ground crew down there. If there were big radio transmitters on Getawehi they'd surely have investigated them by now. So where's their report?"

"There wouldn't necessarily be a report. Communications between ground and the spacewatch have been rather sparse."

"But why? With a laser channel in operation they could have a thousand-way circuit in operation if they chose."

"Except for one thing. A reliable line-of-sight channel presupposes the space end of the transmission to be in a synchronous orbit. But you can't establish a synchronous orbit around something which lollops about in space like Getawehi does."

"I take your point," said Van Noon wearily. "We've just been trying to get some sense out of Getawehi's peculiar rotation scheme. The computer keeps throwing it back requesting further information. We can't find any set of postulates which goes halfway towards meeting the facts."

Jacko stood up. "You know, Fritz, I've followed you into some pretty crazy situations in the past few years. But from the way things are stacking up I have the premonition that Getawehi's going to be the craziest yet."

"And I've a horrid suspicion you're right. No planet is entitled to be as crazy mixed-up as is Getawehi. Even that self-disposing rocket was a highly unusual bit of do-it-yourself. Let's go see what gives with Project Ixion. If it's half as mad as Nash is suggesting, you're going to have company on that long walk home."

Colonel Nash looked up from a report-strewn table as Fritz and Jacko entered. He was obviously not looking forward to the interview.

"Sit down, gentlemen. You've no doubt wondered why I've left it this late to introduce you to Project Ixion. Frankly, it's because we've all been hoping that somewhere down the line there's been a ridiculous mistake. But I'm afraid our last analysis leaves us no such get-out. The improbable is absolutely true."

"Exactly what is Project Ixion?" asked Fritz.

"I'm only an engineer," said Nash. "I don't pretend to understand the theoretical work behind it. It has something to do with determining the possibility of borrowing entropy levels from other parts of the universe. If it could be done, it would place at our disposal almost limitless sources of power without having to expend any of our own resources."

"That I can see," said Fritz. "But why do it on Getawehi?"

"Theory suggested Getawehi as an ideal testbed for the experiment. Geta and its planetary satellite are so far removed from any galactic grouping that they effectively form a miniature galaxy of their own—a universe of two. Freedom from massed stars was something which the experiment demanded. From the theoretical standpoint there's no place in space quite like Getawehi."

"Amen!" said Jacko.

"So what's the problem?" asked Van Noon.

"The Ixion Project consisted of assembling two substantial prefabricated structures on Getawehi. One was a large turntable, and the second was a cantilever dish, which should have mounted on the turntable roughly after the manner of a steerable-dish radio telescope."

"So?"

"So this . . ." Nash threw a clip of message forms across the desk. Fritz picked it up and read speculatively.

GETAWEHI GROUND FORCE . . . TO NASH . . . TYCHO BRAHE . . . YOU OLD IDIOT . . . QUITE APART FROM OUR RIDICULOUS CONFINEMENT . . . MUST INFORM YOU NO UNCERTAIN TERMS THAT NO REPEAT NO PART OF IXION TURNTABLE CAN BE ASSEMBLED FROM PARTS PROVIDED . . .YOU MUST BE MAD . . . EXCLAMATION . . . WOOLEY . . . COMMANDING.

Van Noon turned to the second page and read on.

WOOLEY COMMANDING GROUND FORCE GETAWEHI . . . ASSURE YOU ALL PARTS IXION ASSEMBLED AND TESTED ON TERRA BEFORE TRANSHIPMENT . . . TRY HOLDING PLANS RIGHT WAY UP . . . NASH . . . TYCHO BRAHE.

Colonel Nash shifted his chair uncomfortably.

GETAWEHI GROUND FORCE . . . TO NASH . . . TYCHO BRAHE . . . NO PART OF TURNTABLE FITS EVEN WITH PLANS HELD SIDEWAYS . . . IMPOSSI-

BLE THESE PARTS EVER ASSEMBLED INTO ANYTHING ANYWHERE . . . YOU MUST BE JOKING . . . WHY DON'T YOU RESIGN QUERY . . . WOOLEY . . . COMMANDING.

Van Noon passed the first sheets to Jacko and continued reading.

WOOLEY COMMANDING GROUND FORCE GETAWEHI . . . SORRY TO LEARN OF YOUR NERVOUS CONDITION . . . AM ACQUIRING COMPETENT ENGINEER AS REPLACEMENT SOONEST . . . SUGGEST YOU AVOID ALCOHOL IF YOU CANT HANDLE THAT EITHER . . . NASH . . . TYCHO BRAHE.

There was one final sheet, which read:

GETAWEHI GROUND FORCE . . .TO NASH . . . TYCHO BRAHE . . . ALCOHOL YOU D . . .

The rest of the signal was certified as corrupt by the Signals Officer, but he omitted to indicate whether the corruption was semantic or technical. Van Noon looked up.

"So who was wrong?" he asked.

"Nobody," said Nash. "I saw the completed Ixion structure on Terra and it checked out to specification. It was dismantled and crated by Wooley's own team. The parts space-dropped on Getawehi were one hundred per cent accurate."

"But he says . . ."

"I know what he says—and this is the paradox—I happen to believe him. Wooley's a hell of a good engineer. If he says the parts don't fit, then they don't fit. It's not a question of personalities or expertise. It's simply the fact that something built on Terra will not re-assemble on Getawehi. Don't ask me why."

Fritz considered this in silence for a while. "That takes a bit of swallowing."

"I know. That's why I asked you to come. You specialise

in impossibilities—well here's another one for you."

"What do you want me to do?"

"Do? Brumas wants the construction team rescued from Getawehi. Naturally that's the first priority. But knowing the way you do things, I want you to go one step further. I want you to go down there and finish Ixion itself."

Van Noon examined his knuckles. "That may not be easy. This is a joint Service exercise with divided responsibilities. What sort of backing and resources can I count on?"

"I had a notion you'd ask that. Commander Brumas and I took the precaution of clarifying the position with Gen-Com. You must have friends up there, because their answer was unequivocal. As from the moment of this interview you are appointed Senior Adviser for the whole Getawehi-Ixion project. All units involved will take their instructions from you. Nice work, Lieutenant! As from this instant it's all your show."

With a thunderstruck expression, Van Noon shook the offered hand.

"Seriously?"

"Seriously. There's far too much money invested in this enterprise and far too much to gain to let it fall now. Frankly, this is a vote of confidence in unorthodoxy."

"Very well!" Van Noon turned to Sergeant Hine. "If you can manage to get your mouth closed, Jacko, we've got work to do."

"Like what, Fritz?"

"Like beating the daylights out of the computer, for a start. There must be some reason why that damn planet lollops all over space like that. And unless we can come to grips with the problem I'd guess we're in for a pretty rough landing."

Two days later, standard shipboard time, the *Tycho Brahe* quit hyperspace with a delicious quiver and proceeded on planetary drive to the rendezvous. In high orbit three supply ships circled the innocuous-looking mudball of Getawehi, while far below the solitary pinnace rode the lower circuit making a precariously bad job of maintaining a synchronised station above the ground base. Around them the fiery orb of Geta seemed to trace her possessive path as if guarding her solitary ugly-duckling of a planet. In all other directions the bare inkyness of the great void, shorn of the comforting beauty of individual stars, glowed with the light of a thousand million galaxies. And in one of these, one of countless millions of stars combining to form a solitary visual group, was an unexceptional primary called Sol—one of whose planets nursed the upstart blobs of protein called men who were daring to make space their own.

When the rendezvous was complete, Van Noon abandoned the computer for a telescope and found the results equally uninformative. From any angle of offworld approach, Getawehi refused to deliver up its secrets. Superficially it was a sparsely vegetated, rather uninviting ball of rock and earth. It had never achieved a life-form capable of developing any degree of civilisation and seemed content to go rolling perversely through space until the stars grew cold. Its only claim to activity was on the radio-frequency bands, where its output, inexplicably, was both prodigious and impenetrable.

Jacko watched the pencil being fractured by Fritz's powerful fingers.

"So how're we going to play it, Fritz?"

"I'm not sure yet. We don't seem able to gain any meaningful information from up here, so we'll have to go to where it's all happening."

"To Getawehi? So far they've wrecked every ferry rocket they've sent. Were you thinking of taking the whole UE group?"

"Not initially. Just the two of us, if you're game. I need to get down there to get the feel of the place."

Jacko shrugged. "I've got a pilot's licence, but in the circumstances I make no guarantee about the quality of touchdown."

"That's understood, Jacko. If you can get us down without any broken bones, it'll be the best we can expect."

"Brumas isn't going to be very happy. He's lost too many ferries already."

"He'll be a lot less happy if he goes back to Terra minus his ground crew. Frankly I don't see any alternative. Down there we stand a chance of doing something constructive. With the rest of the UE group still spaceborne we've at least hedged our bets."

"What sort of equipment do you want to take?"

"Just light-engineering kit. If we need anything special they can do a spacedrop."

"Assuming we can get into contact."

"Wooley has his laser link down there, but the thought comes to me that if we can get control of one of those superpower transmitters down there, the communications problem should be over."

"That's the bit that has me worried, Fritz. Where the hell are these transmitters? There's not a sign of them in the telescopes."

"I scarcely expected to find equipment shacks and antennae laid out in a row. Let's face it, Jacko, we're playing in a pretty weird sector of the universe. We're up against so many unknowns that we'd be lucky to recognise a dog before it bit us."

Three

"Can't you hold her, Jacko?" Van Noon was watching anxiously through the ferry viewports as the ground details of Getawehi grew more specific and less stable with their continued descent.

"She's beginning to fight the automatic control system. The inertial guidance platform says that Getawehi is directly under, while Getawehi's gravitation says that it's sideways."

"So who's right?"

"Both and neither. It's all a matter of relativity but it does raise complications. To exaggerate slightly, imagine trying to land a ship on a ramp angled at forty-five degrees from the horizontal. Do you approach at a true right-angle to the surface of the ramp, or do you follow the geocentric vertical?"

"Which way's softest?"

"Either way you're in trouble. If you choose the first, you're liable to topple. If you choose the second you're liable to skid down a one-in-one slope on one landing pad. Throw in the fact that your ramp is not only inconstant in angle but also varies in direction, and you have a rough idea of the dilemma facing both myself and the ship's computer at this moment."

"What happens if we remain controlled by the inertial platform?"

"We crash."

"What happens if we cut the automatics and try to achieve Getawehi's conception of the vertical?"

"We might just make it, if we conserve fuel and don't apply the corrections until the final moment. Only one problem—we don't know what Getawehi's conception of the vertical is. Even with the best of luck we're bound to come down askew on some parameter or other."

"Gyp the automatics and fall by line-of-sight for a while."

Jacko mopped his brow. "Right. I'm cutting all automatics except the stabilisation gyro. We'd have had to do that sooner or later anyway. A small craft like this doesn't have enough fuel to make course corrections on a continuous oscillatory basis."

Van Noon took up station by a viewport and watched the wildly plunging horizon with some dismay. "How far are we aiming to land from the base camp?"

"Under these conditions I couldn't guarantee any position within a twenty kilometre radius. I'm heading far out so that we don't risk putting a jet burn across the camp. The camp's at the foot of the valley, and I'm aiming to come in between those two mountain ranges, about halfway up the pass."

The rising scream from the ferry's outer skin told them of their entry into Getawehi's atmosphere. The laser altimeter raced suddenly alive and began to count down the distance to the surface, acknowledging Jacko's gentle application of the retro-rockets. Through the viewport the horizon spun wildly and disappeared from view. Fritz took one look through the opposite port at the alarming prospect of Getawehi approaching sideways-on, then ducked back to Jacko at the controls.

"If you call that a line-of-sight approach, we'd best go back for an optician."

Jacko took his hands from the controls momentarily. "If you think you can hold this she-devil in control any better, you're perfectly at liberty to try."

The success of this impromptu manoeuvre was dramatic. The ferry immediately ceased its wild swinging and settled into a more restricted pattern of deviation from the geocentric vertical. Jacko looked at the controls in considerable amazement.

"I don't get it!"

Van Noon thought for a moment, then his lips twisted into a grin of amusement. "I think I do. Both line-of-sight and inertial guidance are related to the geocentric vertical. All we did was substitute your reactions for those of the automatics. But we were wrong. All we have operating now is a simple stabilisation gyroscope. Don't you see what that means?"

"No."

"Where does the axis of a gyroscope point?"

"Near a planetary mass? Towards the centre of gravity if it's halfways orientated from the start."

"Precisely! And since Getawehi's gravitational centre is not a fixed point, the gyroscope is swinging the ship to follow the gravitational drift. That was the tendency the inertial guidance system was fighting. But we don't have to fight it—the gyroscope is already giving us the factor we need. It's automatically correcting us to Getawehi's concept of the vertical."

Jacko was not convinced. He concentrated on the task of matching their deceleration to altitude, seldom allowing his hands to move more than a hairsbreadth away from the guidance controls. His caution was proved unnecessary. With a reserve of power still to spare, they continued safely to the point where they were ready to make a soft landing.

But the actual moment of touchdown brought disaster. By virtue of being orientated to Getawehi's gravitational direction, the ferry hit the ground at an angle. The landing mechanisms refused to accept the situation, and the leg servos tried to force the ship to adopt a station at right angles to the terrain. Such a stance was inconsistent with their centre of gravity. The whole structure staggered alarmingly and seemed likely to topple. Van Noon reacted fast, his hands instinctively bringing the fail-safe system into over-riding control.

"Bail out, Jacko! If this thing goes over it's going to do some damage."

Jacko needed no prompting. He hit the emergency release, and jumped as the hatch fell open. Within seconds they scrambled clear of the great bulk of the swaying ferry, and scarcely had they paused to gain breath when the vessel gave a skip and a grunt and toppled disastrously behind them.

Shorn suddenly of the ship walls, they looked at each other in amazement as the full experience of Getawehi's peculiar gravity became a physical reality for them. The first sensation was vertigo, the second, nausea. What had been uphill when they first made touchdown was perceptibly shifting until it became across-the-hill, and, even as they watched, became downhill. Fritz's natural body orientation changed with the shifting direction of "up", and the heavens swung around him in a great arc as he moved into equilibrium with the changing conditions.

"Interesting!" said Fritz at last.

"I hope it's not going to do that often. I expect it when I'm drunk, but cold sober it comes as a bit of a shock to the system."

"I know what you mean, Jacko. On Terra 'up' is up, and it's inclined to remain that way. On Getawehi 'up' not only varies in direction but also in slope according to what angle to the geocentric its gravity is pulling."

"But how the heck does that work?"

"I don't know, but I'll figure an answer to it soon. Of course, even on Terra there's a sight distortion of gravitational direction due to the pull of the moon—hence the tides. But it's so slight it can't normally be noticed. If Getawehi had some extremely massive satellites, that could be a possible answer."

"Except that Getawehi hasn't got any satellites—none detected, anyway. And with the mass they'd need to produce an effect like that it would scarcely be possible to miss them."

"Mmm! We'll come back to that problem when we've had a chance to talk to Wooley's crew. In the meantime, consider the potential uses of a variable-direction gravity. Given a soapbox on wheels and decent set of brakes, you have all you need in the way of low-cost transport. You wait until your destination lies downhill, release the brakes and coast towards it. When your destination shifts uphill you drop anchor and wait."

"You couldn't run wheels over this stuff." Jacko kicked the soft ashy soil moodily.

"I wasn't thinking of it," said Van Noon. "That was purely by way of illustration. Something more in the nature of a sledge . . . to get us to the base camp."

"Moses!" Jacko turned back towards the fallen ferry. It was now a stiff uphill climb, and the ferry that approached from the side looked precariously unsafe. "I've just the thing, Fritz. The plastic cabin liners. Six sections meeting to form a dome. You couldn't have a better shape."

As he spoke the world seemed to rear perilously upwards, ship uppermost, as some new component of Getawehian gravity roughly doubled its field and threw the gravitational angle to something approaching forty-five degrees from the geocentric vertical. Standing now on a hillside plain which fell away below them in a one-in-one slope as far as the eye could see, they stopped in horror. The huge ferry vehicle, its weight now twice that on landing, crushed the soft ash-soil at the edge of the depression it had made for itself on falling, and began to roll murderously down upon them.

Their instinctive reaction was to turn and run down the monstrous incline in front of them. With rare presence of mind Van Noon caught Jacko's arm and forced him to run a diagonal path which took them barely clear of the rolling tail fins as the rogue spacecraft rolled a deep trail in the ash soil. The wisdom of Van Noon's diagonal path of escape was soon apparent. The rolling ship rapidly achieved a velocity which would have fatally outstripped a running man.

Then the angle of the terrain began to flatten again and the intolerable gravity lessened. The ferry rolled to a cumbersome halt as the incline down which it was moving became insufficient to support its motion. Finally the two unorthodox engineers trudged ironically up a slight incline after their errant vessel, approaching it from tail-on lest it should take it upon itself to roll again.

"Lesson one," said Jacko. "First catch your spaceship."

"We seem to be luckier than Wooley's ground crew. At least it hasn't dissolved on us."

"There's still time," said Jacko miserably. "The hatch is on the side. Dare we go in?"

Van Noon cast a wary look at the unstable skyline. "Not for very long. We don't know how often Getawehi goes in for a big pull like that. It'd be fatal to be trapped inside if it rolled again. What we really need is explosives to dig a real big ditch alongside. Once we got her into that we could work inside fairly safely."

"There's explosives in the tool hold."

"Do you know exactly where?"

"I stowed them there myself."

Fritz had been attempting to time the apparent rotation of the highest point of the skyline. Its movement was highly erratic, but there was a certain degree of progression. The coming angle was one soon to place the ship in a position to slip only noseward if it moved at all.

"When I give the word, you try to get in there and out again with the explosives in about seven minutes flat. If you hit trouble, get out without the explosives. But whatever you do, keep inside seven minutes."

Jacko nodded. When Fritz gave the signal he climbed swiftly to the hatch, fought the cover open, and disappeared inside. Van Noon spent an agonising seven minutes which lengthened into eight before a flurry of activity in the hatchway deposited a dozen packets of plastic mining explosive at his feet, followed by a box of detonators. It was ten minutes before Jacko himself got clear, having miscalculated the intricacies of manoeuvring in a space cabin with the gravitational attraction sideways on.

Van Noon was watching the shifting angle cautiously. He waved Jacko away urgently, but although the terrain began to slope in a direction which could have set the ferry rolling again, the angle did not become acute enough to bring the vessel into motion. Van Noon was quick to seize the opportunity. Mentally estimating the circumference of the vessel, he paced out the distance through which the hull needed to rotate in order to leave the hatch at the top.

They placed a chain of explosives across this distance line, with a one-minute detonator at the end. Priming the detonator, they ran across-hill to a safe distance and waited. The explosion ripped a long, deep trough in the soft ash, the edge of which reached almost to the ferry's hull. The shock of the explosion was just sufficient to overcome the forces which kept the great vessel from moving down the incline. Ponderously it rolled into the crater and settled, almost a third of its bulk below ground level.

Now they were able to work on the ferry with the minimum of risk, although the uncertainties of exactly what was "up" were peculiarly unsettling within the confines of the fallen ship. Time and again they were disturbed by the sudden fear that the hull was beginning to roll again, as some sudden change in gravitic direction or intensity made the "floor" apparently shift under them.

It took two hours to cut the cabin liners into sections suitable for two sleds. The shapes they obtained could scarcely have been more suitable for the purpose had they been custom designed. The only brake they could devise was a crude foot-operated device like a ploughshare bolted on to angle brackets at the rear of the sections. On test the brakes proved savagely effective, but the failing light made them put away thoughts of starting their journey before morning.

Very few of the services in the ferry still worked. From the growing acridness of the atmosphere inside, it was obvious that the chemical powerplant had been damaged. For this reason Van Noon decided they would be safer sleeping in the open. They spent the remaining time before darkness removing from the ship various tools and such few items of provisions as could be carried on the sleds.

Night came with explosive suddenness. The night sky was the first tangible reminder of their peculiar extra-galactic location. The only luminous bodies in the crystal-clear heavens were the great galactic clusters, magnificent in their raiment of light but with a unique sparseness and complexity which underscored the alienness of their situation.

They scuffed shallow grooves in the ash-soil in which to settle their sleeping pods, then climbed in, anxious to get some rest to meet the demands of the coming day. Such was their trust in the ecological and atmospheric climate of Getawehi that neither thought to place their face visors over their pods to ward off precipitation or biological attack. Their only inconvenience seemed to be the shifting gravity, which imparted to the pods the feeling of movement, as if lodged in the branches of a vast and slowly-swaying tree.

It was two hours after Geta's rays had set that Van Noon was awakened by a startled cry from Jacko.

"Fritz!"

"What the devil's the matter?"

"Look at the mountains—they're burning!"

Van Noon aroused himself and followed the indicated line. Surely enough, whole sections of the ranks of distant hills were lit with a red glow of such intensity that the sky was saturated with a blood-red cast.

"What is it? A forest fire?"

"Damned if I know, Jacko. That range is best part of thirty kilometres away. It would need to be one heck of a forest fire to be clearly visible from here."

As they watched, the fire on the burning mountains seemed to shift and change with running patterns and pulsations, forming a spectacle more absorbing than the species-long pastime of watching the flickering heart of a home-fire.

"It doesn't look right," said Van Noon after a while.

"Those currents in the flame are moving too fast and too regularly to be true. A forest fire is a set of small burning nuclei—individual conflagrations. But the way the flame out there flickers, it looks as if the mountain is burning *en masse.*"

"Could it be volcanic?"

"Not the kind of volcanism we're familiar with. Anyway, there was nothing about the structure of the rocks by daylight which suggested volcanic action."

"So what's happening over there, then? Don't tell me the whole mountain is made up of paraffin wax?"

"Nothing about Getawehi would surprise me," said Van Noon moodily. "But there's one thing that worries me."

"What's that?"

"There's too much power about. Those burning mountains are a pretty powerful display of something—so is the radio output and the mixed-up gravity. They're all power manifestations of considerable magnitude. But it's always output, with never a sign of the origin. It's as if there's a very much larger force at work—a force so large that it can afford to spill over a few billion kilowatts as side effects and never notice the loss."

"I had the same idea. None of the demonstrations we've seen so far seem lacking for a few billion ergs. I'm not keen on the implications. If there is a large power source around, I like to know where it is and what it is. It helps to know if you have to get out from under in a hurry."

Getawehi swung "up" sideways, momentarily exerted a gravitational pull which almost broke their backs, then reduced its attraction to such an extent that their pods almost left the surface. There was another twist in gravitational angle, then the burning mountains, which had so far seemed to be up a slight gradient, slipped to the bottom of a racing slope of one-in-two. Then, as if to complete the performance, the burning mountains went out—like the turning-off of a lamp.

"You know, Fritz," said Jacko as he sank back into his pod, "Colonel Nash was right. There is no place in space quite like Getawehi."

Four

At first light the next morning they had a trial run of the sleds. By reasonable guesswork their present position from the base camp was about fifty kilometres—an uncomfortable journey if made on foot over the soft ash. For direction they had only to follow the valley floor between the two mountain shoulders to a point where the mountains succumbed to the broad and rocky steppe, the edge of which had been the scene of the disastrous first landing by the construction crew.

To their delight the sleds ran easily over the ashy soil, even when presented with only slight gravitational gradients. The vehicles were prone, however, to come to an unexpected halt on meeting patches of the purple fern which clustered the landscape. A few outcropping rocks were an additional hazard which required careful negotiation. There was no way of steering the flat-bottomed sleds. Wherever obstacles were encountered, it was necessary to halt and manually drag the sled to a new position. Occasionally the gravitational angle produced slopes insufficient to support their motion, and these had to be borne in patient immobility, as did the passing of all slopes other than the one leading in the required direction.

After a survival-ration breakfast they secured to the sleds such items of tools and provisions as they were able to make fast. Then, waiting for the terrain to slope in a suitable direction, they set off. The air was crystal clear and inhabited with a crisp coolness and a heather-honeyed perfume which was decidedly pleasant. Far to their right the burning mountains, now quiescent, stood up glassy and apparently untouched by the conflagration of the night. Nearer and to their left, a vast outcropping of grey-white striated rock formed, with the burning mountains, the shoulders of the valley, some forty kilometres across, through which lay their route.

Their mode of transport proved both exhilarating and predictably hazardous. Swooping down an apparent slope of one-in-three, the ground reared suddenly upwards before them. Fritz managed to drive to a halt, but the momentum of Jacko's sled ploughed it a metre depth into the ash soil before it came to rest. Climbing out from the ditch which he had dug, Jacko's look of murderous reproach threw Fritz into fits of laughter.

However, it was Van Noon who nearly became the first casualty. Driving down a deep slope, where the sled velocity must have been nearing fifty kilometres an hour, the progress of Fritz's sled was suddenly arrested by a patch of fern. Fritz parted company with the sled and proceeded without visible means of support for a considerable distance before he made a spread-eagled landing. He got up, shaken, but miraculously unhurt. Nevertheless much of the equipment he had been carrying on the sled was lost in the ash and could not be recovered.

Despite these and similar incidents and frequent halts while their intended direction lay sullenly uphill or across, they made very good progress. By tacking across their general course they found they could make use of nearly half of the available angles. The mountain shoulders gave them an easy sense of direction without reckoning and at last they reached the end of the broad valley. Before them now began one of the great steppes of Getawehi, a spotted, rock-strewn desert, completely without vegetation. It continued as far as the eye could see—monotonous and inhospitable.

Jacko viewed the prospect critically.

"We could never cross that on the sleds, Fritz. Too many rocks. There's less than a hundred metre straight run anywhere."

"It's fortunate that we don't have to. By my calculation the construction team ditched somewhere between the steppe and the end of the grey-white mountain. If so, we should be nearly within sighting range by now."

They scanned the area anxiously, but found no sign of the base camp.

"Have you got any distress rockets or anything similar in those bits and pieces of yours, Jacko?"

"No. But I've got some plastic explosive left, and a few detonators. We could at least make a big bang."

"That should do the trick. If we can only get some sort of answering signal to guide us we should be able to locate them fairly easily from here. They should be on the lookout anyway, because they must have seen our ferry fall."

They arranged three explosions, separated by a one minute and then a thirty-second interval. After what seemed like a ten minute wait a slight column of smoke rose up near the grey-white mountain's end at about five kilometres distance.

"That appears to be them," said Van Noon. "Let's go over and meet the troops."

By a fortunate coincidence of angle and direction they covered the distance in record time. Swooping from the heights of a big slope they came suddenly across a string of a dozen men labouring on foot up an ashen trail. The party was encumbered with axes, ropes, and miscellaneous rescue equipment. As Van Noon and Jacko braked to a halt, the file of men dropped their loads, and, with a loud cheer, came dashing to greet them.

The teamleader was the first to arrive.

"My name's Wooley. We saw your fire-bucket come down behind the mountains somewhere, but nightfall beat us to it. We were just on our way to find you. Frankly we didn't expect any survivors, from the angle she was making when she hit."

"We were lucky," said Van Noon. "We managed to get out before she toppled." He had the distinct impression that Wooley was not too enthusiastic about their arrival.

"Just the two of you aboard?"

"Yes, but I'm afraid we lost the ship. She'll never make space again. But there's a lot of useful stores and equipment in her if you can get them out."

"We'll get them out somehow," said Wooley. "As for losing the ship, that was a foregone conclusion. The spacecraft isn't yet made which can land undamaged on Getawehi. I don't wish to seem critical, but just what did you hope to achieve by joining the suicide club?"

"I'm Van Noon," said Fritz. "By some mischance I seem to have finished up with the responsibility for this little lot."

"Van Noon?" Wooley screwed up his face. "Weren't you mixed up in that affair on Tazoo?"

"For my sins, yes," said Fritz ruefully. "But by all accounts Getawehi has Tazoo beaten by several orders of magnitude. Jacko and I decided that if we didn't want to spend the next five years driving computers neurotic we'd better get down here and get the feel of it ourselves."

"Then welcome to Getawehi!" said Wooley sadly. "But believe me, you're in for a whole lot more surprises yet."

In the meantime, a few of the construction team had borrowed Jacko's sled and had been making short experimental trips across the terrain whenever the opportunity presented itself. Wooley had watched these antics without much enthusiasm, but one particularly successful run captured his interest. He examined Fritz's sled more closely.

"Did you come all the way on this?"

"About fifty kilometres since sunrise."

Wooley turned and clasped Fritz's hand in a sudden handshake. "Sorry, Fritz! I knew I was being replaced as head of team, but I thought we'd merely get a new boy who'd be making all the same mistakes until he wound up six weeks later in the same situation as I'm in. I hadn't stopped to think of the unorthodox angle. You know, if we'd been at the wreck and wanted cabin liners back at the base camp . . . Dammit, we'd have carried them!"

"Forget it!" said Fritz. "You're not being replaced. It's simply that the overall control for the entire project has transferred itself from its lofty orbital heights to the place where things actually happen."

"You mean they've given you control of the *whole* lot?" Wooley was incredulous.

"Just that. The veritable hot potato."

"No potato that," said Wooley sadly shaking his head. "What they dumped on you was a small star. Come back to base and I'll try to explain it."

"I'd appreciate that," said Fritz. "It's about time somebody gave me a rational explanation of why a group of experienced engineers can't assemble a kit of prefabricated parts."

For a moment Wooley's eyes looked haunted. "I didn't say I'd give you a rational explanation . . . I only said I'd try to explain."

The base camp was a camp in little more than name only. Originally the site of a single space-drop of heavy equipment, it had become the focal point of the endeavours of the construction team solely because there was no incentive to go elsewhere. Behind the site lay the grey-white mountain chain. In front lay the vast mottled steppe. On the ashy no-man's-land between the two, were gathered various space-drop capsules, some of which had obviously contained parts for the Ixion project. Also there were capsules from later drops, clearly marked as having contained emergency survival supplies.

Living quarters, such as there were, had been constructed from well-entrenched girderwork "borrowed" from the abandoned assembly project, overtopped by parachute material from the space-drop canopies. All the men seemed fit, but it was obvious that the prolonged period of enforced grounding on Getawehi, coupled with strict rationing, was beginning to have its effect. The most disquieting aspect was the look of resignation which rested in their eyes.

Fritz looked out over the broad steppe, something about the configuration of ferns and rocks stirring a thread of memory.

"Isn't this the place where your first ferry sank?"

"Sank!" Wooley was incensed. "It didn't sink . . . it was melted."

"You have to be joking!"

"Do I just! You watch this!"

Wooley turned, seized a crowbar from an abandoned toolkit, and tossed it out on to the rock-strewn desert. One end struck the grey sand, while the other touched a protruding rock. There was a blue spark as it touched. For seconds it seemed as if nothing was going to happen. Then to Fritz and Jacko's astonishment the tool began to glow a visible cherry red. Its temperature continued to increase through white heat to a point where the iron bent and fused into a pool of molten iron. The incandescent metal dribbled into a thread and ran apart. The arc which struck as the curious circuit broke was more in the nature of an explosion, and the watching trio ran for their lives as the area was deluged with droplets of red-hot iron and warm sand.

"Convinced?" asked Wooley, when they had retreated to a safe distance.

"Convinced," agreed Van Noon weakly. "It must have taken a couple of thousand amperes to melt a bar like that."

"It must have taken many millions of amperes to melt our ship," said Wooley gloomily, "but it did it somehow."

"But this is ridiculous, Fritz!" said Jacko. "How can you have an electrified desert?"

"Not too ridiculous really. Even on Terra you can find a surprising amount of electrical currents in the earth if you go looking for them. On Terra the source is usually electrochemical—minute differences in electrode potential between regions containing different concentrations of mineral substances. But I don't know of any natural source capable of producing some dozens of volts at many millions of amperes—or why the system doesn't discharge itself."

"We've done some investigating," said Wooley. "The grey rocks you can ignore, but we call the black rocks 'terminals'. Actually they aren't simple rocks at all, but columnar graphite structures presumably reaching down to the bedrock. They have an insulating sheath, a sort of lacerated asbestos, which we theorise came to be deposited by electrophoresis of the soil silicates. But however it came about, it's damned effective in insulating the columns from the rest of the plain. The remaining bulk of the desert is merely a mineralated silicate-base earth, not unlike Terran clay. Average potential difference between the terminal columns and the base land is about twenty-seven volts. But it varies pretty widely and can touch a couple of hundred volts in the high season."

"A.c. or d.c.?" asked Jacko, beginning to recover from the shock.

Wooley began to look rather haggard and turned away for a moment.

"You aren't going to believe this," he said. "Generally it's d.c. with the terminals positive with respect to the baseland. But sometimes you get a.c.—especially on Tuesday and Sunday mornings."

Five

"And if you think that's mad," said Wooley, "wait until you start on the Ixion project."

"You know, Fritz, I'm beginning to get sorry I came." Jacko looked at Van Noon appealingly. "Can't I just go home and sleep it off?"

"Try closing your eyes, Jacko. Maybe it'll go away."

"I tried that," said Wooley. "But it comes back every morning, large as sunrise."

"Well, what *is* the Ixion problem?" Van Noon asked. "The one thing I haven't been able to do is get anyone to talk about it."

"Wait till you've seen it for yourself. I don't think you'll want to talk about it either."

They were approaching a stockpile of carefully classified girderwork, part of the Ixion turntable structure recovered from spacedrop capsules. Wooley consulted a parts list, then drew a few sections from the stockpile and dropped them on the ground.

"A simple demonstration. Girder A measures two metres exactly between hole centres. Don't take my word for it—check it out."

Jacko produced a steel tape from the recesses of one of his pockets and made the necessary measurement.

"Two metres—check!"

"Girders B and C each measure one metre between hole centres, yes?"

"Check!" Jacko looked at Fritz as if seeking release from the infantile nature of what was being demanded.

"Very well!" Wooley was unperturbed. "If you assemble

girder B to girder C, end to end with a suitable rivet, the total length between extreme hole centres should be two metres. Right?"

"Right."

"Wrong," said Wooley sadly. He dropped a rivet on to the ground and waited while Jacko moved the components into line and fitted the fastening loosely into the holes. "If you don't believe me, measure it yourself."

There was no need for measurement. Even viewed from a standing position the combined length of the two half girders was obviously much less than that of the whole one. Refusing to believe the evidence of his eyes, Jacko knelt and carefully measured the combined length of girders B and C.

"One point five seven," he said hopelessly. Again refusing to accept the sum, he kicked the girders apart and checked each carefully before re-assembly. Fritz, who had watched the whole performance with detailed interest, seemed to have withdrawn into a state of deep concentration. At last he took the offered measuring tape from Jacko and repeated the whole ritual for himself. Intrigued by the situation, he found several other objects and measured them individually and together. Then he straightened.

"Incredible," he said, "but very definitely true."

"Then explain it to me," said Jacko. "In all my books twice one is two—and it's never before been in dispute."

"But your books were written on Terra, not Getawehi. On Getawehi they don't apply."

"But that's insane!" Jacko was adamant. "Mathematics is merely a system for expressing the properties and relations of quantities. It's universal, not a local phenomenon. Once one is one, twice one is two. . ."

Van Noon flicked out a slide rule and rapidly reviewed his previous calculations.

"Not on Getawehi. It seems to be different here. Once one is one. . . but twice one is only a bit over one and a half—one point five seven zero eight, to be more exact. And three times one is about two point three six."

"Wooley, you don't agree . . .?" Jacko was still fighting.

The look on Wooley's face, however, convinced him that the battle was lost. "I still don't see how it's possible," he finished lamely.

"It's long been suspected that our mathematics may not be universal," said Fritz. "Dimensionless numbers, for instance, although having an accepted value in the part of the universe where we customarily use them, are more likely to be local coincidences than physical absolutes. But on Getawehi we seem to have hit on something even more fundamental."

"Such as?"

"I'm not sure yet, but for my money it's something to do with unity."

"Unity?"

"Yes. Unity . . . one . . . a whole. I'm no mathematician, but it seems to me there's a dam great hole in our idea of the structure of numbers. We've explored number structure up to infinity and several orders beyond—but something we've always taken for granted is the constant mathematical value of unity."

"But it has to have a constant mathematical value." Jacko's voice was ragged. "Once one is one . . . It can't be otherwise by its very definition."

"So we've always assumed. But what if we happened to be wrong? What if there's a difference between the value of one as representing a whole thing—and the value of one as a mathematical factor. They seem both to be the same in the corner of the universe where our books were written—but one used as a factor on Getawehi is demonstrably only point seven eight five of what it was on Terra."

"You're not right, you know, Fritz. I'll prove it to you."

"How?"

"Take a metre length of iron, cut it in half and then join it together again. By your reasoning we should finish up with a total length only a little above three-quarters of what we started with."

"Let's try it," said Van Noon. "We have to settle this one way or the other before we all go merrily insane."

Wooley provided welding equipment, and they tried it. The

final measurement was a little over point seven eight of a metre.

“But I still don’t see how you can reconcile it with the law of conservation of matter,” said Jacko.

“Where do you keep the alcohol?” asked Fritz Van Noon.

“So what are we going to do with Project Ixion?” asked Jacko the next day.

“I’ve been thinking,” said Fritz. “It’s not going to be easy even if it proves possible. The Ixion assembly is a pretty complex girderwork construction. Every part has to be accurate if it’s going to fit. My first thoughts are to take every girder, cut it in half, and re-join. In that way we might be able to construct what is, in effect, a scaled-down version of the original design.”

“Is that acceptable?” asked Jacko. “Surely some of the parts have a critical size.”

“I don’t know. I tried to put this question to the *Tycho Brahe*, but I don’t think my message was received. Apparently the pinnace can hold our position by line of sight, but it’s not easy for us to track the pinnace because of its unstable orbit. Anyway, I suspect this is a problem for the design team on Terra rather than something which can be settled on the *Tycho*.”

“Then you want me to try cutting and joining the girders?”

“We’d better have a go. We certainly can’t make matters any worse than they are. I’ve a suspicion, however, that the problem isn’t going to be solved that simply.”

“You’re the boss!” said Jacko. “I still can’t convince myself that it happens at all, but at least we’ll go through the motions.”

Six hours later Jacko found Van Noon crouching at the laser terminal trying to maintain sighting on the pinnace. Such was the relative crudity of the ground terminal that sighting on a small and erratic spaceborne target such as the pinnace was so precarious as to be nearly impossible.

Jacko shook his head wearily. “Project Ixion’s no go, Fritz.

We've tried cutting and joining the girders, but it doesn't help. Where the assembly calls for a total span to be formed of thirty components along one edge and only five in another, the whole scheme falls down. Short of cutting every girder into the total number of parts required to form the entire project—and then re-joining them—we don't stand a chance of getting anything to fit."

Van Noon stood up. "I was rather afraid of that. We'd need a computer down here to calculate the operations needed to resurrect the original design, and even then we've no guarantee that the final de-scaled assembly would do the job it was designed to do."

"Is it worth continuing with the work?"

"No. Abandon the whole thing. There *has* to be a more rational way out of this. As far as I can see, Ixion in its present form is destined to be a dead duck. I wonder where the heck they found a name like that for it anyway."

"Mythology—rather symbolic as it turns out," said Jacko mournfully. "Ixion was a character who killed his father-in-law and then tried to make love to Jupiter's wife. As punishment, Jupiter ordered him to be tied to a fiery wheel and rolled forever throughout Hades. Right now I know exactly how Ixion felt."

Van Noon was suddenly alert. "Say that again, Jacko."

"Right now I know exactly how Ixion felt . . ."

"Not that! About the wheel?"

"Tied to a fiery wheel and rolled for ever throughout Hades . . ."

"That could be it!"

"What's on your mind, Fritz?"

"I've just realised how it's done. Why didn't I think of it before?"

"You're way ahead of me. How what is done?"

"The gravity, of course. And the burning mountains, the radio output, and the self-consuming spaceship—they're all part of the same scheme."

"Can we just go back to the start?"

Van Noon was jubilant. "That *has* to be the answer!

Wheels within wheels . . . the fiery wheel of Ixion . . . rolling forever throughout Hades . . . suddenly the pieces all fit together. All we have to do is prove it."

"I'll get them to spacedrop a good psychiatrist."

"Not for me, Jacko. I never use 'em. But if I can get my hands on a good computer and a hyper-radio link with Terra, I think I've just made the Ixion project obsolete."

SIX

"Radio Officer presents his compliments, sir. Requests yourself and Commander Brumas to come to the radio room immediately."

Nash returned the salute and shot a quizzical look at Brumas, who was sitting near him at the conference table. Then he looked back to the courier.

"Is it important?"

"Radio messages loud and clear from Lieutenant Van Noon on Getawehi, sir."

"Radio messages? I thought radio was impossible under these conditions? Dammit!" He looked round at the expectant faces of the officers present at the conference. "In the circumstances, gentlemen, I'm afraid I must call this meeting to a close. It would seem Van Noon has already achieved something of the impossible. There'll be a progress report at twenty-hundred hours ship's standard time. Until then, all sections are to stand in readiness. This may be the break we're looking for."

With Brumas at his heels, Nash reached the radio room in record time. The Radio Officer was supervising a narrow-band lock on the big receiver, which appeared to be tuned to a slowly drifting signal.

"Van Noon to *Tycho Brahe*. Are you receiving me? I say again . . ."

"Can we answer?" asked Nash.

"Not by radio. We haven't anything available with the sort of power that Van Noon's using. All our transmissions would get lost in the mush. We're just linking a relay so that we can answer via the laser circuit on the pinnace. It's easier for us to get messages in that way than it is for Van Noon to get messages out."

"Fine!" Nash waited impatiently for the hookup to be completed. "Hullo, Fritz! We are receiving you perfectly. How the Devil did you come by a high-power transmitter like that?"

Van Noon's voice came over the noise with rare fidelity. "If I told you, Colonel, you wouldn't believe me. Anyway, thank heavens I've managed to raise you. I've been calling for nearly two hours."

"We weren't watching for you on the radio bands because we didn't think it possible for you to use them."

"Anything's possible once you know how."

"I'm glad to hear you say it. How're you making out with the Ixion project?"

"I agree with Wooley that we might as well sell the existing parts for scrap. No one could ever assemble them on Getawehi."

"That wasn't the answer I wanted to hear." Nash was disappointed. "Is there no hope at all?"

"Not for the Ixion structure. But the Ixion *principle* might be a different matter. Unless I miss my guess, we can duplicate the function of the Ixion project without actually building it. But I'm going to need help."

"You name it, and you've got it, Fritz. By the way, Commander Brumas is anxious to speak to you, so I'm handing over for a moment."

"Hullo, Commander! You'll be pleased to know the whole team down here is fit and well."

"I suppose that's some consolation." Brumas was grave. "Did you get around to having any ideas as to how we can get them off Getawehi?"

"Get them off?" Van Noon sounded surprised, then the humour came through in his voice. "I don't think that'll be much of a problem. When the *Tycho Brahe* makes planetfall they can wander aboard just like anybody else."

There was silence for a long moment, broken only by the

hiss of white noise on the radio link and the muted hum of the radio room equipment.

Finally Brumas spoke. "I don't think I quite understood you there, Fritz. For a moment I thought you were suggesting that the *Tycho Brahe* make planetfall on Getawehi. I . . ."

"That's exactly what I did say, Commander. I need the *Tycho Brahe* down here. I need the hyper-radio link, I need the ship's computers, and I need a mass of manpower."

"But you can't jeopardise the *Tycho Brahe*. For pity's sake, Fritz! You know what happens to a ship attempting to make planetfall on Getawehi."

"I know what used to happen, but we've got ourselves a few answers since then."

"You can't be serious, Fritz?" Colonel Nash was back on the circuit. "There's no point in writing off the Labship as well."

"I don't intend to write it off. All I need is a direct two-way speech link with the senior pilot during the talkdown. Given that, I'll guarantee a safe touchdown and that the ship will remain intact after landing."

"I can't permit it," said Brumas. "The risk is far too great."

"Are your recorders on, Commander?" asked Van Noon.

"Certainly. Standard procedure—why do you ask?"

"Because I want this firmly placed on record. I was appointed Senior Adviser for the whole exploit. My considered senior advice is that you should bring the *Tycho Brahe* to planetfall on Getawehi. If you should ignore this advice, I demand that this recording be placed in evidence at any court martial which may subsequently transpire. If you don't do as I ask you have no chance at all of recovering the team on Getawehi."

"Damn you, Fritz!" said Brumas. "Let me speak to Wooley. I want evidence as to the unsoundness of your state of mind."

"You already have evidence. Look through your telescopes. Wooley's out in the valley with his crew, laying out landing markers to guide your descent."

"Very well, Fritz . . . you win!" Nash's voice carried begrudged acquiescence. "It'll take about an hour to put the ship in a state of readiness. After that you can begin talk-down. But I hope you know how much responsibility you're taking on yourself. There's two hundred men aboard the *Tycho Brahe*."

"I know it, Colonel. But I wouldn't put a mouse down on Getawehi unless I was absolutely sure."

"I still don't see how the hell you can be so certain. Every other ship that has touched the planet has come to a sticky end."

"It's just that I'm beginning to gain an understanding of Getawehi. It seems that she and I both have the same sort of outwards-facing-interior approach."

High above them in the uncertain heavens a tiny firepoint denoted the position of the descending *Tycho Brahe*. Its visual distance belied the fantastic thunder of its jets. Even from the extreme altitude the sound carpeted the land with a pattern of thunderous echoes which were reflected and amplified by the valley's throat. With sweat on his brow, and a shielded microphone pressed at his throat, Van Noon was making the critical talkdown. At his side, Jacko, operating both rangefinder and telescope, recited a constant stream of information which served as an informative background to Fritz's constant monologue.

The Labship, its falling now controlled only by braking jets and stabilisation gyroscope, was weaving an erratic course through the lower atmosphere. Its point of destination was a mere approximation due to its curious deviations from the geocentric vertical. Everything now depended on the smooth continuance of the radio link with the *Tycho Brahe's* pilot, and upon the pilot's ready acceptance of Fritz's instructions. In such a manoeuvre the pilot's word was law. It was his decision to accept or reject advice affecting the safety of his ship, and his replies were routed via a laser link from the ship to the ground.

"Make ready for touchdown. Cut outer jets. Full boost on central thruster . . ." Van Noon's voice continued precisely above the wave of sound as the mammoth ship loomed in the air above them. "Gently cut back . . . try for a ve-ry soft landing . . . don't worry about the angle you're making . . . Doing nicely now . . . only metres to go . . . and as soon as you feel the ground, cut jets and cut leg servos."

"Are you mad? With the terrain sloping at this angle?" The pilot's voice came back with swift dissension.

Van Noon was firm. "Do as I say, or you've no chance whatever."

"Check! I can feel the ground. Cutting jets and leg servos. What about the gyro?"

"Leave it running."

"Are you sure?"

"I'm sure about nothing on Getawehi. But leave it running. Oh, and one thing more . . . for Pete's sake don't let your engineers dismantle anything. If they do, they'll never get it reassembled."

The frantic bellowing of the jets subsided and the blinding hailstorm of dislodged ash soil settled in a broad area to reveal the *Tycho Brahe* safely planetbound but leaning at a decided angle to the vertical. Open mouthed, everyone waited for her to topple. Those of Wooley's team who were able to manoeuvre sleds "downhill" came shooting across the valley, convinced they were on their way to a major catastrophe. Van Noon only smiled slightly to himself and mopped his brow, directing Jacko to watch the stability of the Labship's landing pads which were buried deeply in the loose Getawehian soil.

As the uncertain gravity altered its angle and continued its slow rotary progression it became apparent that the towering mass of the ship was not going to topple. Jacko reported that the landing assemblies were firmly planted and showed no sign of wanting to tear out and wander, as had those of the first ferry on Getawehi. With an air of uncertainty the nose-tip of the great craft moved in a broad arc as the angle at which the ship was leaning followed the migrating highest point of the horizon. Even so, it was nearly half an hour before the shipboard establishment cancelled the state of blast-off emergency and could be encouraged to open the hatches and leave the ship.

Characteristically, once the decision had been made, Colonel Nash was first out. He moved thirty paces from the ship, turned and looked dubiously at the huge bulk leaning above him, then set off downhill at a steady run until he was sure he had put more than a ship's length between himself and the metal Nemesis. During the course of the run, what had been downhill became across-the-hill and finally began to curve upwards. He stopped then, shaking his head sadly, and walked the rest of the way to Fritz's control point.

Van Noon wearily laid down the microphone and saluted. "Welcome to Getawehi, Colonel!"

"It's an experience I could well have done without," said Nash. "I must congratulate you on safely conducting our touchdown, but it does raise a few interesting questions."

"Like what, sir?"

"Like how the hell did you do it? Every other craft has either toppled or walked its way to destruction."

"Simple," said Fritz. "I played Getawehi at its own game. If Getawehi wants it that 'up' is angled umpteen degrees from the geocentric vertical, then so be it. Let the ship come down out of vertical, and let it stay that way when it's landed. The thing you mustn't do is try to fight it. It's axiomatic that Getawehi is going to have a last word."

"But won't the *Tycho Brahe* walk?"

"No, and for the same reason. The leg servos, which are responsive to the geocentric vertical, have been cut out. We're not trying to use a stiff leg where a bent one is needed."

"I'll take your word for it," said Nash heavily. His eyes were still nervously watching the trials of the leaning spaceship. Then he shrugged resignedly. "Very well, Fritz! You've got the *Tycho Brahe* down here, hyper-radio transmitters, computers, and all. You've demonstrated that the Ixion structure cannot be built—so now let's hear your plans for an alternative."

"First," said Fritz, "I have to prove a theory. For that I need the computers and a lot of manpower. If I can prove what I suspect is true, I shall then need contact with Terra to verify that Getawehi itself can supply the information that Ixion was intended to collect."

"The entire ship's facilities and the manpower's yours. All I ask is that we can make a getaway from Getawehi in a reasonably short period of time. Which reminds me, you haven't yet explained how you managed to acquire such a powerful radio transmitter."

"I left the details of that to Jacko Hine. But I don't think he much likes talking about it either."

Seven

It took three weeks, with teams ranging over a several hundred mile radius, for Fritz to collect and collate the necessary information. For most of this time the shipboard computers on the *Tycho Brahe* worked continuously, sifting the data from the on-line transducers and from recorders which the sled teams kept bringing in. Piece by piece the pattern which Van Noon had intuitively deduced was verified and described in the mathematical detail which only a high-power computing complex has the ability to construct. From this Van Noon re-drew his simplified models more suited for communication between men. When he was satisfied, he established a hyper-radio link with Terra. For three days more the ship's computers chattered to and were interrogated by their counterparts in the Terran Computing Centre, while Van Noon himself argued on a more prosaic level with the Ixion Project design team.

On the last day he gained the point he had been seeking, and called an immediate conference of all senior personnel concerned. When they were seated, he rose and passed the message transcript round the table.

VAN NOON . . . TYCHO BRAHE . . . AGREE ALL POINTS . . . INFORMATION SUPPLIED PROVES IXION ENTROPY CONCEPT VALID AND VIABLE . . . PROJECT NOW DRAWN SUCCESSFUL CONCLU-

SION . . . THIS MOMENT HISTORIC . . . CONGRATULATIONS ALL CONCERNED . . . IXION CONTROL.

After a few minutes Colonel Nash rose uncertainly to his feet.

"Gentlemen . . . I'm sure we're all glad to know that the Ixion concept is viable. And I'm sure we're all delighted to share in the congratulations for the successful conclusion of the project—especially after it was so nearly a disaster. But I have one important question to ask. Fritz . . . what the hell is going on?"

Van Noon stood up, grinning broadly. "I must apologise, gentlemen, if the last phases of the operation seemed something of a mystery. The trouble was that I leaped to a conclusion about Getawehi which was so unorthodox that I doubt if you'd given me a second hearing had I attempted to explain. Fortunately, events have proven me right. In case any of you haven't already reasoned the position for yourselves, I shall now be happy to explain. Of course, the whole key lies in the peculiar nature of Getawehi's gravity."

"You have an idea of what causes the variations?" Brumas was sharply attentive.

"Yes. I theorised that the effect was consistent with the presence of orbiting satellites of very considerable mass. In point of fact, what we were experiencing was the result of several interacting gravitational attractions rather than the single one to which we are accustomed on Terra."

"Ingenious!" said Brumas. "But not very convincing. To take the main point—Getawehi *has* no satellites."

"I'm afraid you're wrong," said Van Noon. "We have orbital plottings of three major satellites and the reasonable suspicion that at least another twenty minor ones exist."

"Rubbish! I tell you there are no such things." Brumas was becoming annoyed. "Dammit, we've been observing the planet from space for over six months now."

"From space you wouldn't see them. You see, Commander, they happen to be internal satellites—orbiting beneath the planetary surface."

"Nonsense!" Brumas flared with anger. "If this is some sort of a joke . . .!"

Colonel Nash rose and calmed the sudden uproar. "Gentlemen, I think you now see why Lieutenant Van Noon didn't attempt to discuss the matter before. Very few of you have been exposed, as I have, to Van Noon's contempt for orthodoxy. At first sight it always hits below the belt. But somehow the damned idiot always makes it so plausible that I can assure you it's futile to get into an argument with him." He turned back to Van Noon. "I assume, Fritz, that you do have some justification for this amazing statement?"

"Certainly!" Fritz was unruffled. "By the use of weight-loaded strain gauges distributed over a wide area, we have been able to plot the mass, size, and orbits of the three major satellites. The orbital information is precise and all orbits fall well within the mantle of Getawehi. The mass and size figures are enough to make your hair curl."

"Why so?"

"Because the only material known in the universe which could possibly have that mass and density is material which has itself suffered gravitic collapse—degenerate star-stuff—matter so far collapsed on itself that its atoms are virtually in contact with each other."

"As would be material from completely exhausted dwarf-stars?"

"If it were possible, yes. Factually, these small satellite bodies constitute over two-thirds of Getawehi's actual mass. Their orbital speed is low, and the planet is virtually an envelope which lollops around the variable centre of gravity of the satellite group. Getawehi's surface gravity is a compromise between its own weak attraction and the higher, yet mobile, attraction of the hyper-dense orbiting nuclei."

"Are we to understand, then, that Getawehi is hollow?" Nash was puzzled.

"Far from it. Its internal structure is probably not too dissimilar from that of Terra, except that the crust and solid mantle of Getawehi must be many times thinner. Also the whole inner core must be in a molten state—probably molten nickel-iron. It's within this core of liquid metal that the satellites orbit."

"If you say so." Nash settled back and chewed his moustache. "Very well, Fritz! I'll accept that, because I've no doubt that you have it well documented. Now tell us what you used as a substitute for the Ixion assembly?"

"In a moment," said Fritz. "First let me deal with the electrified desert, since it's all part of the same story. There just had to be some natural mechanism available capable of producing substantial voltages at an almost limitless current. I approached the problem by considering what type of winding generator could produce this order of electrical output. The answer was a homopolar generator."

"A what?"

"A homopolar generator—the simplest electrical generator ever devised. It consists essentially of a large conducting disc or rotor, spinning in a magnetic field. Once I had hit on the idea of satellites orbiting in a molten metal core, the answer was obvious. Getawehi has a strong magnetic field, and nine-tenths of her volume is a rotating ball of conductive, liquid metal. Getawehi is a homopolar generator, and one of no mean proportions. The black rodlike terminals apparently project through the solid mantle and act as current pickoffs. I suspect that variations in output are somehow associated with satellite turbulence and to the fact that frequently the whole system gets its axis out of line with the planetary magnetic field."

"But you still haven't built another Ixion," argued Nash.

"I didn't need to. As I thought, the Ixion structure was a massive but fairly simple device, intended to detect some of the oddities of entropy distribution in the continuum by measurement of fairly simple parameters. It was obvious that it was going to work because all the dimensionless numbers relating to entropy calculations are different on Getawehi—and even the dimensional numbers have adapted to follow suit."

"But the hardware . . .?"

"It wasn't needed. The criterion of Ixion was not its complexity, but its size. When I offered Terra not a large turntable but a planet-sized ball of rotating metal complete with current pickoffs, they were overjoyed. They had to recast their parameters, but we were able to feed them in a few days the type of data that the Ixion structure might have taken centuries to produce."

"Hmm!" Nash was thoughtful. "As usual, Fritz, you seem to have all the answers. But I can see some of the technical boys have their toes curling up. I suggest we adjourn for a while to allow them to catch up on the figurework. As for you, Fritz, you're coming with me."

"Where to, Colonel?"

"To show me what the hell Getawehi uses as a high-power radio transmitter. I swear I've examined every square inch of this planet by telescope without detecting even so much as a banana plug."

Van Noon shrugged. "I suppose you won't be satisfied until you've seen it for yourself . . . and you may not believe it even then."

As the sleds neared the range it was possible to see the light from the burning mountains even in broad daylight. Despite a favourable angle of slope, Colonel Nash halted his sled at a distance and took out his field glasses to study the phenomenon, Van Noon drew up alongside.

"How does it work?" asked Nash at last.

Fritz waved his hand. "As with the steppe, the whole ground-mass is electrified. The mountain itself is a great mineral outcrop which consists largely of conductive silicates and laminated strata of various metalloids including gallium and its compound arsenide."

"So?"

"So the whole mountain is electrically alive, with random electrical potentials everywhere. In the high voltage periods the great mountain currents surge through the partially conducting, partially semi-conducting layers, inducing all manner of curious effects. One of these effects is to cause some of the gallium arsenide layers to convert the current flow directly into light."

"Of course—electroluminescence!"

"It doesn't stop there," said Fritz. "None of the metalloid layers are particularly pure, and all of them contain numerous slip-faults. In these circumstances it is inevitable that you find a profusion of naturally formed p and n junctions which would drive a solid-state physicist psychotic. As the potentials vary you get great transistor switching actions with thousands of amperes being diverted up and down the mountainside like the great grand-daddy of all thyristors gone crazy. That's why you get the glow running and shimmering through the mountain like that."

"Fantastic! If I hadn't seen it myself I'd never have believed it."

"You haven't seen anything yet," said Van Noon.

By the time they reached the foot of the mountain itself the glow had died as abruptly as on the occasion when Fritz and Jacko had first seen it. Now the fissured and laminated glassy blocks of the mountain lay apparently lifeless and inert, and only the instrumented probes which Fritz applied to the surface showed the drift and drain of the electrical currents still surging in the mountain.

"Look to the end there," said Van Noon. "Where the mountain reaches down to the steppe there's a silvery outcropping containing a series of thrust faults. That's a typical formation distributed widely over the surface of Getawehi. Like the burning mountain, the lamelar layers show marked transistor action. The outcrop is predominantly laminated silicon semiconductor layers. Subjected to the terrain currents, almost every similar outcrop is a radio transmitter at some state of the current flow."

Nash stopped and wiped his brow. "I won't buy that one, Fritz. I grant you that you have the current and you appear to have the semi-conductor material. But even I know that you don't get a radio transmitter by throwing random transistors into a box."

"No," said Fritz, "but there is a logical explanation. In these fractured semiconductor masses you have potentially every aspect of transmitter function: capacitance, conductance, inductance, switching, amplification, and even piezo-electric oscillation. And you have time."

"I don't see what time has to do with it?"

"Evolution takes time, Colonel. Pass too much current through a transistor junction and you destroy it. Start with an infinity of potential transistor circuit paths and destroy and modify them slowly, and one day you'll strike a circuit which will function—it will dissipate current rather than be destroyed by it. Continue the process for long enough and the only circuits which survive will be those capable of dissipating energy. Thus active circuits will become the rule rather than the exception—by a process analogous to natural selection on a biological level. The burning mountain survives by dissipating the electrical energy in the form of light. The small outcrops predominantly dissipate in the radio frequencies."

"I still find it hard to believe," said Nash.

"When you consider the capabilities of natural selection processes, a radio transmitter is a far less unlikely product than is a human being," said Fritz quietly.

Nash looked at his hands reflectively, then nodded. "And you used one of these outcrops as a transmitter to contact the *Tycho Brahe*?"

"We had to—er—modify it to suit our needs. But yes—that's basically what we did do."

"I see," said Nash. "Your ingenuity does you credit, Fritz . . . but then I suppose that's what we employ unorthodox engineers for."

"In this case," said Fritz, "I can't help feeling that Jacko surpassed himself. He can claim to be the first man—and I suspect also the last—ever to add an audio modulator to a solid state transmitter—with a pickaxe!"

THE BLACK HOLE OF NEGRAV

"The basic philosophy behind the Unorthodox Engineers is simple," said Fritz Van Noon. "As our penetration of deep space continues, so communications and supply lines grow longer, finally impossibly long. And the transport costs of even simple items become disproportionately high.

"For instance, the price-penalties of space-freight are such that a simple spanner required on Aldebaran-seven costs sixteen times its weight of platinum on Terra. Assuming you can afford it, delivery time by hyper-ship can be anything up to three years."

He waited until the buzz of conversation in the audience had died again. Then he continued. At his side, he was aware of Colonel Belling's dark scowl of disapproval; but decided to ignore it.

"If we're to take advantage of the new space-territories the hyper-ships are opening up to us, if we're to build out on the Rim something men can use as the foundations of a colony, we need engineering—and we need plenty of it.

"So who should we send? Mechanics who can't obtain any steel? Engineers whose nearest machine shop is fifty light-years away? Or should we send the men who can make a plough out of a stick, a stone and a length of creeper? The answer's obvious. You can send a few tools; but the thing that counts most at the edge of the galaxy is man's own unchannelled ingenuity—the ability to use anything available to your own peculiar advantage.

"And that, Gentlemen, is the function of unorthodox engineering. It's the habit of breaking with the traditional disciplines and learning how to construct the nucleus of a functional civilisation out of bits of string and matchsticks, if necessary. To hell with what it says in the book. It may not even look like engineering—but if it works, it's justified."

Shortly, the chairman brought the assembly back to order.

"Well, now we've heard both sides of the argument—orthodoxy versus unorthodoxy in space engineering. I'm sure we've all been greatly enlightened, not to mention amused, by Lieutenant Van Noon's account of railways built over small volcanoes, and the use of harps as electrical power generators. While Van Noon's approach may not seem as elegant as some of the precise and mathematical approaches we've heard this afternoon, it's brought some very practical solutions to some very intractable problems. I therefore suggest we conclude this session with an opportunity for questions from the floor. Of particular interest would be a problem which orthodoxy has failed to solve."

At his side on the speakers' platform Van Noon felt Colonel Belling stiffen with anticipation, and knew that his worst fears were about to be confirmed. Belling's consummate hatred of unorthodoxy was almost a legend, and a public showdown before such an influential audience was too good a chance for the Colonel to miss. The next question would be a loaded impossibility. Regardless of who delivered it, Belling would have had a hand in the draft.

A young officer in the uniform of the Space Territories Administration rose to his feet. He was obviously one of the new breed of academic officers not long from space college. He began with his own introduction.

"Captain-Administrator Wilson, Rim Territories Survey. I've been fascinated by Van Noon's treatise on the uses of unorthodoxy. It so happens that out on the Rim we have a good example of one of these intractable problems. It involves a large asteroid called Negrav, which is part of a complex binary-planet system in orbit around the star Springer 218G."

Van Noon stole a look at Colonel Belling, whose expression of smug innocence confirmed his worst suspicions. This problem had been hand-picked by a master.

"Perhaps I should explain," continued Wilson, "that the

companion planet in the binary, tentatively named Leda-four, is a body of considerable interest to us because of its mineral resources. To gain maximum effect from our exploitation of these minerals, however, we require a three-year detailed space survey of Leda. It's impossible to tie up a ship for this length of time, but an ideal observation platform would be the associated asteroid."

Fritz Van Noon listened to this with a patient frown. So far nothing unusual had emerged. Therefore, whatever the problem was, it had to be a honey.

Wilson was deliberately avoiding looking at Belling. "I said the asteroid was called Negrav. The reason for this is that the centrifugal force of its rotation at the equator exceeds the gravitational attraction of its mass. Thus, except at the poles it has a negative gravity averaging about point seven Terrestrial. Unfortunately, because of its spin alignment, it's a point on the equator we need for observation."

"If I understand you rightly," said Van Noon, "yours is a simple problem of securing an observatory on to a surface which exhibits an effective negative gravity. This is slightly more difficult than free-fall work, but not much. Any good adhesive can get you started, and once you've obtained a reasonable foothold, you can surely anchor into the surface by any of a great number of standard methods?"

Wilson took the point sedately, but caught Colonel Belling's eye and was hard-put to restrain the amusement which welled suddenly inside him.

"It's not quite as easy as that," he said, striving to retain his academic pose. "I said that Leda was one of a binary pair. Negrav's only an asteroid, and not large enough to effect the gravitational balance substantially. Rather, it functions as a satellite to the other component of the binary—which is a rather small black hole."

"A what?" said Van Noon, sitting down weakly.

"A black hole," said Wilson, happily, under the approving eyes of his triumphant mentor. "The second component of the binary is a small black hole of roughly terran mass, which has an event horizon of about one centimetre."

"And Negrav is in orbit about this?"

"A very close orbit."

"How close?" asked Fritz suspiciously.

"It actually shaves the surface. Our problem on Negrav isn't getting an observatory to adhere, it's how to stop it being eaten by the black hole in grazing orbit—no pun intended. Orthodoxy doesn't have any good answers. I'd be interested in hearing the unorthodox approach."

Colonel Belling was still laughing the next morning.

When Van Noon received a summons to report to his superior's office at the Engineering Reserve he sensed it was only so that salt could be rubbed into an already smarting wound. It made a change, however, to find his commanding officer in a congenial mood so early in the morning. This was a situation Van Noon had plans to rectify.

"Ah, Fritz! Sit down! I've to congratulate you. Your reputation for unorthodoxy is unimpaired. Nobody ever gave such an unorthodox reply to a question at a Space Engineering Symposium. I was particularly intrigued by what you told him to do with his black hole."

"It was deliberate provocation," said Van Noon. "A put-up job designed to discredit unorthodox engineering."

"Which it did beautifully," said Belling, happily. "I always said I'd show you crackpots up for what you are."

"Then you haven't heard yet?" said Fritz, carefully.

"Heard what?" Belling's suspicion hardened like a forgotten ladle of molten steel passing through cooling-point.

"General Nash was in the assembly representing Space Engineering Command."

"Of course. What of it?"

"Well, the Unorthodox Engineers have pulled him out of several holes in the past. I think he saw the chance to return the favour."

"What chance?"

"That building an observatory on Negrav wasn't entirely a leg-pull. With respect, Colonel, you were so busy looking at the absurdity of it, that you overlooked the possibility there might be a genuine need. It so happens there is a need. The Negrav-Leda complex promises to provide easily-won mineral resources for a large sector of the Rim, avoiding the long hauls from Terra."

"Go on, Fritz," said Belling, grimly.

"Well, General Nash got together with the Director of the Space Territories Administration and offered to build the Negrav observatory for him. The Director was delighted, and an inter-Service contract was drawn up on the spot."

"And?" asked Belling. He had the look of a man who knew what the answer must be, but hoped against hope that the truth could not be as bad as he imagined.

"The contract makes this Engineering Reserve responsible for the building the observatory," said Fritz. "That means it'll be your pidgin."

"I'll never forgive you for this, Fritz."

"But I did nothing. It was you who had the matter raised."

"I still shan't forgive you. It has all the hallmarks of your devious organisation."

"And it raises a good question, Colonel. Who're you going to send to Negrav? An orthodox engineering team—or a bunch of unorthodox crackpots?"

"I still think it was a heck of a tough way of proving your point," said Sergeant Jacko Hine.

Van Noon scowled at his second in command. "Not even Colonel Belling believes me, but I had nothing to do with us being sent to Negrav. The construction orders came down from General Nash, and Belling had to recant on his orthodox approach because there wasn't an orthodox way to do it."

"I suppose it never occurred to you that there might not be an unorthodox way to do it, either?"

"The thought did strike me, but I dismissed it as unlikely. Just how the heck we're going to do it, I don't have a clue at the moment. But at least it puts us marginally up on Belling's approach."

"How do you figure that?"

"Belling's certain it can't be done. I'm certain that it can. So all we have to figure out is how. That simplifies the problem no end."

"Not for me it doesn't," said Jacko Hine. "You'd better clue me up on black holes. If we're to tangle with one, I'd like to know something of the enemy."

"The classical theory's that of the collapse of a burned-out star. Once a star's used up its nuclear fuel the radiation pressures holding it up fall right away. It begins to contract under its own gravity. The size of the star controls how far the collapse can go. But for a star upwards of twice the mass of our own sun, no known physical process can prevent it continuing indefinitely. The whole star's swallowed by its own gravitational pull. It creates a small region with such an intense gravitational field that not even light can escape from it—this is what's known as the event horizon."

"Hence the name black hole?"

"Sure. Light—or anything else for that matter—can be drawn into a black hole by the intense gravity, but nothing, including light, can ever get out again. It's a one-way hole in space."

"What happens to the things it swallows?"

"Virtually crushed out of existence. Everything, including the original star, ends up as a point of infinite density, which is known as a singularity. It's the ultimate state in the compaction of matter."

"So how big is it?"

"We don't know about the size of the singularity; but the size of the event horizon is determined by the mass contained in the singularity. For a collapsed star of around two solar masses, this would be a couple of kilometres in diameter."

"But Wilson was speaking of one about a centimetre in size."

"There's another possible way by which black holes could have been formed. This is in the big bang which began the universe. Theory has it that baby black holes of a mass around ten to the minus five grammes and ten to the minus thirty-three centimetres in diameter could have been formed then and would have been wandering space ever since, consuming whatever mass they chanced to find in their travels. It's entirely possible for one of these mini black holes to be able to eat an entire planet and still not finish up much larger than a marble. At a rough guess that's what's happened to Negrav."

"It gives me a very curious feeling," said Jacko, "to think of a little black hole which could eat a planet. The more I hear of this expedition, the less I begin to like it. As I said just now, I think you've chosen a heck of a tough way to prove your point."

The hyper-ship of the S.T.A. had carried them out to Chronos, on the Rim. From there a slower Navy vessel—though still one with hyper-light capacity—had taken them on to the S.T.A. base on New Australia. By work-vessel it was then only a three week luminal trip to the star Springer 2I8G, with its curious binary satellite and the asteroid Negrav. When they were within two days of the Negrav contact, Van Noon called a conference of his five-man team.

"Now you've all read the preliminary S.T.A. survey report on Negrav. When we get within telescope range, we'll be able to supplement what we know with our own observations. I hope to be able to discover a few items which the S.T.A. observers haven't mentioned because they weren't looking specifically for them. It's highly unlikely that Negrav is totally composed of nickel-iron alloy, or that its entire surface is as smooth and unbroken as the S.T.A. report suggests. Initially we'll need to establish a foothold, and this'll have to be well below the orbital path of the black hole, so what we want particularly is a deep fissure or crack which we can hook into and work safely below the black hole."

"Check!" said Jim Fanning, the U.E. geologist. "But if the S.T.A. photographs are to be believed, you'd stand more chance of hatching ball-bearings than you do of finding fissures in the surface of Negrav."

"I'm aware of that," said Fritz. "The theory's that Negrav

was once a full-sized planet, and all we see now is a remnant of the core. The rest of it's been eaten by that darned black hole. But I'm hoping at least for a blowhole or some form of depression. The frequency with which the black hole sweeps the surface gives us less than thirty-six hours between touching the surface and getting safely tucked down underground out of its way."

"If I judge you right," said Jacko, "you're thinking of building the observatory beneath the surface?"

"We obviously can't build on the surface, because anything on the surface gets eaten by the black hole. Besides which, it makes sense in other ways. Below the surface you don't have to bring in construction materials. You simply carve out the shape of the cavity you want. Also you can make use of the negative gravity, because the centrifugal force'll drift you towards the roof of the cavity, thus producing a semblance of positive gravity. Once the observers get used to making their observations by peering down through windows below their feet, it should be a fairly effective working situation."

"All of which sounds very nice," said Fanning. "But I foresee a couple of practical snags. Like how do we get in deep enough quick enough to avoid being eaten by the black hole? And having got into the surface, how do we carve an observatory-sized cavity in what promises to be a very strong nickel-iron alloy?"

"I admit it may be tough," said Van Noon.

"Tough!" Fanning was aghast. "Blasting won't do much more than deform the surface, and oxy-acetylene cutting could take a lifetime—assuming you could get the supplies. So you're largely back to processes like drilling and spark erosion plus the occasional handfile. At a rough guess, Colonel Belling was exactly right when he said it couldn't be done."

"I've told you all before," said Van Noon, sternly. "Physical limitations aren't absolutes. They're a state of mind. They said iron ships wouldn't float. They reached that conclusion because they hadn't taken all the facts into account.

From this distance I can't see the answer to the Negrav problem either. But I'm sure as hell there is one. All we have to do is find it."

When the S.T.A. work-vessel reached its keep-station around Negrav, subsequent observations did nothing to support Van Noon's optimism. Negrav was a ball of solid nickel-iron, and its surface was flawless and honed to a micro-finish which would have done credit to a precision ball-bearing. Because of its small size, the black hole was not visible even with the most powerful telescopes available. Its relentless orbit around Negrav—or rather the orbit of the asteroid around it, which came to the same thing relatively speaking—had for some millions of years ceased to take more than microns of further material from the surface.

Now the black hole's path hovered millimetres above the surface of Negrav and pursued a progressive rotation which effectively swept the entire sphere over a period of thirty-six hours. The position of the black hole was known with mathematical certainty at any time, but liberation and other effects of the binary on the orbit of Negrav introduced an uncertainty factor. The black hole's progress across the surface had to be described in terms of statistical paths rather than positional lines. In practice this meant that thirty-six hours was the longest period any point on the surface of Negrav could be guaranteed safe from the marauding black hole.

"Which isn't long enough," said Jacko Hine. "Working under space conditions and negative gravity, we wouldn't have time to cut far enough into the surface to be any significant use. We've not only got to get into the hole, but around some considerable corner to prevent being drawn out by the black hole's gravity."

"How far d'you estimate we could penetrate in thirty-six hours?" asked Van Noon.

"If the spectroanalyses of the surface material are correct, we'd be hard put to remove more than a cubic metre with the tools available. And once we get deeper, the work would slow considerably because we could only keep one man at the face."

"That's not good enough," said Van Noon. "I'm going down to Negrav myself to study the problem from the surface."

"If it's not a rude question, how do you intend to hold to the unbroken surface against negative gravity? Chewing gum?"

"No, permanent magnets. Nickel-iron of that structure ought to be highly magnetic. If the negative gravity's only point seven I should get all the attraction I need from a fairly small magnet pack."

"Here's hoping the sunshine doesn't take the surface over Curie point," said Jacko. "Else we're going to have a right game fishing you out of orbit around the small black hole."

If he was being strictly honest, even Van Noon would have admitted his confidence had fled as the little lifecraft dropped him towards Negrav's implacable surface. The nearer they approached, the more smooth and polished the asteroid's surface appeared, until from twenty metres up he could see the perfect reflection of the life craft mirrored in the giant metal ball.

The first problem was to secure a contact with the surface. While the power manoeuvrings of the lifecraft could keep station over a particular point on the asteroid, the problem of trying to attach an assembled magnet package to the surface was akin to trying to throw it twenty metres vertically above his head. It was not until he had experienced the situation that he began to appreciate the reasonings behind Jacko's assertion of impossibility. What he had failed to accept subconsciously was that any work in negative gravity was akin to working on the ceiling, and that any drilling would have to take place in a "hands down, feet out" position, which was both unnerving and extremely tiring. Jacko's estimate of a cubic metre of material removed in thirty-six hours began to look wildly optimistic.

After a series of hair-raising manoeuvres by the lifecraft, the pilot managed to bring Van Noon within striking distance of the metal "ceiling". After a few breathless moments, the magnet package stuck and the long cable trailed outwards with Fritz swinging uncertainly on the end of it. Thereafter he had to climb up the cable to reach his destination, which was no mean feat despite the lightweight flexibility of his spacesuit. This did not accord at all with his ideas on how a conquering hero, even an unorthodox one, should reach the planetary body of his choice.

Having secured himself in a nest on the cable, he began to probe the surface above him. A small drill bit cleanly but slowly into the metal surface, though he was afraid to exert too much pressure lest he should lever away the magnets which held him there. He dutifully collected samples of the swarf which came away, tapped the hole, and screwed in a prepared eyebolt to which he attached a second line. More secure now, he brought up a larger drill and drilled a bole sufficiently large for a second eyebolt to be inserted completely recessed below the surface.

This was the first permanent "foothold" secured on Negrav.

"Getting any ideas, Fritz?" Jacko's voice came over the headphones.

"It strikes me that with the small size of the black hole, the chances of any particular attachment to the surface being eaten in any one orbit are negligible. If we were to suspend an off-standing platform from the surface and attach it by more than an adequate number of cables, we could give ourselves a relatively safe work stage. Furthermore, it would be more comfortable than this fly on the ceiling approach."

"Shall I go ahead and organise a platform?"

"Not yet, because the chances of cutting our way in seem quite as remote as Jim Fanning predicted. There has to be an easier method. Before I leave, I want to see what the explosive charge will do. But I don't really have much hope unless the stuff is a lot more friable than it seems."

"Check! When you get those swarf samples back we'll have some idea of the answers anyway."

Van Noon attached his explosive package to his first eyebolt, carefully levered free his precious magnetic pack, then dropped down the cable from the second eyebolt to make the precarious rendezvous with the lifecraft. When it had stood off to a safe distance, he fired the explosive charge by radio.

The flash was impressive because of the highly reflective surface. The destructive effect was negligible. A further close pass in the lifecraft revealed only the barest depression in the solid metal surface. A slight element of plastic flow had taken place, producing an extremely shallow crater, but there was no evidence that any material had actually been removed.

Van Noon returned thoughtfully to the work-vessel. On the face of it his exploratory trip to the surface of Negrav had been a failure. They had learnt nothing they did not already know, and the few straws at which he had clutched had disappeared like vapour in a vacuum. The problem of building an observatory on Negrav appeared as intractable as ever. As the hours wore on, however, he developed the curious quizzical look at the corners of his eyes which signalled he was far from being beaten.

He acquired the best telescope the work-vessel possessed and spent hours viewing the surface of Negrav, imagining he could see the small black hole as it sped hungrily across the surface. The optical detection of such a small object from this distance was an impossibility, and his patient perusal of the scene began to worry Jacko Hine.

"What's the score, Fritz?"

"One up to Negrav. Our turn to play."

"Are we still in the game?"

"Very much so. Negrav's going to have its observatory, and we're going to build it."

"Crazy like a fox!" said Jacko.

"Am I? You remember my theme at the symposium. The ability of the unorthodox engineer is to do the job with anything he can lay his hands on. Well, Negrav's a classic set-piece—the problem and the answer bound together in a single cosmological package."

"You need to be joking!"

"Think about it. Ours is a problem of method. Cutting's too slow, and blasting's ineffective. But suppose I gave you a tool that'll not only cut nickel-iron without effort, but will also consume the detritus? Suppose this tool needs no external power supply, and the tool wear is so low that it even finishes up marginally larger than it started. And all for no transport costs. Couldn't you do the job with that?"

"Yes . . . but!"

"Our cutting tool's right down there, Jacko. And for a bonus we get an eternally spinning workpiece to go with it. No lathe required. All we need to arrange is the traverse mechanism. With the black hole we can cut a toroidal cavity right around Negrav's equator, and they can build a hundred observatories inside there if they like."

"Fritz," said Jacko, "this time you've surpassed even your own idiot genius. But there's one tiny point you've overlooked. You can't pick up a black hole and use it as a tool. You can't hold it. You can't even approach it. It'll utterly absorb anything you can fling at it."

"All that's accepted," said Van Noon. "But when you've a job to do and there's no conceivable way to do it, there's only one approach left open to you. You have to exercise some good old human ingenuity."

The work-vessel took them back to the S.T.A. base on New Australia. This was the nearest point on the Rim where Fritz could find anything like the computer capacity he needed. He would have preferred to have gone back to Chronos, but was unwilling to waste the time while his enthusiasm was still at fever pitch. Once they had become convinced that Van Noon was intent on going through with the scheme, his team, too, had become infected with his eagerness, and their deliberations had considerably refined and improved Fritz's initial ideas.

The S.T.A. technicians on New Australia listened to Van Noon's proposals with critical alarm, and sent a message by subspace radio to Terra for confirmation that the project could proceed. In the meantime, Fritz's computing was allowed to go ahead.

The message which came back from Terra read:

"IF VAN NOON WANTS TO STICK OUT HIS FOOL NECK ON A SCHEME LIKE THAT, DONT STOP HIM. WE MIGHT GET LUCKY!

SIGNED BELLING,
COMMANDING ENGINEERING RESERVE."

Van Noon could almost picture the gleam in the colonel's eye as he penned the second sentence. Nevertheless, he received all the help he needed from the S.T.A. staff on New Australia. With his precious calculations completed, and sufficient supplies for the job, he returned with his team to the keep-station around Negrav to begin the careful observations on which the success of the operation would depend. It was fairly obvious that the rest of the universe regarded the project as insane. There were moments when Van Noon was not too sure himself. Nevertheless, the future of unorthodox engineering was riding on his back, and having declared his intention, he was unable to retract.

Above all things, timing was critical. The accurate gauging of Negrav's rotation was aided considerably by a huge dye-spot which Jacko managed to produce on the surface. This was achieved in the course of a hair-raising approach to the asteroid in a lifecraft which was carefully manoeuvred while the dye was sprayed on to the metal "ceiling" from pressurised canisters. With the spot in place, the rotational speed of Negrav was determined with an accuracy previously unobtainable, and Van Noon's calculations were complete.

By far the hardest part of the operation was to give the order to proceed. Not only were the dangers considerable, but the timing needed to be immaculate and the positional accuracies held within very small limits. Additionally, there were still a few unknowns which added not only to the hazards but also to the virtual certainty of unorthodox engineering becoming a standard joke throughout the universe if things went wrong.

Having rehearsed and re-rehearsed his team, Van Noon finally reached the critical point, and gave the fateful order. Once the first lifecraft had left the work-vessel and headed towards the surface, there was no turning back. It was only when he had passed this point that he began to appreciate the immensity of the forces with which he played.

Once started, there was no leisure for further thought. Jacko Hine went down with the first Iifecraft and attached his package as specified. The second lifecraft was on its way before he returned. The third and most critical package, Van Noon took down himself.

There being no natural features on the surface of Negrav, he could only judge his position from the radioed instructions from observers on the work-vessel and the relative movement of Jacko's dye-marker. This made easy sense during the long space descent but when the orb of the asteroid began to dominate the sky he lost orientation. In sudden panic he had the lifecraft halted until he could recalculate his bearings. It was this hesitation that probably saved his life.

As he directed the lifecraft to continue the descent, a sudden alarm was issued by the observers on the work vessel.

"Look out, below! You're off course and running right into the path of the black hole!"

The pilot reacted before Fritz had time to formulate his instruction. Veering crazily away in a tight arc, the little spacecraft struggled to escape from the gravitational well of the black hole which was overtaking from the rear. Unless they could build up to escape velocity they were liable to be dragged irrevocably down into this hole to end all holes.

For a short time it looked as though they might escape completely. Then the full power of the lifecraft's tiny motors became insufficient to move them any farther against the intense gravitational attraction which now arrested and began to drag them back towards the surface. There was nothing the occupants of the lifecraft could do except sit helplessly as they were seized and thrown back on to the asteroid.

The touchdown, when it came, was unexpectedly mild. Fortunately their descent had been delayed by the lifecraft's motors just long enough for the black hole to speed on its uncaring way. The friction of the craft against the asteroid's surface was sufficient to prevent them being drawn in the black hole's wake. Almost immediately the gravitational spasm was over, and Negrav's own negative gravity spun them crazily back into space.

Dazed and shaken, Van Noon checked his equipment, while the lifecraft pilot tested his craft. Miraculously there had been very little damage. The lifecraft, though dented, was still spaceworthy even though much of its instrumentation had failed. Van Noon's precious package, which had been the reason for the descent, likewise appeared to have suffered no permanent harm.

His timing, however, had been completely destroyed.

This was a factor beyond recovery. Because of the orbiting black hole, the packages which had already been placed on Negrav had only a limited life expectancy. If his own package was not now put in place, the existing ones would all be destroyed before any new calculations could be made.

Van Noon took a chance. He placed the package with its magnet pack on the nearest part of the surface, knowing that its position was far from being where he had originally intended. The results would be in the lap of the gods, but it was either this or make the long haul back to New Australia for a fresh set of supplies. Then, tired and disconcerted, he ordered the lifecraft to the work-vessel in keep-station above.

Compared to his trip, the rest of the journeys to Negrav seemed uneventful. No less than seven other trips followed, some achieving the desired accuracy, others varying. There was no time left, however, to make any corrections. Fritz had to suffer the errors and hope against hope that some overseeing deity would bring the project through. Otherwise he shuddered to think of the final results.

Then came the final phase. One after another in controlled sequence explosions flared upon the surface of Negrav; appearing as little more than pinpoints of light to the distant observers, yet in reality being massive charges of super-high explosive. The timing was accurate according to the original schedule; but because of misplacement of several of the charges, the net effect would be anything but optimum. There followed a long period of waiting, after which the remaining charges were fired.

As Van Noon read the final collation of results, his heart sank like a stone. He had arranged to check the orbital velocity of Negrav so that it fell into a lower orbit around the black hole. In effect this meant that for a number of rotations the black hole would actually orbit inside the surface of Negrav. Then he had planned to correct Negrav's velocity so that the black hole would return to the surface leaving a toroidal cavity inside the asteroid's equator. Probably due to misplacement of the charges, the scheme had gone disastrously wrong. The black hole had remained inside Negrav . . .

Stupefied, he read the figures; but they no longer registered in his brain. Instead he saw the asteroid of Negrav being progressively eaten from inside by a small black hole so voracious that it could consume its entire host without particularly noticing the meal. Worse, if it remained inside Negrav, the asteroid would disappear entirely. Van Noon did not much fancy being known for the rest of his career as the man who lost Negrav.

He called for the orbit of the asteroid to be monitored continuously, while he searched through the work-vessel's stocks hoping to find sufficient explosive to kick the asteroid's velocity up and bring the black hole again to the outside. A trip to New Australia for fresh supplies was out of the question because of the time involved. By the time they returned, Negrav would have been swallowed whole.

He was unlucky. The explosives he had brought from New Australia had been carefully calculated for the job, and the entire stock had been used. Nor did the work-vessel carry any stocks of its own. The fuel used by the lifecraft was not suitable for the job, and the nuclear-vector powerplant of the work-vessel was too dangerous to be considered. He briefly thought of trying to nudge the asteroid with the work-vessel itself; but concluded that the vessel was unlikely to survive the ordeal.

Disconsolate, he sat down again to check the results of the orbital monitoring. As he did so, he began to brighten considerably. When Jacko found him, he was chuckling uncontrollably, and tears of laughter were streaming down his face.

"You're the first person I ever saw get a belly-laugh out of a computer print-out," said Jacko, warily. "We don't have a strait-jacket, so I'd better give you a shot of tranquilliser. I'd advise you not to struggle."

"Knock it off, Jacko! I've just received proof of the theorem that the deserving don't always get what they deserve. Alternatively, the unorthodox looks after its own."

"Crazy like two foxes!"

"Look at these orbital figures, Jacko. And tell me what it was about the original problem we forgot."

Jacko took the sheets of print-out and looked through them wonderingly. Then he, too, began to smile.

"Negrav's speeding up. If it continues to do that, the black hole'll come outside again of its own accord—and soon."

"Right! We forgot about conservation of momentum. As the black hole removes some of Negrav's mass, the asteroid gets lighter; but its initial momentum remains. Therefore it has to go faster, and climb into a higher orbit. It's a self-stabilising system because whenever the black hole removes some mass from the asteroid, Negrav itself automatically retreats from the attack."

"So what're we left with? The same problem only with a slightly smaller Negrav?"

"No. Unless my figures are wrong, the black hole's been in there long enough to give us a concentric ball and shell effect—like a marble in a table-tennis ball. The increase in Negrav's speed is running up an exponential curve, so that when the black hole does come out it should do so at some considerable angle. With luck it'll only puncture the shell as it comes out, not eat it away. And do you realise the implications of that, my boy?"

"We were lucky?" asked Jacko uncertainly.

"Not only that. It means that Negrav will be safer from attack by the black hole than ever before. And if that cavity's the size I think it is, they'll be able to build a major base in there, not just an observatory. They can mine Leda-four at their leisure, and use Negrav as an on the spot refinery and transfer station from which they can load hyper ships direct. It'll be the most valuable space facility on the Rim."

As the figures had predicted, the black hole did come out of Negrav. It reappeared some thirty-two hours later and finally stabilised with an orbital separation of eleven kilometres. This new orbital distance was a measure of the amount of mass which had been removed from Negrav.

The next part of the exercise was to explore the cavity itself. This was aided by the fact that they could now anchor a structure permanently on to the surface to give them safe working conditions without fear of being eaten by the black hole. With this new facility, the work progressed rapidly. Twenty metres in, they broke into free space inside the asteroid. Van Noon was the first through, followed by Jacko and an assemblage of powerful lamps. Once inside, they gazed into the vastness with amazement.

Fritz's ball and shell concept was substantially true, but random deviations in the rotation of Negrav had not produced a completely clean cavity, but rather one populated here and there with crazy spires and towers and bridges, and many vast columns which rose up to support the central core nearly a kilometre above the inner surface. Every line was curved in representation of some complex mathematical equation, as though designed by a mammoth computer programmed to seek out the ultimate in form and shape; and everything was cleanly cut and polished in flawless nickel-iron alloy.

They made a tour of inspection which lasted nearly twelve hours, and came out so impressed with the wonder of it all that it was difficult to believe that these fantasies had been the results of interference with their own hands. As an S.T.A. base, the situation was, and would be always, without parallel. Had it not been situated on the Rim, it would have been a tourist attraction with no conceivable opposition. They had juggled precariously with Nature, and had been rewarded with a marvellous demonstration of natural design that made them feel humbled and just a little bit afraid.

They found the points by which the black hole had entered and left the cavity, and had these welded closed. Over their original entry point they built a docking hatch and an airlock. Then they radioed New Australia for the S.T.A. to come and take possession of the prize. Captain Administrator Wilson was the first S.T.A. man to arrive. He went in with a disbelieving sneer, and came out so passionately impressed that he broke down and cried.

From then on, the orthodox engineers took charge, ferrying gasses to provide a breathe able atmosphere in the cavity, bringing in power plants and treatment plants and all the paraphernalia necessary to support men's existence in the far reaches of space. Their task done, the unorthodox engineers returned in triumph to Terra.

"You don't have to rub it in, Fritz," said Colonel Belling, when next they met. "I admit I was wrong and you were right. Unorthodoxy does have a use in unorthodox situations."

"Actually we're only arguing about definitions," said Van Noon. "Orthodoxy for us is the tools and techniques which have been evolved for dealing with our local Terran situation. We can't expect these to be the optimum for a completely altered set of conditions. What's orthodox in one part of the galaxy may be unorthodox in another. All that I'm saying is that the most useful thing we can take to any problem is an open mind."

"Well, you've certainly proved your point. The S.T.A. are so delighted with their acquisition that they've asked permission to call their Negrav installation Base Van Noon. I thought it only fair to let you make your own refusal."

"Refusal?"

"That's what I said, Fritz. While you've been journeying back, I've been analysing your figures. As I read it, this was a battle you actually lost, but were saved by a most fantastic stroke of luck. D'you really mean to claim it as a victory?"

"In the circumstances, I take your point. But I claim the right to nominate my own alternative."

"Which is?" asked Belling, ominously.

"How about Serendipity?"

The Colonel's face broke into a huge smile, and he rose from the table to clasp Van Noon's hand.

"I'll go along with that, Fritz. I'll even buy you a drink on it. And while you're here, there's another matter I want to discuss. It concerns the tunnelling problem on Eggar twenty four. Now, I've been thinking that with one of your black holes . . ."

SOMETHING IN THE CITY

Bowman

"Early!"

As she descended the steps from the large military transport helicopter, the first thing Lieutenant Early Annandale saw was a friendly major earnestly trying to attract her attention by waving a clipboard. He hurried to wait for her by the front of the steps.

"Early. I figured it had to be you. There can't be two lieutenants of the same name on WarTech's staff."

"Sandy!" The reunion was both a pleasure and a surprise and both emotions were mirrored in her pert face. "What are you doing in Kunetra?"

The name Sandy was a nickname, originating in a past time when David Bowman's head had been wreathed with ginger hair. Now Bowman had very little hair and he looked older—a great deal older. Kunetra was the sort of place where men aged rapidly, if they were lucky enough to live that long.

He turned her question aside. "Let's have a look at you, Early." He stepped back to gaze appreciatively at her trim figure which, if anything, was enhanced by the cut of the smart green uniform she wore. "My, you're a sight for sore eyes!" Then he noticed the Tactical Intelligence flashes on her shoulders and the joy faded from his face, to become replaced by his latterly habitual look of anxiety and doubt. "You still working for *him?*"

"Colonel Maidment, yes." She was laughing, but only slightly, at the concern in Bowman's eyes. Colonel Maidment, head of Tactical Intelligence, was a particular kind of legend, and not one which suited everyone's palate. In ruthlessly pursuing his duties, Maidment had made a great many enemies, not a few of them on his own side of the war.

Bowman shook his head sadly. "I don't know why you do it, Early. Honest to God I don't."

"There are reasons," said Early kindly.

"Reasons to work for that bastard?"

"And as you know," there was the faintest touch of reproof in her voice, "some of those reasons can never be told."

He shrugged his shoulders, defeated, then turned back to the matters at hand.

"Look, Early," he indicated the giant helicopter now opening its cargo hatches. "I have to supervise the unloading of this lot. All technical stores. Most of it yours, I shouldn't wonder. I'll have a driver take you to the mess. I'll join you there as soon as I can. But listen to me carefully. Stay inside the mess where the driver leaves you, and don't do anything damn stupid like walking out to admire the view. There's a lot needs explaining before you walk out alone in Kunetra."

"Sandy, I . . ." She started to protest but he stopped her with an emphatic wave of his hand.

"Just do it, Early. Later you'll understand. My God, that bastard Maidment! Sending you to Kunetra. There's only one person I'd really like to see here, and that's Maidment himself. Brother, would I really like that!"

Bowman spoke rapidly into his handheld transceiver, and a small half-tracked vehicle detached itself from a park and ran swiftly toward them. He threw Early's personal luggage into the back, waited while she seated herself next to the driver, then signalled the half-track away with the merest nod of his head. The fact that the driver had neither asked for nor was given any hint of destination was something Early noted with only a slight lift of her eyebrows. Such was the state of affairs in Kunetra that unusual precautions to protect the lives of new arrivals had become an unspoken part of their way of life.

The driver was young, barely eighteen Early thought, and, though sweat soaked, his uniform still had traces of newness in it. Furthermore he seemed discomfited by the presence of a female officer, especially by such an attractive and inquisitive female officer as was his passenger. He stammered and never could decide whether to call her "Lieutenant" or "M'am" in answer to her questions. Once, in his confusion, he even called her "Sir." He had been in Kunetra barely two months, one of an emergency-draft replacement for a number of men who had been killed in the city. Already six men out of the original twelve in the draft had been killed, and a seventh had deliberately shot himself in the foot and had to be flown out for medical treatment and Court-Martial for cowardice. The way the story was related no judgements were passed. Men came and went: either they found their own exits or the exits came and found them. And all this had to be viewed against the stark fact that Kunetra was a dead city.

Bowman's intention of joining Early rapidly was thwarted. The technical stores in the helicopter's hold had been accompanied by a Corporal Hammond, who had the look of an athlete and the intellectual air of a university professor. He was tall, wore bifocal glasses, and was obviously out of place as a non-commissioned officer. Corporal Hammond very clearly knew the value and complexity of the instruments in the cases and knew exactly how they should be handled. He patiently ordered the whole operation, apparently unmindful of the fact that Bowman considerably outranked him. Not until the whole consignment had been loaded into the WarTech air-conditioned caravans which had been set on site a few days earlier did Hammond let up—either on himself or on the sweating, cursing men who had been detailed to assist him.

Then he returned to Bowman and saluted thoughtfully. His shoulder-flashes carried the emblem of the WarTech Special Signals School, and Bowman placed him as probably a genius at electronics but one so detached from life that he had failed officer cadet training. Nonetheless, there was something about the man which made him feel vaguely uneasy. He felt reasonably certain about one thing—the fellow did not work for Maidment. Maidment, the arch-liar of the decade, always made his deceptions so immaculately credible.

"Many thanks for your cooperation, Major. Is it possible for me to get a word through to Lieutenant Early?"

"Lieutenant Annandale," corrected Bowman. He hefted the transceiver on the lanyard at his wrist and caught it expertly. "I think that can be arranged, Corporal. Do you want to speak to her?"

"No, Sir. Just a message. All the equipment is accounted for and apparently undamaged. I'll be testing and installing overnight, and the unit should be operational tomorrow morning."

"Just that? I'll tell her myself. Mind telling me what you've got up there, Corporal—if it isn't too much of a secret."

Hammond pursed his lips. "With respect, Major, I don't have the authority to discuss it. Perhaps if you ask the Lieutenant."

"Perhaps," said Major Bowman dubiously. "But I think I'd need to get up very early in the morning to get much out of our Early. If you're working all night I won't bother to fix up your billeting until tomorrow."

"That won't be necessary, Sir. One of the WarTech vans has already been equipped with accommodation for the Lieutenant and myself."

"Separately or together?" The question was a joke.

Hammond smiled shyly. "Separately. As you said, Major, you'd have to get up very early in the morning in order to catch Lieutenant Early."

Rather than recall one of the halftracks which had taken members of the unloading detail back to their quarters, Bowman decided to walk. The journey to the mess where Early had been taken was scarcely more than a mile, and Bowman, as was his mood with increasing frequency, felt in need of solitude. The city of Kunetra depressed him greatly and dominated both his dreams and his waking thoughts. Kunetra was dead, yet incredibly, obstinately it refused to die. It had started to possess his mind to such a degree that sometimes he had forcibly to remind himself that there was still another world outside.

The city, spilled out in its bowl of hills, had been a strategic obstacle to the advance of the Western armies striving to gain a foothold on the eastern plains. Heavily and bitterly defended by the troops of General Quador, Kunetra and its approaches had proven unassailable. Such was its determination not to fall that the stalemate had probably added at least a year to the war and at a cost calculable in millions of lives donated by both sides. To break the impasse the Western Command had finally decided to think the unthinkable. After due warning to allow the occupying forces and civilians to escape, they had detonated a neutron device low over the city. It was a very "clean" bomb: residual radiation levels were acceptably low and the damage it had done to the fabric of the city was scarcely discernible. Yet in that dreadful moment every living thing in the city had died. Kunetra had been sterilized by neutron radiation.

General Quador, too, had been thinking the unthinkable, and with the same brand of ruthlessness and perversity of logic which had made his a name to be feared on three continents. Knowing he could no longer hold Kunetra he determined to make it a costly and regrettable prize, and one which would severely damage the Western cause in the eyes of the rest of the world. Without warning, and with every sign of organizing a mass withdrawal, he had actually permitted only a very few to leave the city. A battalion of nearly a thousand men and most of the civilian population had still been in Kunetra, when the bomb exploded. Troops of the conquering Western army had entered the city rejoicing, and swiftly passed through to the eastern plain with a numb sickness in their hearts and a haunted look in their eyes. War they were used to, but this was massacre on a brand new scale. Perpetrated in their own names.

After the fighting units had passed, the holding troops moved in behind to tackle one of the most nightmarish and soul-destroying jobs in total warfare—cleaning up after a massacre. The trouble with neutron sterilization is that it does not last unless recontamination by airborne bacteria is prevented. The winds and the rain were not helpful. There was no time to bury all of the dead, nor had anyone thought to provide portable crematoria. The answer was hasty funeral pyres ignited with jet fuel, and a room-to-room search of the entire city to remove the bodies of every man, woman, child, dog, cat or other creature that had been in the city at the time of that fateful blast. Most were found before decomposition had advanced too far, others were not; and the smell of death coupled with that of burning bodies contributed a stench which seemed liable to remain in the fabric of the city's walls for all eternity.

And still Quador's thirst for vengeance was not sated.

It was late afternoon before Bowman got the chance to rejoin Early. He picked her up in a half-track he drove himself, and they headed immediately away from the city and up a sloping road to a ledge, from where they had a good view right across the valley. Throughout the entire journey he had been taciturn and withdrawn, and she, recognizing that he was concerned with some inner conflict, carefully restrained her habitual questioning. Then, as the half-track drew to a halt he suddenly became aware of her again. He smiled briefly.

"Sorry, Early. Guess I was lost inside myself. It's this damned place. How much have they told you about Kunetra?"

"Not much. I've read the intelligence reports but they all seem rather confused. That's part of the reason I came. To try and understand."

"To understand Kunetra you have to live here for a while. Then you only understand what it is, not how it does it."

"So what is Kunetra?"

"It's a pathological killer. That's why I didn't want you wandering around until I'd had the chance to speak to you."

"I don't understand how you can call a city a killer."

He swung his hand to encompass the city beneath their feet. "Kunetra isn't dead. It only looks that way. Quador knew that one day we had to come—that all this was inevitable. He knew there was no way we could afford not to come. And he had years to make his preparations."

Far from the east came the almost continuous rumble of a chain of explosions. Bowman gazed toward them speculatively, almost longingly, as though open warfare were the thing he most desired. Then he looked round at the long hills cradling the valley. Already the disc of the sun was half gone behind the distant ice-clad peaks, and the long shadows were striding across the torn city like a blanket being mercifully drawn to hide the hideous wounds of war. His face remained impassive but the crows-feet in the flesh around his eyes betrayed the tenor of his thoughts.

"Quador was like that, Early. Cast in the mould of Genghis Kahn. An innate tyrant. Terrible in victory, terrifying in defeat. He knew he must lose Kunetra, but he's made sure that for us it's a very painful victory. The only thing to be said in his favour is that he remained with his men. He was still smiling when we put his body on the fire."

He turned back to study the darkening roofs of the city itself. From the high slope on which they were standing they had an almost perfect view of the jumbled streets and houses spreading away from the relative orderliness of the old walled city and the citadel which lay at Kunetra's heart. Over the centuries many other armies had fought for possession of Kunetra, but the previous victors had always taken a living city. The city before him now was very, very dead. Yet not dead . . .

"Quador's left something in the city waiting for us, Early. Something inhuman yet intelligent. Something electronic yet programed with all of Quador's own malignant spite. He's left us something which waits and watches and selects—then strikes, always in such a way to cause the greatest distress to the greatest number. Sometimes it strikes massively, when that suits its purpose. More usually it does it with a wry economy. It doesn't need to kill the patient if it can kill the surgeon."

"I still don't understand, Sandy."

"You will. Kunetra has been wired to become the most ingenious death trap in history. Somewhere—and we may never find it—in some radiation-hardened bunker there has to be an advanced computer, programmed to kill. And I doubt if there's a useful room in the whole city that doesn't conceal some potentially lethal device linked to it. The question is, what can we do about it. Because unless we can deactivate it we've no chance whatever of putting a garrison in here."

"Is it really that serious?"

"Worse than serious. It's diabolical. Eighty-three men from the advance cremation party died through drinking poisoned water—water which had previously been tested and certified as fit for use. Some mechanism in the line to that one single tap made an injection of some fungoid toxin at a highly critical time. The men took a week to die, and there was nothing our medics could do for them."

Early shivered suddenly, and it was not only the fault of the evening chill.

"Can't we just abandon Kunetra?"

"No, it's ideally suited for our supply base. And my God, we certainly need those supplies in support of the eastern front offensive. Nor can we just raze it to the ground. Kunetra existed long before the Romans came. They conquered it but they didn't destroy it. They added to it, left something of themselves in it. Christ's own apostles walked some of these same streets you now see before you, possibly even preached from these same heights. Unbeatable in war we may be, but I doubt we're so insensitive to the verdict of history that we'd dare erase Kunetra from the map. After all, it's the quality of the future we're supposed to be fighting for."

Early shivered again, and he put his arms around her shoulders protectively. She delicately but firmly removed herself from the embrace.

"Sorry. I wasn't thinking," he said. "It's becoming colder. I'd better get you back. Before we go, though, I have to talk to you about Maidment."

"Colonel Maidment," she corrected.

"Just so. And Tactical Intelligence. I know Maidment is interested in Kunetra. In fact he's sent five operatives here already. Listen to me, Early. Three of them were dead within twenty-four hours of arrival. All were dead within a week of coming here. Kunetra was waiting for them. So why the hell did Maidment send you here? To make it an even number?"

"Even if I knew, I couldn't tell you," she said simply. "Sandy, I . . ."

"Forget it," said Bowman wearily. He remembered similar arguments too many times before. He removed his cap and brushed his sparse hair back with his hand. "I'll take you back to your caravan."

She looked thoughtfully down at the city, now shrouded by the approaching night. Against the low stone balustrade she turned. "There's still something I don't understand. You mentioned that this something Quador left for us was selective. My impression was that you thought it could respond to particular individuals. Could it do that?"

"It's the only conclusion we can come to. It is selective. I wasn't joking when I said it will kill the surgeon rather than the patient. It actually happens. It kills the surgeon, and both of them die. Two for the price of one. Quador's logic. But I swear it does know one from the other."

"But how could something—a machine—possibly know who was who?"

"You're from WarTech, Early. I was hoping you'd be able to tell me."

She shrugged, buttoned her jacket closely round her shoulders, and climbed into the bucket seat of the half-track. "Don't ask me. I'm only one of the workforce."

Bowman climbed into the vehicle beside her and set it in motion. The surety of their progress down the unlit slopes gave her a hint that this was not the first night Major David Bowman had made the pilgrimage to that particular ledge above the city. She glanced at him, ready to speak, but he seemed to have lapsed back into his previous introspection.

Halfway down the hill, at a point where the roads divided, she saw her opportunity. "What was Quador like, Sandy?

Did you ever meet him? Before the war, I mean."

"Not I. I saw him only once in passing, many years ago. But if you're interested in Quador, why don't you ask Maidment. By all accounts they were fellow students at Oxford together. Shared the same lodgings. If anybody could understand Quador's twisted logic, then Maidment is that man. Small wonder the bastard won't come to Kunetra himself."

Early was saved from having to reply. The half-track's radio, crackling and occasionally bursting into the spontaneous reception of extraneous half-conversations, suddenly became loud and clear.

"Kunetra Control calling Major Bowman. Emergency."

Bowman reached for the handset without halting the pace of their descent down the slope. "This is Bowman. What's the problem, Control?"

"No details, Major. But the Provost wants you urgently. Map reference twenty-three sixty-eight. Repeat two three six eight."

"Got it," said Bowman. "I'm on my way." He turned to Early. "Sorry about this, but I'll have to go straight there. Come to think of it, it may be useful for you to come along anyway. Get a first-hand experience of what our emergencies are like. There's a map under the dash there somewhere. Can you fish it out and see what's at that reference?"

Using the map light, Early explored the folded pages. "It says the Chapel of St. Simenon."

"Damn! That's the one that's been adopted as the garrison chapel." He glanced at his watch. "And the Padre will be just about halfway through his evening meeting . . ."

He did not speak anymore, but concentrated on driving. There was no other traffic, but the streets were completely dark and many were hazardous with fallen rubble. They reached the chapel in about twelve minutes and drove to a halt behind half a dozen half-tracks and trucks. Bowman ran up the steps with Early at his heels, took ten paces inside and then said: "Oh, my God!"

The Padre had been pierced very centrally through the

chest by a steel barb fully eighteen inches long and an inch in diameter. The device which had fired it had somehow been built into the ancient lectern from which he had been reading. The force with which the barb had been projected had carried the unfortunate man back against a large, vertical wooden pillar and pinned him there, where he hung, head dropped forward, a look of incredulity on his face, as if still amazed by the suddenness of his own transition from life to death. The congregation, fully two dozen servicemen and a couple of civilian technicians, had mainly returned to their pews, to continue their prayers alone.

"The surgeon not the patient," said Bowman quietly. He turned to the Provost. "Get your men here and tear this place apart. See if you can find the camera which set this up. And see if you can trace the circuit from that bloody death trap there."

"Tonight, Major?"

"Tonight." He turned away and walked back down the aisle shaking his head sorrowfully. Early followed him.

"What makes you think there is a camera, Sandy?"

"There always is. That's how the thing in the city knows who we are and where we are. That bolt-throwing device could have been placed there years ago, ignoring everything and everyone, until someone it wanted to kill stood just in the right place at just the right time. Eternal patience and a hundred thousand eyes—that's the face of Kunetra the killer."

"Will the camera be difficult to find?"

"Probably. You should see how small they can make them. But it's easier when you know that one is there."

"When you find it, I'd like to have a look at it."

"Surely. But it might take a while." Bowman scanned the chapel's complexity wryly; a wealth of dark beams and fretted screens, an ornate gallery, religious symbols and carved reliefs and statues of saints, a fusion of Christian and Islamic arts. "It has to be up there somewhere. Regrettably, the only time we know where to start looking is after somebody has died. But even then we still have to find it."

"Surely by then the camera has already served its purpose?"

"Early, would you be willing to stake your life on the chance of there not being a second lethal device concealed here somewhere? Or a third? One possibly already targeted on your heart if you take a single step to right or left? I wouldn't." Wan under the chapel lights, he seemed already to have aged another year. "It's already killed five Tactical Intelligence operatives. If I ever catch up with Maidment I swear I'll kill him myself for sending you out here. Come, I'll take you back to your van."

Early

Bowman dropped her off near the tarmac base on which the WarTech caravans were located. All the vans were in complete darkness except for one in which, presumably, Corporal Hammond was doing his night-long stint. Having said goodbye to her escort, Early stood at the edge of the tarmac and waited until the half-track had rounded the bend in the road. Then she went straight to the caravan from which dim lights showed.

The door was unlocked. Most of the equipment which had been delivered by helicopter had been unpacked, but none of it had been installed. In the centre of a mess of packaging, on an improvised couch of poly ether foam, Corporal Hammond lay fast asleep. A half-empty bottle of brandy stood close alongside.

Early grinned mischievously as she approached the recumbent form, and prodded him playfully in the ribs with her shoe.

"The last message I had from you said you were spending all night testing and installing the equipment. Did you break a leg or something?"

Corporal Hammond, alias Colonel Maidment of Tactical Intelligence, sat up and grimaced. "Not exactly. But you know perfectly well, Early, that I can't tell one end of a soldering iron the other."

"You would if you'd ever tried picking one up the wrong way," she said severely. "Instant education." She turned her attention to the scattered modules and began rapidly assembling them into the prepared racks around the walls. When the last was in place she turned the master switch and the whole installation came to life.

Maidment blinked at it curiously. "Don't you have to test everything first?"

"No need. The mean-time between failures on this class of equipment stretches out to somewhere around the time the sun goes cold."

He watched her critically as she trimmed the VDUs and began to load the master program into the computer.

"You know, Early, I sometimes wonder what I'd ever do without you. How did your *tête-à-tête* with David Bowman go? Did I get away with it?"

"As a character you weren't very convincing, but he certainly doesn't suspect that you are who you are."

"You say that with conviction."

"Poor David is very disturbed that you sent me into such a dangerous situation. He swears he's going to kill you."

Maidment laughed softly. "In which he joins an ever-increasing fraternity of hopefuls. Fortunately I'm not easily killable. But if my disguise convinced him, it's a reasonable sign that it may achieve its intended purpose. After all, I hardly went through all that plastic surgery just to convince Major Bowman. Did you learn anything else?"

"Mainly confirmation of what we already know from the intelligence reports. The thing can recognize individuals, and it appears to have an ordered priority for their despatch. It also has a sense of timing. I'm afraid the Padre met with a summary crucifixion right in the middle of his sermon tonight."

Maidment laughed involuntarily. "I love the phrase 'summary crucifixion,' Early. It has a subtle black humour. I sometimes wonder which of the two of us is becoming the harder."

"It's something to do with the company I keep," said Early

darkly. "The point was that it seems able to choose not only the individual but also the occasion. The Padre had read from that same lectern ever since the chapel was adopted. Probably a couple of hundred times. Yet only tonight did it strike him down. Why tonight?"

"Perhaps it was just his turn, in the ordered priority."

"Possibly. Personally I doubt it. Apparently tonight the Padre had his largest congregation ever. Not many, but the best he'd had."

"The principle of the greatest distress to the greatest number. That figures."

"It figures even more if you consider what day it is."

Maidment scowled and searched in his pocket for a diary. "My God! Good Friday. Assuming it's not a coincidence, the implications are pretty far reaching."

"The implications, Colonel, are that the men backing Quador technically have developed AI—artificial intelligence—to an unparalleled degree. Certainly to the human level, possibly much higher. I think we aren't dealing with simple recognition and response. We're dealing with something which can bide its time, act stealthily, and refuse to show its hand until it considers the time is optimum. As David Bowman puts it: 'it doesn't need to kill the patient if it can kill the surgeon.' I think I would add now that it probably won't kill the surgeon until the patient actually needs surgery."

Maidment was staring at the wall without actually seeing it, his forehead creased with the old familiar lines of concentration that even the extensive plastic surgery had been unable to eradicate. His powerful body looked reposed but was actually taut like a coiled spring.

"I hope you're wrong about AI, Early. It could make things very difficult for us."

"And very dangerous, Colonel. Undoubtedly your face is in its files. You've done too much damage to Quador for them to have left you out. You're probably on a priority hit list. But you've come in disguise. The trouble is you'll never know whether or not it's seen through that disguise until the moment of truth. And for you that could be too late."

"Right little Job's comforter this morning, aren't you. Are you trying to tell me all this plastic surgery was probably for nothing?"

"All I'm saying is that you'll never know whether it was or not until the bolt strikes you or fails to strike as the case may be."

"You're doing nothing to improve my confidence, Child. What's the strength of the opposition?"

"Pretty formidable. Quador's head man on pattern recognition and optical character recognition was Abdul Ferenc. Local born but trained in France and America. Came back to this country to join Quador just before the war. We think he was responsible for the personnel recognition system being used here."

"And on the AI side?"

"Not so clear cut. There were two Al men on our lists, but neither of particularly high calibre. Then there was Ibrahim Shaban, about whom virtually nothing is known in the West except that he developed a computer chess program that could beat a Grand Master . . . anytime."

"That makes him a candidate?"

"Inasmuch as he didn't use any of the standard approaches for a chess program. He used an uncommitted AI approach which effectively produced an intelligent and aware machine. Moreover he managed to give the machine a sense of purpose. It was single-mindedly devoted to winning."

"Then Shaban gets my vote. That sounds like the sort of thing we're up against. Cat and mouse, the long-range strategy, I'm beginning to know how a pawn must feel."

"A pawn, Colonel? From the statistical analyses I've done so far, it's reasonably certain that the Kunetra killer computer has two main priority blocks. The first has been prestocked from espionage information. It includes visual recognition patterns for people like yourself and most of the Western high command, senior officers, and the like. A whole group, some of whom might reasonably be expected to come to Kunetra at some time or the other, and whose elimination takes precedence."

"What's the second priority block?"

"The lesser lights. People who happen to have been drafted here just because they were available. Ones who can't be considered to pose any particular threat. Say from Major Bowman down to the latest rookie. They get killed for the sake of causing distress or inconvenience, not because they're particular individuals. I suppose our little underground friend has to make up its own lists for these, based on observation of their roles, and then draw up its own priorities. They're the real pawns in the game."

"Fascinating what you can do with statistics."

"Isn't it. But pay attention to the moral of this tale. You come here with a hopefully unfamiliar face, posing as a corporal. That's your role, and you've probably already been so listed. Providing you continue to act like a corporal you're relatively safe, because you'll stay in the lower priority block. But if you start acting like a colonel, it'll probably take a closer look. It may well promote you to the first block, either by intensive re-examination of its recognition data or simply by deciding to eliminate a potentially dangerous unknown."

"That's why I fetched you along, Early. So I can move around without breaking my cover."

She turned around and concentrated on the screen or a VDU on which was slowly building the trace of a statistical analysis.

"You're a bastard, Colonel Maidment!"

"I know, Early. It's a habit I'm finding difficult to break."

"You knew all that I've just been saying before you ever came here."

"Not in the same words."

"Damn the words! If you've re-written the rules of the game to cast yourself as a pawn, what position have you allocated to me?"

"I rather thought the White Queen," said Maidment softly.

Maidment

Major Bowman looked up in surprise as Corporal Hammond strode into his office almost as soon as the door had been opened. The Corporal had obviously walked all the way down from the Wartech vans; and though it was early the sun was already powerful and the Corporal's jacket was streaked with sweat. Bowman returned a perfunctory salute and settled behind his desk.

"Good morning, Corporal. Manage to finish all your chores last night?"

"I had the whole thing up and finished by five this morning, Major. Lieutenant—ah—Annandale has it running already."

"You can't have had much sleep."

"Not unusual in the Signals, Major." Hammond removed his bifocals and polished them carefully. "Lieutenant Annandale presents her compliments and asks you to give to me the complete personnel records for the Kunetra detachment, officers as well as men, past as well as current."

"Like hell I will! I doubt if she's even entitled to read them, let alone take possession of them."

"Only for twenty-four hours, she said."

"Not for twenty-four seconds if I have my way."

"Then she asked me to give you this, Major." Hammond produced from his jacket pocket a sealed envelope which had been untidily folded in thirds. He straightened it and handed it to Bowman, who regarded the sweat marks on the cover with some distaste.

Bowman read the contents, stiffened, and then said: "It would seem the Lieutenant claims some very powerful friends. I'll have to sort this one out with the C.O. Wait here." He went off down a corridor and returned about five minutes later looking chastened. "You win," he said ominously. "But I'll be having a few words with her later about this. Pulling a trick like that on me."

"Sir?" asked Hammond innocently.

"Oh, never mind! How do you intend to transport them?"

"I thought I might be allowed to borrow a half-track."

Bowman shook his head like a man coming out of a daze. "A half-track and all the personnel records gone, and it isn't even eight o'clock yet. This is going to be one of those bloody days, I know it. I'll find somebody to help you load up. All the officers' records will be in a locked cabinet. Only Lieutenant Annandale is to have possession of the key. Is that understood?"

"Perfectly, Sir."

"Are you staying on in Kunetra?"

"I'm not sure. Depends if the Lieutenant wants me."

"Then speaking of personnel records, I wouldn't mind seeing yours, Corporal. Or hers, come to think of it. After all, you are on detachment here."

"Perhaps the records were delayed in the post, Sir."

"We don't have post in Kunetra. All records and correspondence are handled by facsimile transmission. Bit difficult for that to get delayed."

"I'll mention it to the Lieutenant, Sir. Perhaps she knows."

"Do that." Bowman returned the salute with a gesture which was also a wave of dismissal, and tiredly returned to the job of tidying his desk.

Corporal Hammond collected his laden half-track, briefly considered his route, and decided to make a detour. Thus far he had seen virtually nothing of the city of Kunetra, and accordingly he felt it was in keeping with his assumed character to make a brief if unauthorized exploration. He turned the half-track into the city instead of keeping on the perimeter road, and within minutes was engulfed in the maze of empty houses, shops and covered native *souks* or markets which were so characteristic of the area. The older buildings appeared to be made of a mixture of mud and straw, with a surface skin of something harder, now mainly cracked away. The newer buildings were of reinforced concrete posts infilled with building blocks. They were just as ugly as the old ones, with steel reinforcement rods rising forlornly from their flat roofs on the off chance that somebody might one day want to build above. The whole suburbs had about them the air of a city started but never finished. He wondered vaguely if it ever would be finished now.

The old town proved something of a contrast. Here the houses were taller and the roads even narrower and he had difficulty in taking the half-track through. Typically, on crazy projections of gnarled and twisted wooden beams, the upper stories overhung the frontages to such an extent that the buildings nearly met overhead in the centre of the street. Samuel Pepys might have recognized a similarity between this and the streets of ancient London in the days before the great fire.

Then suddenly the half-track broke out onto a broader, modern avenue, skirted an ornate mosque, and slowed suddenly to a halt as it turned a corner and fetched up short before a gang of sweating sappers engaged in digging a deep channel diagonally across the road.

A provost sergeant waved him back a little. "Sorry about this, Corp. You can either go back the way you came or wait about twenty minutes till they fill the end of the ditch."

"What's going on then?" asked Hammond.

"We're trying to trace the circuit of the device which killed the Padre. They've followed it out to the street. Now they're trying to find where it goes from there."

"Looks a tough job."

"Tough? It's bloody impossible. Look at this."

He handed Hammond a length of black plastic, scarcely a thirty-second of an inch in diameter.

"What is it?" asked Hammond. "Doesn't look like wire."

"It isn't. It's an optical fibre cable. Most of the devices we find are powered by long-life batteries, often topped up by concealed solar cells. But the instructions come in through optical fibres like this. Even the cameras communicate back in the same way, using digitized video signals. The damn problem is trying to trace where the cables are coming from or going to. They've already broken this cable about sixty times just following it down the road. And we know before we start that the attempt is useless."

"Why's that?"

"Because every so often they've run it through a block of concrete. You know where it goes into the concrete, but you don't know where it comes out. And if you smash the concrete, you destroy the cable. There's no bloody way you can follow it. Are you going to turn?"

"No, I'll wait. It's the first time I've seen anything like this."

"You're welcome. I've seen enough to last me a lifetime."

There was some sudden activity at the far end of the trench, now perhaps some forty feet away, and an officer was directing his fatigued and sweating squad to act with caution. Apparently the customary concrete baulking block had been reached, and the theory was that if they could strip the road surface from it carefully enough they might—just might—find the continuation of the cable. None of the men with the pick-axes seemed at all enthusiastic about the idea. Finding a needle in a haystack while wearing boxing gloves seemed a far better bet than locating a fragile black thread in a bed of compacted and tarmac-coated hard-core. Nonetheless the operation was attempted.

Hammond-Maidment's recollection of the next sequence of events was rather hazy. He dimly remembered the concrete block and the roadway opening up, and bodies being hurled into the air. Then he had been smitten by something he could only imagine as an iron bar traveling at a thousand miles per hour, and had reawoken some unspecified time later to find himself dazed, bruised, and bleeding in the roadway with the half-track toppled over against him. Miraculously it had missed crushing his legs by a mere inch, and its bulk had taken the brunt of the blast and the flying debris. The sound of the sirens of approaching emergency vehicles reflected from the buildings around him so many times that he had no idea from which direction they would arrive. The predominant sound was somebody close by screaming. Those who had been at the far end of the trench would be beyond the need to scream.

He struggled to his feet and made his was unsteadily around the front of the toppled vehicle, and stopped, appalled. The scene before him was barely recognizable as the street he had been watching a few minutes earlier. In the centre of the road was a vast crater, and the shops on one side and the chapel on the other had been damaged so extensively that the roofs and frontages were gone entirely. Only the provost sergeant, and the two sappers who had been coming back to start in-filling the near end of the trench, were still alive, and all were injured. Of the officer and the dozen men who had started to clear the road surface from the baulking block there was very little to be seen at all. Just occasional blood-soaked fragments. Pent up in its thick concrete shell, the waiting mine had exploded very violently indeed, and Hammond Maidment knew he was incredibly lucky still to be alive.

The emergency vehicles were quick to arrive—an ambulance, a fire engine and two half-tracks. Bowman himself was in the leading vehicle, and dropped off by Hammond's toppled half-track.

"You all right, Corporal?"

"Shaken. But I'm no emergency."

Bowman pressed on, turning his attention to getting the ambulance closer to the injured men. Then while the stretcher party moved into action he walked to the edge of the crater and came back to Hammond shaking his head.

"It's a filthy business. Any idea how many were there when she blew?"

"About twelve, I think. Any hope?"

"Not for them. Just bits and pieces. They must have been standing right over the bloody thing."

"They were trying to strip the road surface from over a concrete block."

"And something decided to teach them not to be so damned inquisitive. It's done it before. But tracing the cables is the only chance we've got of finding this thing and stopping it." Bowman looked at the toppled half-track, and his own personnel records scattered across the road, as if he had only just seen them. He turned back to Hammond, and there was a questioning speculation in his eyes. "A bit off your route here, aren't you Corporal?"

"Thought I'd have a quick look around while I had the transport. First opportunity I've had."

"That first opportunity was nearly your last. Another twenty yards and you'd have been in the centre of that lot." Bowman nodded toward the crater. "Take it from me, Kunetra's no place for sightseeing." He was peering at Hammond's face as though there was something he felt he ought to remember about it. "That's a very nasty cut above your eye. You'd better come back to camp and let the Medical Officer do something for it. No sense in taking chances."

Bowman was suddenly hurried away to take a call which had come over the radio in the fire engine. Another halftrack with chains righted Hammond's fallen vehicle, and Hammond recaptured most of the personnel documents. In the meantime the ambulance had left with a blare of sirens to take the wounded back to the camp infirmary. All that remained to be done was for somebody to collect what was left of the men who had been close to the bomb when it exploded. Then Major Bowman came back, and the expression on his face was that of a man who had just seen his own ghost.

"Forget about that trip to the M.O. He's dead. Something just shot him through the bleeding heart."

"Q.E.D." said Early. "We are up against AI." She was treating Maidment's cuts and wounds with expert hands. "I wish you executive types wouldn't bleed so much."

"If you must insist on opening up the wounds and rubbing salt in, of course I bleed."

"It isn't salt. And you are going to have an anti-tetanus injection, even if I have to knock you out to give it to you."

"I told you. I'll be all right."

"Yes, you will. You're getting treatment in time. It's those poor devils who were injured who are at risk. With the M.O. gone."

"Isn't there anyone else medically qualified?"

"Not since the last blowup. Skilled medics have a high

mortality rate in Kunetra. Why don't I go down there and fix the men up—at least until they can be flown out?"

"I considered that, and decided against it. It'd be too damn risky."

"Too risky for the White Queen?"

"Especially risky for the White Queen with Tactical Intelligence flashes on her shoulders and a knowledge of medicine among other things. I'm reasonably sure it wouldn't hesitate to strike you down immediately. I can't afford to lose you, Early. Blast!" The exclamation was caused by Early's inserting into his arm the needle of a hypodermic syringe she had prepared behind his back. "Besides, you've got work to do here."

"More important than trying to save the lives of three men?"

"Yes. Like trying to save the lives of the next three thousand. GenStaff is determined to use Kunetra as a supply base irrespective of the cost. We can't locate and destroy every damn device that's been hidden in the city, so we have to go for the thing that controls them." He nodded to the boxes of personnel records. "Let's get those tabulated and into the computer."

"What are we looking for?"

"Heaven alone knows. Everything or nothing. A pattern, perhaps. Somebody who has survived Kunetra too long. Or somebody who didn't survive it long enough. A window onto the thought processes of our enemy. Its strengths and weaknesses. Perhaps even its face."

"I know what its face looks like. David Bowman told me, 'Eternal patience and a hundred thousand eyes—that's the face of Kunetra the killer.' "

"Poetic. But I wonder if it's true." Maidment was examining the hypodermic puncture on his arm. "And if it is, what happens if we make it lose its patience?" He looked up, and the familiar lines of his formidable powers of concentration creased his unfamiliar forehead. "Exactly what does it take, Early, to drive an artificial intelligence insane?"

The next few hours were spent in pure routine. Maidment

accepted the task of transferring to punched cards all the relevant information from the garrison records. Early set up her computers, calling from sub-routines the various statistical analysis routines she wished to have performed, and tailoring these for various methods of display. Finally, while the cards were running through the optical reader, and the computer had begun its task of assimilation and analysis, she turned back to Maidment.

"What was Quador like—as a man I mean?"

"I wouldn't know."

"But you knew him didn't you? At Oxford?"

He grinned like a schoolboy caught in the midst of a prank. "You're not supposed to know about that."

"There's quite a lot of things I know about Colonel Maidment I'm not supposed to know."

"Then I'll tell you. Whole reams have been written about Quador, and all of them are utter rubbish. I knew the man in his formative years and the truth is very different. In all his life the only thing he wanted was peace. In fact he was so passionately devoted to the pursuit of peace that he was prepared to tear the world apart in order to achieve it."

"He certainly did that—tear the world apart, I mean."

"That's the paradox. Quador's logic. Fight to achieve the peace which is the thing you most desire. Was he wrong, Early? If you don't fight for peace, how the hell are you ever going to find it?"

"And how the hell are you ever going to find it if you continue fighting? Annandale's logic," she said critically.

Maidment was looking at her quizzically. "Exactly what made you ask that question about Quador, Early?"

"They say he was smiling when they put him on the funeral pyre. I suppose at least he'd achieved a sort of personal peace."

"What are you driving at?"

"We seem to be looking at an artificial intelligence probably structured on the lines of Ibrahim Shaban's unbeatable chess program. A machine imbued with a sense of purpose. Our job could be a whole lot easier if we could gain some idea of what that purpose was."

"And you're suggesting it might be modelled on Quador's own thought habits?"

"I don't know. Just an idea that occurred to me." She was watching a green trace which was building a graph across the VDU screen. "This first set is from my original figures established back at base labs. The plot is of differences in length of time in Kunetra before being killed. Two very distinct classes. On the left is the first priority block, whose tenure was short, sharp and brutish. On the right is the second priority block—the pawns—whose demise time follows a roughly normal distribution curve."

"No surprises there. Let's have a look at this latest batch of stuff plotted in the same way."

Early tapped a few keys on the keyboard, and a second, red graph line crawled slightly above the first. The two shapes were nearly but not quite identical.

"Nothing," said Maidment, shaking his head.

"Nothing in the similarity, but it would be interesting to know what is causing the mismatch." She bent to the terminal, and for half a minute columns of figures flowed across the screen directed by her expert fingers. Finally a printer chattered and gave her a small set of cards. She read them thoughtfully, then on impulse dropped them into her tunic pocket.

"Learn anything?" asked Maidment.

"Not about the Kunetra killer, but I think about another one. Do you know what caused that mismatch, Colonel?"

"I pay you to tell me things like that."

"So I'll tell you. The mismatch was caused by the deaths of the five Tactical Intelligence operatives who came here before us."

"So the Kunetra killer doesn't like Tactical Intelligence. That's hardly a surprise."

"Think about it, Colonel. They were all non-specialists and were drawn from remote parts of the war theatre. Nobody could ever have anticipated the possibility of their being sent to Kunetra, therefore their recognition patterns wouldn't have been inserted in the first priority memory banks. They were plainly second group candidates who should have been locally evaluated according to their roles. Any idea what those roles were, Colonel?"

"They're on the cards in your pocket," said Maidment, looking nowhere in particular.

"So they are. Two sappers, one driver, one cook, and one medical orderly. Nonentities. Yet three were dead within twenty-four hours of arrival, and the other two lasted five and seven days respectively. That's statistically untenable. Either they didn't maintain their roles and were detected. Or else . . ."

"Or else what, Early?

"Or else they were betrayed."

Maidment bit his lip. "A rather unlikely proposition. Exactly how would you go about betraying someone to the killer of Kunetra? Go to the door and shout his name? Don't forget that nobody who knew those men had any access to Kunetra, and nobody in Kunetra knew who these men were. Not even Bowman—at least until after the men were killed. There has to be some other answer."

"I think there is," said Early. "In fact, I'm certain of it. I've worked with you too long to have any faith in coincidences, Colonel."

"What are you saying, Early?"

"I'm saying that you deliberately set them up for it. I don't know how or why. But I can detect your filthy hand in this somewhere."

"Child, your lack of faith destroys . . ."

"Five lives, Colonel. Your own men. Can you really justify that?"

"Of course I can. You know damned well I always think the excuses out first."

"Then if I'm to continue working with you, I'd appreciate an explanation."

Maidment sighed wearily. "Shortly after the Kunetra breakthrough, one of our advance mobile units captured a small radio station about three hundred kilometres east. Initially we didn't understand its significance. There had once been a substantial encryption facility there, but this had been destroyed in the fighting, and all the staff had either fled or been killed. However, from the orientation of the fixed dish aerials we finally became convinced we had come across the station by which Quador's technicians gave extra instructions to the Kunetra killer complex. We knew by then that it was going to be difficult to find the killer complex physically, but the chance to confuse or nullify it by feeding it false information couldn't be ignored."

Early was staring at the VDU screen as though it was about to give birth to a venomous snake. "Go on, Colonel."

"Our problem was how to use the station effectively. We knew nothing at all about the encryption codes or the access protocol for instructing the Kunetra killer, and we could transmit to Kunetra, but we couldn't receive a response. Thus we had no way of gauging whether our messages were being received or understood. Therefore we had to resort to a trick."

"A trick, Colonel? We're talking about five human lives."

"If it eases your conscience, they weren't Tactical Intelligence men at all. Rather they were known Quador sympathizers we'd detected in our own forces. We hadn't a hope of re-creating the recognition patterns of the type Quador's men had been using, so we tried a long shot. We took one of our suspect group, transmitted from the station in plain language only his name, rank and number plus the false information that he was attached to tactical Intelligence. Then we drafted him into Kunetra, Seven days later he was killed."

"Statistically probable even for a second-group candidate," said Early archly, glancing at her figures. "What the hell else did you expect?"

"Don't anticipate me, Early," said Maidment sternly. "If you have another look at your figures you'll find it's also within the probability span for a first group candidate. On that slender evidence we repeated the operation for a second man. He was killed in four days."

"Oh my God!"

"So you see where I'm leading. On the last three men we achieved a hundred per cent correlation. All of them dead within twenty-four hours of arrival. We had established our link to the Kunetra killer."

"But it's impossible!" said Early. "How can the killer complex identify a man simply by receiving his number, rank and name?"

"That's what we asked ourselves. The answer was shockingly simple. The records of all personnel and personnel movements to Kunetra go via the facsimile transmission. All the evidence suggests that the killer complex can receive and read that too. Seemingly it puts the two pieces of information together and identifies the man virtually from the moment he steps off the helicopter. Then it makes up its own recognition pattern and simply waits for an opportune time to kill."

"Why should it have been slower to kill the first ones than the later ones?"

"We think it's a question of confidence levels. Once we'd struck on the idea it could read our facsimiles' we took to transmitting to Bowman after each death that the individual concerned had indeed been an undercover Tactical Intelligence agent. As you can see, the hit-rate improved remarkably. Confidence established. The Kunetra killer complex now believes everything I tell it."

"Christ! I never thought I should feel sorry for a machine. Now I nearly do. Statistically you had the information you needed after the second death. You used the remaining three just to harden the decimal place. Suspects or not, that was still deliberate murder. I've said it before, but it bears repeating—you're an unprincipled bastard, Colonel Maidment."

"Ah, yes, but a clever one," said Maidment blandly, folding his hands together.

"And this . . ." She waved her hands around the WarTech van and its clutter of computers and instruments. Her voice was rising high. "If you already know so bloody much, what's the point of fetching me out here?"

She looked about wildly, realizing she was near to the point of breaking into tears, then fled abruptly to the toilet cubicle.

Maidment scrutinized his immaculately manicured nails for a long second, his face a mask of something unnameable and lionlike. Then he picked up a Chinagraph pencil from the tray and went over to the graph traces which still occupied the VDU. There, at the very summit of the peak representing the high-priority death statistics he drew a symbol representing a white queen, and tapped the screen thoughtfully with his pencil.

"My dear Early," he said softly to his absent companion, "you still don't seem to realize what a key piece in the game you are."

Early's crisis of conscience lasted all of five minutes. The sound of a halftrack drawing up outside heralded the arrival of David Bowman bearing a small cardboard box. Early emerged dry-eyed from the toilet and took the offering gratefully.

"What is it?" asked Maidment, looking at the slim glass pencil she was still holding after the major had departed.

"One of the cameras which Quador's people installed by the thousand in Kunetra. David managed to get one out intact. Usually they've been cemented in, and the sappers break them instead of trying to preserve them. This one is complete, and ought still to be working."

Maidment examined the prize carefully, then handed it back to her.

"Can you get it running. Hook it up to one of your TV things? I'd rather like to know just how much the Kunetra killer can and can't see—from the inside, so to speak."

"That's what the electronics van was equipped for, but it'll take a while to sort out the digital-to-analogue conversion." She began hunting through a filing cabinet, seeking a particular report. "Actually base labs have already done a lot of work on some of the earlier cameras recovered." She found the sheets and opened them on the table. "Charge-coupled solid state matrix devices. Fixed lens, monochrome, limited resolution. Visual response peaks toward the blue end of the spectrum. Relatively insensitive to reds, completely insensitive in the infra-red region. Minimum utilizable light levels . . ."

"Just a summary will do," said Maidment. "What does all that imply?"

"It means, Colonel, that it can't see all that well in daylight, and at night it's completely blind."

"That's just the sort of news I was hoping for, Early. How soon can you get it operating?"

"You need it urgently?"

"Very urgently. Like yesterday was already too late."

She scowled down at some circuit diagrams. "None of this system is standard, and I'm going to have to half rebuild a monitor to get it to accept the signal. If I work all night, I should have something running about first light."

"That will have to do then. If I'm not already with you by the time you get it going, come and wake me." He reached for the corporal's jacket in which he posed as Hammond, and took up an instant-picture camera and the Kunetra street map. "I'm away down into the city to get some information we're going to need. Better keep your fingers crossed that the killer complex still has me classified as an innocent pawn. God, I hope those plastic surgeons knew what they were doing!"

"And if they didn't?" asked Early, without any particular emotion.

"Then you're going to have to get yourself a new boss and start all over again."

Taking the half-track, Maidment followed a predetermined route which took him about halfway toward the old city and into a broad triangle which had once been hedged by an open food market. Here he left the vehicle after a brief glance at his map, and began to walk. The fruits and wares on the stalls had long since been consumed by insects and decay, yet the tattered awnings which had given the former merchants some protection from the sun still maintained the character of the scene. Now it was a place of ghosts, and had he been fanciful it would have been easy to imagine the *muezzin* call to prayer ringing above the rooftops, or to expect, if he turned into one of the small shops, the proprietor to emerge from some dim recess to begin his bargaining.

Hoisting his camera for an occasional snapshot, Maidment did his best to maintain the pose of a corporal who had snatched a few hours off from his duties and was out to capture some of the local atmosphere. This was not unusual. Off duty troops frequently ventured into parts of the city, and had seldom come to grief. It seemed that the killer of Kunetra was not much concerned with isolated individuals whose perambulations appeared to offer no sort of threat to its installations.

Maidment was acutely conscious that the killer had his own recognition patterns already in the high priority file. If it penetrated his disguise or was not convinced by the fidelity of his pose, then it required but the diversion of a few electrons through an electronic switch to trigger the sequence which would deprive him of his life. He could not see any of the cameras which were watching him, but he was certain that he was under surveillance and that knowledge begat a curious crawling feeling in his spine. As Early had said, he would never know whether his disguise was adequate until the bolt struck or failed to strike. As usual, she was right.

He had a rough idea of the type of place for which he was looking, and his map was ringed with potential sites, the locations of which had been taken from an old directory. None of his information, however, gave him any guidance as to whether or not the marked places were suitable for the purpose he had in mind. Picking the nearest one, he deliberately chose a circuitous route to disguise the pattern of his interests, and wandered off the highway through a minor *souk*. Here rain from a leaking roof had completely spoilt much of the fine cloth which had been on display, and more of the cloth had been soiled by bird-droppings from a noisy colony which nested under the dark eaves. Then he was out on to another highway, contriving not to look too closely at the true focus of his attention. A few snapshots from casual angles, and he came to the conclusion that this was not the site he needed.

The amount of his exposure to the attentions of the Kunetra killer increased with time, and it was obvious to him that the longer he devoted to the project the greater were his chances of being detected and killed. Nonetheless he persisted, camera in hand, gradually making a tour of all the places he had noted on his map. None was perfect, but he came to the conclusion that the last site he visited was probably the best. By this time, however, he was acutely conscious of a sense of growing danger, which was a sixth sense he did not dare ignore.

Thankful to have made some kind of a choice, he turned from his path and trailed rapidly back through the incredibly narrow streets of a sector of the old city once famous for its hand-crafted furniture, and soon regained the halftrack. Only when he was well clear of the city limits, on the perimeter road where no mines or traps were thought still to be located, did he dare relax again. He brought the vehicle to a halt and in the last rays of the setting sun he had a good look at the final snapshots he had taken. What they told him was satisfactory, so he marked the position heavily on his map and then drove the rest of the way back to see how Early was progressing.

She came and woke him at two o'clock in the morning, visibly tired but pleased with the results of her efforts. The camera which David Bowman had obtained was clamped to a retort stand on a bench at one end of the van, and an assortment of cables showed the degree of patching she had had to do in order to use the potential of various pieces of equipment. The monitor had been stripped out of its cabinet, but the screen was live with a view looking down the interior of the van. The display was a trifle jittery, and was streaked with two bright fly-back lines, but nonetheless the image had reasonable clarity and definition.

"For God's sake don't touch anything," warned Early. "I only had time to get it running, not to get it running safely."

She killed the interior lights in the van, and Maidment advanced toward the camera while watching his own image on the monitor.

"Good work, Early! Have you got a chair? A lab stool would do."

She produced one, and he placed it precisely in the centre of the floor.

"Sit on it please, Child. I want to see what you look like to the Kunetra killer."

She sat and watched anxiously as he went to the camera and made some careful adjustments to its angle. Then he turned back and played with the contrast control on the monitor.

"That's about it, I think. A killer's eye view of Early Annandale. Eerie thought. Forget any ideas you might have had about getting to bed tonight. We've a lot of work ahead of us."

Something

He was *something* in Kunetra, a guardian, perhaps. In a sense he was Kunetra. And all he wanted was peace.

His gaze wandered around the city, a floating consciousness that could transfer its vision at will from one eye to the next. Metaphorically he took a stroll around his favourite places, the view from one camera supplanting the next in ordered sequence, almost as though he were actually out there walking or flying through the streets. Under the iron canopy of the *souk* called the Street of the Long Mile the birds had returned to take possession of the rooftop crannies. He did not mind the birds; birds were peaceful. It was people who destroyed his peace.

He wove his way down the length of the *souk* to where the canopy ended and the way again became open above. The bright sunshine forced him to skip the view from a camera which was blinded by direct exposure to the sun. Then he was caught with the view of a different century as he leaped between rows of great stone columns placed there by the hands of the Romans themselves. Finally he reached the place to which he had been heading—the Great Mosque of

Kunetra. An exquisite example of Islamic art and architecture, the mosque had about it an eternal quality, a place in touch and in tune both with the past and with infinity. The very care which had been taken by its builders in preparing the carvings and mosaics, and the overall conception of its form, were proof to him that they too shared this feeling. He knew nothing about the builders. They had all died on the day he first became conscious.

He stopped with his gaze directed across the great open courtyard, with the towers and minarets in clear relief against the sky, and wondered exactly why he had brought his attention to this place. Then he realized the answer was his own disquiet. All he wanted was peace, but people tended to deny him this; and for that reason he had been provided with arms. He knew who his main enemies were, and these he could destroy fairly quickly. Then there were others, not dedicated enemies, but soldiers who tramped all over his favourite places and sometimes tried half-heartedly to find him. They were a nuisance, but he could control them. Occasionally he culled some to keep their numbers down, and occasionally he taught them an object lesson to stifle their arrogance and spoil their morale. But he did these things only rarely because his stock of arms was finite and could never be replaced. But now he was facing a menace of quite a different order—Early. Why, oh why, had they had to bring Early to Kunetra?

For about the millionth time he turned his attention to the files in which details of her identity were lodged. The earliest had been filed in the stilted Arabic format of Quador's espionage agency, but he knew the details so well that he used his own paraphrase: "Lieutenant Early Annandale, Department of War Technology, seconded to Western Tactical Intelligence as Personal Assistant to the departmental head, Colonel Maidment. Outstanding electronics technician with a medical background. The Early-Maidment combination believed to have been responsible for a great deal of damaging espionage and counter-espionage against units of Quador's forces. Recommendation: destroy at the earliest opportunity." He had also received a very full set of her identification patterns.

He moved his attention out of the courtyard then, switching to the cameras in the mosque itself. The site had been a place of religious worship for over three thousand years. The first known was an Aramean temple built to Hadad, god of storm, rain and fertility. Later, the pagan Zeus had been accorded a temple there, then early Christianity had flourished, finally to be supplanted by Islam. And each faith had left a little of itself, either in the fabric, the relics, or in the atmosphere. Now the décor and form was dominated by Islamic art, from the marble mosaics of the floor and lower walls, the gilded designs and frets which continued to the ceiling. Even the arches of the porticoes and colonnades were inlaid with mosaics. A monument of dedication. A monument of peace.

And now they had sent Early to Kunetra to threaten that peace. Why was Early so special?

The second record gave him more of the answer. It had been originated in plain language by somebody called Hammond, and gave exhaustive details of Early's training and capabilities. Somewhere near the end it read: "Early is believed to be a world authority on the uses of Artificial Intelligence warfare. Her multi-disciplinary training and her ties with Western Tactical Intelligence put her in a unique position for countering AI orientated devices in the field, at which she has achieved a hundred per cent success rate."

He could find no information on Hammond himself, but the file entry had come in via the radio link through which he still received updates from the East. The file access codes on the report had been corrupted or were missing, but there was no doubting the validity of the data. Hammond had sent similar entries in the past, and five Tactical Intelligence operatives had been detected and eliminated. He had himself been able to verify that the men destroyed had actually been working for Tactical Intelligence. Ergo, what Hammond reported was obviously to be taken as fact.

And Hammond, too, regarded Early as dangerous.

Suddenly the quietude was not enough. He tried the sensation of motion, swinging his vision suddenly from camera to camera away from the mosque in a simulation of traveling at speed, as he began to consider the facts. In the heart of the Kunetra Citadel was a Roman amphitheatre, almost complete in its state of preservation, and with the sixteen cameras available to him there he took to swinging his field of view round the great open stone galleries like a bird in flight. With part of his mind thus dissociated he felt he could concentrate more readily on his problem. Whichever way he considered it, Early was dangerous to him. She was probably the most dangerous person who could possibly have come to Kunetra.

Facts. Firstly the WarTech caravans had been flown in and set down on the side of a hill where the ground had been so worked by heavy vehicles that none of his own arms there had survived. Then Early had arrived, unannounced by the facsimile transmissions, and brought with her a great deal of electronic equipment. Her companion, similarly unannounced, had all the trim of a fighting man, yet appeared to treat her with deference. Major Bowman had made a particular point of meeting Early off the helicopter, had placed her in a safe situation all afternoon, and had later taken her out to an even safer position where, presumably, she had discussed her plans.

The situation began to look critical. As an element of psychological warfare the elimination of the soldier-priest had seemed ideal, and the timing opposite. The sting lay in the retrospective analysis: Bowman and Early had actually been on their way to the chapel *before* the soldier-priest had been killed. Coincidence possibly? Or not coincidence? Could she possibly have known of his plans to destroy the soldier-priest? If Early was all his records told him, the possibility could not be ruled out. How clever could she be? Take the following day. Her companion similarly had arrived at the scene at which the mine had been exploded *before* the decision had been taken to detonate it. Precognition or analytical genius?

With a flurry which was the nearest an artificial intelligence could come to panic he suddenly terminated his flight of fancy and instantly concentrated his attention on those visual sensors nearest the WarTech vans on the hill slopes, switching his vision there directly instead of taking a sequential route. Currently nothing much was happening. There was no sign of Early herself, although her companion occasionally emerged and went to one or another of the vans, carrying pieces of equipment. He had wondered before about Early's companion, but had been unable to find a valid identity match. He could have killed the corporal half a hundred times as he had wandered round the city, but judged now that he was right not to waste the arms. Early herself was the real danger.

For two hours he concentrated on the scene around the vans, looking for any signs that might give him a clue as to Early's intentions. Then, as dusk was falling, three half-tracks came up from the camp bearing fully a dozen soldiers, with Bowman at their head. They stopped before one of the vans and started to load pieces of equipment into the vehicles. This done, they all sat down and started leisurely to brew a hot drink on a portable stove, glancing occasionally at the disappearing disc of the sun. Suddenly the cleverness of Early's plan became shockingly apparent. She was planning to attack him at night—and after dark he was blind!

There was nothing he could do, no defences he could call on while the group stayed by the vans. Later, as they drove into the city, as he had no doubt they would, he would be able to pinpoint them by the vehicles' lights, and he swiftly reviewed the web of mines and traps available to him on any of the routes accessible from the WarTech vans. He had more than sufficient arms to eliminate her task force several times over, and the satisfactory foreknowledge that in total darkness they were just as blind as he. Perhaps he was worrying unnecessarily about Early.

Then Early herself came out of a caravan and sat among the soldiers, drinking from a large cup and laughing. He captured a set of images of her, deblurred them by fast-Fourier transform processing, and studied the enhancement. Compared with the company she was keeping, nothing about her suggested any kind of menace. True she wore a uniform but she appeared a perfectly normal young woman, even pretty by the standards he had to judge against, and her reactions with the men were light and normal. Some tension inside him ebbed away. He had taken her threat too seriously. Then suddenly he was again unsure, for she had taken up some apparatus and was looking through it at the sky. She was measuring the level of illumination which would be provided by the slim crescent of a very young new moon . . .

The sun dropped behind the hills and the afterglow began to fade. He watched with a kind of fatalistic calm as she called the men to their feet and directed them to their half-tracks, apparently explaining something important as she did so. In the last moments of available useful light he saw her again raise her measuring instrument to the sky, then sweep it around the shades of the slumbering terrain. He managed to capture that image too, and deblurred it. Even the enhancement was poor, but it was perfectly easy to see that Early was no longer smiling.

He was not sure whether he actually saw them start, or whether his own logic told him that the unlit convoy had moved off into the darkness. What did disturb him was the sudden flare of an incoming message over the radio link, which appropriately underscored the seriousness of the situation. Hammond again: "Confirmed Early Annandale now in Kunetra. Imperative you destroy her before she has a chance to destroy you. Suggest her assassination take absolute priority over all other activities, else you are lost."

He never slept, did not know what sleep was: his kind of creature had no need for recuperative slumber. Nonetheless he was used to a period of relative inaction between dusk and dawn, when the only eyes he used were those concealed in lighted rooms occupied by the garrison. This night was different. He ignored the lighted rooms and began to hunt with blind eyes through the dark recesses of the city. Nothing. The ambient light was far too low for his sensors to begin to resolve the scene, and unless somebody showed a light in one of the vehicles he must lose them completely. He lost them. Not even a lighted cigarette tip had betrayed their passage. Now Early was somewhere in the city—his city—and he was able to protect himself no more.

What could she be doing?

With something akin to mechanical desperation he plotted all the likely routes which the group could have taken and estimated the probable distance they might have travelled in the dark. Then, for the first time in his existence, he expended one of his precious road mines without having a target surely in his sights. Even as he did so he realized the move was a mistake. The mine was under a major baulking-block, and sixteen peripheral cameras and the control circuits to a large number of his own arms went out at the same instant. Nonetheless he used the illumination of the flare to scan the road simultaneously for the half-tracks. Nothing. Early had tricked him. His only gain had been to start a fire in one of the buildings which enabled him to keep that part of the road under continuous surveillance.

Where now? Either he had underestimated the speed of the convoy and Early had already passed that point, which was unlikely, or else she had taken a different and less obvious route. Along part of a parallel road he had an automatic rapidfiring gun set to intersect the traffic lanes. He fired off the whole magazine and watched the bright fire of the tracers travel the whole distance without striking anything until they spent their force against a distant wall. He had wasted the usefulness of the armament but gained some information. Of the four possible routes, Early had not used two. The search was narrowing, and he began to feel he still had a chance of winning. In this he was aided by the fire started by the road-mine, which, spreading rapidly through some timbered buildings, was beginning to light the sky by reflection from a dense cloud of drifting smoke.

Dimly, a group of his external cameras began to start imaging again, and he threw himself into the task of examining every area from which he could get a picture, however poor the quality. Then he felt he had her. Having penetrated far more deeply into the city than he had calculated, three half-tracks were drawn up outside a large white building, formerly a government office. He had a camera in every office in the building, and several on the stairs and larger halls. Also, he had an extensive range of traps and single-shot weapons with which he could dispense death to anyone incautious enough to wander into range. He felt his confidence returning. For a supposed expert in the field, Early had chosen a remarkably imprudent venue for her trial of wits and strength.

Immediately, he scanned all the cameras in the building, confident that Early and her group had gone inside, but unable to understand how they had done so without using any form of light. His sensors told him nothing, even though now and then one of them began to image weakly in response to the glow from the fire entering through a window. Then he examined the scene outside again. The half-tracks were still there, but there was no sign of the recent occupants. Ergo, they had to be inside.

Early, he considered, was a clever one, but not clever enough to match him. She had made a serious mistake, and he was determined that for her it would be a fatal one. There was enough light now in the sky outside for him to be able to detect the movement of the half-tracks if she came out and tried to get away, and he had mines and weapons in the road and buildings sufficient to cover most of the available exit routes. If she stayed inside the building he need only await the coming of morning to be able to locate her and then bide his time until she came into range of one of his weapons. Then he would destroy her, and relative peace would return to Kunetra.

A message from Hammond again, the communication coming in as a scream of fast Morse, emphasizing its urgency. "Early known to have quantity of infrared head-sets which enable her to see in darkness. She can move at night anywhere in Kunetra without your knowing, because she can see where you are blind."

The message was timely, informative and disturbing. It explained how the halftracks had been able to penetrate so deeply into the city without detection, and threw some doubt on whether she had actually entered the building at all. Shadowed from the light of the fire by the clustered buildings all round, she could easily have walked away and now be anywhere else in the whole city—his city. He arranged a frenzied scan of all the exterior sensors available to him and came up with nothing new. Only in the area of the fire could he see anything at all, and then only dimly. Now he was beginning to know for sure just how this terrible woman had earned her reputation for being unbeatable. How could he ever find peace while Early was in Kunetra?

Just as disturbing was the realization that he had lost his mastery. Ever since his first moment of consciousness he had been undisputed overlord of the city: to the humans a barely-tangible omnipresence, all-seeing and swift with vengeance. Now Early had changed all that, and it was she who was directing the pattern of play. She MUST be destroyed, and quickly, else there could be no more peace left to him.

Then suddenly he had her! A small and flickering glimmer of illumination in one of the offices in the government building gave him just sufficient light to get an image from one of the cameras. There was Early, moving slowly across the room, and there was a smile on her face. The source of light, probably a match, was extinguished suddenly, and for a few seconds he could see nothing. Then a new match was struck with a bright initial flare, and he could see her again, still moving, and now very near the projection line of one of his weapons. If only the light held . . .

The light did hold, though he was torn between the decisions to fire prematurely in case he lost the uncertain scene or wait until he was sure she was dead-centred in the sights. He waited and had the gratification of seeing the sharpened steel barb, propelled by an explosive charge, penetrate her precisely. Then the wan light failed again.

He concentrated all his attention on that one camera, waiting for the light to come again, and when it did so he experienced the nearest a machine can come to a feeling of relief. Early was pinned against the wall with the barb straight through her chest. Curiously she was still smiling, but that did not alter the fact that she must certainly be dead. He had won, and with a relaxation of the tensions he felt a touch of the promised peace.

However, it was a peace suddenly shattered as a light flared in another room and again the recognition patterns screamed the identification of Early. Impossible! He hunted back to the first camera and there she was still pinned against the wall. Crisis! Could there have been two Earlys? Or did she have some way of replicating, in which case he was fighting a battle he could never possibly win. Nothing in his backup or orientation files suggested that replication was possible, but neither did they suggest it was impossible. This he would have to decide using his own observations and logic. He waited for the opportune moment and killed the second Early by firing the whole magazine of a rapid-firing gun.

Almost immediately a light flared in yet a third room. . ..

He was not exhausted: his kind of creature had no knowledge of the animal sensation of exhaustion. Rather he had reached a condition of knowing, by every application of the logical process, that he could not possibly win. All night he had been taunted by laughing Earlys, and each one he had destroyed when he had the chance. Yet they continued to come in a seemingly endless supply; no matter how many he destroyed, yet another was always waiting for him in the next room or hall or corridor. After a while he understood that it was impossible to kill her. All his weapons could do was to fix her image at that point, but the rest of her escaped somehow and began to haunt him from a new angle.

With the coming of dawn his cameras had shown him that there was at least one Early in every office, and in the great council hall they appeared to stare down from every wall and be entering every door. Just before first light the soldiers had returned to their half-tracks, and he had let them go, because plainly they did not have Early with them. They had left perhaps a hundred of her dreadful patterns behind them in the building, and she was obviously not afraid of remaining in the corridors alone. He quite literally had only one weapon left in the whole building, and though he had her smiling image in the weapon sights he forbore to use the tiny charge of energy needed to make it fire. It was pointless. No barb or bullet or explosive charge could touch her. That much he now knew with an utter certainty.

With the first rays of the sun he disengaged himself from the contact and winged his visual way through old Kunetra, flying through the *souks*, and on between the Roman columns. In the Great Mosque he halted his metaphoric journey, hoping something in the atmosphere would bestow on him a sense of the peace which was all he really sought, but the sojourn was in vain. A visual flight around the amphitheatre was equally distracted, and he kept missing the correct camera sequence to give him the impression of uninterrupted motion. In the space of a few short hours Early had robbed him of his mastery, taken over his city, and proved completely indestructible. He could find no peace while she remained in the city, nor was it within his powers to get rid of her. His purpose was destroyed.

As if to confirm this conclusion, another message came in from Hammond in screaming accelerated Morse and was interminably repeated, as though it had been recorded and run on an endless loop of tape. "You are lost. . . You are lost. . .You are lost. . . You are lost. . ."

In a sudden crisis of indecision he hurled the focus of his attention back to a view of the WarTech vans on the hillside. Early was there, as he had known she would be, and was seemingly untouched by her night of fragmentation. She was sitting on the steps of the van laughing with her companion, as though the events of the night had been simply effortless and amusing. His builders had promised him peace when the job was finished. Now that Early had so thoroughly beaten him from the game there was no more of the job that he could do. This was checkmate, and he had lost. Therefore his task was finished, and he could have his peace . . .

The explosion deep inside the mountain ripped a hundred yards of solid rock, from a cliff face and gave a staccato report which startled everybody in the city. Maidment raised his eyebrows speculatively. It would take weeks of dangerous and careful testing before they could finally be sure that the killer complex of Kunetra was no more, but the coincidence of the timing of the explosion with the transmission of his own last message was highly suggestive.

Meanwhile, deep in the heart of the city a shaft of sunlight, moving imperceptibly slowly across an office floor, began to illuminate the large, shattered photographs of Lieutenant Annandale, and the sticks and strings by which even her photographic image had been manipulated by a master puppeteer and one of the best liars in the business.

A Shot Rang Out — Three decades of reviews and articles by today's Anthony Boucher, Jon Breen. An essential book for any mystery lover's library.
A Smell of Smoke — A 1951 English countryside thriller by Miles Burton.
A Snark Selection — Lewis Carroll's *The Hunting of the Snark* with two Snarkian chapters by Harry Stephen Keeler — Illustrated by Gavin L. O'Keefe.
A Young Man's Heart — A forgotten early classic by Cornell Woolrich.
Alexander Laing Novels — *The Motives of Nicholas Holtz* and *Dr. Scarlett*, stories of medical mayhem and intrigue from the 30s.
An Angel in the Street — Modern hardboiled noir by Peter Genovese.
Automaton — Brilliant treatise on robotics: 1928-style! By H. Stafford Hatfield.
Away From the Here and Now — Clare Winger Harris stories, collected by Richard A. Lupoff
Beast or Man? — A 1930 novel of racism and horror by Sean M'Guire. Introduced by John Pelan.
Black Hogan Strikes Again — Australia's Peter Renwick pens a tale of the 30s outback.
Black River Falls — Suspense from the master, Ed Gorman.
Blondy's Boy Friend — A snappy 1930 story by Philip Wylie, writing as Leatrice Homesley.
Blood in a Snap — The *Finnegan's Wake* of the 21st century, by Jim Weiler.
Blood Moon — The first of the Robert Payne series by Ed Gorman.
Bogart '48 — Hollywood action with Bogie by John Stanley and Kenn Davis
Calling Lou Largo! — Two Lou Largo novels by William Ard.
Cornucopia of Crime — Francis M. Nevins assembled this huge collection of his writings about crime literature and the people who write it. Essential for any serious mystery library.
Corpse Without Flesh — Strange novel of forensics by George Bruce
Crimson Clown Novels — By Johnston McCulley, author of the Zorro novels, *The Crimson Clown* and *The Crimson Clown Again.*
Dago Red — 22 tales of dark suspense by Bill Pronzini.
Dark Sanctuary — Weird Menace story by H. B. Gregory
David Hume Novels — *Corpses Never Argue, Cemetery First Stop, Make Way for the Mourners, Eternity Here I Come*. 1930s British hardboiled fiction with an attitude.
Dead Man Talks Too Much — Hollywood boozer by Weed Dickenson.
Death Leaves No Card — One of the most unusual murdered-in-the-tub mysteries you'll ever read. By Miles Burton.
Death March of the Dancing Dolls and Other Stories — Volume Three in the Day Keene in the Detective Pulps series. Introduced by Bill Crider.
Deep Space and other Stories — A collection of SF gems by Richard A. Lupoff.
Detective Duff Unravels It — Episodic mysteries by Harvey O'Higgins.
Diabolic Candelabra — Classic 30s mystery by E.R. Punshon
Dime Novels: Ramble House's 10-Cent Books — *Knife in the Dark* by Robert Leslie Bellem, *Hot Lead* and *Song of Death* by Ed Earl Repp, *A Hashish House in New York* by H.H. Kane, and five more.
Don Diablo: Book of a Lost Film — Two-volume treatment of a western by Paul Landres, with diagrams. Intro by Francis M. Nevins.
Dope and Swastikas — Two strange novels from 1922 by Edmund Snell
Dope Tales #1 — Two dope-riddled classics; *Dope Runners* by Gerald Grantham and *Death Takes the Joystick* by Phillip Condé.
Dope Tales #2 — Two more narco-classics; *The Invisible Hand* by Rex Dark and *The Smokers of Hashish* by Norman Berrow.
Dope Tales #3 — Two enchanting novels of opium by the master, Sax Rohmer. *Dope* and *The Yellow Claw.*
Double Hot — Two 60s softcore sex novels by Morris Hershman.
Dr. Odin — Douglas Newton's 1933 racial potboiler comes back to life.
Evangelical Cockroach — Jack Woodford writes about writing.
Evidence in Blue — 1938 mystery by E. Charles Vivian.
Fatal Accident — Murder by automobile, a 1936 mystery by Cecil M. Wills.
Fighting Mad — Todd Robbins' 1922 novel about boxing and life
Finger-prints Never Lie — A 1939 classic detective novel by John G. Brandon.
Freaks and Fantasies — Eerie tales by Tod Robbins, collaborator of Tod Browning on the film FREAKS.

Gadsby — A lipogram (a novel without the letter E). Ernest Vincent Wright's last work, published in 1939 right before his death.

Gelett Burgess Novels — *The Master of Mysteries, The White Cat, Two O'Clock Courage, Ladies in Boxes, Find the Woman, The Heart Line, The Picaroons* and *Lady Mechante*. Recently added is A Gelett Burgess Sampler, edited by Alfred Jan. All are introduced by Richard A. Lupoff.

Geronimo — S. M. Barrett's 1905 autobiography of a noble American.

Hake Talbot Novels — *Rim of the Pit, The Hangman's Handyman*. Classic locked room mysteries, with mapback covers by Gavin O'Keefe.

Hands Out of Hell and Other Stories — John H. Knox's eerie hallucinations

Hell is a City — William Ard's masterpiece.

Hollywood Dreams — A novel of Tinsel Town and the Depression by Richard O'Brien.

Hostesses in Hell and Other Stories — Russell Gray's most graphic stories

House of the Restless Dead — Strange and ominous tales by Hugh B. Cave

I Stole $16,000,000 — A true story by cracksman Herbert E. Wilson.

Inclination to Murder — 1966 thriller by New Zealand's Harriet Hunter.

Invaders from the Dark — Classic werewolf tale from Greye La Spina.

J. Poindexter, Colored — Classic satirical black novel by Irvin S. Cobb.

Jack Mann Novels — Strange murder in the English countryside. *Gees' First Case, Nightmare Farm, Grey Shapes, The Ninth Life, The Glass Too Many, Her Ways Are Death, The Kleinert Case* and *Maker of Shadows*.

Jake Hardy — A lusty western tale from Wesley Tallant.

Jim Harmon Double Novels — *Vixen Hollow/Celluloid Scandal, The Man Who Made Maniacs/Silent Siren, Ape Rape/Wanton Witch, Sex Burns Like Fire/Twist Session, Sudden Lust/Passion Strip, Sin Unlimited/Harlot Master, Twilight Girls/Sex Institution*. Written in the early 60s and never reprinted until now.

Joel Townsley Rogers Novels and Short Stories — By the author of *The Red Right Hand: Once In a Red Moon, Lady With the Dice, The Stopped Clock, Never Leave My Bed*. Also two short story collections: *Night of Horror* and *Killing Time*.

John Carstairs, Space Detective — Arboreal Sci-fi by Frank Belknap Long

Joseph Shallit Novels — *The Case of the Billion Dollar Body, Lady Don't Die on My Doorstep, Kiss the Killer, Yell Bloody Murder, Take Your Last Look*. One of America's best 50's authors and a favorite of author Bill Pronzini.

Keller Memento — 45 short stories of the amazing and weird by Dr. David Keller.

Killer's Caress — Cary Moran's 1936 hardboiled thriller.

Lady of the Yellow Death and Other Stories — More stories by Wyatt Blassingame.

League of the Grateful Dead and Other Stories — Volume One in the Day Keene in the Detective Pulps series.

Library of Death — Ghastly tale by Ronald S. L. Harding, introduced by John Pelan

Malcolm Jameson Novels and Short Stories — *Astonishing! Astounding!, Tarnished Bomb, The Alien Envoy and Other Stories* and *The Chariots of San Fernando and Other Stories*. All introduced and edited by John Pelan or Richard A. Lupoff.

Man Out of Hell and Other Stories — Volume II of the John H. Knox weird pulps collection.

Marblehead: A Novel of H.P. Lovecraft — A long-lost masterpiece from Richard A. Lupoff. This is the "director's cut", the long version that has never been published before.

Master of Souls — Mark Hansom's 1937 shocker is introduced by weirdologist John Pelan.

Max Afford Novels — *Owl of Darkness, Death's Mannikins, Blood on His Hands, The Dead Are Blind, The Sheep and the Wolves, Sinners in Paradise* and *Two Locked Room Mysteries and a Ripping Yarn* by one of Australia's finest mystery novelists.

Money Brawl — Two books about the writing business by Jack Woodford and H. Bedford-Jones. Introduced by Richard A. Lupoff.

More Secret Adventures of Sherlock Holmes — Gary Lovisi's second collection of tales about the unknown sides of the great detective.

Muddled Mind: Complete Works of Ed Wood, Jr. — David Hayes and Hayden Davis deconstruct the life and works of the mad, but canny, genius.

Murder among the Nudists — A mystery from 1934 by Peter Hunt, featuring a naked Detective-Inspector going undercover in a nudist colony.

Murder in Black and White — 1931 classic tennis whodunit by Evelyn Elder.

Murder in Shawnee — Two novels of the Alleghenies by John Douglas: *Shawnee Alley Fire* and *Haunts.*
Murder in Silk — A 1937 Yellow Peril novel of the silk trade by Ralph Trevor.
My Deadly Angel — 1955 Cold War drama by John Chelton.
My First Time: The One Experience You Never Forget — Michael Birchwood — 64 true first-person narratives of how they lost it.
Mysterious Martin, the Master of Murder — Two versions of a strange 1912 novel by Tod Robbins about a man who writes books that can kill.
Norman Berrow Novels — *The Bishop's Sword, Ghost House, Don't Go Out After Dark, Claws of the Cougar, The Smokers of Hashish, The Secret Dancer, Don't Jump Mr. Boland!, The Footprints of Satan, Fingers for Ransom, The Three Tiers of Fantasy, The Spaniard's Thumb, The Eleventh Plague, Words Have Wings, One Thrilling Night, The Lady's in Danger, It Howls at Night, The Terror in the Fog, Oil Under the Window, Murder in the Melody, The Singing Room.* This is the complete Norman Berrow library of locked-room mysteries, several of which are masterpieces.
Old Faithful and Other Stories — SF classic tales by Raymond Z. Gallun
Old Times' Sake — Short stories by James Reasoner from Mike Shayne Magazine.
One Dreadful Night — A classic mystery by Ronald S. L. Harding
Pair O' Jacks — A mystery novel and a diatribe about publishing by Jack Woodford
Perfect .38 — Two early Timothy Dane novels by William Ard. More to come.
Prince Pax — Devilish intrigue by George Sylvester Viereck and Philip Eldridge
Prose Bowl — Futuristic satire of a world where hack writing has replaced football as our national obsession, by Bill Pronzini and Barry N. Malzberg.
Red Light — The history of legal prostitution in Shreveport Louisiana by Eric Brock. Includes wonderful photos of the houses and the ladies.
Researching American-Made Toy Soldiers — A 276-page collection of a lifetime of articles by toy soldier expert Richard O'Brien.
Reunion in Hell — Volume One of the John H. Knox series of weird stories from the pulps. Introduced by horror expert John Pelan.
Ripped from the Headlines! — The Jack the Ripper story as told in the newspaper articles in the *New York* and *London Times.*
Robert Randisi Novels — *No Exit to Brooklyn* and *The Dead of Brooklyn*. The first two Nick Delvecchio novels.
Rough Cut & New, Improved Murder — Ed Gorman's first two novels.
R.R. Ryan Novels — Freak Museum and The Subjugated Beast, two horror classics.
Ruled By Radio — 1925 futuristic novel by Robert L. Hadfield & Frank E. Farncombe.
Rupert Penny Novels — *Policeman's Holiday, Policeman's Evidence, Lucky Policeman, Policeman in Armour, Sealed Room Murder, Sweet Poison, The Talkative Policeman, She had to Have Gas* and *Cut and Run* (by Martin Tanner.) Rupert Penny is the pseudonym of Australian Charles Thornett, a master of the locked room, impossible crime plot.
Sacred Locomotive Flies — Richard A. Lupoff's psychedelic SF story.
Sam — Early gay novel by Lonnie Coleman.
Sand's Game — Spectacular hard-boiled noir from Ennis Willie, edited by Lynn Myers and Stephen Mertz, with contributions from Max Allan Collins, Bill Crider, Wayne Dundee, Bill Pronzini, Gary Lovisi and James Reasoner.
Sand's War — More violent fiction from the typewriter of Ennis Willie
Satan's Den Exposed — True crime in Truth or Consequences New Mexico — Award-winning journalism by the *Desert Journal.*
Satans of Saturn — Novellas from the pulps by Otis Adelbert Kline and E. H. Price
Satan's Sin House and Other Stories — Horrific gore by Wayne Rogers
Secrets of a Teenage Superhero — Graphic lit by Jonathan Sweet
Sex Slave — Potboiler of lust in the days of Cleopatra by Dion Leclerq, 1966.
Shadows' Edge — Two early novels by Wade Wright: *Shadows Don't Bleed* and *The Sharp Edge.*
Sideslip — 1968 SF masterpiece by Ted White and Dave Van Arnam.
Slammer Days — Two full-length prison memoirs: *Men into Beasts* (1952) by George Sylvester Viereck and *Home Away From Home* (1962) by Jack Woodford.
Slippery Staircase — 1930s whodunit from E.C.R. Lorac
Sorcerer's Chessmen — John Pelan introduces this 1939 classic by Mark Hansom.
Star Griffin — Michael Kurland's 1987 masterpiece of SF drollery is back.
Stakeout on Millennium Drive — Award-winning Indianapolis Noir by Ian Woollen.

Strands of the Web: Short Stories of Harry Stephen Keeler — Edited and Introduced by Fred Cleaver.
Summer Camp for Corpses and Other Stories — Weird Menace tales from Arthur Leo Zagat; introduced by John Pelan.
Suzy — A collection of comic strips by Richard O'Brien and Bob Vojtko from 1970.
Tales of the Macabre and Ordinary — Modern twisted horror by Chris Mikul, author of the *Bizarrism* series.
Tenebrae — Ernest G. Henham's 1898 horror tale brought back.
The Amorous Intrigues & Adventures of Aaron Burr — by Anonymous. Hot historical action about the man who almost became Emperor of Mexico.
The Anthony Boucher Chronicles — edited by Francis M. Nevins. Book reviews by Anthony Boucher written for the *San Francisco Chronicle,* 1942 – 1947. Essential and fascinating reading by the best book reviewer there ever was.
The Barclay Catalogs — Two essential books about toy soldier collecting by Richard O'Brien
The Basil Wells Omnibus — A collection of Wells' stories by Richard A. Lupoff
The Beautiful Dead and Other Stories — Dreadful tales from Donald Dale
The Best of 10-Story Book — edited by Chris Mikul, over 35 stories from the literary magazine Harry Stephen Keeler edited.
The Black Dark Murders — Vintage 50s college murder yarn by Milt Ozaki, writing as Robert O. Saber.
The Book of Time — The classic novel by H.G. Wells is joined by sequels by Wells himself and three stories by Richard A. Lupoff. Illustrated by Gavin L. O'Keefe.
The Case in the Clinic — One of E.C.R. Lorac's finest.
The Case of the Bearded Bride — #4 in the Day Keene in the Detective Pulps series
The Case of the Little Green Men — Mack Reynolds wrote this love song to sci-fi fans back in 1951 and it's now back in print.
The Case of the Withered Hand — 1936 potboiler by John G. Brandon.
The Charlie Chaplin Murder Mystery — A 2004 tribute by noted film scholar, Wes D. Gehring.
The Chinese Jar Mystery — Murder in the manor by John Stephen Strange, 1934.
The Compleat Calhoon — All of Fender Tucker's works: Includes *Totah Six-Pack, Weed, Women and Song* and *Tales from the Tower,* plus a CD of all of his songs.
The Compleat Ova Hamlet — Parodies of SF authors by Richard A. Lupoff. This is a brand new edition with more stories and more illustrations by Trina Robbins.
The Contested Earth and Other SF Stories — A never-before published space opera and seven short stories by Jim Harmon.
The Crimson Query — A 1929 thriller from Arlton Eadie. A perfect way to get introduced.
The Curse of Cantire — Classic 1939 novel of a family curse by Walter S. Masterman.
The Devil and the C.I.D. — Odd diabolic mystery by E.C.R. Lorac
The Devil Drives — An odd prison and lost treasure novel from 1932 by Virgil Markham.
The Devil's Mistress — A 1915 Scottish gothic tale by J. W. Brodie-Innes, a member of Aleister Crowley's Golden Dawn.
The Devil's Nightclub and Other Stories — John Pelan introduces some gruesome tales by Nat Schachner.
The Disentanglers — Episodic intrigue at the turn of last century by Andrew Lang
The Dumpling — Political murder from 1907 by Coulson Kernahan.
The End of It All and Other Stories — Ed Gorman selected his favorite short stories for this huge collection.
The Fangs of Suet Pudding — A 1944 novel of the German invasion by Adams Farr
The Ghost of Gaston Revere — From 1935, a novel of life and beyond by Mark Hansom, introduced by John Pelan.
The Girl in the Dark — A thriller from Roland Daniel
The Gold Star Line — Seaboard adventure from L.T. Reade and Robert Eustace.
The Golden Dagger — 1951 Scotland Yard yarn by E. R. Punshon.
The Great Orme Terror — Horror stories by Garnett Radcliffe from the pulps
The Hairbreadth Escapes of Major Mendax — Francis Blake Crofton's 1889 boys' book.
The House That Time Forgot and Other Stories — Insane pulpitude by Robert F. Young

The House of the Vampire — 1907 poetic thriller by George S. Viereck.
The Illustrious Corpse — Murder hijinx from Tiffany Thayer
The Incredible Adventures of Rowland Hern — Intriguing 1928 impossible crimes by Nicholas Olde.
The Julius Caesar Murder Case — A classic 1935 re-telling of the assassination by Wallace Irwin that's much more fun than the Shakespeare version.
The Koky Comics — A collection of all of the 1978-1981 Sunday and daily comic strips by Richard O'Brien and Mort Gerberg, in two volumes.
The Lady of the Terraces — 1925 missing race adventure by E. Charles Vivian.
The Lord of Terror — 1925 mystery with master-criminal, Fantômas.
The Melamare Mystery — A classic 1929 Arsene Lupin mystery by Maurice Leblanc
The Man Who Was Secrett — Epic SF stories from John Brunner
The Man Without a Planet — Science fiction tales by Richard Wilson
The N. R. De Mexico Novels — Robert Bragg, the real N.R. de Mexico, presents *Marijuana Girl, Madman on a Drum, Private Chauffeur* in one volume.
The Night Remembers — A 1991 Jack Walsh mystery from Ed Gorman.
The One After Snelling — Kickass modern noir from Richard O'Brien.
The Organ Reader — A huge compilation of just about everything published in the 1971-1972 radical bay-area newspaper, *THE ORGAN*. A coffee table book that points out the shallowness of the coffee table mindset.
The Poker Club — Three in one! Ed Gorman's ground-breaking novel, the short story it was based upon, and the screenplay of the film made from it.
The Private Journal & Diary of John H. Surratt — The memoirs of the man who conspired to assassinate President Lincoln.
The Secret Adventures of Sherlock Holmes — Three Sherlockian pastiches by the Brooklyn author/publisher, Gary Lovisi.
The Shadow on the House — Mark Hansom's 1934 masterpiece of horror is introduced by John Pelan.
The Sign of the Scorpion — A 1935 Edmund Snell tale of oriental evil.
The Singular Problem of the Stygian House-Boat — Two classic tales by John Kendrick Bangs about the denizens of Hades.
The Smiling Corpse — Philip Wylie and Bernard Bergman's odd 1935 novel.
The Spider: Satan's Murder Machines — A thesis about Iron Man
The Stench of Death: An Odoriferous Omnibus by Jack Moskovitz — Two complete novels and two novellas from 60's sleaze author, Jack Moskovitz.
The Story Writer and Other Stories — Classic SF from Richard Wilson
The Strange Case of the Antlered Man — 1935 dementia from Edwy Searles Brooks
The Strange Thirteen — Richard B. Gamon's odd stories about Raj India.
The Technique of the Mystery Story — Carolyn Wells' tips about writing.
The Threat of Nostalgia — A collection of his most obscure stories by Jon Breen
The Time Armada — Fox B. Holden's 1953 SF gem.
The Tongueless Horror and Other Stories — Volume One of the series of short stories from the weird pulps by Wyatt Blassingame.
The Tracer of Lost Persons — From 1906, an episodic novel that became a hit radio series in the 30s. Introduced by Richard A. Lupoff.
The Trail of the Cloven Hoof — Diabolical horror from 1935 by Arlton Eadie. Introduced by John Pelan.
The Triune Man — Mindscrambling science fiction from Richard A. Lupoff.
The Unholy Goddess and Other Stories — Wyatt Blassingame's first DTP compilation
The Universal Holmes — Richard A. Lupoff's 2007 collection of five Holmesian pastiches and a recipe for giant rat stew.
The Werewolf vs the Vampire Woman — Hard to believe ultraviolence by either Arthur M. Scarm or Arthur M. Scram.
The Whistling Ancestors — A 1936 classic of weirdness by Richard E. Goddard and introduced by John Pelan.
The White Owl — A vintage thriller from Edmund Snell
The White Peril in the Far East — Sidney Lewis Gulick's 1905 indictment of the West and assurance that Japan would never attack the U.S.
The Wizard of Berner's Abbey — A 1935 horror gem written by Mark Hansom and introduced by John Pelan.
The Wonderful Wizard of Oz — by L. Frank Baum and illustrated by Gavin L. O'Keefe
Through the Looking Glass — Lewis Carroll wrote it; Gavin L. O'Keefe illustrated it.

Time Line — Ramble House artist Gavin O'Keefe selects his most evocative art inspired by the twisted literature he reads and designs.
Tiresias — Psychotic modern horror novel by Jonathan M. Sweet.
Totah Six-Pack — Fender Tucker's six tales about Farmington in one sleek volume.
Trail of the Spirit Warrior — Roger Haley's historical saga of life in the Indian Territories.
Two Kinds of Bad — Two 50s novels by William Ard about Danny Fontaine
Two Suns of Morcali and Other Stories — Evelyn E. Smith's SF tour-de-force
Ultra-Boiled — 23 gut-wrenching tales by our Man in Brooklyn, Gary Lovisi.
Up Front From Behind — A 2011 satire of Wall Street by James B. Kobak.
Victims & Villains — Intriguing Sherlockiana from Derham Groves.
Wade Wright Novels — *Echo of Fear, Death At Nostalgia Street, It Leads to Murder* and *Shadows' Edge*, a double book featuring *Shadows Don't Bleed* and *The Sharp Edge.*
Walter S. Masterman Novels — *The Green Toad, The Flying Beast, The Yellow Mistletoe, The Wrong Verdict, The Perjured Alibi, The Border Line, The Bloodhounds Bay* and *The Curse of Cantire.* Masterman wrote horror and mystery, some introduced by John Pelan.
We Are the Dead and Other Stories — Volume Two in the Day Keene in the Detective Pulps series, introduced by Ed Gorman. When done, there may be as many as 11 in the series.
Welsh Rarebit Tales — Charming stories from 1902 by Harle Oren Cummins
West Texas War and Other Western Stories — by Gary Lovisi.
Whip Dodge: Man Hunter — Wesley Tallant's saga of a bounty hunter of the old West.
Win, Place and Die! — The first new mystery by Milt Ozaki in decades. The ultimate novel of 70s Reno.
You'll Die Laughing — Bruce Elliott's 1945 novel of murder at a practical joker's English countryside manor.

RAMBLE HOUSE
Fender Tucker, Prop. Gavin L. O'Keefe, Graphics
www.ramblehouse.com fender@ramblehouse.com
228-826-1783 10329 Sheephead Drive, Vancleave MS 39565

Printed in Great
Britain
by Amazon

31383092R00187